Praise f

'All very realis.... ....he faint-hearted'   *Manchester Evening News*

'An enthralling psychological thriller'
                                    Sunderland Echo

'This riveting psychological thriller lays out a power-ful story of conspiracy, murder on a grand scale and corruption at the highest level'
                                    Bolton Evening News

Also by Bill Murphy
Tin Kickers

Fractions of Zero

Bill Murphy

coronet

CORONET BOOKS
Hodder & Stoughton

Copyright © 2001 Bill Murphy

First published in Great Britain in 2001
by Hodder and Stoughton
A division of Hodder Headline

The right of Bill Murphy to be identified as the
Author of the Work has been asserted by him in accordance
with the Copyright, Designs and Patents Act 1988.

A Coronet paperback

2 4 6 8 10 9 7 5 3 1

A CIP catalogue record for this title
is available from the British Library.

ISBN 0 340 76706 5

Printed and bound in Great Britain by
Mackays of Chatham PLC, Chatham, Kent

Hodder and Stoughton
A division of Hodder Headline
338 Euston Road
London NW1 3BH

For Karen Ann

'Take from all things their number and all shall perish.'

Isidore of Seville, AD 600

Conjectura

ST DOMINIC'S BOYS' VILLAGE, KERNVILLE, CALIFORNIA

July 1957

The school motto hung above the boys' coats and jackets in the small cloakroom, reminding them, in deep maroon letters, of their eternal destiny.

Fifteen-year-old Francis Peerey sat in class with the rest of southern California's worst 'incorrigibles'. Even the courts had washed their hands of these boys, an assortment of runaways, orphans and criminals. The legal system was unable to sentence them to regular prison custody, despite their violent behaviour, on account of their youth. The other reform schools, like Father Flanagan's Boys' Town and the Boys' Republic in Chino, would not take them in. Only the Irish priests of St Dominic's were devout or arrogant enough to think that they could save the delinquents' lost souls.

Ninth grade was the only full year Francis had spent in school. He had picked up the rudiments of reading and writing from one of his kinder foster parents and had repaid them by stealing their savings and running away. But now Francis had surprised even himself by the amount he was learning and a part of him would even admit reluctantly that the stringent regime was doing him some good. His options were limited, his freedom curtailed, his choices made. He now had only two guiding codes: safety and fear. Safety came with his chores: cleaning out the sheds, mopping down the latrines, wiring the fences, working in the kitchens and the laundry or stacking the books in the library. He was told what had to be done. Ordered to do it. Do or be done. Life was made simple, easily understood and safe. But fear came in the guise of Christ, punishing brutally and without hesitation. Get it right – or get it wrong and suffer the consequences.

For Francis those two principles met in the person of Fr Ignatius. There was the safety of certainty in his craft, in the pure beauty of the black art of numbers that he taught – and the fear that he dispensed was the fear of retribution, the even purer beauty of random cruelty.

Ignatius entered the room silently as he did every morning. He immediately went to the blackboard and wrote an equation on it. He did this every morning too, to test the boys on what they had learned the previous day. Today it was a rather straight-forward quadratic equation. Francis solved it in his mind in less than a minute and looked around the class, anxious to see if the rest of them looked as confident as him. Most did. For, whatever else he was, Fr Ignatius was a brilliant math teacher. He made the numbers come alive. To Francis he made them dance, perform miracles, explain the inexplicable. *Numbers governed the universe and everything in it.*

He also used them to inflict pain.

A slight, wiry man, pale of complexion, Fr Ignatius had two pink patches on each cheek that, up close, were revealed to be a knitted mottle of tiny veins. He had a thin, almost girl-like mouth, but he instilled fear in every boy in the school. He never used his fists like the other Brothers, or his feet like Fr Paschal, who was rumoured to have broken a boy's pelvis once with one kick, for stealing a brownie from the pantry. Ignatius used a belt strap to administer his punishments. But perhaps even this was not the most fearful part of his sadistic nature. The worst part was the method with which he picked his victims.

'Okay, who shall we have?' Ignatius smiled, his vowels flattened with his harsh Irish accent.

He moved to the sill under the window and picked up his instrument of torture, bringing it back to his desk at the top of the class.

A large white disc, over a foot in diameter, standing upright on a smooth axle with numbers on the edge going right around the circumference, one to thirty. From each number a plastic toothpick stuck out. At the top a drawing compass, its sharp needle stationary, pointed downwards between the toothpicks.

The Number Wheel.

'Right, lads,' Ignatius panted as he spun the disc. It whirred around, prescribing several revolutions per minute, the needle clicking across the toothpicks. As it slowed down the boys stared intently, praying for their number to go by.

The wheel slowed.

Francis closed his eyes.

It stopped.

Twelve.

'Number twelve!' Ignatius announced, 'Michael McClaine, up you get, lad.'

The class sighed with relief.

McClaine was pretty good. He'd get it, no hassle.

McClaine strode to the blackboard and, taking up a piece of chalk, he solved the equation for X and Y.

Simple.

Ignatius smiled. 'Good man.'

But he was already writing the next equation on the board, a complicated one that would require a bit more working-out.

The class tensed as he put down the chalk and spun the wheel again.

The numbers blurred, flickering past the needle. Ignatius watched the class as it slowed, wondering who would be next.

It stopped at twenty-nine.

'Ah, Mister De Rosa, my old pal,' Ignatius cried. He had frequently beaten De Rosa.

De Rosa got up from his desk nervously and went to the board. Ignatius put his thumbs in his belt, standing like a gunslinger, waiting for the boy to mess up.

De Rosa's hand trembled over the blackboard, the chalk sticking to his clammy palm. But he remembered the formula and worked out the problem just before time ran out.

'You remembered, De Rosa, what?' Ignatius laughed as the pupil resumed his seat. 'Well, it looks like I've been teaching you well,' Ignatius said and began writing on the board again. 'But let's see how smart you really are.'

The problem he wrote meant little to most of the boys in the class. It consisted of strange words and symbols. Some vaguely recognized the principle of the problem, the general area of mathematics from which it came. They'd touched on it briefly in the previous day's class but they had no idea how to solve it.

Francis was already working it out.

Without paper.

Running it through the grooves of his brain, the answers sparking in synaptic rapidity.

In his mind he was differentiating the trigonometric function Ignatius had written on the board, using calculus.

The wheel was spinning again.

This time faster, the toothpicks spitting across the needle like a ticker-tape machine.

It seemed to maintain its momentum for an impossible amount of time, an unknown force pushing it around the axle and making the toothpicks buzz.

But it did decelerate eventually, spinning itself out. Each boy's heart beat harder, thumping heavily in his chest, as the clicking slowed.

It stopped.

Jonnie Klensch's number was up.

Ignatius held out the chalk as Jonnie, on the verge of tears, made his way to the board.

The class knew he'd never get it. He wasn't the smartest kid at the best of times.

Jonnie stood staring at the board. The math problem could have been in Chinese for all he knew.

'You're not going to get it, are you?' Ignatius asked him, checking his pocket watch.

Jonnie turned around quickly. Tears were beginning to leak from his eyes. 'Please, Brother, it's not my fault, I can't do it,' he pleaded, his voice ragged, breaking up as his throat choked with phlegm and tears.

Ignatius stared at him, his eyes glazing.

The change.

'I'm sorry, you know the rules.'

'Please, Brother,' Jonnie cried again.

'Sit down,' Ignatius said quietly, softly.

Jonnie knew it was no good and he resumed his seat, burying his head in his arms, sobbing.

The rest of class remained silent.

One of them would have to pay for Jonnie.

Ignatius's voice appeared to change again. His throat seemed tighter, constricting his words, squeezing them out.

'Right, lads. We all know what has . . . to be done,' he said, as if about to undertake a necessary task with grave reluctance.

His fingers trembled and become cold as he touched the wheel. His mouth grew sticky. He began to tremble at the edges of his body as if trying to shrug himself out of a vile, cold skin. He was in a state of high anticipation.

Francis felt the excitement, too. His eyelids grew heavy, hooded with blood.

Letting them close he waited, hating himself for wallowing inwardly in a lustful knot of expectation. Waited.

The wheel went clicking, faster at first, it seemed, purring like an engine, pistons tapping. But soon, too soon, it began to slow, winding down, the constant rattle churning to a series of ever-slowing clicks until there was just one.

. . . *Click*.

The silence seemed eternal.

When Francis opened his eyes the rest of the class was looking at him. Not with pity but with relief.

Ignatius nodded at him and slowly unfastened his belt.

Francis stood up.

The wheel was stopped on number twenty-one.

His number.

He moved quickly to the blackboard. 'Please, Brother, I can solve it,' he said, panicking.

But his teacher pulled the leather belt from the waist-loops of his tunic.

'. . . Please, Brother, I can,' Francis pleaded as he began scrawling out the solution, almost indecipherable in his quivering hands.

This only angered Ignatius more. He caught Francis by the arm, knocking the chalk from the boy's fingers.

'Come on, now,' he said, his head shaking slightly with excited nervousness.

Francis knew it was no good. He could not escape.

'Take the wheel into the cloakroom,' the priest ordered him. 'I will follow soon.'

Tearfully, his hands shaking, Francis lifted the number wheel and took it into the small cloakroom just off the classroom.

Through the narrow window he could see the pinnacles of the church, the flying buttresses topped by the mocking faces of the gargoyles.

Fr Ignatius came in and Francis could hear the whispered chatter of excitement and fear in the classroom until the priest closed the door – and then it was just the two of them.

Moving to the small desk in the centre of the room Francis unbuttoned his trousers and leaned on the table, one of his hands tightly fisted. He could smell his teacher close by, a crisp sterile smell of carbolic.

He felt his trousers being pulled down. A brief moment later his shorts were yanked down too.

Then the priest's hot breath was panting against Francis's back, gusting in warm gasps across the tiny hairs on his skin. Francis glanced up at the wood carving of the school motto, painted in blood red. The bells of the church began a slow ponderous pealing, as if informing the valley of his deserved punishment

As the strap whipped across him, snapping like a firecracker, he tried to focus on the words of the motto. *Suffer one, suffer all.*

But the letters blurred as each blow sent a shock of pain forking up his spine, squeezing tears from his brimming eyes and making the words swim.

In his hand he gripped the compass needle that he'd plucked from Ignatius's precious damned number wheel, enduring the pain of two more lashes – until his fury stirred him to strike back.

LECTURE ROOM 2, BOSTON PSYCOPATHIC HOSPITAL

February 1959

'Vhawt is seven from one hundred, please?'

A moment.

Then the deep male voice answered nervously. 'Ninety-three.'

A student turned away, squinting with a twisted look of disgust.

Another laughed at him, like one who laughs at nothing, trying only to cope with their own giddy nerves. The rest watched with dry mouths, enthralled as the tube was inserted into the head.

'We aim the cannula at the opposing lateral incision.' The surgeon pronounced his words slowly and carefully, perfecting his clipped English.

'At about two to two-and-a-half inches we pause to observe any fluid – the presence of which would indicate penetration of the lateral ventricle.'

He stopped.

The clear plastic tube remained dry.

'How are you feeling, my friend?'

The voice, its owner obscured from view from brow-level down by the surgical screen-sheet, answered that he felt fine.

The surgeon continued and pushed the tube further into the skull, its length gradually disappearing down the small bore-hole whose bony edge was chipped like white slate and streaked with meningeal blood.

'We continue to lower the cannula to the spheroidal ridge at the base of the skull and cleanse the area.'

He nodded and his assistant came close, positioning a small bottle of clear liquid over the hole. The surgeon nodded again and the assistant tipped some of the liquid inside.

'Then we withdraw the cannula and prepare for tissue destruction.'

He retracted the tube carefully and the students steeled

9

themselves for the next part – which they knew would be the worst. Two had already left, one with his hand clasped firmly to his mouth holding back the vomit. The other sat in the corridor outside, his lab coat tight and hot, his forehead sweating coldly.

'Vhawt is seven from ninety-three, please?'

'Er . . . eighty-six,' the voice answered brightly and eagerly.

The surgeon looked up from behind his thick glasses at the students on the benches, his temples creasing as he smiled.

'Iz this correct?'

They answered enthusiastically with a collective laugh, which helped them relieve the tension. Many were struggling to maintain their composure, their foreheads shiny, their faces drawn and shocked. Of course, a few were loving it, scribbling excitedly in their notepads and craning their necks to get a better view.

After giving the tube to his assistant for disposal, the surgeon surveyed his instruments where they lay neatly spread on a surgical tray, glimmering beneath the lights. He picked up a long, blunt-edged knife and held it up towards his audience like Arthur proclaiming his kingship.

'As you can see, it is much like a butter knife in the kitchen.' The words, in his dry German tones, provoked further mirth among the class.

'But you can call it the Killian periosteal elevator,' he added, his glasses lifting as he crinkled his face in a smile.

The stainless-steel blade sparked and flashed as he twirled it under the lights. Behind him his assistant studiously applied a haemostat to the skull and spread a pristine white surgical sheet over the forehead to soak up any blood that might erupt, geyser-like, should the knife encounter an artery.

'Extreme caution must be undertooken,' he began, raising a smile among the students with his mispronunciation. The assistant dabbed the surgeon's head with a cotton cloth as the man poised the knife over the hole recently vacated by the cannula, its dull edge pointing down towards the centre of the head. 'It would be all too easy to damage the major arteries in the proximity of the midline of the brain.'

The surgeon then exhaled and slowly pushed the knife down so that the shaft penetrated about three inches beneath the shaven scalp. Some of the students stood up to get a better look, leaning their bodies over the benches as if they were being sucked in with the knife as it journeyed through the dura mater and into the milky grey folds of the cerebrum.

The surgeon moved very slowly, deftly concentrating his mind on the silver hilt piercing the flesh of the lateral lobe syruped in lemony cerebrospinal fluid. He stopped.

The assistant moved behind the sheet to the body and nodded.

'Vhawt is seven from one hundred, please?' the surgeon asked.

The voice was muffled now, sleepy, struggling for coherence. 'Sheventy . . . sheventy hunthrith . . . sheven . . .'

The patient lapsed into the muttered breaths of fading consciousness and then fell silent as the metal edge plunged deeper into the centre of his head.

Another student left hurriedly, staggering heavy-legged through the lecture-room doors.

The surgeon grimaced and began to move the handle back and forth, ripping across the base of the brain. His accent thickened further, grew guttural with the physical effort.

'The knife is svung from side to side perpendicular to the long axis and along the anterior-posterior plane, cutting the tissue as far to the side as . . . iz . . . pozzible,' he grunted, a bead of sweat falling on the patient's bruised scalp. The assistant quickly dabbed the surgeon's brow but had to move swiftly back as he drew up all of a sudden and pulled the knife out of the patient's head.

The surgeon turned to his audience, sweating, panting with relief and satisfaction. 'Gentlemen, the Freeman Watts Standard lobotomy.'

They all stood and applauded, giddy and light-headed as the surgeon opened his arms in gracious acknowledgement. In his right hand he held the knife, dripping with brain juice. As the applause subsided the door to the pre-op vestibule opened and a tall man in a grey double-breasted suit smiled at the surgeon and motioned politely for him to follow. As this man was the hospital administrator the surgeon quickly obliged and left the theatre to de-gown, leaving his assistant to gather the bone shavings and plug the patient's head.

Two men were waiting outside the administrator's office. In light grey flannel suits and mock silk ties they eyed the administrator suspiciously before stepping aside to allow him into his own room. They saved even more disdainful looks for the surgeon as he followed, wrestling his arms into the sleeves of a tweed sports jacket. There were two more men already inside, older and with an air of authority.

'I found him,' the administrator announced happily. One of the men turned quickly from the window from which he had been looking out over the city as it bathed in a late-afternoon tide of sunshine. He was small, his perfectly circular head perched on a flabby ring of flesh that was his neck. He was smiling as he held out a small, soft, almost baby-like hand to the surgeon.

'Dr Eckhardt, nice to see you again.'

Even his voice seemed squashed and gaspy, as if it was hemmed in by the constriction of his tight cream suit and the strangled patter of his New York accent.

'You don't remember me, do you?' He smiled.

The surgeon smiled back, adjusted his glasses and shook his head.

'You must excuse me . . . I . . .'

The fat man grinned, totally unconcerned that he had not been recognized.

'My name is Dr Edward Shelton and we met at a Foundation party at the Astoria in New York last year . . . Mrs Eisenhower spoke.'

'Ah, you are from the Foundation.' Eckhardt brightened, regaining his slow, almost perfect English pronunciation.

'Yes.' Shelton nodded. 'I'm the treasurer.'

'I hope, Mr Shelton, that our funding will be continued. We are doing some very fine work here . . . thanks to your generosity.' Eckhardt gave a little bow in gratitude.

Shelton bowed back, the smile never leaving his face. 'It's *Doctor* Shelton.'

The administrator, who was hovering impatiently in the background, seized his moment and backed up towards the door.

'Please excuse me, gentlemen, I have some business to attend to on the wards. If you need anything you can buzz through to my secretary next door.'

As the administrator closed the door behind him, Shelton offered the surgeon a seat. He accepted as he had been on his feet all day, performing three leucotomies in succession.

As he sat down, Eckhardt became keenly aware of the other man who had remained silent throughout as he sat beneath the bookcases, his long legs crossed, watching.

'Dr Eckhardt, this is Mr Truscott,' Shelton introduced him.

With a prominent brow and thick black eyebrows, a hook nose and metallic grey eyes, Truscott had the imperious stoop of a bird of prey. He reached out a long arm and flashed an intense, unsettling smile.

'Horace Truscott,' he said, the accent blue-blood Massachusetts, with an attendant air of diffidence.

'How do you do?' Eckhardt answered politely. He had to get up to shake the other man's hand while Truscott remained seated. Truscott held Eckhardt's hand in a tight grip for a moment, as if to impart a subtle but real threat of his power. It worked. Eckhardt bowed his head and Truscott released the surgeon's delicate fingers.

'A coffee?' Shelton suggested, as he leaned, arms folded, against the administrator's large dark oak desk whose top displayed various-sized skulls marked with outlines of the major components of the human brain.

'Thank you.' Eckhardt accepted politely. He hated American coffee.

As Shelton poured a single cup Truscott glanced around the high walls of the office, taking in the bookshelves reaching to the ceiling and full of leather-bound medical texts.

'A lot of books,' he observed, with a hint of disapproval. 'Have they ever been read?'

Shelton handed Eckhardt his coffee. It was cold and too sweet, and he seemed to be the only one having any.

Leaning against the desk again, Shelton pressed his hands together like a minister about to pray.

'Dr Eckhardt,' he began solemnly, 'let me start by saying the Saint Lawrence Foundation is most grateful for your neurological work here at the hospital.'

'Thank you,' said Eckhardt and glanced at Truscott who was nodding an appreciative smile.

'But we feel that your particular expertise might be put to better use somewhere else'.

The surgeon sat up and adjusted his glasses. 'Somewhere else?' he asked, almost unbalancing his cup on the saucer.

'Yes. The Foundation is setting up a new research facility on the west coast, near San Francisco, which we have no doubt that you should head up – given your unique research background . . . I assure you the climate is most agreeable,' Shelton added, the attempt at refinement almost comical in his Bronx accent.

Truscott was nodding in agreement as Eckhardt searched for the correct words with which to decline politely.

'Well, gentlemen, of course I'm flattered but I—'

Still smiling, Shelton took the saucer and cup from Eckhardt, which unsettled the surgeon further.

'Er . . . thank you. As I said, I am most grateful to you and the Foundation but I am very happy here at Boston Psych. It is a very fine city,' he added, looking towards Truscott. 'We are making great moves forward in the neurosurgical field of psychopathology.'

The two other men traded glances of studied disappointment. Truscott tilted his head and furrowed his wide brow in serious deliberation.

'Dr Eckhardt, how long have you been in this country?'

The surgeon became visibly nervous, pinching the frame of his glasses between index finger and thumb.

'Nearly . . . nearly fifteen years,' he said weakly. The words caught hoarsely in his throat.

Truscott's long arm reached behind him and under his seat

to retrieve a black case. His gaze stayed fixed on the surgeon. 'Mmm,' he said. 'Twelve years and three months, I believe,' he corrected him and laid the case on his lap, springing it open. 'And do you . . . like it here?' he asked airily.

The surgeon looked at Shelton who turned away to squint at the books on the shelves.

Eckhardt laughed nervously. The light from the window began to gleam on his pale, bald head, now tacky with perspiration. 'Yes . . . I like it here very much,' he replied, feeling giddy.

'Good.' Truscott flashed one of his smiles again and retrieved a thick manila file from the case. 'You are now privileged to be a citizen of the United States?'

'Yes . . . yes, I have that great honour . . . and I am grateful to this country.'

Truscott opened the file on his lap.

Eckhardt could see the eagle, as he was meant to – the seal of the Luftwaffe high command – and the logo of the Institute of Aviation, Munich.

'Well, this country needs you, Dr Eckhardt,' Truscott said breezily as he began leafing through the file, an assortment of reports, graphs and grim black-and-white photographs. 'It gave you your freedom, and we must all fight to maintain that freedom.'

Truscott paused at a large photo and spread the file open for a closer look. In the photo the agonized face of a man dressed in striped prison garb, wired electrodes clinging to his head like limpets, feeding him with pain, stared out. Truscott shook his head as if disgusted and closed the file quickly.

'Dr Eckhardt, we can give you the chance to use your talents and your intelligence to fight for the cause of freedom against the communist threat that now seeks to contaminate the world. Nearly seventy per cent of our boys captured in Korea and sent to the Chinese indoctrination camps were willing to betray their wives, their families and their country by signing confessions that the US government was corrupt in its participation in the war.'

He shook his head in genuine frustration. 'These boys were all brave men but somehow, in some way, the Chinese got into

15

their heads and turned them around. It's up to us to try and prevent this from happening again.'

Eckhardt looked at the two men blankly. 'Who are you?'

Truscott had no hesitation in answering. He gestured in Shelton's direction. 'This is Dr Shelton, Chief of the Chemical Division, Technical Services Staff, and I am Deputy Director for Plans, Clandestine Services.'

Shelton leaned forward and added softly, 'We're with the Central Intelligence Agency. You used to know us as the Office of Strategic Services, the people who helped you – er – evacuate from Germany at the end of the war.'

The surgeon looked up in surprise at the fat little man. He hadn't heard of the OSS in over twelve years.

'So now we know who everyone is,' Truscott murmured, 'we trust that you will do the right thing and help your country in the battle against the enemies of democracy.'

Eckhardt nodded gravely. It was all so familiar now. Again.

Truscott handed Shelton a letter. Shelton went on with his briefing. 'The Saint Lawrence Foundation, through its parent body, will be funding the refurbishment of the Fursting Primate Laboratory, in Livermore, California. Half the money for the project will be met by matching funds from the government—'

Truscott held his hand up to stop Shelton. 'Let me remind you, Doctor, that when you arrived in this country you signed a secrecy agreement. This programme and all its activities are covered by that agreement and we expect you to observe it. In other words, everything we tell you is classified. Do you understand?'

'Yes,' Eckhardt said quietly.

Truscott nodded for his colleague to continue.

'The research will be conducted under the nominal authority of the Foundation but will actually be directly under the control of the Chemical Division of the TSS. Project designation is MK-Ultra and funding reference is Sub-project 150.'

Trustcott put the thick file back in the case as Shelton continued.

'You will report to the Medical Facility at Vacaville State Prison, California in two weeks' time to oversee the selection of experimental subjects, after which the programme will move to the laboratory in Livermore for clinical tests.' Shelton handed him the letter and a file.

Eckhardt looked over it, just a few paragraphs of meaningless words. 'Do I sign it?'

The two men smiled.

'Never sign anything,' advised Shelton. 'Just familiarize yourself with the aims of the programme.'

Truscott got his full six-foot, three-inch frame up from the seat. 'I'm sure I have no need to restate the need for you to maintain the security of this conversation, Dr Eckhardt.' He waited, towering over the surgeon, who was still staring blankly at the sheet of paper.

'Of course . . . er . . . thank you,' said Eckhardt vacantly.

'Good,' Truscott smiled and left the room.

Shelton picked up his hat from behind the desk. 'Destroy the paper when you're finished. I'll be in touch in the next couple of days to arrange for your travel.'

'Yes . . . yes, thank you,' replied Eckhardt, still quietly shocked.

Before Shelton followed his boss out the door he turned, settling a fawn trilby on his wide crown, and smiled. 'I'm sure you'll enjoy the work Doctor. Welcome to Ultra.'

As the door closed behind the two men, Eckhardt looked at the CIA internal memo, streams of watery gold sunlight from the window bathing the words . . . *unlimited supply of subjects.*

He adjusted his glasses and decided to open the file. The first subject for proposed experimentation was a fifteen-year-old boy who had attempted to kill a priest with a compass needle.

California State Lotteries

Mega Lotto

RESULT

Wed 8th August

| 5 | 7 | 21 | 28 | 41 | 17 |

Defendit Numeris

A manual, Cherie Blaynes reminded herself, flooring the clutch
pedal with a little grunt of effort, and dragging the gearshift
into position, waggling it a few times to confirm that it was in
neutral. She didn't want a repeat of the embarrassing episode
when she'd taken the car out of the forecourt in front of all the
mechanics, trying to smother their smirks in front of her father
as the ignition squealed and the car bucked like a mule, stalling.
She'd forgotten it was in gear. Her father had come running.
Patient but worried.

She turned off the engine and in the silence smiled to herself
with satisfaction. She flipped down the visor, a small tidemark
of dust creeping up the sides of the little vanity mirror. She
moved her head slightly from side to side, checking that her
face wasn't too flushed, touching up her lip gloss, just like her
mom did in the Beemer. She fished her handbag from beneath
the seat and checked all the windows. When she got out she
checked the doors, all of them, even the trunk. In the last rays
of the setting summer sun she walked across the parking lot,
an abandoned jigsaw of parked cars and empty spaces, the
shadows of the buildings darkening against the haze. She looked
back to see her little white Mazda, parked between a blue Buick
and a red Hyundai so it wouldn't be lonely.

Cherie paused at the corner of the shopping mall, about to
step out on to Receda. All the shops that looked out onto the
parking lot were closed, their neon lights humming softly at
the darkening sky. She touched her handbag instinctively and
glanced at the canopy of the ATM at the corner of the building.

She knew she had thirty dollars in her bag. Anyway, Donnie
would be paying, surely.

It was Cherie Blaynes's last night of summer vacation.
Tomorrow she would be entering the daunting new world of
the eleventh grade but on the plus side she would have her
own car. It wasn't a BMW or a new Beetle like some of her

friends had, but it was a car none the less, and it would put her firmly on the scene.

She rounded the corner and stepped onto the wide sidewalk of Receda, the far side shadowy and indistinct while the near side blazed like a wall of pink fire in the dying light of the setting sun. The warmth jumped up from the sidewalk, bringing with it a smell of disinfectant, flavoured with a tang of rubber. Cars swished by at long but regular intervals, as if some law of science spread them evenly apart. It was as if the whole Valley was preparing for school. With one hand she gestured swiftly and flipped her blonde hair behind her ears. Donnie always liked it down. She and her mom liked it up, more pretty, lady-like. Her dad, too.

Turning off the sidewalk Cherie walked under the Aldcott portico into the thin blue light of the mall, increasing her pace as she saw the hands of the clock in the shape of a globe over the cineplex passing eight-thirty. She was thinking about what to wear the next day and the now-possible option of bringing a change of clothes in the car when a large hand closed tightly around her mouth, filling her nose with a sharp reek of turpentine. Her heart bounced to the wall of her chest for a moment.

'Shit, Donnie!' Cherie cried, wheeling around, batting his arm away with her tiny fist.

He fell about, clutching his wrist in fake agony as two more of her friends, a giggling chorus, emerged from behind the QuickSnap photo booth.

'Aw, I'm sorry, honey.' Donnie grinned goofily as he pressed his lips on her face, wet with laughter, wet as his tongue. He gathered her in under his long, tanned arm, teenage-thin.

'We're just waiting for Jared now,' he said, scanning the entrance.

'He's not here yet?' Cherie blushed.

Donnie's tongue was expertly working around his teeth as Cherie kissed the others goodbye, regretting that the next time they met would be in school.

'Got it!' he announced triumphantly after ejecting a fibrous fragment from his mouth and flicking his hands free of salt, the legacy of a jumbo bucket of popcorn.

'That movie was shit,' he declared. 'Pretentious crud,' he added with a critical shake of his shaven head.

'I thought it was good.' Cherie folded her arms. In the three hours since they had gone inside it seemed as if the summer had gone and the sun had shifted south, lowering the temperature of the Valley at least five degrees, cueing the onset of the Californian autumn and the start of school.

'Where you parked?' Donnie asked as another couple of movie-goers slipped by, in the same post-movie glaze that leaves people mouthing small talk.

'Just around the corner,' Cherie replied.

'I'll walk you over,' Donnie decided, putting his arm around her.

'You don't have to,' she replied, already walking, safe against his shoulder.

'Oh, I won't, then. My car's the other way.' He laughed, rounding the corner and walking into the sudden silence of the parking lot.

Cherie smiled and nuzzled into his ribs. He was nearly a foot taller. She liked that.

'Shit, I gotta get some money,' Donnie realized, remembering he owed at least eighty dollars around school. He wasn't going to start off the new term with old debts.

'There's an ATM over there,' Cherie observed, indicating the silver box set in the wall of the mall, its screen dim beneath the bright canopy.

'You'll hold on?' Donnie asked, as his hands roved around his big Adidas sports coat, looking for his cards.

'I'll carry on walking,' she said, thinking again of school tomorrow and sorting things out at home for the morning. 'My car looks lonely,' she added in a baby voice.

The parking lot was almost empty now, just three or four other vehicles among the hundred or so spaces.

They embraced. He stooped, cupping her head in his left hand, his right palm sliding beneath her belt, feeling the firm flesh of her belly, working downwards into her loins, towards the wiry prickle of hair.

25

She moved her lips from his mouth. He tasted salty, like sulphur on a match.

'See you tomorrow.' She smiled and broke away.

'Unfortunately,' he cackled, accustomed to the rebuff, and turned to the ATM.

Donnie took out his ATM card and, placing it to the lips of the machine, saw it sucked in, heard the machine whirring somewhere in its interior works.

He glanced around – Cherie's shape was moving across the lines that marked out the parking spaces.

The machine asked for his PIN. He tapped it in and thrummed the console impatiently, his nails ticking on the steel.

But after a thoughtful moment the machine blinked back, a question mark flashing.

Try again.

Shit.

He stared at the screen.

Hendrix alive in Heaven.

Yeah, that's it.

Thank you.

Six five eleven.

He tapped it in and looked around. She should be there by now.

He squinted. No sign of Cherie. The car stayed quiet.

The machine scrolled up the amount box, gave a choice in a menu for convenience. How much, buddy?

He squinted again at the car: dull white, creamy under the lamps, no figure near it, no light hair, no knee bent to get in.

Then its ignition came on, like two tin plates rubbing together, and the engine took over, revving.

The lights flicked on.

She was already in.

Donnie turned back to the machine.

Tapped in a one and two zeros.

Gotta buy lunch as well.

Behind him he could hear Cherie's car shuffle slowly away.

OVERLAND AVENUE, WESTWOOD, WESTERN LOS ANGELES

Not a sound.

Not even a breath of wind.

Nothing from the trees.

Just Daniel Crebbs Jnr's footsteps on the drive.

Little light.

No moon.

Just a low plasmic dome of orange spreading from the east to the south of the city, far from the comfortable routine silence of the western suburbs.

He looked up. The windows were black behind the panes. The house asleep.

Straightening his jacket, he tried to make the badge more prominent and pressed the doorbell.

A gong somewhere in the heart of the house, deep inside. Remembering the peak of his cap, he tilted it straight.

The porch light came on.

Crebbs Sr turned his body to the camera. Its little eye perched like an owl above the corner of the doorway. The intercom hissed. A sleepy voice, tinny as if it actually lived in the little square box.

'Hello? . . . Is anything up?'

A light was on now in the bedroom.

'I'm very sorry to disturb you, Mr Wiedener,' said Crebbs loudly to the box. He flashed his ScanTec ID to it and then up to the camera. 'But we're letting people on your circuit know that the lines to the base station are down and the relays are not auto-switching to the police lines . . .'

'Eh . . . okay,' was all the little voice said. More technical problems with the system again. Next time just get a dog.

'Sorry, Mr Wiedener, but I have to come in to reset your line for a radio link.'

Crebbs waited, bent down closer to the speaker.

'Sir? Mr Wiedener?'

27

'I'll be down in a minute,' the voice said, boomy, distant from the mike as its owner got out of bed.

'Sorry, sir, but aren't you forgetting—'

'—Forgetting what?' the voice asked, the speaker rasping in its coils.

It was four in the fucking morning.

'The password, sir,' urged Crebbs. 'You should always ask us for the password before allowing admission to the residence.'

A breath from the box, a sigh.

'Oh yeah . . . right . . . the password.'

The intercom went dead for a moment as the man of the house fumbled over the buttons of the ScanTec 7000 Premium Home security system control panel next to the bed – satin ivory, roughly matching the wall trim Mrs Wiedener had picked out. She too must surely be awake by now.

'Okay, I got it.' The little voice returned, brighter.

'Okay.' Crebbs approached within inches of the two-way speaker. 'Today's password is Connecticut.'

'Great,' Wiedener replied, decidedly unimpressed. 'I'm coming down.' He patched out.

Crebbs looked out into the dark, into the garden, the darker recesses under the acacia.

The hall light came on and the door latch opened. Wiedener appeared, wearing a mauve paisley gown that he was tying at the waist. Tallish in his slippers, he raked back his blond hair, patting it in place.

Crebbs smiled, surprised. Pretty athletic for a bank manager.

'I'm sorry for the inconvenience, Mr Wiedener. The company will compensate you, of course.'

'It's a'right.' Wiedener waved it off. They still had the fruit basket from the last fuck-up. Just the week before.

'Where's Jimmy tonight? Isn't that his name?' asked Wiedener, tightening his belt.

'Night off.' Crebbs smiled and entered. He made a beeline for the main controller behind the coat-rack under the stairs. 'I won't keep you long, sir.' He crouched over the panel, removing its cover screws with an Allen key.

'Hope I haven't woken up the rest of the house.'

'Oh no,' Wiedener assured him. 'My wife would sleep through anything.'

'Good,' Crebbs gasped. He flicked the master switch and reached up over his face, the ScanTec hat falling off.

Wiedener's windpipe was suddenly constricted by a thick, black-leather-clad arm that wrenched his head back against the barrel of a Coonan .357 Magnum.

Jeshsus Chrishht!

The words squeezed through his clenched teeth, snapped through a cataract of spit. His nostrils flared, seeking air to feed his pounding chest.

Daniel Crebbs Jnr had arrived.

Crebbs Sr's ScanTec hat was on the floor. His eyes wide in the white holes of a ski mask now stretched over his features, he produced a black handgun from his jacket. He laid it against his own temple, pointing it up, and kissed the index finger of his other hand in a gesture indicating the need for silence.

The black arm tightened around Wiedener's neck, pressing the cold shooter harder against his cranium.

Crebbs looked up the stairs.

Wiedener's eyes, the only part of him that could move, peered in the same direction.

His wife.

Too late for the panic button.

The three men began their slow procession up the stairs, Wiedener in the lead, his head rigid, as if directly connected to the gun.

'All right, honey,' answered Wiedener before they went through the bedroom door.

His wife, alerted by the silence when her husband had gone downstairs, had called out to him, wondering what was going on.

She wasn't stupid enough to scream when she saw the black figures behind her husband.

'Oh my God, what—' she squealed, her voice muffled.

'Shut up!' Crebbs cried, too loud, and brought his own gun to bear on her. The noise unsettled his comrade, who steadied himself on his feet, flexing his fingers nervously around the gun butt pressed against his captive's head.

'Okay, lady, don't lose it.' Crebbs lowered his voice, 'Everything will be fine, we're just taking your husband to make a quick withdrawal.'

Mrs Wiedener sat up in the bed. She kept her eyes on the gun and her mind straight, glancing at her husband. He nodded reassuringly.

'You better get dressed,' said Crebbs, turning to Mr Wiedener. 'Don't want you gettin' arrested for indecent exposure.'

With a jerk of his head, Crebbs called his associate over. 'You keep an eye on the lady of the house.'

The second man kept the gun pointed at Wiedener's head while quickly and awkwardly moving to the bed, his outstretched arm swinging stiffly from one target to the next. A bit amateurish – Crebbs shook his head. He was sure that Mrs Wiedener blushed.

'You keep a *close* eye on this bitch,' he said, his stare meeting hers.

Wiedener was almost ready, fishing the keys from his suit pocket. He turned to say something to his wife but Crebbs nudged him though the door with the gun.

'Let's go, cowboy,' he said cheerfully, herding the bank manager down the stairs. Without looking back he called over his shoulder. 'Make sure your phone's on!'

The other man in the room nodded, keeping his gaze and the .357 on Mrs Wiedener.

'Yeah, I got it,' he shouted back, his nose twitching against the rough fabric of his mask.

Mrs Wiedener could hear the door closing downstairs, sucking air from the house in a gust that rattled the bedroom windows. Then silence fell.

Even in such circumstances humans can still feel the embarrassment of an awkward moment of quiet between strangers. Though she could only see his eyes through the ski mask, Mrs Wiedener knew that this man was young: his eyes were brighter and wider than the other man's.

Fractions of Zero

'You might as well lay back, honey,' he suggested as he slid into the chair next to the bed. 'We could be a while.'

Mrs Wiedener slowly let herself lean back against the head-board, drew up the bedclothes tight around her chest and looked away from the man with the gun who kept his gaze on her, his eyes roving her form beneath the bed sheets.

She seemed a bit younger than her husband. Late twenties, early thirties maybe. Nice brown eyes. Good teeth, though he hadn't seen her smile. Long, dark auburn hair, strands of copper running down the temples, tousled now. He noticed she was wearing a football shirt, huge on her, white with a blue trim. The Cowboys? Was that all she wore to bed? He smiled a grin of yellow teeth, grey-edged along the gumline.

As Wiedener's Mercedes slid onto Olympic a dark Tantura pick-up swung away from the kerb and tucked in a neat fifty metres behind. Crebbs looked over his shoulder and Wiedener could see him smile in the corner of his vision. There was little traffic, as expected.

A black-and-white out of the West LA station cruised past, unconcerned, in the opposite direction.

'Try any shit—' Crebbs showed Wiedener his cell phone '—and my brother will have to cut short his visit with your wife.' A rehearsed smile creased his face, an extra threat.

'Though I think he kinda likes her.'

The bank manager nodded solemnly and the dark pick-up followed them the six miles to the Alliance & Pacific Bank on Nineteenth Street in Santa Monica.

'No kids, huh?'

'No.'

'Why not? Mr Weener ain't got enough swimmers?'

'We just decided not to.'

Mrs Wiedener met her captor's gaze for the first time since her husband had left. She quickly looked away, realizing that the eye contact was making his stare harden.

The Alliance & Pacific Bank was dark, just some dim recess spots threading the perimeter of the foyer in a necklace of light.

Crebbs's breath seemed to tighten in shallow gasps as he watched in the rear-view mirror the dark pick-up as it came to a halt by the sidewalk some thirty metres behind them.

'Okay,' he said finally, his gaze searching the empty angles of the street and the intersection two blocks down. 'Let's go.'

Wiedener got out of the car first and waited dutifully for Crebbs to get out too and come around to the kerb, the barrel of his gun now hidden in his jacket pocket. They made their way to the glass doors of the bank. A master key allowed them into the foyer and to the biometric access system. Wiedener turned on the retinal scanner and waited while the tiny invisible laser combed his right eye's vascular pattern and cross-referenced it with the staff database. A green light prompted him to key in his security PIN and with a simple twist of the knob he disarmed the pressure pads, acoustic pick-ups and breach beams that protected the building from intrusion. The anti-robbery door unfolded its interlocking steel arms and allowed them into the public area of the bank, a smell of fresh carpet shampoo hanging in the dark warm air.

'Do you want lights?' Wiedener asked, forgiving himself the stupidity of the question given the circumstances.

Crebbs just shook his head and the gun emerged once again from his pocket. He fixed his eyes on the thick pine staff door at the end of the service counter.

'Come on, let's keep going,' Crebbs urged, nudging the bank manager in his stomach with the gun. With another master key, Wiedener led his captor through a succession of doors to the vault room at the rear of the bank.

Crebbs's eyes seemed to bulge and redden as he scanned the room. On one side the cashbars stood behind the ATM, gently humming, the cash cassettes deadbolted with a framework of iron bars. Beside the ATM hung the blue night-deposit sacks, bulging like Christmas stockings beneath the drop chutes. But Crebbs had no interest in these and he knew the bank manager would not have any way of accessing them. On the right stood the manifest room, a small glass cage, just large enough for two people and a couple of million dollars in any denomination. Supposedly bulletproof, it was completely empty, just a counter top and a typist's chair. Crebbs turned his eyes to the left side of the room and smiled at the eight-foot-high battleship-grey door dimpled with a smooth bulge from which protruded the hand clasp and the 'valve wheel'. On the wall next to the steel door was a small squat number pad and a miniature LCD screen.

Crebbs fished out his cell phone and gave the all-clear. Thirty seconds later Wiedener instinctively stood back as three men in old US army jackets and black ski masks entered the vault room. One carried a sawn-off shotgun while another carried an AK-47. The third, a small man, toted a large holdall in one hand and a small oxygen tank in the other.

'It's on a time lock,' Wiedener told them.

This amused Crebbs as he gave directions to the two gunmen to take up station at the entrance to the room. 'We ain't got time to hang around,' he laughed. 'We got our magic lantern.'

The small man knelt down in front of the vault, carefully lowering the tank on its side. From his holdall he took out two long thin rods of magnesium and twisted them together. He was about to attach the oxygen tube to the joined rods but suddenly they all turned towards the rear wall as one of the night sacks shuffled on its hook. The movement looked like a ferret caught in a bag and a metallic thud sounded somewhere outside.

'What the fuck is that?' whispered one of the gunmen, nervously aiming his AK-47 at the back wall of the vault room, alert for any sign of movement.

Wiedener raised his hands to calm them. Crebbs shot a glance at him, looking for an explanation, and fast.

'It's just a night deposit!' the bank manager explained, with a nervous, placatory smile.

Crebbs watched the wall, the deposit bags once more hanging silently from the chutes, the ATM buzzing quietly in its interior circuits.

They all lowered their guns again and the kneeling man pushed the rod into the clear tubing that ran like an umbilical from the oxygen tank.

Crebbs put his gun down. 'Okay, Mr Wiedener, your job's nearly over.' He held out his hand.

Wiedener was puzzled for a moment.

'The *keys*, fuckhead!' Crebbs screamed at him.

Wiedener handed them over and was rewarded with a punch in the ribs that made his stomach lock in spasm, choking him. He was about to fall over when Crebbs caught his arms from behind and wrenched them behind his back. He could hear his muscles tearing and the faint gasps of laughter from the other raiders.

Crebbs ripped some telephone cord from the wall and bound them around Wiedener's wrists. He dragged him to the glass door of the manifest booth and, jangling through the keys, found the right one and opened the door. Wiedener was still gasping for air as Crebbs tied him to the typist's chair with more phone cord, tightening the flex so hard around his wrists that the bank manager could no longer feel his hands.

Today was Friday, he thought. Last year's FBI figures demonstrated that nearly twenty-two per cent of all armed robberies in California occurred on a Friday.

Crebbs pulled out his cell phone, tapped in seven letters and held it up in front of Wiedener.

'Any shit from you and I'll press the send button.'

He locked the bank manager in the counting room as the magnesium torch ignited in a low blowing roar and its operator set its cutting flame against the steel.

Mrs Wiedener looked at her watch as she pulled back her sleeve with her index finger.

'So what time is it?' her captor asked, looking at her sleek fingers, her nails not too long but well manicured.

'Three twenty-nine,' she answered and squeezed her knees together to stop them from trembling.

'Cold?'

She nodded.

He got up and, smiling, went to the walk-in closet, all the time keeping the gun on her.

'Let's see,' he said, quickly glancing around the clothes, neatly stacked on the shelves. 'What could you put on?'

At the back of the closet he found her dresses, hanging on a rail. 'A bit dressy.' He smiled, holding up a short black chiffon dress in front of him. He stared at her in the bed and his smile became fixed as he drew the dress back against his chest and arched his hips against it. Then he broke into laughter, dropped it on the ground and swept his free arm across the shelves, littering the floor with clothes. He picked up a pair of jeans and walked slowly to the bed. Mrs Wiedener gathered herself even tighter, burying as much of her body as she could under the sheets.

'Come on, honey, put these on,' he said, flinging the jeans on the bed in front of her. 'You said you were cold,' he sneered, a white cheese of spit in the corner of his mouth, as he waited for her to remove the bedclothes.

She was shaking, trembling under the hot weight of his gaze.

'I'll need a belt for these,' she pleaded feebly.

The bright plume from the magnesium torch slowly traced a black scar down the face of the steel vault door. The gunmen turned their heads back and forth, nervously searching the dark foyer of the bank and the street outside the windows. Crebbs watched patiently, almost transfixed by the dazzling blade of fire slicing the cold metal in a loud whooshing noise like a steam hose.

A noise made him start. A metal thunk, like a dustbin lid.

One of the night sacks stirred again.

He lowered his gun.

The small man operating the torch stopped for a moment to lift his ski mask and wipe his brow. Crebbs looked around to see if Wiedener was watching, but the bank manager was out of sight. Crebbs noticed a hissing sound just before the torch was brought to bear on the door again. From one of the blue night sacks thick columns of white smoke billowed, filling the air with a biting smell that made Crebbs's throat tighten and his eyes sting with tears. CS gas.

There were voices, muffled shouts from outside. The man with the shotgun jerked back as a red column of fire issued from its barrel, blasting into the dark. A stuttering response of automatic gunfire peppered the vault-room walls, splintering off the steel surfaces.

The man with the torch ducked for cover. The two gunmen at the door fired indiscriminately at the moving shadows outside that were the source of the shouting voices. The man with the AK-47 took a hit in the shoulder blasting a string of blood against the wall. As he fell his gun loosed a few bursts that dug a string of bullet holes in the ceiling. Then his head fell back and a small puff of smoke spurted from his ski mask. The man with the shotgun tried to reload but a short rip of gunfire made his body jerk before a single shot to the head stilled all movement and he went down.

Crebbs shot into the dark square of the doorway at the shapes of men running through. Then he turned and shattered the glass of the counting booth with a single shot. He raised his gun to execute the bank manager.

The air was full of choking smoke and the bank manager was coughing violently in front of him. Voices surrounded him, gas masks, black-helmeted, faceless assassins with yellow letters on their shields, muffled orders to surrender.

Then it felt like someone was prodding with a hot poker. Crebbs couldn't move – it was as if the bank manager's pleading face, running with tears, was somehow sucking the life from his body. The pain grew like a hot plume of fire from his abdomen up his chest.

He couldn't pull the trigger and dropped the gun. Instead, he pulled out the cell phone.

All feeling shrunk to a burning point on the back of his head. Then everything blew out red.

The masked raider ran from the closet back into the bedroom, the .357 Magnum trembling in his hand as he raised it to Mrs Wiedener's head.

A window smashed somewhere in the house, sprinkling glass on a wooden floor.

Feet pounded up the stairs.

He cocked the hammer.

She flung off the bedclothes for him.

Her fine tanned legs.

Between her thighs the black eye of a Glock-17 muzzle,

winking as a 9mm round left the barrel and spat in his face. The crown of his head lifted for a moment, then fell to the floor in pieces. His knees collapsed and he fell forward on top of her. His weight squashed her gun into her abdomen and snapped her wrist in one second. Her fingers locked and the gun gave a smothered thud, making his crumpled body spasm once more, his shattered skull clinking in its retaining mask of skin like a bag of broken crockery.

As she writhed in the searing agony of her fractured wrist she shouldered the limp form off her. He fell on the floor, fanning a small spray of blood across the pine.

The back-up agents found her sobbing on the bed, her broken-wristed hand still clutching the gun. On the floor at the foot of the bed, her attacker lay, leaking heavily, his black ski mask turning burgundy, pushed in like a punctured football.

ASSISTANT DIRECTOR'S OFFICE, FEDERAL BUILDING, WILSHIRE BLVD, LOS ANGELES

Agent Ramirez sat with Kronziac while Phillips paced the office, shaking his head, muttering and occasionally grimacing with pain when he forgot the livid bruising on his wrists.

'Why in the fuck did they give your name?'

Kronziac shook her head and scanned the report in the *LA Times*.

> Four of the Bitteroot Woodsmen, a Montana faction of anti-government activists, were killed in an FBI sting. Two of them were brothers, Daniel Crebbs, 25, and his 17-year-old brother Matthew.
>
> The operation was led by Special Agent Nancy Kronziac of the FBI's Domestic Terrorism Unit.
>
> The Woodsmen captured an undercover agent who was posing as a bank manager, and gained entry to the Santa Monica branch of the Alliance & Pacific Bank to steal money to fund their armed campaign.

Kronziac closed her eyes for a moment and tried to smother another yawn.

'You okay, hon?' asked Maggie, leaning close. 'Yeah, fine,' Kronziac replied tersely. '. . . Thanks,' she added, as gently as she could.

Maggie Ramirez was twenty-four years old, a psychology graduate from the University of Miami with a year's postgrad work at the John Jay College of Criminal Justice. She was just six months out of training at Quantico. Maggie was petite, athletic like a gymnast and very pretty, with bright brown eyes and short black hair. With her ever-enthusiastic attitude and an obvious bent for investigative analysis she was quickly endearing herself to everyone in the office. Somehow she seemed to have latched on to Kronziac as some sort of a role model and tended to copy a lot of her mannerisms – like holding the steering wheel of her car with one hand at the six o'clock position or reaching for a cigarette packet when she got annoyed with something.

She'd been the first to find Kronziac after the shooting in the bedroom the previous day. Her sympathy was genuine but cloying. Kronziac now felt like telling her to get away from her, to walk around the room like Phillips. That was one of the many things she liked about Phillips – he rarely sympathized in the sickly hand-on-the-shoulder way with her or gave in to the politically correct fashion of apologizing for the sometimes brutal nature of their job.

The door snapped open and Assistant Director-in-Charge Leonard Foley strode in, carrying a cup of coffee, tinkling on its saucer. A short, square man in his fifties, Foley had been Director of the LA field office for nearly ten years and had wondered if he would ever get the call to return to Washington as Deputy Director of the whole Bureau. He was beginning to suspect his age was acting against him. Kronziac quite liked him. He always seemed fair, though he had little to do with the Unit – reckoning that domestic terrorism was something of an isolated threat to the nation's peace. He still kept a large portrait of Hoover on the wall behind his desk and dusted it every week.

He stopped abruptly and put the cup to his lips, taking a judicious sip of the coffee. He turned and smiled to his secretary outside. 'Perfect, Miranda, thanks,' he said and continued into the room.

Following him was the tall figure of Nathan Sedley. He was quite good-looking, Kronziac had thought on seeing him the first day he arrived: handsome in a conventional way with a severely angular jawline and a square brow. His manner was thoughtful and reserved, and he had yet to join them for a beer or cocktail at their local watering holes. But he seemed nice enough and on occasion talked to her about his wife and two kids. Phillips, of course, disliked him, not only because of his cool efficiency and easy competence, but because he reckoned Sedley had taken his, Phillips's, job, parachuted in from the Violent Crimes Unit at the Chicago field office to take over as a Deputy Assistant Director. It made Kronziac smile: whatever else Phillips was, a DAD he was not.

Sedley glanced at Kronziac, a searching look.

'You okay, Nancy?' he asked.

'Fine.' She smiled thinly and put the paper down. He was still calling her by her first name.

'Sit down, Phillips,' instructed Foley. But there were no more seats left as Sedley had sat down in the last one on Foley's side of the desk. 'Or just stop . . . pacing.'

Phillips complied. 'Yes, sir.' He leaned against one of the oak bookcases that housed the Director's columns of law books.

Foley picked up the paper and glanced with raised eyes at Kronziac.

'I'm fine,' she stated again, putting up her right hand as if swearing in.

'Well,' Foley began, 'I first want to say thank God that none of you were hurt . . . too seriously,' he added, acknowledging Kronziac's wrist. 'In many respects I suppose the operation was a success. Four less bad guys on the streets.' He smiled unconvincingly.

He paused for a sip of coffee and clicked his lips as if trying to put a year on the bean.

'However, as you know, there has to be an internal inquiry about what happened and since Nathan was actually there he will submit a report for the DOJ . . . for the record. And that, I should say, will be the end to it.' He dipped his head and sipped again from his coffee.

Sedley took his chance.

'I don't think there's anything to worry about.'

Kronziac stared at him.

What the fuck is this?

Phillips could not keep silent. He stood up straight.

'What do you mean? We didn't actually do anything wrong. The operation was cleared, procedures were observed, the HRT boys did what they do and that was that.'

Sedley reflected solemnly. '. . . And five civilians are dead. One of them just seventeen years old,' he added in the direction of Kronziac and kept his eyes on her to see if she had anything to add. She remained silent.

'Are we under investigation?' asked Phillips cautiously. The question made Maggie look around at him.

Sedley waited for his boss to say something but Foley kept his eyes down as he sucked the rim of his cup.

'It's a standard report, nothing to worry about,' Sedley assured them.

Phillips seemed to be more angered by Sedley's evasiveness.

'Are we on suspension?'

Sedley laughed. 'Of course not. But . . .'

Kronziac looked up at him.

But.

'You both were subjected to a traumatic encounter yesterday and so I . . . we . . . think it would be in your own interests to take some leave.'

Kronziac looked at Foley.

He nodded. 'Yes, I agree,' he said. 'Get away from things here and don't worry.'

She did not like the way they kept telling them not to worry but all she said was, 'Fine.'

'Another thing,' Sedley began, with an air of caution. 'We reckon their older brother Lucas Crebbs might be—' he didn't seem to know quite how to phrase it '—might be gunning for you, Nancy. He'll want revenge for the deaths of Daniel and Matthew. Jones in the Twin Falls office is keeping an eye on the Crebbs homestead and said Lucas hasn't made a move yet but you should be aware.'

Kronziac seemed unresponsive to the news that Lucas Crebbs, one of the most violent and notorious of the Woodsmen, was probably going to come after her for the death of his brothers.

'We'll drop in on her,' Maggie assured Sedley and Foley.

'Good,' Sedley replied, like one who'd just averted a crisis. He looked up at Phillips who was shaking his head again and looking decidedly pissed off with the whole idea.

'Okay,' he said, shrugging. 'Holiday time it is.'

Maggie felt a bit stupid but still had to ask.

'No, Maggie, you're still on duty,' Foley informed her, smiling apologetically.

She got up and followed Phillips out the door.

Kronziac was left wondering if there was more. She got out of her chair slowly. But before she could say anything Sedley stood up.

'Thanks, Nancy. You get some well-earned rest.'

She turned to Foley but he was sipping his coffee again, though it was stone cold by now.

2434 ABRAMAR, PACIFIC PALISADES, CA

Kronziac thought about it the whole way home and was still thinking about it as her blue Explorer four-by-four squeezed to a stop in the garage. In the darkness of the car port she tried to shake from her head the image of Matthew Crebbs, lying on the floor, the top of his head blown off, an oozing soup of brain and skullbone neatly packed like a pudding in his ski mask.

Did I react too soon? Could I have waited another second or two for Maggie and the others to enter the room? He might have surrendered.

As she got out of the car the sudden white blast of morning sun chased her to the front door and into the cool refuge of the house where she leaned against the door and took a deep breath.

She was home.

Couched on a verdant mesa between Temescal Canyon to the east and Marquez Knolls to the west, the house had been inherited by Kronziac from an actress aunt who had bought the property in the 1950s for seven thousand dollars, the exact fee she'd got for landing a small part in a Joe Mankiewicz movie. Kronziac always told everyone, or at least those she was trying to impress, that she was her aunt's favourite niece. Then she added, with a breezy laugh, her *only* niece. She kept to herself the suspicion that her inheritance had more to do with her aunt's desire for revenge than with her affection – revenge on a wayward husband, a barman and bit-past actor who was rumoured to have had flings with every female extra on the Warner lot.

She threw her keys in the little rosebud bowl on the hat stand by the door and, going into the kitchen, she plucked a bottle of water from the fridge.

Hector watched her go by with a swivel of his cold glassy eyes.

The real-estate people were always haranguing her, saying she could get nearly a million for the place, half a million alone

43

for the view. She turned the key in the French doors and walked out onto the veranda and leaned her palms against the clay-red deco tiles that fringed the patio, warming under the noonday sun.

My informer told me they were committed, twisted sons of bitches but would avoid using their guns at all costs.

She watched the snaking threads of traffic, from Santa Monica up the golden arm of the Pacific Coast Highway, hugging Topanga Beach and stretching beyond the cupped hand of the Malibu Colony shore. Pulling back like a camera she held the view of the ocean, a pale blue vee framed by burgeoning ranks of California oak on each side, a bank of *bougainvillea glabra* with its legions of cyclamen-coloured flower bracts marching up the foreground, pushing up the sloping garden from the smoky green haze of the pine bluffs. She held in her gaze a Signac painting, a living idyll of Medea – worth half a million bucks.

She turned around to her children, their little faces coloured medals of light in the sun, nodding like an audience in the wind – a chorus of day-lilies, the Scarlet Orbit sopranos, their high colour merging melodiously with the crimson pistils of Kwanso Flore Pleno and the cooler tones of *citrina*.

She would water them later, lest the sun should scorch them through their tears.

Lowering herself onto the sun lounger, its blue stripes faded as old denim, she rested and was pulled into sleep as the sun licked her face, a tongue of fire.

BLACKJACK

'I've explained how to play . . . I'm the Dealer and you're the Player. Basic house rules: five dollar minimum, Dealer stands on seventeens, faces up . . . *for the beginner*,' he added graciously.

He reached down and picked up the shoulder bag. Unzipping it, he rooted around and tossed out its useless contents: a Snoopy diary, a driver's licence, some magazine coupons, a stick of lip gloss.

He let the bag fall when he found the purse. He split it open, fishing for the money.

'Okay . . . no high rollers tonight,' he observed, fingering two bills and running a cursory glance over the assorted change.

'About fifteen bucks,' he surmised, pocketing the money. 'Three reds it is.'

From a small black tray on the table he carefully selected three red chips from a row of red, green and black columns and slid them across the cloth.

'I don't have any whites,' he giggled.

He picked up the cards and began to shuffle.

'Now remember, an ace is either one or eleven and the jack, queen and king are the same as ten. Reach twenty-one before the Dealer and win your bet. Get twenty-one on your first two – and Blackjack!' he announced with hollow jubilation. His hands stopped and he looked up at her.

'. . . And I might let you go,' he said softly.

She trembled. The duct tape clung to her mouth like a skin graft, pulling the flesh of her cheeks down over her face, squeezing it over her mouth, making her nostrils suck and blow for air.

'Ready?' he asked, about to deal.

She trembled helplessly.

'Five-dollar bet,' he announced and pulled back one of her chips into the middle of the table.

'Ready?'

She squeezed her eyes shut.

Too long for a blink.

Not long enough to wake from the nightmare.

'Good,' he said, 'let's begin.'

He dealt her one card, face up – a seven.

Then his own, face down.

Her second – an ace.

And his second card, face down.

He turned his first over.

A queen.

'Okay, Player has a soft seventeen and Dealer a ten,' he observed. 'Stand, hit or double-down?'

His fingers thrummed the deck.

Staring at him, her neck pulsed with a pleading moan from her trapped voice.

'I'm sorry.' He put the deck down. 'Don't let it be said I don't play by the rules.'

The stool squealed as he turned to the tool chest on his right. His hand crawled down the drawers past the hammers, the wrench sets and the drill bits until he came to the cutters.

As he pulled the drawer out she could see a neat arrangement of handles lying on the soft yellow bed of chamois – pliers, wire-cutters, secateurs and scissors. His fingers danced an inch above the instruments as if he was a judicious surgeon or someone looking for their favourite chocolate. Next to a shiny, long-limbed scissors sat the ugly, squat grey 'X' of a wire-cutter.

The curved claws tightened and the red three-core electrical flex snapped open. A snort rushed from her nose. She flexed her red fingers and rotated her blanched wrist robotically, its veins cooling with the blood rush. He was speaking again.

'Remember, tap for a hit, two taps for a double-down and a flat wave for a stand.'

He gazed at her, frowning, his brows twisted with impatience. Her head shook, eyes half blinking, and she tapped the table once.

Another card.

A queen.

'Hit or stand?'

She couldn't work it out. Her paralysed brain wanted to collapse.

'You've eighteen. Now, hit or stand?' he insisted.

She shook her head wearily.

'I take it you're standing.'

His cheeks dimpled as he turned up his own second card and beheld a king of spades.

'Twenty! Dealer wins!' he trumpeted and cleared the table. With exaggerated movements he picked up the red chip and placed it in the tray with all the others. Shifting excitedly in his seat like someone expecting a roll he began dealing the cards again.

'Oh, almost forgot,' he sniggered, affecting a childish awkwardness. Reaching over, he slid back one of her two remaining chips into the middle.

'Five bucks again. Don't want to bleed you dry.'

Her head fell forward with exhaustion and a plain unwillingness to watch him any more.

But he dealt her a jack and a queen this time.

His first card was a four.

'Want to split your hand?' he offered cautiously, aware he was about to lose.

Her hand moved towards her mouth and tears were dripping from her lowered face once more. Her bottom eyelids were stretched in the grip of the tape, making her eyes sore and cold.

'I might let you go,' he said quietly, like a remorseful child chided for being cruel to the family dog. Then his face flushed with anger.

'Come on, Alison!' he roared. 'Hit, stand or double-down?'

Her head lifted and in her red-rimmed eyes a last flicker of hatred flashed. An anguished, throaty roar reverberated behind her duct-tape gag.

He snatched the cutters from the table. In one swift movement he grabbed her free hand, holding it tight as she tried to wriggle it free. Then he simply snipped her index finger off.

'You're standing,' he decided calmly, sitting down as she slumped in shock.

He flicked over his own cards.

An ace.

'Fifteen soft,' he smiled and dealt himself another.

This time an eight, eight of hearts, scarlet red.

'Back to thirteen now.'

Flicked over one more.

A nine of spades.

Dealer busted.

He looked at her.

Her anger now gone, a hollow moment of defiance, all muffled sound and fury. Her hand shivering, the stumped knuckle bending as if trying to locate the rest of itself. A strand of her blonde hair fell down over her glistening brow. He saw her legs were open, the smooth denim sheathing her inner thighs gathering in a tight bunch between them. Her sweat settled like dew on her neck and he could see her swallow. His stomach began to burn, a light balloon of heat, fingering up his chest, tightening his throat, filling him with desire. He looked down between his legs. Nothing.

He shot up.

She was watching.

The silver mask on her mouth grinning.

Her eyes leaking tears of laughter.

The hot flame rushed up him in a wave, lifting his arm so that it lashed out like a whip, his hand snapping first from the table, then across the side of her head.

There was a small cracking sound, like the fibres of a stick of celery being twisted in two.

He stood up instinctively as her shoulders fell forward and her head slumped down over the table once more. Some liquid was running somewhere, dripping below.

He looked at his hand and exhaled with a breathy, nervous laugh.

In his fist lay the wire-cutters, their jaws clenched like lovers' hands, now dripping with rich claret.

He dropped them and looked at her.

She was moving, silently riding the steady tide of her breathing. Unconscious.

He sighed as the inner boy, disappointed with the game being over, drew back, shouldered aside by a now more inquisitive little demon.

A red wet mass was covering the side of her hair and a new shape was dangling below, rolling in the hollow between nose and cheek.

He bent down.

From the black slit of her eyelids, gently bobbing with her breathing, her right eyeball hung on a pink, gutty string of tissue. The impact of the cutters had severed the orbital bone and flicked the eyeball from its socket. He watched a streak of clotted blood run down it like red mercury, over the white orb networked with veins like crazed porcelain. He slanted his head, like a curious dog – and reached for the scissors.

DEVONSHIRE COMMUNITY POLICE STATION, 10250 ETIWANDA AVE, NORTHRIDGE, CA

Jerry Blaynes led his wife for the third time in two days up the steps to the flat functional concrete and red-brick facility of the police station. Desk Officer Linda Kempechne was shuffling through the morning mail as they came through the doors. She recognized them immediately and reached for the phone.

As they waited in the front area Cynthia held on to her husband tightly. A small woman with long loose waves of straw-berry-blonde hair, many mistook her for her daughter's older sister as they walked, laden with shopping bags, through the mall on Saturday afternoons. This, of course, delighted Cynthia but she wasn't sure whether her daughter liked this confusion. Like her own mother used to say: underneath, kids like their parents to be parents – forget the modern psycho-crap about trying to be your child's best friend.

But now, up close, the wrinkles around her eyes and mouth had deepened in the past thirty-six hours, the lines hollowed out by a cycle of tears, worry and no sleep. Her husband, Jerry, much taller than her, held her close like a child. Though his hair was still jet black with no signs of grey his face was begin-ning to sag, especially under his chin, now scratchy with two days' growth of beard.

'Morning, folks,' Detective Sergeant Cunningham greeted them as he emerged from a door beside the front desk. Carrying a file under one arm, he extended his free hand to Jerry who thought they were past that act of formality. He liked Sam Cunningham, who, as director of the Devonshire Police Activity League Supporters, had approached Jerry to see if he would take on some kids from one of the gang areas to work in his car lots. Reluctant at first, Jerry took a couple of fifteen-year-olds from Panorama City who were found by the LAPD with a stolen Ford in an overpass under the 405.

Cynthia told him he was mad and revived her campaign to move the family from their reasonably safe neighbourhood in

Twin Lakes to Riverside or Glendale or further up the Valley, anywhere so long as it was far away from the gangland areas of Northridge. They could well afford it, after all, and if not for themselves then for the children. For the first time ever Jerry was beginning to take her seriously and hoped to God it wasn't too late.

Cunningham led them down the corridor past the Squad rooms. A tall, pear-shaped man with narrow shoulders, it was as if all his muscles had melted and slid to his waist where he now carried a noticeable ring of flab. His manner was calm, almost breezy as he talked with a considered but distracted drawl as he looked for a quiet place for them.

Jerry didn't like it. Quiet places to talk usually meant bad news. But he kept his large frame tall, striding firmly, his voice steady.

'A fine station,' he remarked to his wife distractedly.

They found an empty interview room near the cell block and the fluorescent light flickered before coming on. The detective smiled and arranged the only two chairs in the room on one side of the small interview table. Jerry couldn't help fearing the worst and wanted to remain standing but Cynthia held on to his hand as they sat down.

'You found something,' she said, unable to wait.

Cunningham nodded, opening his file.

'One of our patrols found her car early this morning over near Porter Valley. Not far from where she was last seen, actually,' he said. 'Maybe a mile, mile and a half.'

'Sure it's hers?' Jerry wanted to know.

'Licence plate matches. A yellow Mazda,' the detective confirmed.

'And no sign of Cherie?'

'No,' was all Cunningham could say. But he quickly went on as he saw Cynthia set her lips, trying to keep herself from breaking down. 'But there are no signs of a struggle or anything being forced. The patrol officers have sealed off the area and are treating it as a—'

He realized the words 'crime scene' would push Cynthia over the edge.

'Well, they're sealing it off, just in case there are any clues to her whereabouts.'

Looking down at the single sheet in his file he asked, 'So, is there any reason why she might be in that area? Any friends, acquaintances she might be going to see? Any place of interest to her there?'

They were both shaking their heads.

'None,' said Jerry. 'None that we can think of.'

Cunningham pressed on. 'Something to do with school maybe? Her boyfriend?'

He glanced at the file. 'Donnie?'

Jerry was still shaking his head. 'Well, he lives quite near us, but I don't know, you'd have to talk to him.'

Cynthia touched the corners of her eyes with a tissue to soak up her brimming tears. 'And you've heard nothing, nothing at all about her?'

Cunningham closed the file. 'It's still early yet. We're doing everything we can. Our detectives are on it and I spoke to Missing Persons at Division, and though officially they don't handle minors they'll let me know if they come across anything. All our patrols have a description and copies of her photo are being distributed. We'll find her,' he added confidently. But Cynthia's bleary stare made him fidget with the file once more.

As Cunningham continued to search for more comforting assurances on the measures the LAPD could use to find one sixteen-year-old girl in a city of thirteen million Jerry reached into the breast pocket of his jacket. 'Maybe these might help,' he said weakly, almost embarrassed.

He took out an assortment of photos of his daughter: her sixteenth birthday, smiling in a green silk dress, her arm around her younger brother; one at Disney two years ago riding a roller coaster, and one of her junior prom taken with her father, the one he would show buyers at the car lot to close a sale.

California State Lotteries

Mega Lotto

RESULT

Sat 6th October

5 30 18 39 3 24

STAFF PARKING LOT, FEDERAL BUILDING, WILSHIRE BLVD

Though she was glad to get there in one piece, Nancy Kronziac winced in pain as she unclamped her right hand from the steering wheel. Laying the heavily braced wrist on her lap she took off her shades with her good hand and rubbed her eyes. She felt weak and flushed with a clammy wave of nausea. Three days of nothing but fitful sleep and waking with haunting flashes of masked faces and the black tunnel of a gun barrel running through her brain had left her drained of energy. Around her other cars moved in and out of the spaces like robots and people walked by with stolid faces, eyes narrow and squinted against the sun. She felt strangely isolated from the world, like someone who has been hospitalized for months only to emerge fearful, like a stranger, into the indifferent bustle of the city. The pain in her wrist was subsiding as she got out of the Explorer and headed for the bright edifice of the Federal Building.

The ride up to the seventeenth floor was uncomfortable and claustrophobic as she shared the elevator with an excited gang of interns. Kronziac had never before been worried about confined places but she watched tensely as the floors passed until the indicator light for seventeen blinked and she quickly pushed through the group of the noisy youngsters into the cool public foyer of the FBI offices.

The floor buzzed with a low hum of activity as she made her way down the corridor to her own room in the south-west corner. She wondered whether she should check in with Foley or Sedley to let them know she was in but she was anxious to get to her phone and try Jimmy again. Maggie Ramirez was standing over the to-and-fro light of the copier when Kronziac entered the DTU open-plan office.

'Hey, hey,' she called out. 'Look who's back.'

Phillips, on the phone, nodded, a slightly puzzled look on his face, and continued his conversation.

'I thought you'd be out for a few more days,' remarked Maggie, looking Kronziac up and down, quickly assessing the fitness of her boss.

'I was goin' nuts sitting around at home.' Kronziac waved it off and continued towards her office.

Maggie followed. 'I tried calling a few times.'

'Yeah, I just left the answering machine on.' She liked Maggie a lot but her chirpy little voice and positive attitude was something Kronziac was not up for at the moment. As she passed Phillips he quickly scribbled on a post-it and pinned it to her jacket. Kronziac tore it off and squinted at the scrawl – *What the fuck you doing here?*

She balled it up and dropped it in the bin, smiling. 'Are there any messages for me?' she wondered as they entered her office, which seemed cold and unlived in.

'Just the usual mail.' Maggie motioned at a pile of correspondence on the desk.

Kronziac quickly dug out the phone messages and scanned them quickly. 'Nothing from Jimmy Soton?'

Maggie shook her head doubtfully. 'No, not that I know of.'

Phillips appeared at the door. He seemed fresh and tanned, like he always did. Kronziac always marvelled at his ability to recover quickly from trauma. Like her, he too could easily have lost his life three days ago.

'Foley's gonna carve you a new butt,' he warned with relish, 'if he finds you're back on duty already.'

'Oh, I missed you guys too much,' she shot back. 'Especially your deep concern for my ass, Phillips.'

Maggie moved close to Kronziac and gently lifted her heavily braced right arm. 'How's your wrist?'

'Still a little tender,' Kronziac answered, dumping her messages on the desk.

'You were lucky,' sang Phillips. 'Could've been a compound fracture. One of the strongest bones in the human body, the radius. Tribes in the South Seas used it as a short-reach lance for taking down barracuda or whatever else they wanted to eat.'

'Thanks, Doctor Moreau,' Kronziac chimed.

'Nothing from Jimmy?' asked Maggie.

Kronziac shook her head. 'Gone to ground, I guess. Can't really blame him.' She sat down, taking her arm back from Maggie.

'Where's the Bitteroot Surveillance file – we might need to keep an eye on the rest of them, could be reprisals,' she added, fishing about on her desk.

'Against us?' Maggie asked, surprised.

Kronziac didn't answer. Not because she didn't hear, Maggie figured. In her three months at the DTU Maggie had learned that Kronziac rarely liked to sensationlize or overreact to a possible threat, something that seemed to be shared by all members of the unit. It took her a while to get used to their sometimes black, even morbid sense of humour.

'I thought I left the file on my desk,' said Kronziac, still searching under the piles of paperwork.

'Sedley has it, I think,' Phillips informed her.

'Sedley?'

He moved towards the window, looking out at the buildings of downtown partly obscused by a grey and copper haze of smog. 'Yeah. In your absence he's been looking over all the Bitteroot case materials.'

Kronziac got up. 'I've only been gone three days!'

They all turned around as Sedley's voice sounded from the doorway. 'We thought you'd be out for the rest of the week.' He was smiling.

Maggie moved quickly and scampered past Sedley like a squirrel. 'Anyone for a coffee?' she said loudly.

She was gone before they could all refuse.

'Can you give us a minute?' said Sedley quietly.

For a moment Phillips didn't realize Sedley was talking to him.

'Oh yeah, sure . . . I'll be just outside if you need me,' he added for Kronziac's benefit.

Sedley nodded and smiled in appreciation as Phillips went out. Then he entered the office himself, closing the door behind him.

Kronziac hated the door being closed.

'Am I losing command of the Bitteroot case?' she asked, bluntly.

Rolling his head, Sedley gave a false laugh. 'God, you're paranoid.'

'Well, am I?' She wanted to know.

He looked at her straight, composing himself again. 'The AD and I feel you should get a rest, take some leave. You've had a narrow escape.'

'It's always a narrow escape when it comes to these nuts,' she said.

'Jesus, Kronziac! You almost got shot in the face!' he reminded her. 'We know you can handle it but there's no harm in taking time out, to take it easy, to recover mentally from the trauma . . . and there *is* trauma.' He looked at her intently, as if the evidence was before him.

'Shit, so I'm going insane now.' She wobbled her head, mimicking madness, and sank into the chair.

'You know what I mean,' he said, annoyed. 'You can't even drive a car at the moment with your wrist . . . or you *shouldn't* be driving,' he added, knowing full well that's exactly what she had just done.

She had no answer for him, admitting to herself he was probably right.

'I just think you should take some time off, you deserve it,' he went on.

'I'm fine, really,' she assured him, holding up her bandaged arm and flexing her fingers slowly.

He remained unconvinced.

She put her arm down. 'It's more than just getting some rest, isn't it?' She sensed he hadn't yet told her everything.

The long moment of silence confirmed her suspicion. 'Look . . .' he started.

She began nodding, knowing what was about to come.

'It's just a formality,' he continued. 'Still, Inspection Division do have to conduct a procedural enquiry into the operation. We have five people dead,' he explained.

'Five terrorists,' she reminded him.

'Sure, that may be. But the DOJ has to make sure the

58

operation was conducted within the parameters of the Attorney-General's guidelines on engagement.'

'So I'm under investigation,' she concluded flatly. 'Is that it?'

'You might be,' he confessed after a moment of thought. 'Matthew Crebbs was found with a gunshot wound to the head and two in the stomach.'

'I know. He fell on top of me,' she said, exasperated, and held up her broken wrist again as evidence.

'Well, they have to make sure there's no question of excessive force having been used,' his words tailed off, as if he was embarrassed by the implication.

Kronziac was slowly shaking her head. 'He had the shooter at my fucking head – what was I supposed to do? Tell him to hold on while I phoned the AG's office and asked them if I would be infringing his rights by stopping him from blowing my brain to pieces?'

'You're preaching to the converted,' Sedley replied, his voice shrill with annoyance. He began pacing the room, like Phillips usually did when in a bad mood.

'If I'm not officially on suspension, then . . . then I can continue with my work until someone tells me otherwise,' Kronziac stated firmly.

Sedley swung around. 'That might be unwise,' he warned her.

'Unwise?' Kronziac laughed and shuffled papers aimlessly on her desk as though looking for something. She stopped. 'Look, I don't want to be a pain in the ass about this—'

'Good,' he interrupted. 'Then go home. Go visit your family, play with the dog, walk on the beach. Just stay out of here until we give you the word to come back.' The directness in his voice made her pause and consider doing what he said.

'Okay, okay.' She got up, 'I dunno what the hell is going on but . . .' She held her hands in the air in surrender and left the office.

'Listen, give me a call,' said Sedley in his best buddy-buddy voice as he followed her out.

She walked quickly enough to stay a few steps ahead.

Maggie was standing by the coffee-maker, trying to look busy as Kronziac passed.

'Sedley said he'd love a cup,' Kronziac said softly, almost whispering. Maggie wasn't sure what was going on but poured a mug from the coffee pot anyway.

Further down the corridor Kronziac stopped for a moment at Phillips's desk. 'Is there another NCIC terminal anywhere else in the building, outside the squad offices?' she asked furtively.

He was surprised by the request and had to think about it for a moment.

Kronziac was aware that Sedley was watching and moving close but Maggie stopped him with the steaming mug of coffee.

'Oh . . . thanks,' he said politely.

Phillips was still thinking, then realized the obvious. 'The front desk has a terminal,' he said excitedly. 'Fully linked.'

'Thanks. I'll call you later,' said Kronziac and quickly headed on down the corridor.

Maggie shouted goodbye after her.

Luckily the public foyer was empty – no callers and only one secretary from admin behind the front desk, a temp whom Kronziac barely recognized.

'Hi . . . Cara, isn't it?'

The girl smiled back. 'Tamara,' she said and continued putting some Bureau circulars into a stack of envelopes.

'Okay if I use the station?' Kronziac enquired politely, standing in front of the computer terminal.

'Sure,' the girl replied. 'Can I do anything for you?' she asked, seeing Kronziac's wrist brace.

'Nah, I think I can handle it.' Kronziac bent over the keyboard and tapped in her code to access the National Instant Criminal Background Check System database. This was hosted by the huge servers in the Clarksberg, Virginia FBI Criminal Justice Information Services division.

'I'll just be behind the partition.' The secretary excused herself and left the front desk, much to Kronziac's relief.

'Okay, thanks,' she said as she quickly tapped in a name on the search screen. Her wrist twinged with pain from the movement. Five seconds later Jimmy Soton's criminal record blinked on screen and Kronziac scanned the rap sheet: possession . . . arms violations . . . assault. How did he manage to ever get a job with a security firm, she wondered. She found what she was looking for, a contact address . . . *damn!* . . . 323 Cabrillo Avenue . . . she knew that. Had already tried it but got no answer. Her eyes darted to the *Known Aliases* file . . . two entries . . . Lee Martin and Leroy Tardell. She clicked on Martin, grimacing again at a stab of pain.

'Excuse me, ma'am!' A male voice made her jump – she thought it was Sedley. She looked up to see a tall dark-haired man leaning over the counter.

'Excuse me, ma'am,' he said again, 'but I wonder if you can help me.'

'Someone will be with you in a moment,' she said quickly, trying to be polite, and got back to her search. A long list of 'Lee Martins' appeared and she tapped in 'Los Angeles district' to narrow it down. Her wrist stung with pain.

'I know this may not be under FBI jurisdiction,' the man continued, 'but my daughter has gone missing.'

Kronziac was scanning the new shortened list of names, about ten of them.

'You've reported it to the police?' she asked, distracted.

He smiled weakly, dimpling his fleshy cheeks.

'Of course. But I thought you guys might have come across something or might help in the search . . . I dunno,' he said like a man in a daze, clutching at straws. 'I thought I'd come down here myself and see if any more can be done.'

Kronziac was trying to look at the screen and answer the man. 'I'll call someone for you,' she said and tried to remember the secretary's name. Her right hand was now throbbing.

'Hello!' she shouted 'Tara?'

But there was no response from behind the partition.

'I have some pictures,' he said taking out some photos, 'and I've typed out a detailed physical description.'

'Okay,' Kronziac replied and called again for assistance. But no one came. She finished reading through the 'Lee Martins' and decided the best thing to do was to print them out. She punched the print button and the printer buzzed into life.

'Her name is Cherie Margaret Blaynes,' the man went on. 'I'm her father, Jerry Blaynes, from Twin Lakes in the Valley.'

He threw his business card on the printer in front of Kronziac.

'She's sixteen years old,' he went on, 'and disappeared four days ago from the Aldcott Shopping Mall on Receda.'

Kronziac was tapping in the second alias.

'I can offer a reward,' he said hopefully and asked, 'You have a website, don't you? For Missing Persons?' Maybe you could put her photo up.'

Kronziac's wrist was aching, her fingers stiffening as she swiftly stabbed the keys specifying all the 'Leroy Tardells' in the Los Angeles area.

'Do you have a special Missing Persons department?' He persisted with his questioning.

'Listen, sir, I'll get someone for you, okay?' Kronziac snapped at him loudly, shocking him into silence.

Immediately she regretted it. But it was he who began apologizing. She could see he was on the verge of tears. She was about to say sorry to him when Assistant Director Foley's voice stopped her.

'That's enough, Nancy,' he said coldly.

She turned around and saw Foley standing by the partition, a murderous look in his eyes. Behind him were Sedley, Phillips and Maggie, all of them looking embarrassed.

'Agent Ramirez, can you look after this gentleman?'

Maggie led Blaynes to the other end of the counter as Foley fixed his stare on Kronziac. 'I think you better get yourself home and rest or I'll put you on suspension,' he warned, bunching his eyebrows.

'I'm sorry, sir,' Kronziac said wearily, clutching her throbbing wrist.

'Phillips, you make sure she gets home okay,' Foley said and walked away, shaking his head in annoyance.

Sedley stayed put, watching Kronziac.

Before she left she managed to turn and log off from the database. She saw just the one entry for a Leroy Tardell on screen.

Same address in Cabrillo Avenue.

'You can leave that,' urged Sedley before she could memorize it.

She snatched up the Lee Martin printout, folded it quickly and put it in her pocket as Sedley stood over her shoulder.

'You're not doing yourself any favours.' He shook his head gravely as Phillips led her away like an invalid.

DEVONSHIRE COMMUNITY POLICE STATION, 10250 ETIWANDA AVE, NORTHRIDGE, CA

The morning mail had arrived and Officer Kempechne had sleepily worked her way through nearly forty pieces of post – everything from Department circulars to citizens' complaints. She checked her watch. Only twenty minutes left on shift. She opened the last piece of mail with a certain amount of satisfaction and threw the envelope in the bin beneath the large wood-chipped counter.

It was a missing-persons notice.

Or it looked like one.

A printout from the Devonshire PD website.

MISSING PERSON

Cherie Margaret Blaynes

Missing from Aldcott Shopping Mall, Northridge, California September 2nd.

DOB:	August 12th, 1985
Race:	White
Sex:	Female
Hair:	Light Blonde
Eyes:	Blue
Height:	5' 3"
Weight:	112 pounds

Cherie was last seen at approximately 11.30 PM on Sunday September 2nd getting in to her car, a yellow Mazda 323 Hatchback as she left her friends in the Aldcott Shopping Precinct carpark on Receda, Northridge.

She has not been seen since.

Remarks

Cherie was wearing blue denim jeans, white blouse, red sweater and white trainers. She was carrying a shoulder bag with personal items and identification.

Anyone who has seen Cherie Blaynes or has any information as to her present whereabouts please contact the Devonshire Police Department or the LAPD headquarters.

Fractions of Zero

Kempechne shook her head and wondered why anyone would send them a printout of a missing person without a cover note or any other attachment.

She turned it over and found a small paragraph that she hoped would explain it.

But the words made no sense.

In fact there were no words, just jumbled letters.

RMDEGZWQZRDAYFTQTQMXFTKNDQMFTUDREFOXQMDQ
PARTQMHKHMBAGDENQFIQQZRAGDFQQZMZPQTMDNAG
DQNUZFTQEXQQBKIQEFXMKHMEFMZPQPSQIMKEXUWQM
PUEYMXOUDBGQFANQ

2434 ABRAMAR, PACIFIC PALISADES, CA

Nancy looked at herself in the full-length mirror, twisting to look over her shoulders to check out her butt. *Ah, what the hell*, she decided. They were her favourite Bermudas, once a deep maroon, now a faded rust colour and a little frayed around the pockets. But who was going to see? She always felt she looked good in them, not too grungy and definitely not too preppy – more beach chic. She put on a black Nike tank top, easing it carefully over her bandaged right hand and tugging it tightly across her breasts.

Though a heavy curtain of fog was stubbornly lingering over the ocean, creeping up the cliffs over the PCH, it was unusually humid, with the midday temperatures up in the low eighties.

She fixed herself an orange-and-pineapple juice at the Hawaiian bar and was tempted to light up a cigarette. But she decided it would spoil the clean healthy regimen she had endured for the past three days since being escorted out of the office. She still couldn't believe she'd been sent home like an unruly delinquent suspended from school. As she walked out on to the veranda a small excited flock of gulls were wheeling over the bluffs further down. Her neighbour Mrs Peters was throwing scraps of bread into the air and the birds were trying to catch them like winged seals going after flying fish. Mrs Peters turned around and waved up. Nancy balanced the prospect of her neighbour calling in to talk incessantly about her two sons at college back east against the excuse it would give her to have a convivial smoke with the old woman.

She waved curtly back and looked out over the sea. The grey-blue ocean merged imperceptibly with the dwindling veil of fog and the white plume of a yacht's spinnaker punctured the mist. After three days of complete rest, sleeping twelve hours a night, watching TV, watering the plants and flowers, making calls to her parents in Chicago and her sister in Dayton – she was beginning to go stir-crazy. Even the visits to Pluto's Bar over in Malibu to see the waitresses for a chat or going to the sauna up at the Country Club where she met another neighbour, the secretary of the residents' association who berated her gently for missing meetings had not relieved her of the boredom that was beginning to gnaw at her nerves.

She had considered going down to the beach with her board to catch some waves but the doctor's words echoed with the twinges of pain that still reminded her of her fractured wrist. No strenuous activity, he'd warned her. 'That's the rock climbing up in Rustic Canyon out, then? she'd asked him cheekily.

Carefully rotating her injured hand, she was relieved that some movement was coming back. The improvement stirred her to get back to some unfinished business.

She found the folded sheet of paper in the pocket of her dark work suit and wondered if Sedley had seen her take it. It contained contact addresses for the twenty or so Lee Martins with a criminal record in the Los Angeles area. One of them, she thought – or hoped – might also be an alias for her Bitteroot informer Jimmy Soton. She put down the cordless phone beside her and started circling the names, checking to see if one of them was Soton.

The sun began to burn through the veil of cloud and shone brightly on the white mosaic of the Zellig table. As she opened the creased folds of paper she glanced around, looking for her shades. She couldn't find them. But Nancy did find a small white business card lying in the middle of the sheet of paper.

The guy at the counter, she remembered.

She turned it over.

Northridge Premier Autos ran in large letters along the top, a BMW badge on one side and a VW colophon on the other. Underneath was his name – *Jerry Blaynes, Managing Director. Finest new and used luxury cars in the Valley.*

She reached for the cordless and dialled the phone number on the card but hung up before it rang.

He deserves more than that, Nancy thought to herself, and got up to change again.

The traffic was busy, the cars sweeping by without a break between them. Nancy Kronziac took the time to look up and down the road as she waited at the Nordoff Street intersection to join Corbin. About two hundred metres down on the left side she could see a large blue-and-white BMW sign with 'Northridge Premier Autos' in black lettering beneath. She forced herself in between a gas truck and a removals van that indicated its displeasure by blasting its shrill horn. She held up her hands in a gesture of innocence and accelerated down the street. The driver of the van gave her another hoot as she turned and drove into the car lot, shaking his head in anger as he sped by.

Passing a row of twenty or so brand new BMWs, gleaming like toys in the afternoon sun, Kronziac parked the Explorer outside the sales office. For the first time she wondered if this was a really bad idea. She could have just rung Blaynes or, better, maybe left him alone altogether. Besides, he probably wouldn't even remember her – or he might remember her only too well and show her the door before she could apologize, reporting her to Foley for harassment. Still, she got out of the car anyway and nearly banged the shining flank of a light metallic blue convertible.

'Yes! I can see you in it!' a young male voice declared behind her. 'The new M3 convertible, just out this year, 350 horse-power, inline-six, sequential gearbox—'

She looked at the speaker blankly and he decided to change tack.

'. . . Plenty of room in the back,' he added slyly, waving his arm over the open cream-leather seats. 'For kids, for the dog, for the shopping,' he sang like an amusement-park huckster.

He was small, with a compact squashed build; tight trousers, slip-ons, fake Rolex and hair as solid as if it was moussed with glue.

'Sorry, out of my range,' Kronziac confessed and glanced at the beautiful car. She *could* see herself in it – tripping to the country club, parking it on the marina or zipping up the PCH for a weekend in Carmel.

'Only forty-five grand,' he tempted her, 'and we've a great finance plan, give you something good for that . . .' He nodded, poking a finger at her trusty Ford.

She swung her bag over her left shoulder and threw back her hair. 'Tempting . . . but no, thanks,' she said politely.

Even if pigs began flying and she suddenly got that sort of money she wouldn't give this little butt-lick the commission.

'Is Mr Blaynes around? Jerry Blaynes?' she asked.

The kid's expression changed to concern, almost fear. She knew the boss. 'Yeah, sure,' he answered. 'He should be in the office. I'll show you.' He led the way like an eager puppy.

Jerry Blaynes was trying to concentrate, looking through a parts manifest, when his junior salesman appeared at the door.

'Sorry, Chief, there's a lady here to see you.'

At first Blaynes didn't recognize the woman in the long sleeveless summer dress, her dark hair falling loosely over her shoulders.

Kronziac wasn't sure how to introduce herself. It wasn't official business.

'Hello, Mr Blaynes. I don't know if you remember me. My name is Nancy Kronziac.' She walked into the office as Blaynes dismissed the young salesman.

He thought he recognized her, all right, but couldn't quite place her.

'You came into the FBI offices . . . in the Federal Building.' She tried to remind him.

'Yes . . .' he said blankly. 'Last week.'

'I was behind the public desk . . .'

He suddenly remembered her. She looked completely different – her clothes, her hair, her demeanour. 'Oh yes . . . you were under a bit of pressure at the time, I think,' he said gently.

Kronziac felt grateful and embarrassed all at once. 'Yeah, that was me, I'm afraid,' she muttered, feeling herself blush slightly.

Blaynes got up and rushed around, setting a seat in front of his desk for her. 'Sit down, please.'

'I don't want to take up your time,' Kronziac began before she sat down, 'but I really just wanted to come over and apologize for my . . . outburst. I feel really bad about it.'

He shook his head, dismissing the matter. 'Forget it. We all have bad days.'

Kronziac asked cautiously, 'Have you heard anything more about your daughter?'

He smiled, obviously making an effort to keep himself from breaking down.

'No . . . I thought that maybe you . . . or someone else from the FBI had something for me.'

He looked at her intently, making her sorry once more that she'd come, giving him false hope.

'Oh, I'm not with Missing Persons,' she said hurriedly.

He smiled again and it seemed that he understood.

'I'm sure everything is being done . . . they'll find her.' Kronziac found herself saying the words she knew everyone else was telling him but there was nothing else to be said. People had to be positive.

'They found her car,' he mentioned, the words coming out quietly and slowly as if loaded with a heavy weight of dread.

Kronziac knew it wasn't a good sign. 'And no clues from the forensics people?' she asked.

He sighed, exhausted. 'Nothing . . . not a damn thing.' His frustration was apparent as his mouth tightened with anger.

'We keep going over everything, my wife and I . . . over everything that Cherie did that day, what she said. Everything . . . just can't understand it.'

Kronziac shifted in her seat, thinking that he was going to break down. 'A lot of kids run away for all sorts of reasons that we have no explanation for,' she offered by way of comfort. 'She might turn up today, hungry and feeling stupid for having run away,' she added lightly.

But he looked at her straight, his eyes moistening, his large frame bowed over the desk, shaking ever so slightly with a deep, deep rage.

'Not Cherie . . . not Cherie,' he repeated with absolute certainty. 'That's not her.'

Kronziac had no words of comfort for him. He had obviously heard it all before and nothing had brought his daughter back yet.

'I'll call my colleagues at the Bureau and see if there've been any sightings.'

'Thank you,' he murmured. 'You're very kind.'

Kronziac moved into investigation mode. She was never much good at counselling or comforting relatives. 'Sorry to be so pragmatic,' she began, 'but keep thinking about it and you might come up with something that could help explain her disappearance or that might help the police find her . . . anything at all, even if you think it's insignificant.'

Blaynes seemed to perk up, enlivened by her directness. 'No, that's what we need here . . . I'm sick of fucking crying . . . of feeling sorry . . . sick of feeling so goddamned helpless . . .'

He blinked and inhaled deeply to keep the tears from flowing. 'Shit . . .' He gasped and wiped his eyes. 'I'm sorry. Excuse my language.'

Before she could assure him that it was quite all right, he pulled out the vanity drawer under his desk and handed her a single sheet of paper. On it was a missing-persons report.

'Devonshire PD got this in the post,' he informed her.

Kronziac quickly scanned the page carrying Cherie's description.

'Someone sent it in the post?' she asked, puzzled.

Blaynes told her to turn it over.

On the other side she saw the group of letters. 'What is it?' she wondered.

Blaynes was shaking his head. 'Beats me. I think it's some code or something.'

She looked at it closely. Four lines of continuous letters – letters, that was all, no words.

Have the police any idea what it's about?'

'Nope.' He shrugged. 'Not a clue, they don't even know if it's anything to do with Cherie. Could be a hoax, could be a mistake, could be anything.'

Kronziac suddenly placed the paper on the desk.

'Is this the original?' she asked, faintly annoyed that any latent prints or other trace evidence would now be destroyed.

'No, it's a copy.' Blaynes allowed himself a bleak smile. 'The detectives have the original.'

She picked it up again, studying the letters closely. 'Mind if I have a copy?'

'Sure. Take that one, I've several more.' He smiled and stood up. 'Thank you so much for calling in, Miss Kronziac. You really didn't have to, but I appreciate it just the same.'

Kronziac stood up, too. 'Okay, Mr Blaynes—'

He interrupted her. 'Please call me Jerry. Not many people are that considerate.'

'I'll have some of our people take a look at this and we'll be in touch,' Kronziac promised him as she left the office.

'You know, the worst thing,' he said as he walked her to the door, 'is the thought that she might be suffering.' He looked at the ground, his mind churning again with the living nightmare of his daughter's disappearance, turning it over and over in his mind, never getting any respite.

'I know, Mr Blaynes,' was all Kronziac could say. 'I know.'

The cars flashed by on the street as they did all day, every day, sweeping through the warm air, the hum of the city thickening with the onset of rush hour. As Kronziac swerved her car out the forecourt, past the lines of glittering autos, she caught a glimpse of Blaynes in his office. He was sitting at his desk again, looking drained, eyes closed, his hands cupped in prayer like someone who has lost everything.

MAGNOLIA APARTMENT BUILDING, BONANZA ROAD, LAS VEGAS, NV

A trash can clattered and the dog began barking again. The oily smell of cooking burgers rose through the building and a stereo pounded two floors up – no discernible music, just a constant muffled thump like a giant ball rhythmically bouncing on the roof of the apartment block.

Ellen Holby held her hands limply as if her wrist muscles had been severed. Then she blew over the purple nail varnish and shook her fingers through the air. As she waited for her nails to dry she glanced out of the frosted window of the bathroom, slanted slightly ajar, out over the labyrinth of passages in the back lots to the city beyond.

The casinos and hotels on the strip looked dull, their glass façades smoky in the bright unflattering midday sun, like beached cruise ships waiting for the dark tide to set their lights ablaze. In the distance Ellen could see the Spring mountains, their peaks patched with snow, riding the northern horizon, and nestled beneath them the pale pastel gated communities of Sun City with their single-storey stucco homes, red-tile roofs and easy-care desert gardens. Populated by mostly out-of-state retirees. Ellen felt aggrieved that her late husband's Air Force pension from twenty-five years as a mechanic at Nellis wouldn't even buy her a walk-in closet in Sun City or any of the other sixty-something colonies that fringed the Las Vegas Valley. Only a jackpot on the slots would release her from the Magnolia building – a cinder-block shanty of overcrowded families and poor native pensioners. But today was Thursday – day-release. Connie from 506 would be calling and they would meet the other girls in half an hour at the Hacienda for the $7.99 Champagne Brunch special followed by an afternoon on the Jungle Fever slots, a five-dollar cold buffet for supper and an evening with Bud Thorpe and the BlueLites Dixie Jazz Band.

There was banging at the door.

Ellen hurried out of the bathroom, waving her hands in the

air. 'Okay, honey!' she said loudly and carefully unlatched the door, keeping the chain on.

She saw wheels, like a trolley, and stopped herself from unhooking the door chain.

But then she was looking at her hand and was puzzled. Her nails were fine, dry now, holding the door, but on the wrinkled crest of her hand there was a dot of blood, the thin silver line of a needle pushing between the white tendon strings of her fingers.

She looked up, questioning, like a stung child, shaking her head, falling away from the door.

The ground hit her and she sighed like a heavy sack. Immobile, her senses shrinking to a tiny focus of terror, she could hear only her own breathing, sounding like heavy waves of gas in the chambers of her chest.

As her eyes fluttered, slowly closing, she saw an arm curling around the door. A large shape moved across her, looming over her like a dark moth.

ROULETTE

The world flickered back into focus like the leader frames of a film – dim, confined, dark in the corners. She tried to get up from the seat but her head was held fast in a harness that was like an old leather football helmet, keeping her rigidly in place. She looked down and saw that her wrists were tethered to a table, straining vainly, and her legs were bound to the chair, lashed tight by some electrical cord. A small green baize cloth covered the table, patched with dark stains like continents on a map. In the centre lay a smaller, darker-green rectangle of cloth, yellow numbers marked on it. To the side a black disc, like a deep plate, fringed by a ring of numbers in red and black squares.

A voice came out of the dark and its owner's face entered the dim cone of light beneath the overhead shade.

He sat in front of her across the table.

'Good morning, Mrs Jackson,' he smiled.

She blinked. Her mouth was clamped shut with a fat band of tape, rendering her silent.

'Good morning . . .' he said again, the smile gone, expecting something in return now.

Squinting her eyes shut and snapping them open again as if to push the terror away she realized it was real, it was all real. Her breathing thickened, strident, flushing through her nose. Her body shuddered, struggling, futilely in its harness.

He shook his head reproachfully.

'Okay, if you don't want to remember me . . .'

On the table in front of him lay a small grey lever attached to a spring-loaded steel arm, about two feet long. He pushed the lever and a loud click sounded in her left ear. Straining her eyes left, she still couldn't see what had made the noise. It was too close, just behind her field of vision.

'Good,' he said, satisfied that the test worked, and reached over her left shoulder. 'Thought you'd get away,' he muttered, unlocking something close to her head. 'Moving all the way out here.'

A different click now, something released, unclamped. He sat back, with something black in his hand, L-shaped, with a wooden handle.

'I suppose you couldn't resist the games.' He smiled and flicked the thumb piece. The cylinder fell out on its side, its chambers empty.

She screamed, but the effort produced no sound, just a whimper at the back of her throat and a sustained heave in her chest.

'This time you're gonna have to play,' he told her as he took a bullet out from beneath the table. 'Can't just watch from the window, friggin' yourself with a broom handle.'

He smiled knowingly and placed the bullet in one of the chambers, twirled the cylinder into a blur and snapped it shut into the pistol's frame.

'Time to play!' he announced happily and fixed the revolver back into the clamp next to her head. He snapped it into place as if doing nothing more than replacing a blown fuse and sat back in the chair.

'Now, this is for you.' He pushed the small metal lever close to her right hand. 'Careful,' he cautioned. 'Don't want to set it off too soon and ruin the game . . . and the carpet!' he added gleefully.

Picking up a small black box from beneath the table, he placed it beside the disc. This, she now realized, was a miniature roulette wheel and the yellow numbers on the dark green mat a roulette table – just like a child's toy.

Opening the box, he took out six red chips and stared at the table for a moment. 'This is going to be difficult,' he declared quietly, as if in deep concentration.

She struggled in her harness again, the straps biting at her face. She had no idea what time it was – not even if it was day or night. As he muttered distractedly to himself she glanced about, searching for some clue as to where she was. But all she could see was darkness beyond the shroud of light that fell across the table like a mosquito net. A little of the light reflected on some metal shelving to the sides and she glimpsed the plastic handle of what she supposed was a large electric drill on the floor.

He seemed to have made his mind up about something and placed the chips in front of her. 'It's a bit complicated,' he confessed, 'but it's all for a bit of fun.' He grinned, glancing to the side of her head and his smile turned leery, his eyes dulling. 'That's what he used to say before he began, wasn't it?' His expression changed to one of excitement once more as he pulled the roulette wheel directly into the middle of the table.

'I know this might be a bit un-American,' he began, 'but we're gonna play European roulette – pretend you're in Monte Carlo.' He winked. 'With no double-zero – that way the House advantage is down to just over two per cent! Very good for you,' he added, darting his glance again at the gun to the side of her head.

'Since you forgot to bring money with you I'll loan you thirty dollars in five-dollar chips . . . so don't spend it all on one number,' he joked, amusing himself.

'The House rules are that if you make sixty dollars – in other words, win thirty bucks, the amount I loaned you – then you can go.' He waited for some reaction but she just closed her eyes, the rims now black with smudged mascara.

'But for each chip you lose,' he warned her, 'from the six I gave you, then we play the other roulette.'

Her eyes opened, wide like a gazelle's. She could see the excitement growing in him as he picked up the chips again.

'Of course, I'll have to place your bets for you but you can just nod.'

Trying to shake her head, she twisted her face against the unyielding leather, glistened with her tears.

'Okay, inside bets – one chip for starters,' he began. 'Red or black?' he asked, looking at her. But she was sobbing heavily in her bonds.

'Okay, Red it is.' He shrugged. He placed a chip on the red diamond marked on the mat. 'House pays one to one, true odds 1.1 to one, edging 5.26,' he sang. 'No more bets!'

Pressing a small plastic button just under the wheel he made the disc spring to life, spinning swiftly around, turning the numbers into a continuous red-black band. He dropped a white ball, no bigger than a small ball-bearing, onto the rim and it bounced through the grooves for a few moments before hopping into red twenty-one and settling there. He clapped his hands.

'We have a winner! You just won yourself five bucks and another chip!' he cried, rewarding her with another red. 'Now I think you're being very shy with your bets,' he declared slyly, getting quickly on with it. 'This time we'll put down three outside table bets.'

Straining her neck against the restraints and bucking her knees she tried desperately to get away from the stupid game and her captor's cruel leer. Each time he looked at her or asked a question she turned her eyes away, searching the darkness behind him for some hope.

'Red or black?' he asked, impatiently. 'We'll stay with red, I think,' he decided, getting no response from her. 'Even or odd?'

Again no sign as she looked away and shut her eyes tight.

'Odds it is.' He placed another chip on the *Odd* rectangle.

'High or low, one to eighteen or nineteen to thirty-six?'

Not even looking at her he placed another of her chips on *1 to 18*.

He tapped the table with a fourth chip. 'Now . . . dozens, I think . . . pays two to one . . . could help you on your way.'

Making his mind up quickly, he slipped another red on the rectangle marked *2nd 12*.

No more bets!' he declared, his lips dry with anticipation. He stabbed the button and sent the wheel spinning. The little ball dropped and danced around the rim, rattling against the cheap plastic, descending slowly for six or seven revolutions. Then it hit the grooves and hopped over the numbers, springing off the sides, and finally fell to a rest in a black notch as the wheel drew slowly to a halt.

He rubbed his hands. 'Let's see, what does this mean – black thirty-one. Player wins on Odd, but loses on red, one to eighteen and second twelve . . . brings your total to eight minus three . . . down to five,' he figured, delighting in her loss.

'Time for the next level,' he suggested, swallowing tightly. He edged the small lever over so that it lay directly beneath the fingers of her tied right hand.

She squirmed in the seat, roaring and screaming soundlessly inside her trapped body.

'Pull the lever,' he said quietly, hardly able to say the words as his breathing grew shallow.

Again, she shut her eyes tight and curled her hand into a little fist.

His anger loosened the constricting grip of excitement from his throat and he shouted at her, sprinkling her nose with warm spit.

'Pull the fuckin' lever!' he screamed.

The old woman sobbed, her breathing a rough snort through her nostrils, wetting the duct tape over her lips.

About to pull the lever himself, he broke away from the table and hurriedly opened a drawer in the tool chest. Picking out a blue-handled pincers he sat down again. 'You have to play the game, remember,' he insisted. 'We always had to play by the rules.'

But she kept her eyes closed, each socket a nest of wrinkles, black with mascara. She struggled like a trapped animal in the harness as he forced open her fisted hand and caught one of her little fingers in a sharp bite of the pincer jaws.

He squeezed the handles just enough to break the skin and draw a ring of blood around the finger.

'You'll lose it if you don't pull the lever,' he said, shaking with barely stifled anger.

Tears ran in black tracks down her cheeks, making her face look like the mask of a sad, grotesque clown.

He squeezed the handles a little more, bringing them closer together.

The flesh, pinched white, gave way softly.

Then a snip.

A dull little nick, like clipping a fresh flower stalk.

Her body convulsed for a moment, knees jumping. Her head jerked back and he could hear a demented animal-like squeal in her throat.

She stopped moving and all colour drained from her face as if a plug had been pulled. Her head floated limply in the harness.

She had passed out and her little finger, the skin dry and

loose, lay on the table, lifeless, almost fake like a prop, a broken part, the table cloth growing dark beneath the hand. The white core of the bone stump was exposed, a pink jam of muscle and blood around it like Swiss Roll.

He slapped her face and her eyes fell open. Dull now, barely focusing, rubbed sore by a mist of red pain.

'Pull the lever,' he hissed and poised the grey teeth of the pincers over the next finger.

'Pull the lever,' he whispered, tempting her.

Though her head was shaking how, shivering with pain and shock, she could see her amputated finger an inch from where it should be, its nail perfect. Now it was the only part of her body not trapped in the black box of his world.

She pulled the lever with her shaking thumb.

He blinked in vague annoyance as if someone had surprised him with a cream pie in the face.

Wiping the blood spray from his eyelids, he shook his head to banish the sudden ringing in his ears.

The side of her head nearest the gun was perfect – just some smouldering from the small scorched hole in the temple. But the left side was out, gone, replaced by an ugly blood-streaked grey bladder of brain-flesh that hung like a small saddle on a bowl of fresh skull bone.

He began laughing, shaking his head with amused disbelief.

'One-in-six chance, first shot and bang! How shit unlucky is that?' he asked the empty night.

2434 ABRAMAR, PACIFIC PALISADES, CA

Phillips shook his head.

'Fucked if I know,' he offered and settled back in the sun lounger.

Maggie took the sheet of paper from him. First she glanced at the picture and description of Cherie Blaynes, then turned it over.

'It's like some sort of a code,' she remarked after studying it for a few moments.

'That's what I thought,' agreed Kronziac as she came through the French doors onto the veranda with a tray of drinks.

'Guys, it's not FBI business,' Phillips informed them, slipping his shades over his eyes, helping himself to a beer and tilting his face to the bright sun.

'Have you shown it to Questioned Documents over at Westwood?' Maggie asked, bringing the paper closer to her eyes.

'Yeah, I left it in with Taggart at Forensics.'

Kronziac sipped her Long Island Iced Tea and sat down on the other lounger while Maggie stayed sitting at the Zellig table, lightly sipping an orange juice.

'Like Mr Sensitivity over there said,' Kronziac went on, 'it's not really our case.'

'Hey, all I'm saying is we can't help every schmo with a runaway daughter we feel sorry for,' Phillips said defensively. 'Leave it to the PD.'

Maggie shook her head. 'You're an asshole, Phillips,' she told him. But he just smacked his lips and shifted in his lounger as if about to fall into a blissful sleep under the warm heavens. 'I still think it's some kind of a code,' she went on.

'A code for what, though?' Kronziac wanted to know. 'It is kinda strange.'

Maggie looked up suddenly, straining her ears. 'Did you hear that?'

Kronziac put her drink down.

'A phone,' Maggie decided. 'Not mine.'

Kronziac jumped up and ran inside the house.

'Tell 'em I'm not available!' Phillips shouted after her, as he always did when the phone rang, any phone, even the one on his desk in the office.

Maggie put the sheet of paper back on the table. 'You think Nancy's okay?' she said quietly.

'Kronziac? She's fine. Don't worry about her,' Phillips reassured her.

'Sedley said she was still under investigation,' she confided, keeping her voice low.

'Fuck Sedley,' muttered Phillips, not wanting to talk about it. He sucked a long drink from the bottle.

Maggie was about to say more but Kronziac came out again and placed her cell phone very slowly and carefully on the table as if thinking hard about something.

'Everything okay?' Maggie asked.

'That was Jimmy Soton.'

Phillips sat up and snapped his shades off. 'He's still alive?'

'Yeah,' confirmed Kronziac, a little amazed that her informer had crept out of the woodwork at last. 'He left a message on my secure box at the office you set up.'

'And?' Phillips asked impatiently.

'Wants to meet me tomorrow morning,' said Kronziac.

'You shouldn't go,' Maggie interrupted. 'You're still on leave, remember?'

Phillips stood up and followed Kronziac to the clay balustrade that overlooked the garden and the steep bluffs below.

'Where?' he wanted to know.

'At the LA Zoo at twelve-fifteen p.m. tomorrow. The Reptile House,' Kronziac told him, her voice slightly nervous.

'I'll go back-up,' he said. But Kronziac shot him a warning look.

'Like hell you will,' she warned him. 'If we scare him away again we'll never pin the connection with the dealers to The Club.'

MATERIALS & DEVICES UNIT, FBI FORENSICS LAB, WESTWOOD PARK, LOS ANGELES

A compact five-storey white-plastered building not far from the Federal Building Westwood Park served the forensic needs of the Bureau and its field offices on the West Coast. Since its opening over two years ago the facility was fast gaining a reputation as one of the finest crime labs in the country. But its speciality was terrorism-related evidence examination. Even the FBI's mammoth laboratory in Washington sometimes sent material evidence to Westwood for expert examination. The Materials & Devices Unit, housed on the second floor, used an immense array of equipment, from gas chromatographs and spectrum analysers to 3-D facial modelling systems and electron microscopes, to extract the tiniest traces of evidence or clues to help the Department of Justice in their cases against organized crime, fraudsters, serial murderers – and, of course, terrorists.

Phillips called it the most expensive chemistry set in the world. Indicative of the Bureau's recent policy of attracting younger recruits into the FBI's forensic services, the average age of the Westwood lab staff was late thirties. Andrew Taggart, ten years younger again, was peering at a monitor showing a multi-legged monster roaming a parched, rock-littered landscape – the magnified surface of a carpet fibre.

'How's the wrist?' he asked.

'Coming along.' Kronziac smiled.

Pale-skinned and rosy-cheeked, Taggart could have easily been mistaken by casual callers for an intern or a twelfth-grader on work placement. But Kronziac regarded him as one of the most incisive of the 'whitecoats' at Westwood.

'Heard you had a bit of a tussle with the Woodsmen.' He grinned knowingly.

'Yeah . . .' was all Kronziac would say. One thing she didn't particularly enjoy was talking with him about the actual events of a crime or an operation: Taggart tended to grin like a kid,

83

describing a shoot-out as if it was a movie, maxed up for thrills. She liked him best when he stuck purely to the science of evidence.

'Can you give me anything on the sheet?' she asked hopefully, glancing at a plastic sleeve lying on a shelf above the microscope that contained the copy of Cherie Blaynes's Missing Persons notice.

He took it down from the shelf. 'Er . . .' He hesitated, smiling.

'Come on, Andy what is it?' she said directly.

'I tried,' he began, 'to get the guys up at QD to see if they could make anything of it but they wanted a case number and a case officer and when I mentioned your name they—' He stopped again, curling the sheet nervously in his hand. 'They said you were on suspension. Been a bad girl?' He smirked.

Kronziac shook her head, sighing wearily. 'Okay. Thanks, Andy,' she said and grabbed the sheet from him, 'I gotta go. I'm already running late.'

Taggart, surprised by her abruptness, got up from his stool and hurried to the door after her.

'Look, Kronziac.' He stopped her. 'It's a code, all right? So what you need is a cryptographer,' he suggested. 'Maybe someone up in the Computer Crime Squad, they do a lot of encryption and math sorta shit.' He began shrugging. 'Worth a shot.'

But Kronziac wasn't too cheered. 'They're putting the freeze on me,' she said dejectedly.

But Taggart was smiling again. 'Nobody puts the freeze on you.' He grinned, like a kid.

Kronziac nodded gratefully. 'Thanks, Andy.' She remembered the time and rushed out the door.

Taggart returned to his electron microscope on whose screen two dust mites clashed like rhinos over a flake of skin.

134 (VENTURA) FREEWAY, EASTBOUND

As the Explorer drew gently to a halt behind a long line of cars Kronziac lowered the window to find out what the hold-up was. She could see a white tour bus at an angle across the arm of the Victory Boulevard exit, a small Toyota wedged beneath its chassis. The paramedics were casually treating the sobbing driver of the Toyota as the CHP tried to bounce the little car from beneath the bus. It was already twelve-fifteen.

There was nothing Kronziac could do but hope that Jimmy Soton would still be there when she arrived.

She picked up the sheet of paper, still shrouded in the protective plastic sleeve from the lab, from the passenger seat. It annoyed her – four little lines of impenetrable code.

'Damn it,' she said decisively and pressed the directory on her car phone. Scrolling through the names she poked the send button when Fred Stranski's work number came up. She waited in the traffic as the phone hummed in Washington.

FAA OFFICES, INDEPENDENCE AVE, WASHINGTON DC

The secretary found Fred Stranski at the elevator where he was saying goodbye to a senior captain with Air Florida. As head of the Human Factors Study Group, Stranski, a psych graduate from Harvard and a behavioural expert, advised the Federal Aviation Administration on the psychological evaluation of flight-crew environments. Before taking up his present position he had spent some time in private practice in Syracuse and before that had worked for a couple of years as a visiting lecturer at Cambridge University, England and then for a year at the Behavioural Science Unit at the FBI Academy in Quantico where he had awarded nearly top marks in Criminal Investigative Analysis to a certain female cadet from Chicago.

'Fred, there's a Nancy Kronziac on the phone for you!' the secretary called to him as he shook hands with the pilot.

A tall man, at least six-two, he loped down the corridor back to his office and snatched the phone from the hook, breathless.

'Nancy . . . how the hell are you?'

134 (VENTURA) FREEWAY, EASTBOUND, VICTORY BLVD EXIT

The bus rocked as three CHP officers bounced the Toyota free and the passengers began clapping.

Kronziac held the phone with her good hand. 'Yeah, still chasing the bad guys,' she said lightly. 'Fred, I got a favour to ask,' she went on, a little nervously as if her credit with him was stretching. 'No, I don't need a prescription . . . well, not yet.' She laughed. Looking at the sheet of paper lying on her lap, she asked, 'Do you know anyone good with codes?'

Stranski thought she'd said 'coats'.

'No, *codes*,' she repeated. 'I need a cryptographer.'

REPTILE HOUSE, LOS ANGELES ZOO, GRIFFITH PARK

'Jimmy and his goddamned reptile obsession.' Kronziac cursed under her breath and looked away from the pit. Below, amid the sandy outcrops, lit by warm spots, the giant lizard crawled slowly behind a hollow log. It stood there for a moment conscious of its audience peering from their safe positions behind the thick glass of the viewing platform. Its tongue shot out, wriggling from the dripping mouth, tasting its surroundings.

Kronziac looked at her watch again.

Nearly one o'clock.

It was a warm sunny day and the zoo seethed with a mass of tourists, school trips, senior junkets and families – all slowly circulating through the hundred or so acres of enclosures. Groups were led by guides and volunteers in khaki, peddling biofact carts and imparting information about the resident wildlife through loud hailers. A conservation drive spread volunteers through the park, costumed as endangered species, looking for donations and distributing leaflets.

The Reptile House, dark under its low black wooded ceiling, was hot and stuffy. Children were clouding the glass pens with their breath and melting soft-serve ice cream. They crowded through the passageways, pointing and squealing in disgust at the pythons and adders, the bright emerald tree boas draped like bright rubber streamers on their perches, the gekkos motionless, swivelling wet bulbous eyes.

The two Komodo Dragons were recent arrivals and wards of court, a notice informed the public, while the Department of Fish and Wildlife pursued an exotic-reptile collector through the state judiciary. In the pit one of the Komodos strode heavily over the sand, his low body swaying like a flattened sumo, the tail swinging pendulously in a wide arc behind.

Kronziac looked away again. The huge reptiles gave her the creeps and her nose twitched, smarting with the stale smell that hung in the air, leathery, like dead skin. She wasn't sure if it was from the people or the reptiles.

'One swing of his tail and he could send you across the room,' said a man next to her. He was still staring through the glass, marvelling at the beasts, as Kronziac turned around.

'And break your neck in two,' he added with a degree of satisfaction. He turned to her. 'How are you, Agent Kronziac?'

'I'm fine, Jimmy,' she replied, relieved, 'I was sure I had missed you.'

He seemed unconcerned. 'I had a good walk around,' he said. 'How's Hector?' he asked suddenly, as if enquiring about a sick child. 'You feeding him right?'

'Oh, he's fine,' she answered, without much conviction and a little unsettled that Jimmy Soton had such knowledge of her personal life.

'Chameleons need proper food, you know,' he informed her, a hint of reproach in his tone.

Jimmy wasn't a very big man, for a security guard – about five-nine, 160 pounds. Though he had the weasely demeanour of the petty criminal that he was. His face was rounded and dark, swarthy. Even when he shaved he always seemed unkempt. Today he wore a tight, light blue T-shirt and tatty jeans. A patch of his hair over the forehead was turning prematurely grey, which prompted people on first seeing him to ask if he was painting a ceiling or something. He had worked for ScanTec Securities for nearly seven years and had contacted the FBI when he over-heard one of his colleagues plan to kidnap an A&P bank manager to fund the Woodsmen's campaign of anti-government insur-rection in the Bitteroot Mountains of northern Idaho and Montana. Kronziac herself had to go to Washington to meet with the Assistant Director to sanction 'facilitation' money to pay Soton for all the information he had on the kidnapping. She didn't like him much, didn't like the way he looked her up and down or stared at her lips while she talked. She reckoned he fitted right in here at the Reptile House. But at least she always knew where he stood – wherever there was money to be had.

'What do you want, Jimmy?' she asked directly.

He remained silent, watching the Komodo slither into the dark hole of its cave. The spectators moaned in disappointment and moved on to the snake pens.

'Let's grab a coffee,' he suggested, 'the Gorilla Grill or the Safari Café?'

Kronziac shook her head. 'Whatever.'

The sun grew warmer and the zoo swelled with a mass of people moving like a slow river along the walkways between the enclosures, pointing at and delighting in the animals. A line of volunteers at the entrance to the park dressed as polar bears handed out leaflets and pestered people for donations. The Safari Shuttle, a long tram with the black-and-white streaks of a zebra pulled off from the Flamingo Exhibit as Kronziac and Jimmy found a table in the Safari Café just vacated by a messy family of humans who left a stack of burger cartons, half-eaten doughnuts, and soupy globs of jam. Kronziac had to repeat their order of two coffees to the waitress as a noisy birthday party arrived, festooned in hats and plastic bags from the gift shops.

Jimmy fidgeted with one of the cracked plastic cups left behind on the table. 'I need protection,' he said, nervously looking around as someone dressed as an ostrich patted a toddler on the head and made the child turn its head in to its mother's armpit and cry.

'We can't give you any more money,' Kronziac told him, sensing that his idea of protection was twenty grand of federal funding and a one-way ticket to Puerta Valarta.

'Look,' he said insistently, 'even those dumb-ass fuckin' hillbillies can put two and two together and come up with yours truly.'

The parents of three perfect, blonde-haired kids at a table nearby looked disdainfully in Jimmy's direction, the mother utterly appalled at his language.

Jimmy leaned in over the table. 'I don't care where you send me,' he whispered. 'I don't care, just get me outta LA.'

Kronziac shook her head doubtfully as the waitress came back and landed their coffees in front of them. She waited for her to pick up the other litter on the table.

'That's up to the Justice Department,' Kronziac said. 'We'd have to prove that you are in imminent danger and you'd have to testify in a federal court when and if—' she raised an eyebrow '—*if* it all came to trial.'

'That's bullshit!' Jimmy snarled, attracting more looks of disapproval from the Brady Bunch at the next table.

Kronziac looked at the ground, a little embarrassed.

'You've got to help me,' he continued, the tilt of his head and the edge on his voice suggesting a threat.

Sipping at her steaming coffee, Kronziac considered her response as the crowd at the Aquatic Centre nearby clapped and cheered.

'If they get to me they get to you,' he surmised with slow deliberation.

She stared back at him. 'Don't try that shit on me,' she warned him softly. 'Remember you came to me with the information.'

'And you were damn glad to take it,' he retorted. 'And now I'm on the run. I had to leave my apartment, quit my job . . . I can't go any place quiet . . .' He shook his head and rubbed his rough chin. 'I'm pissin' in my pants when I go to the liquor store, in case one of those crazy fuckers finds me.'

Kronziac had to admit, at least in her own mind, that he was indeed in danger. They all were. Crebbs and his family played for keeps. She wanted to help but wouldn't promise anything she couldn't deliver. She knew putting Soton on a witness-protection program wouldn't fly with Foley or the brass in DC.

'Why don't you just get out of town yourself?' she suggested. 'Leave the country if you have to.'

He seemed disgusted, sitting back in his chair, appalled at the betrayal. 'With what?' he asked, 'I've got about a hundred bucks left.'

Kronziac had difficulty keeping quiet herself. 'Jesus, Jimmy! We gave you ten grand!' she gasped. 'Just a couple of weeks ago. What the hell did you do with it?'

He didn't answer, just looked around with a haunted scowl on his face.

Kronziac shook her head, took out her cheque book and scribbled Jimmy a cheque for five hundred dollars.

Before he could thank her Kronziac's cell phone purred dully in her purse. The line crackled with a distant voice and she pressed her other hand against her free ear.

'Hello? . . . Hello?' She suddenly smiled as she realized that the caller ID was 202 – Washington.

'Fred! I didn't expect to hear back from you so soon,' she said loudly as two quads carrying animal feed droned past.

Jimmy stood up impatiently and gestured to Kronziac that he was going to the gents' over by the Alligator Pen. Kronziac nodded curtly as Fred Stranski told her about a friend of his who might be able to help her and glanced up as Jimmy's blue T-shirt disappeared into the crowd by the mall. She asked Fred to repeat his friend's name as the crowd at the aquatic show cheered again. She awkwardly retrieved a pen from her purse and tried to write down the name with her left hand as she pinched the phone between her cheek and shoulder.

'Okay, go ahead.' She nodded, scribbling down the name. 'James Ellstrom . . . Department of Mathematics . . . What? What Center?'

One of the conservation volunteers in a white polar-bear outfit came over to the table and shoved a clipboard in front of her face.

'Save endangered species, ma'am! Fifty dollars for the World Wildlife Fund could help us save a Sumatran phinoceros or a pair of Californian condors!' the male voice in the suit sang and shook a white pouch in the shape of a bear paw in front of her.

Not now, asshole. She wanted to shout at him but just shook her head.

'Sorry, Fred. 'She turned back to the phone. 'Can you repeat that? Science Center . . . yeah . . . at Harvard University . . . Cambridge, Massachusetts . . . and the number?'

Jimmy Soton stood in front of the urinal, breathed out slowly and closed his eyes. He was glad the old man next to him had finished and had left him alone in the restroom.

Jimmy always found it hard to piss if there was another guy right next to him and the more conscious of it he became, the more stubborn his bladder. He could feel the satisfying tickle of release in his lower abdomen when the heavy inner door into the lavatories opened and one of the costumed volunteers walked in. Dressed in a fawn acrylic kangaroo suit, complete with a pouch below the midriff, the newcomer took up position at the urinal next to Jimmy and pushed his hand into the deep pocket in the front of his costume.

Jimmy heard him say something and turned to ask him to repeat it. That was when the blade of a gutting knife flashed out of the pouch. It plunged into Jimmy's neck, piercing his windpipe with a short, sharp squelch as it cut through the gullet. He hung there for a moment, his body spasming in surprise around the hot pain in his throat. Then the knife was pulled out again, further ripping the muscles of his windpipe, and he collapsed, heavy like a corpse from the gallows. Another man, this one dressed in a black gorilla suit, entered the toilet as Jimmy gasped on the cold floor, choking in his own blood. The kangaroo and the gorilla dragged him through a side door and out the back of the toilets to a service yard that led to the rear of the alligator pen. Jimmy could hear the dolphins chittering in the distance, then a splash of water and a wave of clapping. Above him he could see a mosaic of eucalyptus leaves against the bright blue sky. They dragged him in under a dark passage and a heavy wooden door clunked open and he was pushed and fell into the bright world again. He could feel his elbows breaking like dry sticks as he hit the tarmac banking and rolled over endlessly downwards until his useless, convulsing body stopped, trapped in a thick warm sludge.

He lay there for a moment, struggling to understand the bright open space and the smell of rotting, slimy unguent that covered him. He struggled to hold his gaping neck wound closed to stop himself from bleeding dry.

But Jimmy was already beginning to lose consciousness as something clamped his thigh and began tearing at his leg.

'All right, Fred, thanks again for your help,' Kronziac shouted and flipped her phone shut. She looked up to see if Jimmy was coming back but could see only the constant movement of strangers in the sunshine.

The guy in the polar-bear suit had left a pamphlet on the table. She picked it up.

It had some beautiful colour photos of wild animals: a majestic Bengal tiger lazing beneath a cool umbrella of banyan leaves, a polar bear adrift on an ice floe in the Arctic sea, a condor aloft on an Andean breeze.

He had left another pamphlet under the first.

This one was ugly, a crude printout.

Large red letters, dripping like blood:

SPECIAL AGENT NANCY KRONZIAC
FBI
WHORE OF THE ZIONIST GOVERNMENT

A grainy photograph beneath. A woman standing on a patio balcony, drinking from a glass, a riot of wild bougainvillea climbing up to meet her.

Overprinted on the picture were the cross-hairs of a rifle. Beneath this were the words:

WANTED DEAD . . . (OR BARELY ALIVE!)

Nancy Kronziac reached for her purse to take out her gun but forgot for a moment that she hadn't carried one for weeks. Her seat fell back and rang against the concrete like a dropped cup as she ran from the restaurant towards the lavatories.

The crowd at the aquatic centre laughed, cheered and whistled in appreciation as a trio of dolphins rode their tails across the blue water.

But someone was screaming near the back of the alligator pen.

Kronziac followed the scream.

Some keepers were also running at the back of the pen, out of view of most of the onlookers.

She went as far as she could around the side of the wall, topped with a ten-foot wire-mesh fence.

Someone gasped and said they could see a body inside.

Kronziac scanned across the broad curve of mud, about a half-acre in size, a wide band of stagnant water sweeping through the middle, the long shapes of the alligators basking on the banks like idle blunt torpedoes.

Fractions of Zero

But in the back, half obscured by the mud bank, a few metres below the feeding hatch there was some frantic movement. Whipping alligator tails.

Then one alligator swung away, tossing the L-shape of a human leg in its mouth.

Three stayed, a frenzy of jaws and tails around a shape, slicked with mud – a patch of blue fabric, hair, a face being devoured.

Red oozed like fondant on the grey mud as the alligators fought over the torso. The others on the bank, stirred, slipping into the water, cruising in for left-overs.

ADIC'S OFFICE, FBI, FEDERAL BUILDING, WILSHIRE BLVD

Foley was shaking his head.

He was reading the photocopied words again

Wanted dead or . . . barely alive.

Kronziac sat quietly in front of the big dark mahogany desk, her arms wrapped tightly around herself as if trying desperately to keep herself warm. She shuddered each time the image of Jimmy Soton's half-devoured chest flashed across her mind. His ribcage hung with ragged flesh, the alligators pulling pieces of him away.

The shoulders of Foley's grey suit bunched up as he sat back in his high-back leather chair. He was still shaking his head.

'We'll assign you protection,' he pronounced.

Maggie was perched on a chair next to Kronziac, attending to her with close care and comfort, wrapping her sweater around her friend's shoulders.

'I can stay with Nancy for a while,' she offered gently, almost as if she didn't want Kronziac to hear.

'Yeah, and I'll stay around as much as I can.' Phillips spoke up from the back of the room where he leaned against the bookcase.

'All right, good,' Foley agreed. 'Crebbs and his family – they won't stop,' he added gravely. 'What were you thinking?' he asked Kronziac, his concern turning to frustration.

She didn't answer.

'Going there on your own . . . what did you hope to gain?' He was about to turn on Phillips to ask if he knew about the meeting when there was a knock on the door.

Nathan Sedley, all business, appeared like an eager news hack, carrying a small notepad in his palm. But the sight of Kronziac seemed to take the wind out of his sails and he stopped before opening his mouth.

'What is it, Nathan?' Foley asked.

'Er . . . I just talked to the LAPD about Soton and they said they found some— something on him,' he replied awkwardly.

'What?' Foley barked. 'What did they find?' He glanced at Kronziac, knowing it was something to do with her.

'I gave him some money,' she uttered wearily, her first few words since they'd sat her down in the office.

Sedley was nodding affirmatively. 'They found a cheque with "N. Kronziac" on it,' he said.

Foley's lips tightened as he fixed his stare on Kronziac. 'This is just getting better,' he gasped. 'How much?'

Kronziac looked back at him. 'Five hundred dollars,' she replied, 'I needed some information and it's always a pay-in game with Soton.'

'And you decided to pay him yourself!' His voice became ragged with anger. 'Your own personal snitch fund, special interest rate . . . what the fuck do you need us for? Hell, the FBI is just getting in the way, isn't it?'

Maggie glared at the Assistant Director, wordlessly pleading with him to ease off. She could see Kronziac was on the verge of breaking down.

Foley shot up out of his chair and paced to the windows, one hand on his hip, the other massaging the nape of his neck to try and stem the headache that was beginning to grip him like a claw.

'Any idea how it happened?' Phillips asked Sedley quietly.

But the blank expression on Sedley's face suggested there wasn't that much to go on yet. 'They reckon he was knifed in the toilets, then dragged out back into the service area and dumped through the feeding hatch.'

'Sounds like an inside job or someone with knowledge of the park,' Phillips said.

'Yeah, they're talking to the keepers and the staff but haven't got any leads yet . . . it was a busy day at the zoo.' Sedley shrugged.

Foley turned around. 'Okay, Nancy,' he began purposefully. 'This is really for your own good as much as anything but you can now consider yourself officially on administrative leave. And,' he continued swiftly, expecting her to interrupt him with a protest, 'if I hear of any further involvement by you on the

Bitteroot case then we'll talk about reassigning you to the Anchorage Field Office's clerical unit!'

He opened his eyes wide, as if challenging her to try his patience any further.

'Do I make myself plain? Do I sparkle? Am I transparently clear?'

Fuck. Phillips glanced worriedly at Sedley.

But Kronziac, tired, worn, her nerves like abraded teeth, nodded gratefully.

'Thanks, sir,' she said quietly – and seemed to mean it.

Foley calmed down and returned to his desk beneath the rounded eyes of Hoover. As they all left he advised Kronziac, as she reached the door, 'Might be a good idea to get out of LA for a few days.'

California State Lotteries

Mega Lotto

RESULT

Sat 27th October

5   43   11   33   22   8

SCIENCE CENTER, HARVARD UNIVERSITY, CAMBRIDGE, MA

Kronziac couldn't help feeling a little disappointed.

'This is it?'

The cab driver nodded. 'Yeah, the Math Department is in there.'

She gave him the fare and got out into the cool air. Though she had spent a week in Chicago with her parents, a couple of days in Dayton with her sister, and a night doing all the bars in Manhattan with her twenty-four-year old brother and his buddies, Kronziac was still not used to the bracing East Coast autumnal air. She pulled the collar of her coat around her chin and followed a stream of students up the wide path to the Science Center. The sidewalks were littered with brown faded leaves that ran with a hushed rustle each time the wind blew.

Kronziac was amazed to see how young some of the students looked. To her they seemed as if they were high-schoolers, not Harvard Freshmen. She hadn't quite imagined finding gangs of undergraduates, scarves wrapped jauntily about them, gowns billowing behind, clutching books to their sides and singing 'Fair Harvard' as they hurried to class. But now she half expected a line of SUVs to pull up with Moms waiting to collect their kids for softball practice.

Even the Science Center building itself, with its early seventies modernity, struck an odd pose, like the dissected superstructure of a liner, the funnels and decks replaced about each other haphazardly. The main centre of the building tumbled like a descending stair of glass steps, framed by a lattice of precast concrete. As a law grad herself, Kronziac was familiar, through the many books about Harvard, with the great buildings that were most associated with Ivy League institutions. Whether she would have admitted it back then, she'd often dreamed of traipsing through Harvard Yard during Fall semester, taking opening argument in the romanesque grandeur of Austin Hall or discussing amendments by Pound and Derschowitz or

Chafee and the Freedom of Speech bill under the imperious portal of Langdell Hall.

Once inside, Kronziac began to appreciate the bright, airy atmosphere provided by the large windows and high ceilings louvred by white fans of steel. She also began to let the doubts about the wisdom of this visit climb to the front of her mind. But the memory of Jerry Blaynes's voice pleading with her on the phone when she rang him from New York to find out if the police had any news on his missing daughter had cast the doubts from her mind. He'd begged her to help in any way she could.

She asked directions to James Ellstrom's office from a bright attendant on the information desk. He directed her to Lecture Room 507, giving his instructions with an air of friendly alertness.

As she rode the elevator she repeated to herself that it was private business, nothing to do with the FBI, nothing that would contravene the terms of her probation as laid down by her boss.

Lecture Room 507 was half full with an assortment of professors, junior faculty members and undergraduates. Kronziac found a seat at the back of the room and smiled at a couple of young male students next to her, one looking remarkably like a junior Bill Gates. They smiled broadly at her, welcoming the presence of a single female. Apart from two other women up front, both in large nunnish-like pinafores, Kronziac seemed to be the only representative of her gender at the gathering.

At the front, talking to the gallery from the dais, was a tallish blond man, grinning as he referred to himself as an explorer in the fascinating world of ellipses. An overhead projector beside him illuminated a large black book cover on the screen behind. It showed a splash of lines and curves, as if drawn by a child on a spirograph, the title running in dull grey across the top: *Diadems are Forever – Infinite Elliptical Journeys in a Modular World* by Professor James Ellstrom.

The speaker was in his late thirties, possibly early forties, Kronziac figured. With his pale Nordic complexion and large blue hooded eyes, he reminded her of a young Michael Caine, an impression further enhanced by his English accent – not London but certainly southern, Home Counties.

'Let me finish,' he said, closing a copy of the book, 'by paraphrasing, if I may, Galileo in *Opere II Saggiatore*.' He affected a theatrical pose as if about to slip into a Shakespearean monologue.

'The world cannot be understood until we have learned its language and become familiar with the characters in which it is written. For it is written in mathematical language, and the letters are triangles, circles and other geometrical figures, without which means it is humanly impossible to comprehend a single word.' Then he bowed.

He actually bowed, Kronziac thought to herself. The crowd clapped and cheered. Some of the older academics rushed to him and shook his hand heartily and patted him on the back. And then they all made for a table set up beside the dais, lined with bottles of wine, plates of potato chips and tubs of dip.

As Ellstrom leaned against the dais, handing out signed copies of his book, Kronziac sipped on a plastic cup of tart red wine, waiting for an opportunity to speak with the mathematician.

'It's not a very good book,' someone next to her remarked.

Kronziac turned around and saw a corpulent man with a grey bush of hair, which seemed to grow sideways instead of down, filling his mouth with a chip generously heaped with a dollop of sauerkraut.

'Oh, I'm sorry, are you from the publishers?' He smiled nervously at her.

'No.' Kronziac smiled back.

He narrowed his eyes, trying to figure her out. 'You in the Math Department?' he asked.

Kronziac laughed. 'No, no,' she said. *Christ, no*, she thought, but hoped her denial wasn't too eager. 'I'm just a friend,' she added breezily.

The man stuffed another potato chip covered in creamy chive dip into his mouth and carried away three plastic cups to a group nearby who were discussing quietly and conspiratorially the flaws of the book.

The two young guys who she had sat next to had been joined by a third at the drinks table and were gulping down the wine as if it was soda.

Kronziac overheard the tail end of a joke one of them was telling between mouthfuls of the cheap rosé.

'. . . And I write this seven-digit number on the board,' he said eagerly and made a grating nasal sound, pushing an imaginary buzzer with his thumb. '"Wrong," she said, "wrong answer." But I said 'No, right answer – if the question is . . . what's my telephone number?"'

His friends broke out laughing, one of them sinking a straw into his wine.

Kronziac moved quickly away and saw that Ellstrom was handing out his last book, giving it to an appreciative colleague.

'Sorry, last one.' He smiled smugly as she came up to him. 'But there will be more on sale at the Cabot Library for the rest of the week and I think the *International Journal of Mathematics* will be publishing an abstract soon.'

Kronziac smiled. 'Great,' she said, wishing to appear impressed.

Ellstrom quickly realized that she didn't seem like the usual type of math groupie who attended the regular 507 seminars or book launches.

'I wonder if you can help me?' Kronziac asked sheepishly, glancing at his name projected large on the screen, 'Professor Ellstrom.'

'Of course, if I can,' he said brightly. 'But if it's to do with the Taniyama Shimura Conjecture and the relationship between *E-series* and *M-series* alluded to therein then I will have to refer you, reluctantly, to one of my colleagues.' Kronziac's dumb smile made him laugh.

'No, it's not that, – whatever it was,' she said, lost, but remaining polite, hoping he might still help.

'I didn't think so.' He smiled condescendingly, amused at her obvious ignorance of the subject.

Kronziac just continued to smile back, nodding. *So you've written a book about child-doodles and have to hand out free copies to a bunch of geeks whose idea of fun seems to be sucking*

cheap wine through a straw and making jokes that at a real party
would have you thrown out without the benefit of the door being
actually open first.

'A friend of mine,' she began politely, 'Fred Stranski in DC,
said you might be able to help me.'

For a moment he seemed to search his memory banks as his
gaze drifted over her shoulder.

'Of course!' He turned back. 'You mean Freddie, Freddie
Stranski, yes, we were both teaching at Cambridge together –
Cambridge, England, I mean,' he added, having, of course, to
allow for her probable ignorance of geography as well as math.

'Good old Freddie,' he stated fondly. 'How is the guy?' His
accent wavered between an English and a Massachusetts accent.

'Oh, he's fine,' Kronziac answered and took out a folded sheet
of paper from her jacket. It was a photocopy of the rows of
letters sent to the Devonshire Police Station, on the back of
Cherie Blaynes's Missing Persons Notice. 'He told me you knew
something about cryptography,' she said coyly, handing him
the paper.

One of the junior faculty members, a small guy in a cheese-
cloth shirt and mauve chords, quipped as he walked by, 'Watch
out, Ellstrom. Remember, women divide, but men must
multiply.'

Ellstrom began laughing again. 'Joe's a topologist,' he said
to Kronziac. 'Can't tell the difference between a bicycle wheel
and a Polo mint!' he shouted after his friend.

'All comedians, huh?' Kronziac remarked, her patience
wearing thin, as Ellstrom opened the folded paper and studied
the letters for a moment.

'Is it some sort of a code?' Kronziac asked eagerly.

'Well, cryptography is more of a hobby for me, number theory
being my real thing.' He rambled on, distracted by the lines of
letters. Then he swiftly folded the sheet into a small rectangle
again and handed it back to her.

'Looks like a simple Caesar Shift to me,' he said dismissively.
'Tell Freddie he should work out his own riddles.'

Kronziac put up her hands defensively. 'Hold on, can you tell
me what it means?'

Bill Murphy

She remembered that Stranski had warned her that Ellstrom was a difficult man and that to hold his attention she might have to challenge his intellectual integrity or at least leave the problem with him. Sooner or later he would have to solve it, no matter how easy or hard it was.

'No, of course I can't.' Ellstrom shook his head, 'I would have to run a frequency analysis.'

She took what looked at first glance like a blank business card with her LA number handwritten on it, from her coat and thrust it into his palm.

'Well,' Kronziac said, 'if you *can* work it out, please give me a call at this number.'

'*If* I can work it out?' Ellstrom repeated, a bemused smile of incredulity stretching his features.

Kronziac bowed gracefully. 'Nice to have met you, Professor. Hope the book does well for you!' She smiled and walked away before he could say anything else.

He watched her disappear out the door, then flipped her card over.

The FBI seal made him wonder.

LAS VEGAS METRO POLICE DEPARTMENT, 400 E. STEWART ST, LAS VEGAS, NV

Detective Ernie Mazzalo was peeking under the stacks of files on his desk, searching for a missing Missing Persons Report. He was legendary as being one of the best people-finders in the department but was equally infamous as one of the worst at keeping his records in good order. His corner of the office was affectionately known as the Paper Jungle by his fellow detectives – a place where files went to gather dust and collectively imitate the New York skyline in miniature on his desk. One of the new temps dropped a single sheet of paper on one of the stacks as she scurried by.

'Eh – what's that?' Mazzalo barked, raising his wide brown-eyed gaze to her.

Taken aback, the young secretary cleared her throat guiltily. 'The Desk Sergeant sent it up,' she squeaked.

He picked up the sheet. 'What is it?' he repeated.

'A missing-persons notice,' the secretary replied blankly.

Mazzalo began twisting open the top button of his shirt. 'I know that,' he wheezed. 'But what am I supposed to do with it?'

She began to edge further away from the desk. She had other files and reports to deliver. 'I was just told to bring it up to the Missing Persons Detail – to your desk,' she said loudly, making her getaway down the corridor.

Mazzalo was about to say something else but he began nodding to himself. He'd recognized the description of the old woman.

THE LAS VEGAS METROPOLITAN POLICE DEPARTMENT IS
REQUESTING THE PUBLIC'S ASSISTANCE IN LOCATING THIS

MISSING PERSON

Ellen Tiffany Holby was last seen on the night of 9th October in the Magnolia Building on Bonanza Rd where she lived.

66 years of age Mrs Holby is described as 5' 5" in height of thin build, with blue eyes and silver hair.

Anyone with information that may help locate this missing person is urged to call at 800-LOST or Det. Ernest Mazzalo at LVMPD Missing Persons Detail.

The notice reminded Mazzalo to call Homicide. He remembered that the crime-scene report had said her apartment door had been found open by responding officers but that nothing had been missing, just the old woman. It seemed decidedly suspicious.

As the phone buzzed at the other end he turned the sheet of paper over and found in the middle of the page an array of letters, no spaces, printed in three lines and making no sense.

LVEFASDPFZUWNRZMGANTMUROLRGCZSCRXJVLHRASUKO
SBFZXAGBFZWITBUGSBBPFPWRYIWMVOAYMGANTIOBZEFBP
ZWTBZSIYTBQO

FOREST SERVICE ROAD 53, UMATILLA NATIONAL FOREST, OREGON

The day began to close and the sun blinked wearily as the dark clouds moved low over the Blue Mountains, crawling on a million legs of rain.

Peter Kelley checked the meter.

Almost thirty dollars already. He smiled to himself. Thirty dollars to travel the Scenic Byway out of Heppner past Willow Creek Lake, the glass sheen of its surface tickling with trout and bass, and up into the pine-and-fir-gloved hills of Umatilla Forest. He stopped the cab outside the old Ranger hut at the northern edge of Cutsford Park. The last rays of sun split a seam of molten gold in the cloud and sent a blade of light across the peaks.

Checking in with Dispatch, his wife Dorothy playfully chided him for enjoying the scenery when he could be in town picking up fares. But Peter told her he would wait for fifteen minutes for his pick-up, a hunting party from Portland, before heading back to Heppner.

Getting out, he ran a cloth along the flank of the Buick, polishing the large green shamrock and the words *Kelley's Kabs.*

A light wind brushed the tops of the trees like a giant hand-stroke. A quail scurried, flapping fussily through the under-growth, spooked by the shifting air.

Dorothy hated the name – too cheesy – but Peter assured her it was catchy and swish. Besides, it wasn't as if they had much competition. Kelley's Kabs was the only taxi company in Morrow County, serving its mostly farming population of three or four thousand.

Peter was polishing the side windows as another creature rattled through the trees. It sounded larger, a deer or an elk maybe, or even more dangerous – one of the weekend hunters from Seattle or San Francisco, all gear and no stealth. A small commotion in the bunchgrass left him relieved as another small creature sprung unseen into the gathering darkness of the forest.

He continued to the windshield, wiping a greasy film of dust from the glass.

As he pulled up one of the wipers he felt a hot, sharp pain driving through his thigh. A gloved hand cupped his mouth, suffocating all sound. He could feel a man's body, strong, behind him, pinning him against the car for a moment before his own limbs buckled and his head wobbled loose into unconsciousness.

BACCARAT

To seize up the human heart by electric shock generally requires in excess of 2,000 volts of alternating current. Upper-brain functioning and lucidity can be destroyed at about 1,500 volts but the more heavy-duty workings of the heart, as serviced by the body's autonomic nervous system, need a charge of at least 500 volts more. Some individuals of over-average weight who have an inherent and peculiar resistivity may require a charge of up to 2,400 volts. At this level a careful regulation of the current should be observed to avoid *cooking*.

Peter Kelley weighed about 195 pounds.

He swung into consciousness with a hazy awareness of danger, confused by the absurdity and totally unreal nature of arrival. This clouding of the cognitive processes was burnt away by the bright sun of acceptance as he saw his captor, a shadowy outline tinkering at the wires.

With the frantic level of activity of a crisis centre, more messages poured in from around his body. He could feel something heavy pressing down like a millstone on the top of his head. The helmet confining it felt damp and restrictive around the temples. His wrists were strapped to the stout wooden chair arms, his hands clenching in restive fury while his legs strained against their own set of shackles. His right leg also felt damp, wet in a patch and with something steely clinging to his calf like a brass compact. His jeans had been cut to the knee and he was beginning to notice that he couldn't open his mouth: his lips were pinched by a prickly bond of tape. The dark air bore the tarry ether of thick oil. Peter's eyes followed the wires that led to the crude transformer and the coiled apparatus of his impending execution.

A scream clucked uselessly in the smothered hollow of his mouth.

'Well, well, look who's awake!' his captor's voice rang out, rejoicing.

Bill Murphy

A young-looking man, he sat down at a small desk in front of Peter, entering the cone of dim light that swam with minute fibres.

The table was covered by a dark green baize cloth, heavily stained. A deck of cards stood in the centre, perfectly aligned so that it looked like a little box.

'Hope the chair's comfortable,' the young man said. 'I built it just for you. You remember me, don't you?' His eyes were dull. A heavy gaze, memories sodden with hate. Peter could not recall ever seeing him before.

'I'll explain as we go along – just like you used to before you raped us.'

Picking up the deck, he began shuffling the cards into to a blur, fanning them like an accordion.

'But first—' he smiled and put the cards down '—we need to prepare.'

Peter was roaring behind his gag, his face congesting under the helmet, his breath huffing through the nose.

His captor stood up and, stooping, checked the connections on the chair, the straps and the electrodes attached to the head and the leg. The caustic methyl of a skin cream permeated the air around the other man as he brushed against Peter.

'Shouldn't forget this,' he sneered, placing a large, fat-burnt tray beneath the seat of the oak chair. 'Drip pan,' he said, and went off into the darkness beyond the canopy of light.

Something clicked and Peter could hear the black vat of oil hum beneath the table. A crude step-up transformer made of four iron bars bolted together in a square. On one side of the iron square wound a single coil of copper wire that fed into the vat via two brass terminators, the domestic supply. 110 volts AC. On the other limb of the square three smaller copper coils, tightly wound. All submerged in fifteen gallons of electrical oil, like thick marsh-water, and resting on ceramic insulators fixed to the bottom.

'The primary system is energized,' the young man croaked, fidgety because of his excited nerves.

Trailing from the transformer was a plexus of 1.5mm^2 copper wires – six in all, connected in series to three heating elements pinned to small clay bricks, to draw the load. Behind the elements were three single-pole switches. As the electricity swirled around the circuit the first heating element slowly blushed amber, heating up its coil.

'One Kv,' he said, delighted with the simple demonstration that the circuit was working.

Carefully picking up a small olive-coloured box that was connected to the heating coils, he laid it on the table next to him. Well insulated, it housed a single switch, a fat black square the size of a domino.

From the circuit-breaker a wide-gauge black lead ran under the table and disappeared somewhere beneath Peter's legs. What he couldn't see was that the cable was spliced and each copper strand connected to the electrodes by a turn-screw. This secondary circuit would be completed by the conductive properties of bone and musculature – and the considerable amount of fluids therein.

'Ever wonder why birds can land on the overhead power cables without frying? No?'

Peter wriggled in his fetters, soundlessly yowling.

'Potential difference is zero, no current,' his jailer explained and quickly picked up a plastic red ammeter from the ground, like a child's lunchbox, its needle waving at about five amperes. He set it down next to the cards.

'Now, again – the rules,' he said, picking up the deck again. 'I chose baccarat because I know it was your favourite – good for playing us off against each other.'

He knew Peter was pleading behind his gag.

Squirming throaty sounds.

Tears beginning to come.

The young man began to deal.

'Three bets, for you, always on the player's hand, closest to nine wins, all tens and face cards equal zero, aces are one and other cards as they are – clear?'

Peter's body was tensed, against his cage of leather and the wet crown of brass.

The young man dealt them each two cards and set down the deck.

A glowing bar of orange, the element created a warm insulation of air around itself.

Leaning in, he picked up Peter's cards. 'Two and an ace equals three. We'll draw you another.'

He flipped him a third card. 'Ooh, another ace! That's four! Let's see what I got – five and a two!'

Gleefully, his eyes already on Peter. 'Time to test the circuit.'

He pulled the large switch towards himself, holding the switchbox between forefinger and thumb.

'You made us feel as if we wanted it – the game,' he slurred, mouth thick with lust for vengeance.

On pushing the button for about five seconds he fed Peter's body with a spiking charge of electricity. The ammeter's needle quivered just below five amps and the transformer purred on its ceramic shoes, vibrating in its dark bath of oil.

All of Peter's muscles seized as each nerve was electrified and a deep magnetic pain sucked at his bones. His heart squeezed as if grasped by an animal's taloned claw.

The switch flicked off.

Peter fell back, the electric grip suddenly gone, his heart now fluttering, his head pulsing against the brazen plate.

It hadn't killed him. The load had only been 1,000 volts and the current had dipped due to the body's resistance.

Flicking the switch on the second heating element meant that the primary circuit drew another Kv and the coil ticked, heating up with the current.

The cards were sailing again as Peter tried to catch his breath.

Two for the player, two for the dealer.

The young man tipped Peter's over.

A six.

His own an eleven.

'Banker wins again!' he cried, hovering at the main switch.

'Remember when you had me with a power drill? The bit covered in a rubber shroud . . . did some damage . . . not too much – but enough for you.'

He tripped the switch.

2,000 volts.

Peter's chest jumped, his own fingernails driving like pins into his palm, his lean calf beginning to sizzle like a strip of bacon.

Then it stopped, released him like a sprung lock.

Part of his brain was scorched, broiled in the kiln of his skull, and he was near unconsciousness. Another switch and now all the heating elements were on, three rods of amber hue, warming the air, bringing out the aromas of hot oil and singed hair.

The dealer's nose was twitching with the acrid smells and the transformer murmured in the vat, the wires buzzing, carrying the whisper of electricity.

He dealt Peter a fifteen and himself a perfect nine.

There was no hesitation in flicking the switch. He pushed it hard, as if to increase the power of the 3,000 volts that now played through Peter Kelley's body, contorting him as if he was possessed, filling him with the electric snake. The ammeter wagged its needle finger at about seven amps, an applause-O-meter registering the excitement in the coils.

The clothes began to burn in spreading black patches, a dry, flameless burn. Blood and rendered tissue-fat began to drip sizzling in the tray and the eyeballs spat like onions on a pan.

'Remember me now!' he shouted at the thing in the chair as its head began to hiss.

2434 ABRAMAR, PACIFIC PALISADES, CA

Kronziac dropped her bag at her feet and flounced onto the couch. A thick fog at Logan had delayed her flight by almost four hours but she was glad to leave the frigid grey gloom of the East Coast and to be back home under the copper-blue skies of southern California.

On the coffee table stood one of her crystal vases blooming with a spray of golden lilies and fern. A small card placed beneath said 'Welcome Home' in a big flourish. Kronziac smiled, recognizing Maggie's writing. Before checking on Hector she reached over, punched the play button on the phone-set on the table behind the sofa and listened to a succession of messages from her mom, her sister, two short hellos from Phillips, a reminder from the doctor about her wrist brace and a couple of hang-ups. The last caller fumbled over his words like someone who hates leaving messages on a machine but she recognized Ellstrom's accent straight away and was surprised to hear from him so soon – or to hear from him at all.

'Eh, hello, this is Professor Ellstrom, from Harvard.'

On the phone he sounded like a man twenty years older. 'I've had a quick run over the cipher you gave me and have managed to crack it,' he continued, his voice less formal. 'It was quite simple really, though of course a little tedious, but frequency analysis yielded an applicable occurrence pattern to establish the cipher alphabet. Anyway, I will now recite the plaintext to you.'

Kronziac jumped up, searching for a pen and pad in the drawer of the pine rifle cabinet. She had to press replay and endure again the mathematician's self-congratulatory introduction on how he cracked the code.

Kronziac had to write quickly to keep up with Ellstrom as he delivered the lines of verse.

'Well, there it is,' he concluded. 'I hope it makes some sense to you. Tell Freddie I'll call him soon. I have to do a bit of travelling to universities around the country to give some talks on my book but I promise I'll call him soon. Goodbye Miss . . . Kronziac.'

He took his time pronouncing her name, as if reading it from the card, and then hung up.

She looked at the scribbled lines on her pad.

Though the words made up some sort of verse, like a short poem, they still made little sense.

1597 LOCUSTA STREET, NORTHRIDGE, CA

Jerry Blaynes shook his head, brushed his dark hair back and read it again, slowly.

'I've no idea,' he said, turning to Kronziac as he laid the small page with her transcription of Ellstrom's message written on it.

'Me neither,' she concurred. 'It might have nothing at all to do with Cherie – but I thought you would want to see it in case it made any connection.'

'Yes, of course,' Jerry replied gratefully. 'It's like a riddle, a math riddle or something.'

'Yeah, it is,' Kronziac said. 'But it still doesn't mean anything to me.'

'Could your friend, the guy who decoded it, could he—' Jerry stared at the message again in a last effort at understanding. '—Could he work something out of it?'

Kronziac wasn't sure if Ellstrom would help her again. 'I suppose he might,' she replied hesitantly.

The front door opened and a woman with long reddish blonde hair, tied up with an emerald bow, entered the living room, cradling a grocery bag in one arm. Following her was a young boy carrying another, smaller bag. At first she looked at Kronziac with apprehension. Though dressed in canvas jeans and a short raincoat the woman sensed something official in Kronziac's demeanour.

'Hi, honey,' Jerry stood up, 'I'd like you to meet Nancy Kronziac.'

His wife put down the groceries.

'Hello.' She extended her small hand, 'I'm Cynthia Blaynes. How kind of you to help.'

Kronziac felt embarrassed. 'I haven't done anything.' She blushed.

Cynthia turned around and introduced the small boy standing quietly behind her. 'This is our son James.'

Kronziac went over and shook his hand as she would with an adult. 'Nice to meet you, James.'

'Hi,' was all he said, smiling nervously. 'Have you found Cherie?'

he asked directly, the slightest note of hope in his voice.

The three adults traded quick looks of concern.

'Not yet.' Kronziac smiled gently.

'She'll be coming home soon,' Jerry announced confidently as his wife put her arm around James's shoulder and guided him out of the room.

'Come on, James, help me put the groceries away.' Before they left she stopped and, apologizing for her husband's forgetful manners, asked their guest if she wanted a coffee.

'No, thank you, I'm fine,' Kronziac answered.

Sitting down again, Jerry looked at the small scrap of paper, reading it over one more time.

'It's hitting them hard,' he remarked, almost casually.

'Of course it is,' Kronziac said, looking around at the family photos on the sideboard.

'Cynthia tries to keep herself busy. The house is spotless,' he added, glancing up from the paper. 'I just don't know what to say to her any more,' he said quietly. 'She just seems to have given up.'

Kronziac realized Blaynes needed to talk to someone about what he was going through, but she wasn't sure she was the right person. She hardly knew the man.

He began laughing, a pitiable, forced laugh. 'When Cherie was younger we used to do a double act, a magic show, we called ourselves Jerry and Cherie—' his voice began to waver as he said the names, '—I used to make her disappear under the table in the kitchen.' He curled his mouth tightly, keeping in the pain. 'Sorry, it's not fair to dump all this on you,' he said, regaining his composure.

Kronziac knew it was selfish in a way, but she prayed for his wife to come back in soon. She wouldn't know what to do if he started to break down.

'Maybe if I show you her bedroom,' he suggested brightly. 'Might give you some background.'

Hiding her reluctance, Kronziac agreed.

The room was bright, a large window on the street side permitting a white rectangle of sunlight to spread itself brilliantly across the light cream carpet. It was full of the usual items any sixteen-year-old girl would have in her room – teddy bears and dolls ranked in a line on the pillows on the bed, posters of pop bands and movie stars, a TV and a tower of videos. The dresser was crammed messily with variously sized perfumes, moisturizers and lipsticks, the mirror was strung with necklaces, a black beret and some dried flowers. In a small open box lay a wad of letters, tied with ribbon, a lock of blonde hair cellotaped to a card, a baby tooth rattling in a matchbox and a small bracelet, made of two thin strips of leather. Cynthia had found the box under the bed, Cherie's private box, just like any other schoolgirl would have.

But for all the light, the warm colours of the walls, the patch-work duvet and the bright dresses and T-shirts hanging motion-less in the wardrobe – the room was cold, the emptiness tangible, almost like a presence in itself.

'The detectives had a quick look around,' Jerry said, prop-ping up a Beanie Baby that was slumped precariously at the edge of the bed.

All Kronziac could do was smile sadly. 'What a lovely room,' she observed.

They stood there quietly for a moment and she wondered if he was expecting her to start poking around or start dusting for fingerprints.

'You've talked to all her friends?' she asked.

Jerry nodded gloomily.

'Several times, and the police have interviewed them.'

'Did she have a boyfriend?'

'Yeah, a young guy called Donnie,' he confirmed. 'He was the last to see her at the parking lot the night she disappeared.'

'And he didn't see anything suspicious or out of the ordi-nary?'

She knew all these questions would have been asked several times already but she couldn't think of anything else to say.

'Yeah, he told us and the police all he could remember,' Jerry answered. He decided to keep to himself the fact that he hated the goofy little shit. Jerry always wondered at the way Donnie would put his arm around Cherie when they were going out at night. The little punk would turn around and assure her father that he would take care of his daughter and, with a little smile, he would flick his tongue out between his grinning teeth, quickly, almost imperceptibly, subtly hinting that he was doing things he shouldn't to Jerry's baby girl. Cynthia accused Jerry of not only being an over-protective father but a borderline racist, not liking the idea of his blonde blue-eyed girl going out with the Puerto Rican boy.

'Poor kid's as cut up as the rest of us,' he said vacantly.

The phone began ringing downstairs and after answering it Cynthia came up to them.

'Jerry, it's someone from the garage,' she informed him as he rushed downstairs to take the call.

Cynthia smiled at Kronziac in the room but wouldn't herself go in, staying at the doorway.

'Showing you her room?'

Kronziac felt like an intruder. 'Yeah. He thought I should see it.'

'It's funny, you know.' Cynthia leaned against the door frame, her gaze fixed but distant. 'When I wake up in the morning, for the first few moments it's any ordinary day, like it was before. Jerry snoring next to me, the kids up, watching TV or getting ready for school. But then—' She squinted her eyes and fixed her gaze on another invisible point. 'Then I remember. Cherie – she's not in her room, she's not out with her friends staying the night, she's not at camp—'

Cynthia looked up, her gaze now on Kronziac. 'She's just gone – gone for ever . . . only I can't tell him that.'

She began smiling, as if thinking of some silly half-sad joke. 'He thinks she's still alive . . . it's all he's hanging on to.'

Kronziac nodded solemnly. 'I know,' she said.

They could hear Jerry coming up the stairs again.

'Please don't take that away from him,' Cynthia pleaded. 'Not yet.'

2434 ABRAMAR, PACIFIC PALISADES, CA

The eaves dripped through the dark hours as a thick, drizzling fog nestled itself for the night in the Santa Monica bay, enveloping all the houses along the coast in a mist that smelled of rusted iron. Kronziac had tossed and turned, fearing that a masked woodsman would run out of the dark at her, ready to plunge a knife into her chest. Several times she regretted her decision not to take up Maggie's offer to stay with her. Getting up at about four, she made hot milk and sat down in an old Dodgers shirt to work on the riddle, to try and make some meaning out of the mysterious rhyme. She couldn't explain exactly why but she *knew* it must have something to do with Cherie's disappearance. People don't just send cryptic messages on the back of Missing Persons notices without there being some reason behind it.

At about seven she dragged herself to bed and finally fell asleep as the windows slowly faded up with the light of dawn. It was about midday before she stirred again.

She picked up the scrap of paper and read it again for about the hundredth time and gave up again, shaking her head in despair. She was beginning to think she was helping the Blayneses out only because she had nothing better to do. The house was cleaned from ceiling to floor, she had sifted through a mountain of clothes and discarded anything more than a year old, the flowers and plants in the garden were pampered like spoilt children, even Hector eyed her suspiciously as she polished to a sparkle the inside of his cage. Even her wrist was on its way to recovery. She picked up the rubber ball the doctor had advised her to use and began squeezing it in her right hand, the wrist twinging with pain.

She suddenly dropped the ball on the duvet, sat up quickly as she heard the front door open and glanced over at the dressing table where she kept her gun. But, hearing Maggie's voice, she relaxed again and jumped out of bed.

Fractions of Zero

'Hi, Nance, it's only us!' Maggie shouted.

'In here!' she shouted back and quickly fussed over the bedclothes in a vain attempt to cover up the fact that she had spent all morning in bed. She never slept in, even during vacation.

Phillips shouted hello from the living room while Maggie popped her head round the bedroom door, some food containers in her hand.

'You okay?' she asked. Kronziac was tying up her hair and squeezing into a pair of old denims.

Maggie came into the room, looking around as if sensing Kronziac had just got up. Seeing her younger colleague dressed in a smart suit, with a hint of make-up, not too much but enough to enhance her clear, tan complexion, Kronziac felt like a mess. But it was too late now to change into anything else. She yearned to go back to work, to join the real world again.

'How was your trip back east?' Maggie wanted to know.

'A bit tiring,' Kronziac answered sluggishly, fixing her hair in place with pins. 'You know, trying not to worry my parents too much about what's happening.'

'You didn't tell them anything about your suspension and the death threats, did you?' Maggie asked, concerned.

Kronziac smiled. 'No way,' she said. 'They're better off not knowing, believe you me.'

Maggie didn't pursue it and held up one of the see-through food containers, displaying the bright colours of a salad. 'Hope you haven't had lunch yet.'

'Haven't even had breakfast,' Kronziac admitted, settling into her sandals and following Maggie to the living room.

Phillips was, as usual, making himself at home, reclining on the sofa and looking at the maps, tourist guides and dictionaries Kronziac had left on the coffee table. The computer, on all night, ran across its monitor screen a saying about living each day one at a time, posted by the novelty screensaver.

'Going on a trip?' he asked.

'No,' Kronziac said, helping Maggie with the plates. 'Just trying to figure something out.'

123

'What?' he asked, puzzling over a map of west Los Angeles, the Santa Monica region circumscribed by a marker.

She felt a little stupid, as if obsessed by some silly project, and began explaining vaguely.

'It's the cryptogram that we got from Blaynes.'

Phillips recalled it. 'That jumble of letters on the back of the MP notice?'

'Yeah, I got a math professor from Harvard to take a look at it. He's a buddy of Fred Stranski's,' she added, hoping it would make whole thing sound less absurd.

'A math head from Harvard?' Phillips repeated with amused incredulity.

'And?' Maggie urged Kronziac eagerly, emptying the contents of the salad box into a dish.

'And . . . he deciphered it.'

Maggie was about to put a juicy twig of celery in her mouth but stopped. 'What did it say?' she asked impatiently.

Kronziac knew they were on duty but offered them wine anyway.

'Water's okay for me,' Phillips said, loading a fresh bread roll with ham. 'Got any Thousand Island?'

'Come on!' Maggie badgered Kronziac to tell. 'What did it say?'

As Kronziac gave Phillips a jar of dressing and sat down herself she pulled out the deciphered text from her pocket, the paper now well worn, and laid it on the coffee table among the strewn maps and reference books. She decided to have a glass of wine herself and sipped a dry Bolivian white.

Not needing to look at the paper, she recited the riddle by heart.

> far sunken from the healthy breath I rest
> cleared then of heavy vapours between fourteen and e
> harboured in the sleepy west
> lay vast and edgeways in a dismal cirque to be

Phillips and Maggie remained silent for a moment.

'*Far sunken from the . . . whatever . . . I rest?*' Phillips repeated after a moment of thought. 'You think it's the girl?'

Fractions of Zero

Maggie answered him immediately. 'Has to be,' she declared, took the cryptogram from the table and began reading it herself.

'Could be a crank,' Phillips suggested, 'or just a coincidence.'

'Could be,' Kronziac agreed calmly and bit into her sandwich.

They were both being cautious, experience having taught them that it was easy to get over-excited about these things. Still, their experience at the Bureau had also shown them over the years many cases of cryptic clues being sent by a murderer to lead the authorities to the body of the victim. A classic tease.

'*Harboured in the sleepy west . . .*' Maggie read out the third line again. She glanced at the map on the table.

'Mean anything to you?'

Kronziac shrugged. 'I've looked over it a hundred times and still can't get it. I thought line two would really give it away.'

Maggie read it out loud. '*Cleared of heavy vapours between fourteen and e . . .*'

After a pause Phillips said, 'Is it something to do with pollution?'

No one answered, a different part of the cryptogram running through each of their minds.

'*Fourteen and e?*' Phillips said, wiping his mouth with a napkin. 'Could they be streets?'

Kronziac gestured at the map, nodding. 'There's a 14th Street in Santa Monica, runs from San Vicente to Ashland. But the *e* . . .' She shook her head forlornly. 'Can't find an E Street.'

Maggie turned over the index on the flip side of the map. 'Could be East Boulevard or East Way in LAX.'

'Either of which,' Kronziac added, 'gives us a huge area.' She got up and tossed a sliver of tomato into Hector's cage. The lizard looked at it contemptuously for moment, not wanting to appear eager or grateful for the morsel of food.

'Besides, the fourteen could mean a lot of things – fourteenth district, a date, a building number and the *e* could mean thousands of things,' Kronziac continued, closing the top of the cage.

Phillips put down his sandwich and picked up the cryptogram from the table. 'What else does it say?' he said, almost to himself,

125

and began reading it over. '*Far sunken from the healthy breath I rest . . .* what the fuck does that mean?' He looked up at the others with a pained expression.

'*The healthy breath*,' Maggie suggested. 'Something to do with fresh air?'

'The wind?' Phillips mused, pleased with himself.

'*And harboured in the sleepy west*,' Kronziac recited. 'Some place on the west side?'

Phillips had taken up his salad roll again. 'Could be West Side, could be the whole of west LA, the West Coast or just the west as in Wild West, bang-bang, them dar injuns are a-comin'.'

Kronziac threw Phillips one of the looks she reserved for him whenever he contributed something stupid to a conversation.

Maggie read out the last line. '*Lay vast and edgeways in a dismal cirque to be.*' She furrowed her brow in concentration. 'Well, a cirque is some sort of a circle, right?'

Kronziac agreed. 'Dictionary said it was an old name for a circle or a semi-circular lake with a sloped bottom.'

'Any lakes out near the bay?' said Phillips.

'Well, there's Ballona Lagoon down in Marina del Rey,' Kronziac confirmed, having found it on the map the night before. 'And the marina itself, I suppose.'

Phillips leaned over the map, his fingers circling the blue squares of water, denoting the docks of Marina del Rey.

'Hey, there's a Basin E there!' he announced, thrilled.

The phone rang in the kitchen like a chorus of approval for Phillips's discovery and Kronziac jumped up to answer it.

'What about the fourteen?' Maggie asked.

'Could be a mooring,' Phillips offered, off the top of his head.

Maggie referred back to the cryptogram again, squinting to make sure she was reading it right. 'How does it tie in with the heavy vapours and the healthy breath part?' she asked.

'I still think it's referring to the wind,' he stated resolutely. 'And the marina is a safe place from the wind.'

'It says sunken, not safe from the healthy breath,' she reminded him.

'Well, the body could be under water,' Phillips replied.

They looked at each other, Phillips beginning to smile. 'What are we doing here? This is absurd.' He looked at his watch.

'Time we were heading back to the office.'

But Maggie, still intrigued, was looking at the riddle once more as Kronziac emerged from the kitchen. She was looking at her hand.

'What is it?' Maggie asked. 'Your wrist okay?'

'That was Cynthia Blaynes – the missing girl's mother,' Kronziac explained. 'She's a schoolteacher.'

'So?' Phillips tried to prompt her to go on but she was staring at a word scribbled across the palm of her hand.

'She teaches tenth-grade English and when Jerry showed her the cryptogram she thought she recognized some of the lines. They're not entirely complete quotes,' she added, 'but they do come from a Keats poem.'

Maggie scrutinized the cryptogram in her hand to make the connection. 'Which one?'

Kronziac held up her hand to them. 'It's called *Hyperion*.'

Phillips reached for a fat dictionary that lay heavily on top of the coffee table and began fanning through the pages, hunting for *H*.

'With a Y?' he asked. 'H – Y?'

Kronziac spelled the word out for him and she took the cryptogram from Maggie to see if the new information helped unlock the riddle.

Maggie stood up and walked to the French doors, the name turning over in her mind. Beyond the veranda and the garden the vast bowl of the sea lay still, like molten lead beneath the heavy, cloudy sky.

Phillips ran his finger down the page past *hyperinflation* and *hyperinsulinism*. 'Got it!' he shouted. '*Hyperion* – Greek myth, a titan, son of Uranus and Gaea, father of Helios.'

Maggie swung around from the patio doors. 'Shit! of course!' she cried, smiling broadly and flattening her palms against her head in sudden realization.

'What?' asked Kronziac, surprised at Maggie's outburst. She rarely swore.

'*The heavy vapours* . . .' Maggie blurted and rushed to pluck the cryptogram from Kronziac. '*Far from the healthy breath . . . harboured in the west . . .*'

Phillips and Kronziac were watching their younger colleague with bemusement.

'The treatment plant!' she declared, 'the Hyperion Water Treatment Plant – out by the airport – in the bay.'

She hurried over to the table and, kneeling down, flattened the map out with her hands. Trailing her finger down the coast from Venice to Dockweiler State Beach she tapped a small rectangular box marked in black.

Phillips read the key beside the box. *Hyperion Sewage Treatment Plant.* 'It's in Playa del Mar,' he observed.

Kronziac began nodding, pursing her lips, considering Maggie's idea.

'A sewage plant?' Phillips looked at Maggie, disdainful of the idea. 'I still think the marina's a runner,' he said.

But Maggie wasn't letting go. '*Far sunken from the healthy breath? Cleared of heavy vapours? Harboured in the west?*' She recited the lines, animated by the discovery.

'What about fourteen and e?' Kronziac wondered. 'And the dismal cirque?'

Maggie shrugged. 'Well,' she said, putting it to them. 'Only one way to find out.'

Kronziac looked over at Phillips. 'Might be worth a look.'

But Phillips's gaze was drifting aimlessly over the map. 'You're forgetting, guys – this isn't our case,' he reminded them.

HYPERION WASTE WATER TREATMENT PLANT, 12000 PLAYA DEL REY

The guard at the truck service gate advised them to go to the public entrance on the western perimeter, so they found themselves again on the highway turning left as they hit the beach road on to Vista del Mar. Signs along the road informed motorists that the beach was closed due to storm-drain run-off and they could see small clusters of surfers huddled forlornly on the bluffs overlooking the grey scowling sea.

Kronziac rubbed tenderly her wrist. 'Should be able to get out on the waves myself pretty soon.'

Maggie clicked on the left indicator and they turned in at the wide public entrance and stopped at the security island. The security man informed them politely that they had just missed the tour, which began at nine a.m. sharp. Maggie flashed her ID and he raised the barrier and pointed them to the Administration Building.

'Looks like a small city,' Kronziac commented as high industrial structures and towers mixed with some office blocks rose above them like a miniature downtown metropolis. At the intersection beyond the security island there were road signs pointing to such areas as the Contaminate Storage Drain Facility, Primary Batteries and Power & Blower Buildings.

As Maggie parked the car outside the Administration Building, Kronziac tapped her on the shoulder and pointed at one of the signs.

Maggie squinted at it. 'Service Water Facility.' She read it out slowly, trying to grasp the significance.

'Yeah, and look underneath,' Kronziac said.

Maggie's eyes brightened. 'Eleventh Street!' she announced, 'You're right, it *is* like a small city. They've even got street numbers.'

'Do they have a Fourteenth Street?' Kronziac wondered excitedly.

'It's a bit creepy.' Maggie sniffed, noticing there were very few people around – just the odd truck driving through or some plant personnel in hard hats scurrying between the buildings, which hummed with the low vibration of subterranean industry.

EDUCATION CENTER, ADMINISTRATION BUILDING, HYPERION TREATMENT PLANT

The brand new visitor centre on the roof of the Administration Building resembled an air-traffic control tower: a pentagonal wall of tinted glass permitted a 360-degree view of the massive facility. In the centre of the floor computer screens blinked with graphics and hidden speakers rumbled with music and sound effects overhead.

Devised mostly for school trips, a multimedia show starring Perry, a chirpy little computer character, pink and shaped like a stretched peanut, described with the aid of colourful animations the workings of the plant to visitors.

Kronziac couldn't help smiling as she watched Maggie staring at a monitor that showed Perry, complete with a little hard hat, flying over a virtual representation of the 144-acre site and describing the various processes used in the treatment of LA's daily output of nearly one billion gallons of raw sewage.

The door into the centre opened and in bounded another perky character.

'Barry Foster,' he said, smiling widely, 'Director of Education, LA Bureau of Sanitation. Welcome to the Hyperion Treatment Plant.'

Kronziac smiled back and shook hands with him while Maggie remained coolly formal, flipping her ID.

'Special Agent Margaret Ramirez.' She took Foster's hand and shook it stiffly.

Foster was a tall man with a long reach, receding hairline and ready grin. However, his public smile dropped off his face as he looked at Maggie and then at Kronziac for some hint that this was a joke.

'FBI?' he asked, startled, looking back again at Kronziac.

'Sorry,' Maggie said. 'We didn't tell them at reception downstairs who we were.'

'Yes.' He laughed awkwardly. 'I thought you were teachers organizing a trip,' he explained and gestured at the AV displays, Perry the pink electronic turd leading his invisible audience through the anaerobic digestion of primary sewage influent.

'Is there something wrong?' he asked, suddenly concerned, his wide brown eyes darting between the two FBI agents. He was obviously not sure who was in charge. Maggie's slight build and girlish looks always drew expressions of surprise when she told people she was with the FBI. But it was a drawback she dealt with admirably, her easy intelligence soon winning people's confidence.

'Well,' Maggie began. 'We were hoping you could help us with a small and—' she began smiling, helping Foster to relax '—a rather strange enquiry which has to do with an ongoing investigation.'

Foster didn't quite know what to say and glanced at Kronziac. She met his look with a sweet persuasive smile. She knew if Phillips was here he would be really pissed off. He always said the female agents tended to get more help from the male population. Of course, she denied using any such ploy.

'Sure,' Foster replied willingly. 'If I can help at all . . .'

'Great,' Maggie said and took out the piece of paper with the cryptogram on it. This was her own copy – she'd transcribed it neatly from Kronziac's worn original.

'It's a long shot,' Maggie explained further. 'But we thought this note we received might refer to somewhere here in the plant.'

She read out two of the lines: '*Far sunken from the healthy breath I rest . . . cleared of heavy vapours between fourteen and e.*'

She could see he was beginning to get a little concerned again, his dark eyebrows tightening, his face struggling between a smile and a frown.

'Fourteen and e,' he mused. 'Fourteen and e.' Then, suddenly, the smile won out.

'This might be it,' he said, excited. He rushed over to a touch-screen beneath the glass wall and pressed an icon marked *Map*. Perry danced across the screen and pulled a schematic of the plant after him. Near the southern end of the facility Foster ran

132

his finger along a straight line that ran between a group of circles.

'This is E Street,' he told them and his finger turned and moved along another line running perpendicular. 'And this is Fourteenth Street.'

Maggie and Kronziac traded excited looks.

'Between fourteen and e!' Kronziac said, feeling they were getting close.

'It's the quietest part of the plant,' Foster went on and led them over to the window that looked out on the southern end of the facility.

'We call it the farm,' he said, an amused note in his voice, 'with all the secondary treatment facilities, the settling tanks and oxygen reactors.'

Kronziac looked out at the eighty- or ninety-acre rectangle of land. On one side, sunk in the ground, were about thirty large discs like draughts on a game board, their surfaces black and liquid, slick as old vinyl records. On the left side were lines of low square buildings joined by a matrix of pipes and gantries, all criss-crossed by a network of small service roads.

Foster pressed his finger against another monitor on the wall and zoomed in on the southern perimeter.

'Where's Fourteenth and E?' Kronziac asked.

Foster pointed to the far end of the plant. 'Near the southern retaining wall by the Hazardous Waste Storage,' he said.

Maggie was studying the cryptogram again, reciting it quietly to herself. '*Lay vast and edgeways . . .*'

Foster zoomed in on the junction of two of the service roads. 'Fourteenth and E,' he said.

Maggie looked up at Kronziac, her voice strained with frustration. *Like a dismal cirque to be*?'

Zooming in further, Foster pointed at the corner of Fourteenth and E Streets. 'There it is,' he said, calmly.

'What?' Kronziac asked, 'There what is?'

Foster turned around from the monitor, slightly embarrassed. 'Er – 2B,' he said shyly and a smile slowly opened on his face as if his features didn't know what else to do. 'I thought you said "2B".'

'*A dismal cirque to be*?' Maggie repeated.

Foster pointed at a group of circles on the map, each indicated by a number and a letter.

'The clarifiers,' he said. 'The top right-hand one is Clarifier 2B, right on the corner of Fourteenth and E Streets.'

Kronziac glanced at Maggie, whose expression barely hid her growing excitement. 'What are these clarifiers?' she asked.

Pressing another icon on the screen, marked *Secondary Treatment Equipment*, Foster explained. 'Basically, they're huge water tanks sunk in the ground and used for sedimentation.'

He pressed another icon marked *Clarifiers* on the sub-menu and Perry slipped across the screen, opening another animation graphic.

With two blade arms rotating like a giant propeller squeezing a dotted layer of thick substance labelled *Activated Sludge* down the sloped bottom of the tank, the clarifier looked like a giant mixing bowl.

'What exactly are we looking for here? A dead body?' Foster's curiosity finally overcame him but his attempt at flippancy fell flat.

Maggie and Kronziac were still staring at the screen. 'Any chance we could go down and see the real thing?' Kronziac asked.

SECONDARY WATER TREATMENT FACILITIES – *THE FARM*, HYPERION W.W.T. PLANT

Kronziac sat in the back of the white Bureau of Sanitation Bronco with an electronic tableau, a small slim multimedia unit with no keyboard, resting on her knees. She was able to continue to learn on the move about the various pieces of equipment used in the plant simply by touching the video screen and calling up Perry who would buzz annoyingly around the display, guiding his viewer with cheeky enthusiasm through the fascinating subject of sewage treatment. Maggie sat up front with Foster as they pulled away from the Water Service Building. The hum of the pump stations and blowers receded behind them as they headed down a long service road, marked E Street. Foster, out of polite nervousness, gave them the tour-guide commentary.

'Here at Hyperion we treat nearly a billion gallons of sewage daily,' he declaimed proudly. 'That's about eighty per cent domestic and twenty per cent industrial waste. We have full primary and secondary facilities refining up to ninety per cent Biological Oxygen Demand and suspended solids from the raw waste,' he chirped.

Kronziac glanced at the screen and wondered for a moment if Perry was based on Foster, his human counterpart.

'The clean dechlorinated effluent is pumped to an undersea canyon five miles out in the bay,' he continued as Maggie nodded appreciatively.

'How come the beach is closed today?' Kronziac asked, busting his balloon.

'Storm run-off and heavy-metal contaminates,' Foster answered gruffly, glancing at her in the rear-view mirror.

Maggie feared that Kronziac was going to start bitching about pollution in the bay and its effect on local surfing, so she pointed to the line of low square buildings to the left.

'Oh, they're the Oxygen Reactors,' Foster informed her cheerfully. 'That's where the aeration chambers allow micro-organisms to break down the waste.'

He waved his hand over the steering wheel, pointing to the right. 'And on this side we have the clarifiers.'

The clarifiers looked like giant concrete boiling pots half sunken in the ground. Kronziac and the other two could not see the surface of each tank, just their thick curved walls and iron access stairways.

As Kronziac pressed another button, Perry told her that basically the clarifiers were large settling tanks. An animated graphic scrolled up, showing the internal workings of a clarifier on screen.

They passed about ten of the huge tanks before they came to the end of the road. At the intersection ahead Maggie could see a sign marked 14th Street.

'Well, here we are,' Foster announced. 'Clarifier 2B.' He pointed at a sprayed sign on the wall of one of the tanks.

As they got out of the Bronco they noticed another white van parked around the side of the huge concrete vat.

'I radioed one of the plant engineers to meet us here,' said Foster, leading them to the base of the tank.

'It really is quiet out here,' Maggie remarked.

Kronziac agreed. She could feel a light breeze coming off the ocean, which voiced its hushed presence periodically as a wave tumbled and spread with a swish on the beach below the highway that ran along the side of the plant.

An African-American man wearing jeans and a check shirt emerged from the van, fitting a hard hat over his dark head. Not tall, he was nonetheless powerfully built, his arms and legs thick. But he was in his early fifties and his body was softening around the belly and under the chin.

'This is Irv Holgreen.' Foster introduced him. 'Chief maintenance engineer for the clarifiers.'

Holgreen tipped his hat. 'Ladies.' He greeted them with characteristic Deep South courtesy.

'Agents Ramirez and Kronziac.' Foster ushered them closer. 'From the FBI,' he added with mischievous relish and stared at Holgreen for some signs of astonishment. But the engineer just smiled shyly as Maggie and Kronziac said hello. A field civil engineer, he was more at home working with his maintenance crew on the sewage tanks than he was dealing with outsiders – or 'non-technicals' as he called them.

'They have some questions for you,' Foster continued, 'about the clarifiers.'

'Sure. Let's get topside,' he said and jumped onto the lower rung of the steel stepway that spiralled up the ten-foot flank of the clarifier like an ivy runner.

'I'll bring the tableau,' Foster said, sticking his head in the back window of the Bronco while the others followed Holgreen up to the top of the clarifier.

'This is it,' said Holgreen as they joined him on the rim of the tank.

Like a giant circular swimming pool with a clear surface, the clarifier water was constantly moving, flowing smoothly over a small weir that ran around the entire circumference of the tank. In the centre was a large concrete hub to which a steel bridge with a gangway reached from the side where they were standing.

Fourty-four metres in diameter.' Holgreen pointed across to the other side. 'With a side-wall depth of five metres. We have thirty-six of these clarifiers currently constructed on site, each with an operational overflow rate of 1.75 metres per hour.'

Kronziac looked out over the side wall to see the thirty-five other clarifiers stretching like rows of huge black plates across the landscape.

They followed Holgreen across the bridge to the centre of the pool. The water beneath them moved quietly, like dark lava, to the side and tumbled in a gentle, almost soothing, cascade over the weir plate. Kronziac leaned over the railing and peered into the water to see what lay in its dark depths but she couldn't see past the reflection of the grey skies on the glassy surface. A few small agglomerated particles popped up in the water like miniature surfacing bathyscapes and were carried off to the sides to be caught in the baffle screens.

'I thought there'd be more of a smell,' Maggie remarked, instinctively twitching her nose.

'All the nasty stuff is well under water,' Foster assured her.

As they reached the centre of the clarifier Holgreen pointed beneath the central column. 'This is the feedwell through which the influent is pumped and spread radially below us.'

Looking down, they could see, below the surface and agitated by currents of water, clumps of grey porridgy matter shooting out the feedwell and then falling away into the depths.

'The heavy bio-solids fall to the bottom of the tank,' said Holgreen, 'and the scraper arms push them through the sludge outlet to be returned to the oxygen reactors to maintain the microbe colonies that biologically consume the waste.'

Even Foster seemed to be listening intently, as if learning something new.

'The clearer water is drawn out over the effluent weir,' Holgreen went on, running his outstretched hand along the edge of the tank, 'and piped out for tertiary treatment and eventual release into the sea.'

Kronziac looked up at the engineer, something preying on her mind, something she didn't like the sound of.

'What is the scraper?'

Holgreen searched a moment for the right term to help explain. 'Well,' he began, 'it's basically a huge propeller revolving at the bottom of the tank. The official name is a loga-rithmic-spiral curve arm on a peripheral drive.' He felt slightly embarrassed by his use of technical jargon. 'Yeah, a big propeller,' he said again, happy with that description.

'How fast does it move?' Maggie asked.

Holgreen answered, 'Just under a meter a second.'

They all looked silently again into the dark waters, as if peering into a bottomless well. Kronziac wondered with dread if Jerry Blaynes's daughter lay somewhere hidden in the black deep. She knew it was time to level with these guys and broach the real purpose of their visit. Holgreen and Foster began to fidget and kick their feet against the bridge, too polite to come straight out and ask the agents what the hell this was all about.

But it was Maggie who spoke up first. 'If a large solid, say,' she began cautiously, 'was in the tank—'

'Any *large* solids are caught at primary screening,' Holgreen interrupted defensively.

'Well, let's just say a large solid fell into the pool here,' she hypothesized as the two men nodded vaguely.

'How big a solid?' Holgreen asked.

Maggie tried to remain casual, as if hers had been just an academic question. 'Oh, about five foot long.'

Holgreen nodded and considered it, lifting his hard hat off the crown of his head to let some air in. 'You mean a body, don't you?' he said directly.

Maggie became uncomfortable and wasn't sure what to say.

'Yes, a body,' Kronziac said, matching Holgreen's directness.

A smile on Foster's face seemed to broaden with hopeful excitement. 'Shit, we better call the Plant Manager,' he panted.

Holgreen grabbed the tableau out of his hands and called up the graphic with the clarifier workings displayed. He pointed to a point at the bottom of the tank. 'The heaviest material settles down at the end in the tank,' he stated. 'But a body would not fit through the outlet pipe.'

He tapped a dirty fingernail at a point on the bottom of the clarifier next to the rising column of the feedwell and the narrow aperture of the outlet pipe. 'I reckon here would be most likely for it to lay.'

'How about the scraper?' Kronziac wanted to know. 'Wouldn't it cut it up? The body, I mean.'

Holgreen pursed his mouth. 'No,' he said. 'The scraper would just push it out of the way since the arms move so slowly. Your biggest problem,' he went on, 'would be the biological breakdown.' He looked up from the tableau at them. 'How long could this body have been here?'

'Two months or so,' Kronziac figured.

The engineer began shaking his head solemnly. 'The material at the bottom is full of micro-organisms,' he said. 'Bacteria, nematodes and various fungi . . . be lucky if anything but bone was left.'

Foster grimaced as though he'd just swallowed someone else's spit.

'How would we actually find out if there's anything down there?' Maggie probed delicately, presuming it would be a big operation.

Holgreen shrugged. 'Well, it would be buried in the sludge blanket,' he declared, shaking his head slowly. 'That's a thick zone of . . . sludge,' he said, unable to find a more suitable term. 'We would have to shut down the feedwell and drain off the water.'

'We'd need to okay it with the Plant Manager,' Foster warned them.

But Kronziac looked at Holgreen. 'How long would it take?' she asked.

He considered for a moment. 'Plant capacity is down at the moment, due to a chromium leak. So—' he raised his eyebrows '—we could take this pool off-line.'

'Presuming we had permission,' Foster said sharply. But the chief engineer didn't seem to take much notice, pushing the tableau back against Foster's chest.

'About five hours to drain off excess and a couple more to hose down the sludge,' Holgreen said. 'Shitty work,' he added, straight-faced. 'But we'd have it done by tonight.'

Kronziac leaned once more over the side of the little bridge to look down into the black circle of the pool. But all she could see was her own reflection, wavering on the surface as if caught in the wake of a giant creature fluttering its fins far below.

She turned to Foster. 'Can you call the Plant Manager?'

FBI OFFICES, FEDERAL BUILDING, WILSHIRE BLVD

It was late. Phillips was one of the last agents left in the office and he knew he shouldn't have answered the phone.

It was Kronziac, asking him to do something he shouldn't. Again.

He looked at his scribbled notes, summarizing her instructions.

Run search on all Cal state law enforcement databases and networks for any 'stops' on mysterious notes received by PDs. Post notice requesting any personnel to report any such occurrences . . .

He gathered his jacket and headed for the network terminal out at the front desk.

CLARIFIER 2B, HYPERION WASTE WATER TREATMENT PLANT

Kronziac put her cell phone away, after calling Phillips.

'We could be joining you.' Maggie shivered, contemplating her future. Like a little girl wearing her father's coat Maggie huddled in the back seat of the Bronco, wrapping about herself a large white anorak that Foster had lent to her.

'How do you mean?' Kronziac turned around, whispering so as not to wake up Foster who had nodded off in the driver's seat.

'Foley,' Maggie replied, peering out the window into the dark gloom. 'He might decide that I need an involuntary holiday too when he finds out about this.'

'You'll be okay,' Kronziac assured her, not too convincingly, and turned around again.

They had been sitting in the jeep for nearly nine hours, waiting as Holgreen's men drained the clarifier and began dredging the bottom of the tank. Like a miniature football stadium, the tank was surrounded by a ring of portable floodlights that threaded the rim in a bright necklace.

'What time is it?' Maggie asked, her mouth gaping as she yawned.

'Twenty after eight,' Kronziac said, glancing at the clock on the dash. She looked over at Foster. His head rolled to the side and soft rhythmic choked-off snorts began to sound from the back of his throat with every deep indrawn breath.

'He's gonna start snoring again,' Kronziac warned.

Maggie sat up quickly. 'This might be something,' she said, as the figure of Irv Holgreen came down the stepway from the clarifier. Kronziac lowered the window as he walked towards the jeep.

'Might wanna take a look at this,' he said, a disturbing note of icy understatement in his voice.

They both got out of the jeep and were about to climb the steps when Holgreen stopped them. He opened the back of his van and grabbed two face masks, the type industrial painters use to protect them from noxious fumes.

'You guys will probably need these,' he said and handed the masks to them.

As they climbed the steps a gust of wind rushed in from the sea and swirled about the deep void of the tank, blowing Kronziac's hair into her face.

The clarifier looked completely different from when they'd seen it earlier that day. Drained of water, its side walls were stained with layered bands, as though strange tidemarks were indicating the different zones of settlement. A couple of metres from the bottom, drying filaments of sediment clung to the concrete like flakes of peeling paint. From the centre of the tank the feedwell rose in a large cement pillar from the muddy base. Two men in waders and face masks stood in a couple of feet of sludge, hosing channels in the mud at the bottom next to the feedwell. Above them on the side walls some security men, all in masks, looked on, silent spectators. There was no variation of colour anywhere – everything was a metallic grey under the ring of arc lights.

The wind died down, fleeing inland, and now the only noises were those of the rattling engines of the pumps and the high-pitched gush of the hoses as they slashed channels through the sludge. A rancid odour rose like a hot invisible swell from the pit of the tank: the bitter, mealy stink of concentrated sewage. Maggie's chest heaved, convulsing as if she was about to vomit, and they both quickly fixed the masks over their faces.

'Down there.' Holgreen pointed to the centre of the tank beneath the feedwell pipe.

Two workmen stood beside a black shape that jutted from the sludge. One of them carefully hosed water around the shape, clearing away the grey soup of sewage. The other workman tilted his mask off his face and craned his head up to them.

'Looks like a sack!' he shouted, his voice echoing hollowly about the walls of the sunken cauldron.

Foster had woken up and now joined them on the bridge that spanned the clarifier.

His face grimaced with disgust. 'Found something?' he asked, muffling his mouth and nose with a cupped hand.

But nobody was quite sure how to answer.

'Better find out,' Kronziac said decisively. 'How do I get down?' she asked Holgreen.

'The ladder over there.' He nodded at the side wall from which a flimsy-looking chain ladder hung, leading down into the tank.

Kronziac followed the engineer back over the bridge to the side of the clarifier.

'You'll have to wear these,' he instructed, picking up a pair of thick oilskin waders.

Kronziac bent her shoulders into the straps of the waders while Maggie helped her pin up her hair under a hard hat that Foster had given her. Lowering herself backwards, she carefully placed her boots onto the ladder rungs.

'Hold on tight,' Holgreen advised her. 'The ladder can swing and you don't want to fall into that . . .' His words tailed off as he realized the obviousness of his warning.

Kronziac wondered if her recovering wrist would hold up. But, slowly and sometimes precariously as the ladder swung under her weight and clattered against the wall, she made her way to the bottom. Hesitating for a moment, she moved her left foot from the last rung and held it poised over the mud.

'Yeah, right there,' one of the workmen directed her. 'You'll be standing on the scraper blade.'

Kronziac lowered her foot. As it sank through the sludge she feared that the muddy sump she was about to enter would swallow her whole.

Her mask felt warm against her nose as she let out a breath of relief when her foot came to rest on a solid surface about nine or ten inches under the sewage.

Feeling as though she was walking through porridge, she moved slowly towards the centre of the tank, dragging her waders heavily through the glutinous ooze until she reached the others.

'We haven't opened it,' one of them said loudly, his voice muffled beneath his mask. The other man operating the hose cleared the last traces of obvious sewage from around a sack that poked up from the mud. He signalled to the compressor operator up on the bridge to cut the pump. As the slashing noise of the water hose subsided and the compressor wound down, the giant tank seemed to settle lower in the new silence under the chalky light of the lamps. Kronziac could hear the sludge beneath her seething faintly – like brewing yeast – as the bacterial colonies slowly digested the waste.

She leaned down close to the sack, careful not to overbalance. The black plastic of the sack shone with a thin coat of slime and she could see the small opening at one of the corners.

Kronziac turned and looked up at Maggie and Holgreen. 'Gloves!' she shouted through her mask, her voice sounding as if it was encased in a cardboard box.

Holgreen leaned over the bridge directly above and carefully lobbed a pair of thick rubber gloves to her. She put them on and asked one of the workmen for a torch. The guy with the hose unholstered a small black Maglite from his tool belt.

On her haunches, Kronziac twisted the torch head on and waved the bright disc of its light beam over the sack. Edging closer carefully, she steeled herself and pointed the small torch in through a small opening in the corner of the sack. At first she couldn't see much, just more grey sludge, streaked with run-off.

Above her, Maggie, Holgreen and Foster leaned over the railing, peering intently at the scene below.

With her left hand, Kronziac gently poked the torch further inside, rotating it around the interior. She saw the shape of an arm, black, like a rotten tree branch. Trailing the light up it, she could see some mud-streaked fabric, a dull red, showing through the grey phlegm. Moving the torch's beam up further, over the hump of a shoulder, she jerked her head back in shocked recoil as the light travelled over the features of a flesh-less face, the skull masked in a clotted emulsion of waste. One of the workmen swung away, having caught a glimpse of the head in the sack.

'Is it her?' Maggie shouted down.

Holgreen and Foster gripped the railing tightly, afraid to look but unable to turn away.

Her eyes squinting, Kronziac opened the sack a little further and could see a matted filament of human hair, slicked back over the ear-knub in an obscene treacle of mud.

ADIC'S OFFICE, FEDERAL BUILDING, WILSHIRE BLVD

'Would someone mind telling me what agents from the Domestic Terrorism Unit of the FBI were doing in a sewage tank in the middle of the night?'

Foley rubbed the back of his neck and repeated the question as if talking to himself.

'Could someone please help me out here? Could someone possibly do that? Must be my age or somethin' . . . because I just don't understand.'

He picked up some message notes from the side of his desk. 'I've had calls from the Bureau of Sanitation and the plant manager at the Hyperion facility, wondering why we were digging up bodies in his plant. I got a call from a Detective Cunningham out of Devonshire asking why he wasn't called in earlier. Even the guys at Harbour PD were on the horn bitchin' about how they were left out.' He looked at Kronziac and Maggie in turn as they sat silently in front of the desk.

'We called Cunningham and Harbour after we found the body,' Maggie said limply.

'Why not before?' Foley asked, widening his eyes in amazement.

'Well.' She hesitated. 'We weren't too sure what we were looking for . . . I mean, we just had this note that had these cryptic directions—'

The Assistant Director glanced at her in a manner that suggested she ought to shut up now. Then he turned his look on Kronziac.

'Anything to say, Agent Kronziac?'

He always tended to call her 'Agent Kronziac' when he came the heavy. True, Foley could be a tough boss, but she always thought they got along fine, most of the time. She could push him to the brink, maybe, but once she paid him the courtesy of letting him know what was going on in the DTU he pretty much left her to run the show they way she wanted. It was an unspoken agreement that had evolved over the years. It didn't hurt, either, if she called him 'sir' once and a while, especially in front of the others.

'Sorry, sir,' she said, suitably chastened. 'I was passed on some information from the victim's father.'

Foley held his hands up, his eyes shut tight as if unable to keep up. 'The body has been id'd?'

Kronziac was reluctant to answer. 'Er – not yet,' she confessed.

Foley nodded smugly, the point won. 'Go on.' He urged her to continue digging her own hole.

'Well, the father passed on a communication received by his local police station in the form of a—' She hesitated again. 'A riddle – a cryptogram,' she added, trying to redeem herself with fancy terminology.

'A riddle?' Foley raised a greying eyebrow.

'Yes,' she replied, moving on quickly. 'We thought it was a long shot but it did actually lead us to recover a body.'

But Foley wasn't about to let her off that easily. 'And you just couldn't pass it on to the appropriate police authority?'

'Well, they didn't know what to make of it,' Kronziac explained, 'or whether it was anything at all to do with the girl's disappearance.'

Foley shook his head, not wanting to argue the matter all morning. Instead he decided just to pull rank. 'Correct me if I'm wrong,' he began. 'But I put you on suspension – I mean, I did do that, didn't I?' he asked, looking at both of them briefly before turning back to Kronziac. 'I didn't instruct you to use the resources and personnel of the FBI to set up your own private investigation agency to go around solving riddles – did I?'

'No, sir,' Kronziac replied quietly.

The admission seemed to free the anger and impatience that had built up in Foley. 'Jesus, Nancy! How do you get yourself into these things? First Soton, now this!'

Kronziac had begun to think about it when there was a tap on the door and the tall figure of Nathan Sedley appeared.

'Good,' Foley said as if he'd been waiting for Sedley's arrival all along. 'Come in, Nathan.'

A perfect example of what an FBI agent should look like, Sedley was dressed in a black, well-pressed suit, his hair neatly cropped, accentuating his square features. *Super-agent Nathan Smedley*, Phillips called him.

'Nathan here,' Foley announced with exaggerated satisfaction, 'is now in direct command of the DTU.'

He turned to Maggie. 'You so much as go to the can without his permission and you can join Kronziac here on an indefinite holiday,' he added menacingly.

'So I'm still on suspension?' Kronziac asked, not surprised.

But Foley glanced up at Sedley to deliver his answer. 'IAD haven't made a decision yet on the Bitteroot sting,' he confirmed. 'They're still considering everyone's report on the operation.'

'So I still can't do my job?' Kronziac protested.

Foley nodded. 'You stay at home,' he cautioned her sternly. 'It's the safest place for you.'

'Is it?' she wondered doubtfully.

'We keep in contact with Jones up in Montana on a daily basis,' Sedley assured her. 'They're keeping a close eye on Lucas Crebbs and the Woodsmen, but we can still cover your protection,' he added, seeming to be genuinely concerned.

'That's up to you, Nancy,' Foley intervened, 'if you want it.'

Kronziac looked at Sedley, a little surprised at his concern for her. 'I'm okay.' She shrugged.

'Okay,' Foley said, beginning to move some other paperwork on his desk. 'Everyone hit the door, I've got work to do.'

As they came out of Foley's office Phillips was on the phone. When he saw Kronziac he put his hand over the mouthpiece and called her over.

'A detective from Vegas here,' he whispered and picked up a pen to write down some details. 'Responding to the notice you asked me to put on the police net . . . says he got a weird set of letters on the back of a Missing Persons sheet a few days ago.'

Before Kronziac could say anything she felt a large hand on her shoulder.

'You should get home,' Sedley advised her. 'Get some rest.'

Though he was smiling, there was something in his voice that made her think she should take his advice.

1597 LOCUSTA STREET, NORTHRIDGE, CA

Though the house seemed quiet, there were several cars parked outside. Kronziac opened out the collar of her raincoat as she rushed onto the porch. While the West Side basked in sunshine the valley languished under a low base of cloud that sprinkled heavy showers from the Hollywood Hills to the San Gabriel Mountains.

A little boy answered the door. His hair was neatly parted and combed and it was obvious that he had been dressed up by his parents for the visitors.

'Hi, James,' Kronziac said, smiling. 'Are your Mom and Dad around?'

He just nodded and held the door open.

Kronziac could hear the hushed chatter of people in the living room, subdued whispers of condolence and comfort. As she followed James inside into the hall she was relieved when Jerry Blaynes called to her from the living room. He excused himself from a group of older women who were sipping delicately on glasses of juice. A young teenage girl took James by the hand and led him upstairs, asking him to show her his computer games.

'Nancy,' Blaynes said, putting his arm around her, obviously cheered by her arrival.

'I'm so sorry,' she said, kissing him lightly on the cheek.

He closed his eyes and nodded, the pain of his grief barely kept at bay. 'How nice of you to call,' he said and guided her into the quiet dining room.

'I don't want to intrude,' Kronziac apologized.

Jerry shook his head. 'It's just some relatives and neighbours over to give their condolences,' he assured her.

She sat down at the table and asked him quietly, almost cautiously in case it upset him, when the funeral was.

He seemed unsure. 'She's still at the morgue, I think.'

The words obviously pained him and his large dark head shook as his eyes shut once more – somehow trying to squeeze

149

from his mind the thought of his daughter, her mutilated body lying on the cold steel table of the Medical Examiner.

'Maybe I should go,' Kronziac said, feeling her presence was making him worse.

His eyes flashed open. 'No,' he said. 'Please stay a little while. You're the only one we can really talk to.'

She stayed still and nodded. 'How is Cynthia?'

He took a deep breath and gathered himself together. 'She's good,' he answered. 'Under the circumstances, very good. I don't know if it has all sunk in with her yet,' he continued, 'but she's being very strong for me and James.'

'I suppose it's hard for him to know what's going on,' Kronziac said sadly.

'He kept asking if Cherie would come home for Christmas.' Jerry tried to smile but failed: his face tightened in a tortured look.

'We were able to identify her by the clothing,' he said slowly. 'And by the necklace we gave her on her fifteenth birthday.'

He began shaking his head, his swollen eyes fixed in a frozen stare. 'I . . . I couldn't look at her,' he jabbered. 'I just couldn't look at her – it wasn't her . . . not how I knew her.'

His hands were trembling and Kronziac thought she should call for his wife.

'It's just not her,' he repeated, shaking his head in horrified disbelief. 'It wasn't my daughter – that black twisted—'

He stopped himself by pressing his palms against his forehead, almost physically pushing the terrible image of Cherie's body from his mind.

Kronziac could hear footsteps coming quickly over the wooden floor of the hallway from the living room.

Dressed in a neat dark skirt and jacket, her hair tied in a black bow, Cynthia stopped at the door into the dining room. Seeing her husband weeping, she paused, preparing herself before she entered.

'Hello, Nancy,' she said, trying to sound bright. Her eyes were bloodshot, the skin around them dry and wrinkled. 'Can I get you anything?' she asked Kronziac, resting her hand on Jerry's shoulder to comfort him in any small way she could.

'No, thank you,' said Kronziac and started to get up, ready to offer her condolences once more and leave. But Cynthia closed the door behind her and took a seat next to Jerry. 'It's nice of you to call,' she said thinly, patently weakened by her grief.

'Not at all,' Kronziac replied softly.

'We want to thank you,' Cynthia said. Jerry nodded in full agreement, taking a handkerchief from his blazer to wipe his eyes.

'We'll pay whatever it costs to find whoever did this to her,' Cynthia continued, her voice steady.

Kronziac shook her head and moved her chair back from the table. 'This is a police matter, really,' she told them.

'And they're doing the best job they can. Cunningham's a good guy—' said Jerry.

'They spent the last couple of months doing tests on her car and handing out flyers,' Cynthia interrupted bitterly. 'They've plenty of other cases on their hands. But we're only interested in Cherie and you're the only one who's really helped – you found her for us.'

But Kronziac was still shaking her head. 'I'm sorry, it's up to the detectives,' she insisted. 'The FBI can help in investigating her kidnapping but I'd leave it to PD Homicide.'

'The first time I met you,' Jerry said, 'at your office – you were angry about something, angry as hell.'

Kronziac remembered the occasion when she had bawled Jerry out at the front desk a few weeks previously, having other matters on her mind at the time.

'That's what we need,' said Cynthia, 'not sympathy, not comforting words, we need someone who's angry – like we are.'

Kronziac had no reply.

Cynthia turned to her husband. 'Please, honey, can you get the file?'

Jerry nodded and got up from the chair. 'Excuse me,' he said and went out the door, closing it behind him.

After a moment of silence Cynthia spoke again. 'You must think I'm very cold.'

Kronziac shook her head. 'Not really,' she said. 'I've seen quite a few families of victims and everyone reacts in different ways.' This seemed to comfort Cynthia.

'Jerry cut his finger the other day,' she reminisced, smiling at the silly accident. 'He was chopping some tomatoes for dinner. A nasty little nick, seemed quite painful,' she added, 'but he just left it to bleed.'

Kronziac's puzzled look prompted Cynthia to explain why she was telling her this. 'He wanted to suffer,' she said, her eyes beginning to sting. 'He's not a very religious man, but he wanted to suffer. He thought, in some crazy way, that if he did God would lessen the pain Cherie suffered when she died.'

Kronziac put her hand on Cynthia's. She felt cold, her fingers blanched and trembling. But the grief passed again like a wave and anger returned.

'We can't help her now,' she whispered. 'But we *must* find whoever did this to her.' Her voice was ragged, edged with rage. 'I want to see them – to look into their eyes and ask them why.'

Kronziac, still holding on to her hand, just nodded. The Blaynes were fully entitled to their anger but she just wasn't sure if it would help them heal the wounds – not this soon, anyway.

The door opened and Jerry came in, carrying a black ringbinder thick with paperwork. 'We called the Department of Justice's Office for Victims of Crime, and they advised us that we could appoint an outside law-enforcement officer or a lawyer as a mentor to help us with the investigation. It's a new initiative,' he told Kronziac, 'aimed at keeping the families of victims of violent crime in the picture. The investigators can be compelled under federal statute to give you relevant information on the case.'

'Me?' Kronziac asked, never having heard of this before. 'You want to appoint *me*?'

'Please,' Cynthia pleaded, holding Kronziac's hand tight. 'We're begging you to help us.'

There was a knock on the door, a sound that Kronziac felt thankful for.

Fractions of Zero

'That them?' Cynthia asked her husband.

He nodded and got up to open the door.

Four teenagers walked in quietly. Two girls and two boys. They seemed subdued and were dressed sensibly and conservatively for the occasion.

Cynthia turned to Kronziac and introduced them. 'Jared, Rhiannon, Joanne and, of course, Donnie . . . these are Cherie's friends. They want to help all they can.'

2434 ABRAMAR, PACIFIC PALISADES, CA

Tossing her wetsuit onto a sun lounger on the veranda, Kronziac took a beach towel and began drying her hair, which hung in strands around her glistening shoulders. Clad in a one-piece *SurfGirl* swimsuit under a cerise sarong, she headed back indoors, her flesh peppered with goose bumps. That morning she had enjoyed her first dawn surf in nearly three months, catching a nice set of four-foot rollers off Malibu Pier that had curled under a nice south-westerly.

She slipped into one of her navy blue FBI sweatsuits and, having got a juice from the bar, she settled on the other lounger on the patio. Some small clouds, like spun floss, drifted lazily inland on the salty Pacific breeze. She thought she should write some Christmas cards but instead picked up the black ring-binder that the Blayneses had given her and opened it. She felt a heavy sense of self-reproach, asking herself the same question Foley had asked her.

How in the fuck do I get myself into these things?

As she flicked through the various police reports, background information and statements Kronziac was again struck by the Blayneses' organizational skill and by their determination to find out who had killed their daughter. Each section in the binder was carefully labelled and indexed. She found a neatly drafted itinerary of Cherie's last known movements on the day she had disappeared.

TIME	LOCATION
18.15–18.45	Dinner with family – Jerry, Cynthia & James Blaynes
18.45–19.05	Cherie goes to her room to get ready to go out to buy some school supplies and meet friends for movie. Phone rings at about 19.50. Cherie answers in her bedroom.
19.07–19.10	Leaves in car (yellow Mazda hatchback) wearing light blue jeans, red sweater, runners

154

	and shoulder bag. Last seen by Cynthia pulling out of driveway.
20.24	Car parks in Aldcott shopping mall. Seen by security cameras on main building and ATM.
20.32	Cherie meets friends Donnie Claterios, Joanne Fisk, Jared Macapelli and Rhianon Bodine at the Movie Planet cineplex in the Aldcott mall.
20.35–23.05	Watches movie *Whole Lotta Love* with friends.
23.07–23.12	Walks to parking lot with Donnie.
23.19	Car seen on ATM and security video, and witnessed by Donnie Claterios leaving parking lot and turning onto Receda.

Kronziac closed the file and picked up a small secateurs. She clipped some dead bearded iris that spilled from the clay pots on the balcony. Instinctively, she glanced down the garden, scanning across the small lawn and into the smoky green obelisks of yew trees, wondering for a moment if one of Crebbs's henchmen was watching. She put the thought from her mind but nearly dropped the secateurs when a shrill voice called out to her.

'Morning, Nancy!'

Kronziac shivered after the little shock. 'Hello, Mrs Peters!' she shouted back to her next-door neighbour who was leaning out her bedroom window, about fifty feet from Kronziac's house. Still in her dressing gown and holding her first cigarette of the day, Mrs Peters had just got out of bed.

'Had a nice dip?' the woman asked, spotting the wetsuit lying on the lounger.

'Very nice!' Kronziac replied.

Mrs Peters, for reasons only known to herself, always referred to any water sport as a 'dip'. She never went near the beach and her skin was the colour of an onion's, darkening to a grassy yellow between the fingers with which she held her cigarette.

'Wanna come in for a coffee and a smoke?' she asked, waving her cigarette enticingly.

155

Kronziac was about to say yes when the phone buzzed inside the house. 'Can I take a rain check?' she asked and dropped the secateurs on the Zellig table.

'Sure, honey,' Mrs Peters shouted back. 'You know where I am.'

Phillips spoke with hushed excitement, as if not wanting to be heard by the other people at his end.

'What is it?' Kronziac asked, squeezing the handset closer to her ear.

'*That Vegas detective, the guy I was onto when you left yesterday?*' Phillips whispered.

'What about him?'

'*He sent me a fax of a weird set of letters he got on the back of a Missing Persons notice.*'

'Anything like the last one?' she asked impatiently.

'*Weirder-looking shit this time,*' Phillips said. '*Don't know if it's got anything to do with anything but I thought you'd want to know.*'

Kronziac couldn't help wondering if this message had been sent by the same person who'd sent the riddle about Cherie's body. 'Can you get it to me?' she asked hopefully. 'I don't think it'd be a good idea for me to show up at the office right now.'

Phillips paused. '*Foley could start bustin' my ass,*' he warned. But Kronziac remained quiet, hoping he would talk himself into it. '*Sedley's watching us like a hawk.*'

'Sure, I understand,' she said, graciously disappointed.

'*Oh fuck it, what the hell,*' Phillips said suddenly, '*I'll try and get it out to you this afternoon.*'

'Okay, Phillips,' Kronziac said and before she could say thanks he had hung up.

Kronziac was about to do the same. But instead she reached across the counter top to her shoulder bag and with one hand fished among her things to find the scrap of paper with the Harvard Math Department's phone number on it.

The squad room was loud with ringing phones and chatting voices. At one desk three *cholos* from a Hispanic gang sat like weary schoolchildren, listening to a Community Law Enforcement officer lecture them on a weapons violation. At another desk a drunk was throwing up into a waste-paper basket that one of the detectives was holding out at arm's length.

Front-line policing, Kronziac thought to herself. *No, thank you.*

Detective Cunningham pointed her to a rigid wooden stool in front of his desk while he plonked himself heavily onto a typist's chair that squealed briefly under its burden. His forehead shone with a thin coat of sweat, his thinning hair still damp, hanging limply over his temples.

'Just had a workout,' he explained and patted his soft midriff.

Keep it up, Kronziac thought to herself, and just smiled cordially back.

He opened a thin folder, and took out some stapled sheets of paper and tossed them on the desk. 'ME's report,' he stated flatly.

'You don't mind?' Kronziac asked, picking them up.

'Not at all.' He waved his hand, 'I know Jerry Blaynes, he's helped us over the years with our various community programmes. We'd like to help him all we can.' He shook his head dolefully. 'It's such a damn tragedy.'

Kronziac scanned down the cover letter. 'Bob Vesoles conducted the examination?' she asked, recognizing the signature of the coroner.

'You know him?' Cunningham asked.

Kronziac nodded and, seeing a highlighter on the desk, picked it up. 'May I?'

'Go ahead,' Cunningham said obligingly as she began marking in the salient points of Cherie Blaynes's autopsy report.

Forensic Science Laboratories Division

USC Medical Center
1200 North State

AUTOPSY REPORT

NAME: Blaynes, Cherie Margaret
DOB: 8/12/85
AGE: 16Y
SEX: F
PATH MD: Vesoles
AUTOPSY NO: OIC – 17561

FINAL DIAGNOSIS:

    I.   Craniocerebral injuries
       a. Severe fracture of right orbital bones at zygomatic, palatine and sphenoid.
       b. Subdural hemorrhage
    II. Ligature radial abrasion on both wrists and ankles.
    III. Right hand index finger severed at proximal phalanx
    IV. Unidentified markings on frontal skullbone (glabella).

Toxicology:
blood ethanol – none detected
scheduled drug screen – none detected.

(Upper torso and face badly decomposed. Lower extremities exhibit substantial autolysis and decomposition)

CLINICOPATHOLOGY:
Cause of death for this 16-year-old female was severe craniocerebral trauma and resultant hemorrhaging.

'Jerry said you were on vacation from the Bureau,' remarked Cunningham.

But Kronziac wasn't listening. Looking further on in the more detailed notes of the autopsy she searched for more specifics on the fatal head injury.

'I was thinking of joining the Bureau myself a couple of years ago,' Cunningham reflected. I was gonna do night classes for a law degree at UCLA and all – but I'm happy here.'

He looked around as a huge man, heavily adorned with tattoos, was bundled past the door by several officers making for the holding cells.

'She died because of a bad bang to the head?' Kronziac asked. 'A fracture of the right orbital and subsequent haemorrhaging?'

'Yeah,' Cunningham said. 'The right eyeball is missing – don't know if it happened because of the blow to the head or if it was destroyed in the sewage tank. Pretty fuckin' gruesome, though, either way.'

Kronziac continued to pore over the notes on the head injury.

'You think the attack was sex-related?' Cunningham asked. 'They found a cervical cap in her.'

Kronziac flicked through the pages to the appropriate section. '"Latex cervical cap – but no discernible traces of spermatazoa",' she confirmed. 'You wouldn't expect to find any after that amount of time and given the decay.'

Cunningham sat forward over his desk, fishing out another slip of paper. 'Actually, Forensics were able to trace the manufacture of the cap. It's called a—' he squinted at the scribbled note '—FemiForm cap – made by Harmonex Healthcare Products.'

Krenziac quickly flicked through the pages to the clothing section. 'No traces of torn clothing,' she commented, a little surprised.

'You think it was consensual?' Cunningham asked, a little indignant at the thought. 'She had ligature marks on her wrists, and was tied up in the sack.'

Kronziac ignored Cunningham's presumption. 'What did the boyfriend say?' she asked, 'Were they together that night?'

'You mean did they have sex?' he asked, furrowing his brow. Kronziac nodded.

Cunningham inhaled heavily in disapproval and opened his file again, retrieving a witness statement. 'Didn't mention it,' he said dryly. 'But I suppose it's not exactly something he'd fess up to, besides they'd hardly have the time,' he added. 'They left the others at ten after eleven and her car pulled out nine minutes later. Not much time,' he smiled, 'not even for a horny seventeen-year-old.'

'Mmm . . . not much time,' Kronziac agreed, seeing his point.

'Anyway, we have it all on tape.' Cunningham closed the file again.

'Security cameras?' Kronziac asked.

Cunningham nodded. 'The mall's outside cameras and the ATM security cam,' he confirmed. 'She just drove off, not a sign of anyone else near her,' he said, his expression mystified.

Kronziac sat quietly, looking over the report cover sheet for any further clues.

'You should get Vesoles to check out this unknown marking on the forehead bone,' Kronziac suggested gently.

'You get long vacations with the Bureau?' Cunningham asked.

LOCUSTA ST, NORTHRIDGE, CA

Donnie recognized the silver seven-series BMW parked outside his house.

The door swung open.

'Hello, Mr Blaynes.' Donnie greeted the large, dark-haired figure of Jerry Blaynes as he got out of the car. Plucking the tiny headphones of his minidisc player from his ears, Donnie smiled nervously as Jerry came towards him.

'How's school, Donnie?' Jerry barked.

'Er – okay, I guess,' Donnie replied, a little surprised at the question and the sharp manner in which Jerry asked it.

'Good.' Jerry smiled. 'How are this year's tenth-graders? Any nice pieces of ass?'

Donnie wasn't sure if he'd heard right. 'I'm in twelfth grade,' he said, a little shocked.

'Yeah, but you like 'em young, don't you? Surely you've already checked out the little honeys.' Jerry laughed but his voice was edged like a razor. 'And they probably can't resist you, huh?' He looked Donnie up and down, his expression one of disgust.

'What's wrong with you, Mr Blaynes?' Donnie recoiled, thinking that Cherie's father was drunk.

'One thing you may have overlooked,' Jerry hissed and pushed Donnie against the wall. 'Ever hear of the California Penal Code? Sections 261 to 269?'

Donnie shook his head, freaked out by Jerry's onslaught. 'Jesus! Take it easy, Mr Blaynes!' he pleaded.

'It's an offence to have sex with a minor under the age of eighteen!' Jerry spat angrily, pinning Donnie against the wall. 'Did you know that, you little prick? Thought you could just get away with it?'

Shaking his head vigorously, Donnie pleaded with Jerry, instinctively putting up his hands in defence. 'What are you talking about?' he cried.

'You know what I'm talking about!' Jerry yelled at him, his

face reddening, barely keeping himself from lashing out. 'She was only sixteen, for Christ's sake, just a little girl!' he roared.

'I never touched Cherie!' Donnie replied distraughtly. 'I swear to God I never touched her!'

It was all Jerry could do to keep from driving Donnie's head against the hard concrete of the wall. But he gestrained his anger, holding it back as though in a sling.

He stepped back, shooting up his finger like a gun, pointing directly into Donnie's face. 'If you had anything to do with her death—' he began sweating heavily with the heat of his anger '—I'll fucking kill you myself!' he warned. He turned and walked away quickly before he carried out the threat there and then.

'I had nothing to do with it!' Donnie sobbed, lowering himself to the ground. 'I loved Cherie! I loved her!' he cried as Jerry's car screamed away.

ENCOUNTER RESTAURANT, THEME BUILDING, LOS ANGELES INTERNATIONAL AIRPORT

'It really *is* like a spaceship!'

Ellstrom stood staring in awe as Kronziac led him up the sidewalk under the rounded legs of the Theme Building. In the fading light of evening the parabolic arches began to slowly fade from rich magenta to a vivid green as the computer-controlled wash luminaries wrapped the curved structures in a slowly changing kaleidoscope of colour.

'Like a svelte lunar module,' he went on, describing the distinctive LA landmark.

'I always thought it looked like that thing that came out of the ocean in one of the Bond movies,' said Kronziac.

'*The Spy Who Loved Me*?' Ellstrom guessed.

'The one with Curt Jurgens as the baddie, I think,' said Kronziac.

'Yeah, Stromberg!' Ellstrom stated, excited at their little exchange of movie trivia.

Ellstrom ordered a char-grilled steak and a beer while Kronziac settled for an espresso. Looking around the restaurant, Ellstrom marvelled open-mouthed at the electric-blue ceiling and the curved, moulded walls. By one of the large windows some of the staff were putting the last touches on the Christmas tree, the fairy lights blinking like the landing lights of the aircraft outside that were making their descent to the airport. At the crater-shaped bar small lasers flashed against the ceiling each time one of the bartenders poured a drink through the bar guns.

'It's the canteen on the *Enterprise*,' Ellstrom commented gleefully.

Kronziac smiled but reckoned for a moment she was dealing with a thirty-nine-year-old kid. Still, under the radiant blue light she thought he looked quite handsome – even better-looking than the young Michael Caine he reminded her of. 'Yeah, I

163

think the guys at Disney designed the place,' she told him.

A waitress leaned over them and placed a large plate, almost entirely covered by a grilled slab of meat, in front of Ellstrom, along with a side bowl heaped with fries. She lifted a fat pitcher of cold beer and a tall glass from her tray and placed them next to the steaming plate, completing the instant all-you-can-eat heart-attack supper.

In front of Kronziac she rested the dinky espresso cup that tinkled on its saucer.

'Thanks, honey.' Ellstrom beamed.

Kronziac shook her head slightly in bemusement – that phony half-American accent again.

As the waitress smiled back and thanked him for thanking her, Kronziac pulled out a copy of the cryptogram Phillips had received from the detective in Vegas.

'That's what I like about America,' Ellstrom said, his gaze rolling greedily over the huge plate of dead cow in front of him. 'Big portions.'

'This your first time in LA?' Kronziac asked, unfolding the sheet of paper.

'Yes.' He nodded, stabbing the meaty disc with a steak knife. 'I go to San Francisco the day after tomorrow, up to Berkeley and Stanford.'

'I was lucky I caught you just before you left Boston,' Kronziac said, taking a sip of coffee. 'Could have missed you.'

'Odds weren't that high, actually,' he remarked, dunking a large chunk of meat in some black-pepper sauce.

Kronziac laid the cryptogram flat on the table and was going to ask Ellstrom about it when he managed to get out another question between mouthfuls.

'How long have you been here?' he asked. 'Are you a native Los Angelean or whatever they're called?'

'Angelinos, I think,' Kronziac corrected him. 'I'm from Chicago originally but I've been here seven years now come . . . February,' she calculated.

'I thought you'd be more tanned and . . .' He paused, smiling cheekily.

'More what?' Kronziac asked.

'Blonde,' he said quickly and stuffed his mouth with a squat triangle of meat.

Kronziac smiled graciously, again finding herself having to remain patient with him.

'Too much sun's not good for you,' she told him. 'But I suppose it's not something you have to worry about too much, being from England.'

Ellstrom didn't make a sound when he laughed but his shoulders shook while his mouth chewed busily.

'I would love to try surfing,' he said finally, swallowing his food with the aid of a swig of beer.

'I'll take you out some time,' Kronziac suggested nonchalantly, waiting for his expression of surprise. Only one thing amazed people more than the fact that she chased terrorists for a living and that was that she was a surfer.

'Wow,' Ellstrom said dumbly, clutching his glass of beer.

'What part of England are you from?' she asked, waiting for his answer as he took another drink.

'Outside London,' he gasped, the fizzy beer pinching his nose. 'A small town called Denham, actually now called Old Denham – it's in Buckinghamshire. My father used to work as a colour grader in the Rank Labs nearby.'

Kronziac's puzzled look made him explain.

'Grading master film prints,' he said. 'Balancing the colour and brightness – he was in the movie business, you could say,' he added lightly.

'Sounds nice,' she said, slowly sipping her coffee as Ellstrom attacked his food with the steak knife again.

'Well, at least you didn't say cute,' he remarked acidly, reminding Kronziac of the smug condescending math professor she'd met at Harvard.

'You a film fan, then?' she asked.

Again, Ellstrom could only nod, his mouth stuffed with some fries. 'What's your favourite film?' he blurted, eventually swallowing.

Kronziac thought about it for a moment. 'Dunno if I have a favourite . . . *One Flew Over the Cuckoo's Nest*, maybe, or *Doctor Zhivago* – or *Breakfast At Tiffany's*.'

'Really?' he asked, surprised.

'What?' Kronziac wanted to know. 'What's wrong with those?'

'Nothing.' He smiled cheekily. 'Nothing at all.'

'Oh, let me guess – I suppose your favourite is *Star Trek – Part—*' she searched for a number '*—Part 57 – Beyond the Hairpiece.*'

'No, actually,' Ellstrom corrected Kronziac, amused at her sassiness. 'I just thought you'd like – you know, *The X-Files* or *Silence of the Lambs.*'

'Oh, right, the FBI thing.' Kronziac caught on. 'Well, I don't like violent films and besides, being an FBI agent isn't all just about guns and serial killers.'

Damn. Kronziac cursed herself for getting sucked in but she always hated it when people made comparisons between real life and what they saw on TV or in the movies. She decided to change the subject.

'So how long have you been in the States?' she asked, waiting as he chewed his food.

'Just over a year,' he answered. 'Got an opportunity to combine my research with a teaching fellowship at Harvard.'

'And what do you research?' Kronziac asked, not sure she wanted to sit through the answer.

'Numbers,' he said simply, 'Number Theory.'

Kronziac watched him sever a long strip of meat from a thick belt of gristle.

'That sounds pretty broad,' she said. 'I mean, I thought that's what all math people did – basically just study numbers. You know – plus and minus . . .'

'I explore the *theory* of numbers,' he stated firmly, cutting her off and putting down his knife and fork. Dabbing the corners of his mouth with a napkin, he grinned back at her. 'Besides, being a mathematician is not all just about numbers and plus-and-minuses.'

Before she could acknowledge his riposte he finally pointed at the sheet of paper on the table.

'Another little riddle?' he asked. 'What's it this time? Little Bo Peep?'

'I doubt it,' Kronziac answered quietly.

'And what about the last one?' he asked, settling back in his chair, satiated at last. 'Did we win a little prize or something, or is it just a hobby of yours, Special Agent Kronziac?'

'The last one?' Kronziac played nervously with her cup of cold coffee. 'The last one led us to the body of a murdered sixteen-year-old girl,' she said with deliberate flatness.

Ellstrom flinched, nearly knocking over his glass. Then he smiled.

'Is this a joke?'

'You want the autopsy report?' Kronziac offered, making a move to pick up her bag.

Ellstrom leaned forward over the table. 'You're not jerking me around, are you?' he asked, not smiling this time.

Kronziac turned over the sheet of paper with the cryptogram on it. On the other side was Ellen Holby's Missing Persons notice from the Las Vegas Metro Police Department.

Ellstrom drew close, picked it up and read the details. He glanced at Kronziac for a moment, checking one last time for any signs that it was all a trick. But her dark eyes held his gaze without blinking.

He turned the sheet over again and studied the rows of letters, already scanning for patterns.

*RMDEGZWQZRDAYFTQTQMYFTKNDQMFTUDREFOXQMDQP
ARTQMHKHMBAGDENQFIQQZRAGDFQQZMZPQTMDNAGD
QNUZFTQEXQQBKIQEFXMKHMEFMZPQPSQIMKEXUWQMPU
EYMXOUDBGQFANQ*

'I'll need a box of 3B lead pencils, a book of graph paper and a quiet place to work,' he said.

ALDCOTT SHOPPING MALL, RECEDA, NORTHRIDGE

The piped strains of 'Jingle Bells' and other Christmas staples shook from the ceiling like pennies jangling in a pocket.

Kronziac glanced at her watch and craned her head up at the globe clock over the Movie Planet Cineplex. For a moment she imagined she could see the small pretty figure of Cherie Blaynes rounding the corner of the entrance into the mall, dressed in her red sweater, the necklace that her parents had given her shining in a button of gold on her neck. Instead, shoppers walked briskly by, clutching bags packed with brightly parcelled boxes, and Kronziac shuddered at the prospect of doing her own Christmas shopping. Still, at least there were a few days to go yet.

'Agent Kronziac!'

A voice, the ragged-edged burr of a teenage boy, made her start.

She turned around and the lanky figure of Donnie Claterios loomed over her.

'Sorry,' he said. 'I came in the other way.'

'Thanks for coming,' said Kronziac and shook his bony hand, which was heavily adorned with rings. He was dressed in sports gear with chunky luminous-soled trainers on his feet and a black peaked cap tugged low over his closely shaved head. She thought he was a nice enough kid but suspected Jerry Blaynes wouldn't have particularly liked the idea of his daughter dating someone who looked like Donnie. But what father would?

'I know you've gone over this with the detectives,' Kronziac began, 'but I want to get a clear picture of what exactly happened the night Cherie disappeared.'

'Sure,' Donnie nodded eagerly. 'I understand.' He looked around, a little lost as to where to begin. 'Where do you want me to start?'

Kronziac glanced towards the main doorway from Receda. 'When you first saw Cherie that evening,' she suggested, 'or if you saw her earlier on that day.'

'Well.' Donnie thought about it. 'I didn't actually see her all day. I had band practice with the guys,' he added with an expectant smile, obviously hoping she would ask him more about his music.

'So here,' Kronziac pointed at the ground, 'is where you first met her that day?'

He nodded. 'Yeah, though I talked to her on the phone earlier.'

Kronziac took out from the inside pocket of her coat a copy of Cherie's itinerary that the Blayneses had drawn up. 'What time?' she asked.

Donnie held his chin in his left hand, rubbing the rough beginnings of a sparse goatee. 'About ten before seven,' he said thoughtfully.

'Right,' Kronziac concurred. Jerry had noted the phone ringing about then also. 'What did you talk about?' she asked gently.

He curled his lips, trying to recollect. 'Nothing much,' he replied, 'just kinda general stuff on how her day was and our arrangements to go to the movie. Like I said, nothing much.'

Kronziac nodded sympathetically, letting him slowly wind out his memory.

'Some stuff about going back to school,' he went on, 'I told her how practice was going and that was all there was time for.'

'In a rush?' Kronziac smiled.

'No, she had another call waiting.'

Kronziac glanced at the sheet. No mention of another call. But then, the phone wouldn't have rung, would only have beeped to tell Cherie there was a call waiting.

'Who was it?'

'Joanne, I suppose,' he answered. 'Or maybe Rhiannon ringing up to see what was going down.'

'Okay,' said Kronziac, moving on. 'What time was it when you met her that night?'

Donnie stretched out a long arm. 'About eight-thirty, just about here.'

'How did she seem to you?' Kronziac asked.

'Same as usual.' He shrugged, a sad smile broadening his lips. 'Though I kinda gave her a bit of a fright when I jumped out at her from behind the photo booth.'

'And you didn't notice anyone following her or hanging around?'

'No.' He shook his head blankly. 'But then, I wasn't exactly looking out for anyone else.'

'So you went straight into the movie?' Kronziac continued.

'Yeah, after Jared arrived. We all sat together.' He added, with a sour grin, 'It was a crap movie, though Cherie seemed to like it.' His smile disappeared again.

'What happened after the movie?' Kronziac continued her questioning.

'Well,' Donnie answered, looking back at the door into the movie theatre, 'we came out here, all of us doing our Siskell and Ebert on the film and we walked out of the mall onto Receda.'

'Show me,' Kronziac told him.

'What?' asked Donnie, puzzled at first.

'Take me through it,' Kronziac said.

Donnie began moving towards the large glass automatic doors of the entrance to the mall. A cheery and rather slim Santa Claus was pushing a collection box under the chins of passing shoppers and patting their unimpressed kids on the head.

'Okay, we walked outside.' Donnie described their movements as Kronziac followed him out the door under the portico with the large crescent-shaped words of the Aldcott Mall. Donnie stopped in the middle of the sidewalk, looking around to find the exact spot. The traffic on Receda slowly filed past, the car engines muttering stolidly.

'We said goodbye to the others who headed north since Joanne's car was parked across the road,' said Donnie, pointing up the street. 'And Jared's car was parked up on Lassen, I think.'

Kronziac raised her eyebrows, amazed that out of the five kids that night four of them had their own cars. 'What did you and Cherie do then?' she asked.

Donnie began walking in the other direction towards the

parking lot. As they turned left into the car park, which was crammed with cars, he continued his commentary.

'We stopped here for a while,' he said, and then pointed at the ATM. 'I had to go get money for school the next day,' he continued. 'I asked Cherie if she wanted to wait and said I'd walk her to the car.' He turned to Kronziac, his expression tight as if he was in pain. 'But she didn't want to wait,' he added quietly. 'We kissed and she walked off to her car – somewhere over there.' He pointed to the other end of the car park.

'What time was that?' Kronziac asked.

Donnie answered immediately, having already told the police several times. 'A quarter after eleven.'

Kronziac nodded. Cunningham had told her the bank records for Donnie's withdrawal at the ATM registered 11.16 p.m. 'And that was the last time you saw her?' She asked.

Donnie nodded slowly, pensive. 'While I was at the ATM I looked over my shoulder and I saw the car lights come on and she drove away.'

'You didn't notice anything or anyone else in the parking lot?'

Donnie just shook his head. 'Nothing,' he said desolately. 'Nothing at all.'

'No other cars and nobody hanging around?' Kronziac asked, trying to get the last ounce of information from him.

But Donnie continued to shake his head, adamant that he couldn't remember anything out of place.

Women with heavily laden trolleys trundled noisily by to find their cars and fill the gaping mouths of their hatchbacks with groceries and Christmas parcels. Kronziac found it difficult to visualize the car park empty, quiet and dimly lambent under the street lights that night in September.

'Donnie,' she began cautiously. 'Look, you don't have to answer this but I've got to ask.'

The teenager looked at her, his boyish features drawn with the strain.

'And this is strictly between you and me,' she assured him, making him even more apprehensive. 'Did you and Cherie—' she began, finding herself surprisingly nervous. 'Did you guys ever have sexual relations?' she jabbered, as if spitting out a bad piece of food.

Donnie closed his eyes and began smiling, an ironic grin, and let his chin fall against his chest.

'It's absolutely none of my business, I know,' Kronziac went on, trying to put him at ease. 'But it would help clear something up – and, like I said, you don't have to answer me,' she reminded him. She knew Cunningham was going to have to ask him and she definitely knew Jerry Blaynes was going to ask once he saw the autopsy report.

Opening his eyes, Donnie looked up at her squarely. 'No,' he said quietly.

Kronziac knew she had to be sure. 'You didn't have sex with Cherie on the day she disappeared?' she persisted, hating having to do it.

Donnie shook his head again. 'Not that day or any other day,' he stated. 'Cherie was a virgin,' he added firmly. Then he suddenly stopped shaking his head, his gaze boring into Kronziac. 'Did—' he stuttered, realizing the purpose of the question. 'Did the bastard who killed her – did he—?' He couldn't bring himself to say it and Kronziac knew it. She put her hand on his shoulder and took out her business card.

'I'm sorry to have put you through this, Donnie,' she said, pressing the card into his hand, 'I've written my home number on the back.'

Donnie broke away, punching the air with his bony fist. 'Motherfucker!' he spat, drawing inquisitive looks from some shoppers hurriedly loading their car nearby as a light rain began to fall from the sky.

California State Lotteries

MegaLotto

RESULT

Wed 19th December

2   20   13   25   17   6

2434 ABRAMAR, PACIFIC PALISADES, CA

They emerged from the car into a downpour where the wind blew billowing sheets of rain that chased them to the door.

Ellstrom shook himself like a dog, laid his briefcase on the floor and spread his arms to survey his wet clothes.

'Bloody 'ell,' he cursed. 'So much for the California sunshine.'

Kronziac threw her keys in the rosebud bowl and shimmied out of her raincoat. 'Yeah, the weather's a bit crazy at the moment,' she said, bone dry beneath her waterproof outer garment and faintly amused at Ellstrom's sorry state. 'You want a towel?'

'A Scotch would be more like it,' Ellstrom answered, taking off his blazer and leaving it to drip dry in the hall.

'Wow, nice pad,' he exclaimed, impressed by the pine floors and the huge Aztec alpaca rug in the living room. He glanced enviously over the pine gun cabinet with its rows of clay and wood Meso-American figurines, the wide three-seater soft-fill couch and the hexagonal commode coffee table. His eyes widened further as he saw Kronziac squeezing behind the small counter of the Hawaiian bar beneath its straw hutch.

'FBI agents must do pretty well for themselves,' he commented.

'We do okay, I guess,' Kronziac said, ducking down to find the Scotch bottle. 'But I inherited this house from my aunt a few years ago, as a matter of fact.'

'Must have been her favourite niece,' Ellstrom decided, catching the vista of the bay through the French doors.

'Yeah, I suppose.' Kronziac smiled and took out a couple of glasses from the rack.

'Got your own bar, even.' Ellsrom came over and examined the large blackboard that lay on the floor against the counter and listed in colourful chalks a selection of exotic cocktails.

'An ex-boyfriend of mine built it for me,' Kronziac explained, pouring his whisky.

'Let me guess – a barman, a Hawaiian barman,' said Ellstrom, resting his elbows on the polished counter.

175

'He was a fireman from Milwaukee, actually,' she informed him. 'But I don't know—' she looked around her, at the small thatch of straw above, the rows of bottles and the paper flowers on strings, '—I sometimes think it's a bit too trashy for the house.'

'No,' Ellstrom said judiciously. 'I think it gives the place character.'

Kronziac pushed his whisky over the counter. 'Thanks for being polite about it,' she said with irony. 'How did your lectures go?' she asked, filling her own glass with Sprite.

'USC was fine,' he answered unenthusiastically. 'But the guys at the MSRI in Berkeley were a bit snooty,' he added wearily, consoling himself with a quick sip of Scotch. 'But then again, most of them were physicists.'

Kronziac wasn't going to ask what the difference was. 'So what are your plans for Christmas?' she asked as she went into the kitchen.

'I was thinking of going back to England,' he answered. He walked over to the French doors and looked out at the darkening sea, the lamps on the PCH threading like a beaded string up the coast towards Malibu. Pursing his lips, he relished the sharp taste of Scotch. 'But I reckon I'll just hang out in Boston and take it easy.'

'What time is your flight?' Kronziac shouted from the kitchen, rifling through the contents of her fridge to see what to make for dinner.

Ellstrom suddenly let out a roar from the living room, a shocked, hoarse cry.

Kronziac ran out.

'Fucking 'ell!' he exclaimed, standing to the left of the French doors, 'What is *that*?' He recoiled in disgust.

After a moment of bewilderment Kronziac realized what he was staring at. 'Oh, that's just Hector,' she said, relieved, and flicked a switch, illuminating the cage with an incandescent basking lamp.

Ellstrom looked at her as if she had suddenly sprouted an extra head. 'You keep a *lizard* in the house?'

Kronziac smiled. 'He's in a cage,' she assured him, 'and he's a Jackson's Chameleon.'

'He's a lizard!' Ellstrom insisted and suddenly stepped back from the cage. 'Can he get out?' he asked worriedly.

'Of course not,' replied Kronziac. 'He's no bigger than your hand and even if he did get out he wouldn't harm you.' Though she couldn't really back up this statement as she herself hardly ever let Hector out of the cage and he, thankfully, never showed any signs of wanderlust.

Ellstrom scanned the room, nervously searching the corners in case a snake came coiling out from beneath the couch or a spider suddenly scuttled across the pine floor, heading for his ankles.

'You don't keep any other . . . *things* in the house?' he asked, a look of abhorrence still evident on his features.

'No,' Kronziac told him. She lowered her voice. 'I don't much like having him here either. But it was part of my aunt's will that he could stay here in the house as long as he was alive.'

'How long do they live for?' Ellstrom asked, reluctantly looking back at the chameleon who was now hiding motionless behind the fleshy lobe of a hibiscus leaf, somehow sensing he was the subject of attention.

'Don't know.' Kronziac shrugged and walked off back to the kitchen.

'Do you have time for dinner before your flight?' she asked. 'I was thinking of shepherd's pie – might remind you of home.'

'Sure, that'd be great,' answered Ellstrom. 'So long as we can eat in the kitchen,' he added, following her promptly.

Watching him scoop up the last remnants of pie with an elbow of bread crust, Kronziac commented, 'You certainly like your food.'

Ellstrom mumbled in agreement, his mouth full. 'You don't look like a Nancy,' he said finally, clearing his mouth with a swig of red Venezuelan, a bottle of which he was quickly finishing off all by himself.

Kronziac stuck to her Sprite. 'Don't I?' she smiled.

'Or a Kronziac,' he went on, exaggerating the vowels.

'Oh?' she wondered. 'What should I look like?'

Ellstrom pondered it for a moment. 'I dunno,' he said. 'With

177

a name like that you should be much taller – you know, basket-ball-player size, with a huge hooter, big feet and glasses that look like TV screens. And you should sound like Marge Simpson on steroids.'

Kronziac nodded slowly, not quite sure whether he was complimenting her or not.

'Still, I suppose it's a good name for an FBI *Special* Agent,' he went on.

She hated the way he emphasized the 'special' part – it made the whole thing sound childish. Getting off her stool at the bar where they had decided to have their meal, she began clearing the dishes.

'So is it just domestic terrorists you investigate?' Ellsbom asked.

'Yep, pretty much,' she replied, opening up the dishwasher.

'You don't hear too much about them these days,' he remarked, buttering a last slice of bread. 'Oklahoma was the last big one, I suppose, and that's a good few years ago now.'

'Oh, they're still active,' Kronziac informed him, coming back out of the kitchen with a cafetiere.

'Are they organized?' he asked, slightly incredulous. 'I mean, they seem like just a bunch of rednecks holed up in shacks in the mountains or just a few skinheads with acne problems.'

Kronziac plonked the pot heavily next to him, shaking her head. 'Much more to it than that,' she informed him with a dismissive laugh. 'We watch everyone from the extremist mili-tias, the Klan, the white supremacists right up to the clandesdine right-wing political groups that would like to destabilize the government. We've been chasing The Club for years, a Chicago-based group who have deeply infiltrated the government.'

But this only prompted Ellstrom to ask more questions. 'But what's their aim? Who's their enemy?'

Kronziac laughed again. 'I don't think we've got the time,' she said. 'The extremists such as the Bitteroot Woodsmen from Montana – well, basically they just hate the Federal government and all its institutions – they call it ZOG.'

Ellstrom had difficulty swallowing the last piece of bread. 'ZOG? What the hell is that?'

'Zionist Occupied Government.' She spelled it out. 'They believe the government is a Jewish pawn of the New World Order that seeks to deprive America of its sovereignty.'

'In other words, they're whackos,' Ellstrom concluded.

'*Dangerous* whackos,' Kronziac added, in case he was still taking the idea too lightly. 'You want to take your coffee outside?' she suggested.

'Yeah, sure,' Ellstrom replied as he hopped off the bar stool and moved into the living room.

'What time is your flight to Boston again?' Kronziac called from the kitchen where she was loading the rest of the dinner plates into the dishwasher.

Getting no answer, Kronziac made her way out from the kitchen and found Ellstrom sitting silently on the couch, staring at Hector in the cage. 'You'll never win,' she advised him. 'He can stay motionless without blinking for about two hours.'

Ellstrom shuddered and got up to get his briefcase from the hall.

'Well, I got you some pencils and graph paper,' Kronziac said. 'They're over by the computer.'

'No need,' Ellstrom replied, placing his case on the coffee table. 'I had a bit of free time after my talk today and I worked out the plaintext on the plane down from Frisco. It took about four hours, of course, but . . . here you go.' He took out a sheet of paper with four lines of text scribbled in pencil on it.

Kronziac took it carefully from him, pausing a moment before reading it. 'Does it make any sense?' she asked him warily.

Ellstrom jigged his head and lowered the corners of his mouth. 'Well, it's in English,' was all he would say.

Kronziac spread the paper out on her knees, swept her dark hair back over her ears and began to read.

> like sad clymene flying still embraced in the arms
> of her father eighty above her loved one
> lying on the shores of ragtown

'I had to draw up the Vignere Square of twenty-six different alphabets,' Ellstrom said, trying to impress upon Kronziac that it was no easy task. 'And as the Vignere is impervious to frequency analysis I had to employ the Kasiski, or the Babbage cryptanalysis method, as I prefer to call it.'

But Kronziac wasn't listening to a word he said, just reading the lines over and over again. 'Any idea what it means?' she asked, finally looking up from the sheet of paper. 'Seems to me to be another riddle, like the last one.'

'Mmm . . .' Ellstrom mumbled distantly, taking a long sip of coffee.

Kronziac placed the riddle on the comode table and, using a pen, underlined the words *clymene* and *ragtown*. 'These are our only two definite clues,' she stated, her eyes still fixed on the sheet of paper.

Ellstrom looked around the room for any books. 'Got a dictionary or an encyclopaedia?' he asked.

Kronziac pointed at the bookshelf over the computer desk.

'I'll take "Clymene",' he said, getting up from the couch.

'Well, I guess I'll take "Ragtown", then,' Kronziac said, following him to the computer.

Ellstrom thumbed through a thick encyclopaedia while Kronziac ran a search on the Internet.

'Here we go,' Ellstrom announced, running his hand down the page. 'Clymene . . . clymene dolphin, formerly classified with spinner dolphin, a deep-water dolphin found in the tropical and sub-tropical Atlantic Ocean—'

'I've got 987 matches for "ragtown",' Kronziac chimed as Ellstrom continued down the page of the encyclopaedia. 'Clymene . . . Greek mythology, meaning "famous might", daughter of Oceanus, wife of Iapetus, mother of – well, a whole load of gods . . . also believed to be mother of Deucalion, survivor of the Flood, also married to King Merops of Egypt, married to Helius, mother of Phaeton – either she was a rather liberal woman or there were several Clymenes.'

Kronziac was reading through the web matches. 'I've got a Ragtown in California, a Ragtown in Texas, in Toledo Bend; one in Ohio; a clothing company in New York; there's a Ragtown in Churchill County, Nevada; a Ragtown Road in the Ozarks and one in Black Canyon, Nevada.' She looked up at Ellstrom who was standing over the desk still reading the encyclopaedia.

'Well, I think we'll forget about the dolphin for the moment,' he decided, shaking his head with amused disbelief at what they were doing, 'and concentrate on the Greek goddess.'

'I think I'll narrow it down to the Ragtowns in California and Nevada,' Kronziac decided, turning back to the screen.

Ellstrom placed the riddle next to the entry in the encyclopaedia.

'*Clymene . . . in the arms of her father*,' he recited the line again. 'Well, her father, according to this is – Oceanus.' The thick encyclopaedia nearly fell from his hands as he turned to the index at the back.

'Okay,' said Kronziac, connecting to a tourist site for ghost towns of California. 'Ragtown, off Highway 40, between Steadman and Ludlow – a deserted mining town,' she said. 'Could be it.'

Ellstrom had found another entry. 'Oceanus: winding stream of water covering the world, together with his wife – mother of our dear Clymene, presumably,' he remarked. 'With his wife Tethys, he produced the river of the world and the three thousand ocean nymphs – busy chap,' he added breezily.

'Next is Ragtown in Churchill County, Nevada, off US Highway 95, along the Carson River, part of the California Gold Rush trail of the 1850s,' Kronziac announced.

'That sounds even better,' said Ellstrom, leaning over her shoulder.

'Why?' Kronziac asked, looking closely at the information on screen in case she had missed something.

'Well.' Ellstrom began to explain. 'Clymene is *flying still embraced in the arms of her father*.'

Kronziac gave him a questioning look.

'*Embraced in the arms of her father*?' He repeated the line.

Kronziac began nodding slowly, catching on. 'The river.'

'Could be,' Ellstrom agreed.

Turning back to the computer screen, Kronziac clicked on the next link. 'Could also be this one,' she noted. 'Ragtown in Black Canyon, Nevada, on the banks of the Colorado River. A town sited for the workers on the Hoover Dam in the 1930s.'

Casting his gaze over the riddle once more, Ellstrom tried to find another clue that might point them in the direction of one particular Ragtown. *Eighty above her loved one lying on the shores of Ragtown . . .'*

'Eighty what?' Kronziac wondered. 'Eighty miles, eighty feet – she's flying eighty feet above Ragtown?' She tried to make sense of it, turning swiftly around to Ellstrom who was still studying the riddle. 'What time is your flight?'

Ellstrom looked up from the sheet of paper, then glanced at his watch. He began smiling. 'In about three minutes,' he said slowly.

'I'm sorry,' Kronziac said. 'It's my fault for keeping you here.'

'Yes, it is,' Ellstrom said. But he was still smiling. 'Now you've got me all caught up with this nonsense.'

Kronziac wasn't sure what to say. 'You're . . . you're more than welcome to stay the night – if you want,' she suggested, hoping she wasn't blushing. It had been a long time since a man other than Phillips had stayed the night.

'You sure?' Ellstrom asked. 'I can sleep on the couch.' His resolve seemed to weaken as he glanced in the direction of Hector who was dozing on the floor of his cage.

'Not at all – I'll make up the spare room,' Kronziac said emphatically. She got up from the desk. 'I'll drop you at the airport first thing on my way.'

'On your way where?' Ellstrom asked, closing the encyclopaedia.

'To the Hoover Dam,' Kronziac replied sharply and picked up the empty cups on her way out of the room. 'You wanna get your stuff from the car?' she said.

2434 ABRAMAR, PACIFIC PALISADES, CA

Golden rectangles of sunlight slanted across the pine floor and refracted up the light-coloured stucco walls. Kronziac paused at the kitchen window to watch a large naval ship crawl across the bay like an ugly animal sloping home, sailboats like white moths flurrying out of its way.

Sipping on her pineapple juice she tipped half a cup of mealworm, chopped cricket and fruitfly into a small dish.

'Jesus! What's that?' Ellstrom snorted, trying to suffocate a yawn as he traipsed wearily in his bare feet from the spare room.

'Breakfast,' Kronziac declared happily, showing him the dried-insect goulash. 'For Hector,' she added after a pause that caused Ellstrom's face to contort agonizedly, as if he was about to get sick.

'Christ.' He shook his head and moved to the French doors in the living room, blinking in the bright light.

'It's a beautiful day,' remarked Kronziac, opening the corner of Hector's cage and placing the dish inside.

'The view's even better in daylight,' said Ellstrom, impressed, 'and I didn't realize you had such a nice garden.'

Kronziac joined him at the French doors. 'You should see it in summer,' she said proudly. 'There's not too much colour now but I like the varying greens of the agave and yucca. Want anything for breakfast?'

Another yawn stretched Ellstrom's face wide. 'I'd better have a black coffee,' he said sleepily. 'But first, I think I'll take a shower – if that's okay?'

'Sure,' Kronziac said. 'You'll find fresh towels in the linen closet, next to the bathroom.'

Kronziac was about to fill the kettle when she remembered that opening the faucet in the kitchen lowered the water pressure in the bathroom and thus increased the water's temperature, usually scalding the person in the shower.

She put the kettle down and checked the bagels browning

under the grill. She started when someone knocked loudly on the front door.

Kronziac was surprised to find Phillips standing there, still hammering on the knocker as she opened the door.

'Morning,' he sang and held up a bag of fresh bagels.

'Hi, Phillips,' she said, opening the door for him. 'Maggie not with you?'

'Nah,' he answered, making quickly for the kitchen. 'Sedley's got her busy doing up some end-of-year reports.'

'How did you escape?' Kronziac asked.

'Oh, he asked me to do a report on NCP enactment for the Attorney's office last week.'

'And you gave him a real stinker,' Kronziac said, knowing Phillips's total inability to produce a readable report or any other official paperwork.

'Worst he ever saw,' he declared proudly, 'He won't make that mistake again.'

As they entered the kitchen, Phillips shouted a quick greeting to Hector who was greedily feeding on his breakfast of mealworm and insects.

'Looks like I just caught you in time,' said Phillips, sniffing the bagels lightly toasting under the grill. 'Never mind that packet stuff,' he admonished and turned off the oven.

'Any news on the Woodsmen?' Kronziac asked cautiously, having managed lately not to think about the threat to her life.

Phillips shook his head. 'Jones up in Twin Falls has got them under constant surveillance. They can't so much as take a crap in the woods without us knowing.'

'Any leads on Jimmy Soton's death?' she asked.

Phillips shook his head. 'ME's report stated he suffered a stab wound, was dragged over ground and then – well, you know the rest,' he said. 'There wasn't exactly that much of him left after the gators had done their stuff.'

'Any idea of the type of blade?' Kronziac asked quickly, trying to take her mind off the memory of Jimmy Soton being devoured in front of her eyes.

'Large, eighteen to ten-inch, serrated,' he confirmed. 'A typical hunter's knife.'

'The Woodsmen, all right,' Kronziac concluded quietly to herself. 'Somehow Lucas Crebbs's men were in LA, probably slipped the FBI surveillance in Montana.'

'And the guys at Q-docs couldn't find anything on the leaflet with your . . . death threat,' Phillips went on, picking up the kettle. He was about to turn on the tap when Kronziac shouted at him.

'Hold it!'

'What?' Phillips yelped, turning around. 'I was just gonna make the coffee.' A worried expression spread across his features. 'Is there someone in the shower?' he asked quietly.

For some reason Kronziac felt guilty, or a little awkward at least. 'Yeah, I have a guest,' she said, sounding as if it was a confession.

'Should I leave?' Phillips wondered.

'Jesus! Of course not!' Kronziac barked, annoyed with him. She knew Phillips always looked out for her, like a big brother, and she was ever mindful of making sure he knew that was how she saw him – and as nothing more. He had a string of beautiful, mostly blonde girlfriends, leggy, giggly types he met in bars. But she always suspected he had a long-standing soft spot for her.

'Who is it?' he asked, trying to be nonchalant. 'If you don't mind me asking.'

As if on cue Ellstrom appeared at the doorway, a long white bath towel around his waist. He was drying his hair with one of Kronziac's colourful beach towels 'Good morning,' he said casually, seeing Phillips.

'Hello,' Phillips replied with a transparent smile.

Kronziac introduced the stranger. 'This is James Ellstrom,' she said. 'Professor James Ellstrom.'

Phillips raised an eyebrow. This guy was a professor? 'Pleased to meet you.' Phillips extended his hand. 'John Phillips – I, er . . . work with Kronziac.'

'Another special agent?' Ellstrom smirked as he shook hands.

'You English, huh?' asked Phillips, noting the accent.

'Yep.' Ellstrom smiled.

'Great.' Phillips nodded, a sarcastic grin on his face.

Kronziac grabbed the kettle and banged it under the tap. 'Breakfast will be ready in a couple of minutes,' she said loudly, trying to break the awkwardness. 'Hope you like bagels?'

Ellstrom nodded. 'Yeah, sure, sounds great.' He began stepping backwards, still drying his hair. 'I'll just go and get dressed.'

'Good idea,' Phillips suggested smartly.

Ellstrom stopped for a moment, not quite sure if he'd heard Phillips right. 'And I'll ring the airport to see what time the next flight to Boston is.'

'Okay,' Phillips said, encouraging Ellstrom to do just that.

'You can use the phone in my room,' Kronziac told him, plugging in the kettle.

Phillips watched as Ellstrom disappeared down the hall into Kronziac's room. 'You do know you've got a naked guy in your room?' he said.

'Yeah. So?' Kronziac answered.

'What's he doing here, anyway?'

'Helping me with the—' Kronziac hesitated '—with the crypto,' she said, mildly embarrassed.

'The crypto?' Phillips laughed.

'Yes,' she said indignantly. 'The cryptogram we got from the Vegas PD. Ellstrom's a math professor – a number theorist.'

This made Phillips laugh even more. 'A math teacher!' he said condescendingly.

'He's a professor at Harvard University,' Kronziac corrected him as she took out the bagels and placed them on a large plate. 'He stayed the night because he missed his plane back to Boston,' she continued, hating having to explain herself.

Phillips took a bite out of his bagel and leaned against the counter top.

'Got any other news for me?' Kronziac asked, hoping to change the subject.

'Oh yeah, almost forgot,' he replied, acting all cool. 'The real reason I called over—'

'What is it?' Kronziac asked as Phillips took something out of his pocket. 'My Christmas present?'

Phillips grinned. 'Close,' he said and held up another piece of paper in front of her. 'E-mail from our detective friend in Vegas.'

She grabbed it out of Phillips's hand as Ellstrom re-entered the kitchen, fully dressed.

'I'm starving,' he exclaimed, smelling the fresh bagels.

'What time's your flight, Professor?' Phillips asked.

'The next available seat direct to Logan is tonight at a quarter past nine,' Ellstrom said, pinching a bagel between his fingers. 'The earlier flights are all booked out.'

'Christmas rush, I guess,' said Phillips impassively and then quickly looked at his watch.

'Speaking of which, I gotta hustle,' he said and made to leave.

'You won't stay?' Kronziac asked, looking up from the e-mail printout. 'For your own bagels?'

'You enjoy 'em,' Phillips smiled.

'I'll walk you out,' Kronziac suggested, leading him out of the kitchen.

'See ya, man!' Ellstrom shouted after him and helped himself to coffee.

As they reached the front door Kronziac opened the door for Phillips.

'You sure it's wise, having this guy here?' he asked her, keeping his voice low.

'Don't worry,' Kronziac replied wearily. 'He's not going to try anything.'

'That's not what I meant,' he corrected her. 'He's in danger staying here. Remember, Lucas Crebbs and the Woodsmen probably have a contract out on you – and they know where you live.'

Kronziac hadn't thought about it that way. Phillips was right.

'He'll be leaving today.' She tried to pass it off.

'Whatever you say.' Phillips shook his head doubtfully. 'Stay outta trouble,' he shouted over his shoulder as he walked to his car in the driveway.

Kronziac leaned against the door after closing it and in the cooler light of the hall she took out the e-mail Phillips had given her.

Ellstrom was calling from the kitchen, asking where she kept the maple syrup, as she began reading the initial police report on Ellen Holby's disappearance – no signs of forced entry, no immediately discernible traces of a struggle or abduction.

VISITORS CENTER, HOOVER DAM, NEVADA WING

Ellstrom squirmed uncomfortably in his shirt, which was stuck to his back with perspiration.

'I can't believe it's only three days to Christmas. It's so bloody hot!' he groaned as Kronziac drove the Explorer onto the third floor of the parking garage. 'It's probably snowing in Boston,' he added, still amazed at the heat.

'It's seventy-nine degrees,' Kronziac informed him, glancing at the temperature readout on the dash. Dressed in shorts and a *Surf Diva* T-shirt under a sleeveless sailing fleece, she had enjoyed the drive from LA through the warm bowl of the Mojave Desert to Nevada.

'What's that in English money?' Ellstrom asked, flicking a dimple of sweat from his hairline. 'Twenty, twenty-two degrees Celsius?'

'About twenty-six,' Kronziac figured. 'You didn't have to come,' she reminded him as she pulled the car into an empty spot.

'And do what instead?' he retorted crankily. 'Stay in your place and watch that reptile of yours flicking his tongue at me? No, thank you. So long as I'm back in time for my flight I might as well see a bit of this great country of yours.'

'Well, come on – let's get a move on,' Kronziac urged impatiently, realizing it was almost two in the afternoon already.

But before they got out of the car Ellstrom paused, staying in his seat. 'What if we find something here?' he asked, suddenly remembering the real purpose of their journey. 'I mean, what if we find this—' he instinctively lowered his voice '—this missing old lady.'

Kronziac just held her door open. 'Chances are we won't find anything at all,' she said dismissively. 'It's a long shot that we're even in the right place.'

Another car parked close by and three kids rushed for the exit, shouting for their parents to hurry up.

'At least you'll get to see one of the greatest pieces of engineering in the world,' she told Ellstrom, evading the possibly macabre reason for their day trip to the dam.

Ellstrom relented, jumped out of the car and immediately noticed a rack of pamphlets pinned to the wall. 'I'll grab one of these,' he said, plucking a self-guided-tour booklet from the rack.

They headed out of the garage to the escalators. Ellstrom's mood improved as the large metal towers of the dam's crane system came into view.

'Largest cableway in the world, it says here,' he observed gleefully, looking at the massive cables slung like giant telegraph wires across the canyon. Like an excited child, Ellstrom rushed to join a group of tourists at the rubble-masonry retaining wall at the near edge of the canyon.

'Holy shit!' he gasped as he looked out over the vast 1,200-foot gulf of Black Canyon, its rugged volcanic flanks plummeting nearly a thousand feet to the narrow valley floor where the mighty Colorado flowed gently, like a stream, having been tamed by the dam.

Kronziac smiled to herself as Ellstrom stood, mouth agape and one hand shielding his eyes against the bright light.

'And there she is,' he said, with quiet awe in his tone, as he panned left and caught the bright white sweep of the dam, curving in a smooth arc of six million tons of concrete wedged between the parched grey cliffs of rock. On top of the dam, two lines of cars slid past each other in opposite directions, their windshields sparkling like flashguns in the sunlight.

'Come on,' Kronziac urged, tugging his shirt. 'We've got to find Ragtown, remember.'

Reluctantly, Ellstrom broke away from the canyon observation point and they made their way up the escalators towards the safety island. Here they could see the glimmering expanse of Lake Mead shored behind the dam, a giant mirror of deep jade, shimmering in patches when the light wind touched its surface.

Ellstrom stumbled as he climbed the steps. He couldn't take his eyes off the massive dam. It was indescribably huge, a giant stopper holding back an inland sea.

'We'll ask this guy,' Kronziac decided, pointing at a tour guide from the Bureau of Reclamation who was wearing a bright red Santa's hat and talking to a huddle of tourists around the dam's art-deco monument.

Set in against the rock, a 140-foot flagpole rose between two bronze angel-like figures sitting with vertically raised wings on a base of polished coal-black diorite.

'Their wings are thirty feet high,' the tour guide said loudly, 'and made of four tons of statuary bronze, designed by the sculptor Oskar Hansen to symbolize the power of man.'

Some people were rubbing the feet of the angels, one old guy laughing that it would bring him luck at the casino in Vegas that night.

The tour guide continued his talk as Kronziac edged closer in the hope of asking him where Ragtown was.

'If you look down on the floor—' the guide directed his audience and addressed them in a deadpan, rehearsed tone of voice '—you will notice the star map embedded in the terrazzo. The brass discs denote the exact location of the brightest stars visible in the heavens on the thirtieth of September, 1935, the day President Roosevelt dedicated the dam.'

Obviously in a hurry and probably on his umpteenth tour of the day, the guide looked at his watch and prompted his party to follow him away from the monument.

'Okay, ladies and gentlemen,' he called to them. 'We'll now move on to the Old Exhibit Building and the Nevada Spillway.'

As he marched off Kronziac took her chance and caught up with him. 'Excuse me!' She stopped him. 'I'm sorry, but I'm looking for a particular place that I believe is near the dam.'

'What's it called?' he asked, swinging the white tassle of his Santa hat over his shoulder.

'Ragtown,' Kronziac answered, eliciting a smile from the tour guide.

'Ragtown?'

'Yes,' she replied, hoping he had heard of it, 'an old encampment for the dam workers in the 1930s, I think.'

'Yeah, I've heard of it,' he said, still smiling.

Kronziac gestured at Ellstrom who had caught up with them.

'We just wanted to see what it looks like now,' she explained, trying to make out that she and Ellstrom were just a couple on a day out.

'Any idea how we get there?' asked Ellstrom hopefully.

'Sure.' The tour guide grinned, revelling in some private joke. 'If you've got a submarine,' he added.

'What?' Kronziac cried, not finding it funny.

'You're quite right,' the tour guide went on. 'Ragtown *was* a workers' camp but when the dam was finally built the town was flooded by the reservoir – now it lies about 500 feet under the lake's surface.'

Ellstrom came closer to Kronziac, nudging her in the side. 'Remember,' he whispered, 'the riddle said she is *flying still* over Ragtown – probably means she's *floating* over the town.'

The tour guide's smile seemed to fade and his expression changed to one of bemusement at Ellstrom's hushed mutterings.

'Can we get there by boat?' Kronziac suddenly asked.

'I suppose,' the guide replied hesitantly. 'It's about a mile upstream from the dam in Black Canyon.' He thought about it for a moment. 'Rich Crandal,' he said suddenly and decisively.

'Who?' Kronziac asked.

'Crandal's Dive Shack,' the guide replied. 'A boat and dive hire place over in Kingman Wash. He's your man,' he enthused. 'Knows a lot of the history of the dam and the lake . . . yeah, go talk to him.'

By now a few of the other tourists had gathered around, thinking they might have been missing something.

'How do we get there?' Kronziac asked.

'Go across to the Arizona side, follow the highway for a couple of miles, look out for the Kingman Wash Launch and take the turn-off. You'll find him down the right side of the beach. Can't miss him – beat-up trailer,' he added.

Kronziac smiled. 'Thanks,' she said. 'You've been very helpful.'

'Sure.' The tour guide smiled back. Kronziac knew he thought they were nuts but she didn't care. She had other problems now. The tour guide walked off down the steps, followed by his gang of chattering day-trippers.

'All right, let's get back to the car,' Kronziac mumbled, heading back towards the Visitors Centre.

Ellstrom followed her, tripping along happily.

'What are you smiling about?' she asked him.

'We get to drive across the dam,' he beamed and began reading the information pamphlet again.

'There's enough cement in this thing to build a two-lane highway from San Francisco to New York,' Ellstrom read out as they followed a slow line of cars across the road that swept in a broad band of asphalt along the top of the giant arch-gravity dam.

He pointed to the left at two towers that jutted from the lake like huge, louvred lighthouses.

'The Nevada intakes.' Ellstrom quoted from his tour booklet. 'Rising 395 feet from the side of the canyon wall.'

'Come on,' Kronziac grunted impatiently as the line of cars crept slowly towards the other side of the dam, their drivers trying to peer over the retaining barriers at the lake.

'Lake Mead!' Ellstrom announced like a carnival crier. 'The largest man-made lake in America, 247 square miles, enough to cover the state of Pennsylvania in a foot of water.'

He craned his head over Kronziac's shoulders to have a better look at the lake. It spread like a vast green stain, filling the jagged inlets and rock ledges of Boulder Basin, the surface creased with the white-feathered scars of boat-wakes and jet-ski trails.

'Just coming into Arizona,' Ellstrom pronounced, seeing the brass plaque in the centre of the dam that marked the border and commemorated the dam as one of the greatest feats of engineering in the history of mankind.

'Change your watches!' he cried. 'We're on Mountain Time now.'

'Well, at least the traffic's a bit better,' Kronziac remarked with relief as the cars in front speeded up, heading past the Arizona intake towers and off the dam towards the mountains.

A few minutes later, as they followed the road east around

the volcanic outcrops, Kronziac found the National Park Service sign for the Kingman Wash Launch and swerved the Explorer left off the highway onto the clay-red dirt road.

'A bit like Mars,' Ellstrom commented as the car bounded down the track through a rocky landscape of low, red, sandy hillocks, clothed sparsely in rough cresote and brittlebush.

'And they must be the Martians,' Kronziac observed caustically as they passed a troupe of holidaymakers, suburban families scooping lunch from Tupperware under the awnings of their gleaming RVs.

The lake came into view again as they scudded down the track and onto the beach of a shallow cove. A few other cars and campers lined the shore, kids paddling noisily in the water as a small cruiser grumbled slowly past the shoreline.

'Ain't exactly Miami Beach,' remarked Kronziac, looking around for a place to stop.

'Down that way to the right,' Ellstrom instructed her, seeing a small dry plank of wood, trimmed at one end to a point and with the words 'Crandal's Dive Shack' burned onto it, nailed to a post.

'That must be it,' Kronziac said, lips pursed, not particularly impressed by the fact that Crandal's boat and dive-equipment hire concern was headquartered in a 'shack'.

The car bumped down the gravel, heading towards a trailer hitched to a decidedly neglected pick-up truck. A dull tin lean-to canopy was hung with wetsuits and masks, and a six-pack of air tanks huddled by the back wheels.

As the car halted with a crunch on the loose dirt and shingle behind the trailer, Ellstrom watched a powerful speedboat skip by the shore, bounding over the dark iron-blue surface, dragging the rigid, slanted figure of a water-skier behind, straining tautly against the tether through a fantail of spray.

'Doesn't seem like a safe place for diving,' he commented as they got out.

They found Rich Crandal sitting in a wicker deckchair propped against the sun-bleached side of his pick-up. In his sixties, Crandal had a face that was red-brown, rough and weather-worn, shielded by a frayed red fishing cap. Talking to a couple of young guys, their wetsuits rolled to the waist, he spoke with a hard, clipped voice and chewed gum thickly like it was a wad of tobacco.

'Looks like an old Forty-niner,' Kronziac observed quietly as they walked up to Crandal.

'Merry Christmas, folks,' he saluted them, tipping his hat at Kronziac.

'Hello.' She smiled. 'Rich Crandal?'

''Fraid so.' He grinned broadly. 'Come to do a bit of diving?'

'Maybe,' Kronziac said as the two young guys said goodbye and coolly sloped off, dragging a windsurf board up the pebbled beach.

'Maybe?' Crandal said back, half smiling, half squinting in the light, trying to figure out these two. A pretty-looking woman, sportily dressed, right enough – but the guy with her, tall, pale and dressed in slacks with a white shirt and loafers, he didn't seem like a water man.

'You guys ain't from the Department of the Interior, are you?' he asked, suddenly a little concerned.

'No,' Kronziac answered with a reassuring smile.

'No,' Ellstrom echoed and nodded in his companion's direction. 'She's with the FBI.'

Crandal stood up slowly as Kronziac slung a sharp look at Ellstrom.

'FBI?' said Crandal, obviously uncomfortable.

'Look, it's nothing,' Kronziac replied, trying to laugh it off as best she could. 'I'm just doing some background research.'

Crandal was now looking at Ellstrom. 'You too?'

By the smile that was beginning to crease the corners of Ellstrom's mouth Kronziac was afraid he was going to say yes.

'He's just a friend,' she said sharply and quickly moved on. 'One of the guides up at the dam said you were an authority on the lake and the local history. The best around,' she added, hoping the flattery would relax him, get him on side.

It worked.

'Could be, I guess.' He grinned modestly. 'My dad was a young engineer in the construction.'

'Wow,' Ellstrom cooed. 'Excellent.'

'Well,' Kronziac began, but not sure where to start. 'We're looking for a place called Ragtown.'

The mention of the name made Crandal's face light up, bunching his wrinkles into a broad smile.

'Well, Ragtown's kinda hard to see these days,' he said.

'I know,' said Kronziac. 'It's now under water, isn't it?'

'About 450 to 500 feet below the surface, depending on the intake up at the dam,' Crandal confirmed.

'Do you know its exact location?' asked Ellstrom.

This seemed to amuse the old guy even more.

'Well, it's a town, covered a good few acres in its day.'

'Can you get us over it?' Kronziac wondered.

'Yeah, sure, it's about a mile, mile and a half upstream from the dam.'

'Can you take us there now?' Kronziac know she had to push, seize the momentum.

Crandal seemed to search for a reason to say no but couldn't really find any.

'Sure, why not?' He shrugged. 'But we come fifty dollars an hour,' he added, pointing at a small white diving launch, moored near the shore.

Ellstrom turned to Kronziac. 'You got fifty bucks?'

She nodded.

'Good,' Crandal butted in. 'In advance, please.'

Crandal's boat bobbed, slapping the surface of the lake as they accelerated away from the shore. Beneath them giant boulders lay in the shallow depths like pebbles in a fountain.

'What's the FBI doing, trying to find a dead sunken ol' town, anyhow?' Crandal shouted, twirling the wheel and banking the boat left to follow the line of the shore.

Kronziac glanced at Ellstrom who was clinging on to the side of the boat as the seventy-horsepower outboard bit into the water and the craft rode high in the water.

'Ah, it's just a routine background check on some historic information,' she answered vaguely. She could see Crandal smiling to himself but he didn't ask any more questions.

It was hard to see the edges of the lake as a fine screen of sun haze slowly drew itself across the vast basin. Only the near shoreline remained distinct, with its rugged outcrops steadily climbing to the black-grey andesite cliffs of Black Canyon.

'How will you know when we get there?' Ellstrom shouted over the throbbing anger of the engine.

'I know the lake like the back of my hand,' Crandal replied. Then he pointed at a rack of navigation equipment on a shelf in the cab over the helm – a GPS read-out, a depth-finder and the green line of a sonar, sweeping from side to side like a windscreen wiper drawing patches of green on the small monitor.

'These will also help.' Crandal grinned. 'We're about two miles from the dam now,' he shouted, throttling back as they rounded the corner of the cliffs and the sandy white line of the dam wall came into view in the distance, the intake towers standing like lanterns.

Ellstrom noticed another speedboat clipping across the water not far behind them, vaulting over their wake.

'How near the dam are we going?' Kronziac asked, watching the line of the dam spanning the gaping mouth of the canyon downstream.

'Not much nearer,' said Crandal, cutting the engine. The boat settled on the water, drifting to a stop just before the jaws of the canyon narrowed. Kronziac and Ellstrom couldn't help looking in awe at the towering walls of rock, frighteningly beautiful.

'Welcome to Ragtown,' Crandal announced, waving his hand over the wide body of water behind them. '500 feet below and hasn't seen the light of day since 1935.'

'It's underneath us right now?' Kronziac asked, wanting to make sure.

'Yep,' Crandal confirmed. 'Obviously, you can't see anything of it from the surface – and if you went down you wouldn't see much, either.'

'Water's washed it all away, I suppose,' said Ellstrom, looking over the side into the bottomless depths.

'Thousands of workers lived there, mostly in tents,' said Crandal. 'It was a hell of a place, by all accounts. People died in the heat out here before they moved the workers to Boulder City.'

Ellstrom tried to imagine the canyon and the basin emptied of its water and what it must have been like here all those years ago in the baking heat of the Nevada summer.

'Five thousand men worked at one time building the dam,' Crandal went on, 'and eighty-nine of the poor souls lost their lives, falling off the canyon walls, in explosions and other accidents . . . "They died to make the desert bloom",' he said quietly, reciting a line from the bronze commemoration plaque on the monument at the dam.

As Crandal seemed to drift off down memory lane Ellstrom came closer to Kronziac, taking out a scribbled copy of the riddle from his shirt pocket.

'*Eighty above her loved one lying on the shores of Ragtown,*' he read out the last line quietly so Crandal couldn't hear. 'Well, there's Ragtown,' he pointed at the wavering blue water beneath them. 'So what do we do now? If she's eighty feet above Ragtown, then she's about 400 feet below us.'

Kronziac thought about it for a moment, staring at the piece of paper that shook in the light breeze. 'It says she's eighty above her *loved one* on the *shores* of Ragtown – so we've gotta find out who her loved one was.'

'Take your pick,' Ellstrom said as he took out another scrap of paper with the information he'd got from the encyclopaedia about the Greek goddess Clymene.

'Everything okay with you folks?' Crandal called from the bow.

'Yeah, we're fine,' Ellstrom replied.

'Do many people come up around this part of the lake?' Kronziac shouted back.

Crandal pulled at his cap. 'Well,' he began thoughtfully, 'as you can see, it's pretty quiet here now. It's not the best place for boating or windsurfing. Though some hotheads go wherever they want,' he added, obviously hating the intrusion of some of the more careless water users.

'What about divers?' Kronziac asked.

Crandal seemed doubtful, shaking his head. 'Well, there's

Diver's Cave, up nearer the dam – quite a good site for those with cave certification but it's a bit cold this time of the year . . . Yeah, that's about it around here,' he concluded. 'There are more popular sites over in Calville and Hemenway where there's a sunken boat in about fifty feet of water, much more accessible than the one here.'

Kronziac and Ellstrom looked at each other.

'What one here?' Ellstrom asked.

'It's just an old maintenance barge that went down in the early nineties,' Crandal said defensively. 'She lies in about eight metres of water on a ledge, a little beyond recreational diving to my mind.'

He began smiling. 'Nobody was lost or anything,' he assured them. 'But I knew the skipper of the *Iapetus*.' His smile turned to a laugh. 'He couldn't navigate his way around a bath.'

Ellstrom moved swiftly up the boat to Crandal. 'What did you say?' he hissed, shocking both Kronziac and the old man.

'Er – I said he wasn't much of a navigator,' Crandal confessed, afraid that Ellstrom was somehow related to the captain of the sunken barge.

'No, the name of the boat – what name did you say?' Ellstrom desperately wanted to know.

'The *Iapetus*,' Crandal said quietly, taken aback by Ellstrom's intensity.

Grabbing Kronziac by the arm, Ellstrom brought her to the back of the boat, leaving Crandal to wonder if he should take these two strange people back to the shore.

'What the hell is wrong with you?' Kronziac asked, puzzled by his sudden excitement over the name of the boat.

'Iapetus was Clymene's husband,' he informed her. 'Her *loved one.*'

Kronziac grabbed the scrap of paper from him as if to read it but her mind was racing over the possibilities. Again it was all too coincidental.

'Where is it?' she shouted at Crandal.

'What?' he replied, dreading what they were going to ask him to do next.

'The wreck,' Ellstrom said impatiently. 'Can you take us to

the *Iapetus*? We'll pay you for another hour's time,' he added enticingly.

Kronziac wasn't sure if she had another fifty dollars on her to back up Ellstrom's promise but she kept her mouth shut for the moment.

'Okay.' Crandal relented, shaking his head and turned the key in the ignition. The engine snarled into life.

'It's just around this corner of rock anyway,' he said. 'Should only take a couple of minutes.'

As the boat picked up speed and ploughed through the water, part of Kronziac reminded her that she really shouldn't be doing this, that she should hand over all details to the Vegas detectives investigating Ellen Holby's disappearance. But her doubts were banished when Crandal shouted and pointed to a small yellow buoy in the water about twenty feet from the canyon wall on the left side of the channel, chained to the rock.

'That's the wreck buoy,' he said, throttling back again, leaving the boat to drift gently close to the yellow ball under the dark overhanging rock.

Crandal looked up at the depth-finder tracing a rough contour of the lake beneath them. 'She's in about eighty metres of water below us now,' he confirmed.

Ellstrom shot Kronziac a knowing glance. They both moved to the side of the boat and peered into the water, its depths steely black in the shadow of the canyon wall.

Crandal watched them with curious interest. 'You won't see her,' he advised them and for a moment Kronziac thought he was referring to the missing old woman.

'Too far down,' Crandal said, 'and there's quite a bit of silt build-up.'

Kronziac whispered to Ellstrom. 'If the body is floating eighty metres above the wreck,' she said, referring to the riddle, 'then she should be on or near the surface. But I can't see a damn thing.'

Ellstrom nodded, gazing intently at the water around them.

Crandal applied engine power for a moment to keep station with the buoy since the current was trying to pull the boat downstream.

'I'm gonna take a look,' Kronziac decided, prompting Ellstrom to turn to her in stark surprise.

'What are you doing?'

'What does it look like?' she replied sharply, sitting against the side-rail and untying the laces on her trainers. 'We can't come all this way out here and not get a closer look.'

Watching from the helm, Crandal warned her. 'This ain't the middle of summer, Miss – water temp's only about fifty and it's dark down there.'

'I won't be too long in,' Kronziac assured them, pulling off her fleece top and handing it to Ellstrom.

'Are you sure?' he said, watching her helplessly.

'I'm a good swimmer,' she replied and stepped onto the taffrail, diving in immediately before she could change her mind.

The water thundered in her ears as she pierced the surface and entered the cold darkness of the lake. Her chest muscles tightened, gripping her ribs as the sudden change of temperature made her lungs gasp, forcing her to expel a gulp of air bubbles. Visibility was about ten to twenty feet, beyond which the dim light faded into a gloomy underwater cloud. She held on to the dark brown chain of the buoy with one hand and circled around it, waving her legs to propel herself. But she still couldn't see anything, just the chain trailing to its anchor on the rock. With her lungs straining in her ribcage she burst up to the surface, her body shaking for air.

'Any sign?' Ellstrom shouted, his face leaning down from the boat.

All Kronziac could do was shake her head. She had no breath for words. She reached up to him and he helped her aboard where Crandal wrapped a towel around her dripping shoulders.

'Are you two looking for treasure or something?' he asked, getting a little annoyed that they weren't telling him what this was all about.

Ellstrom was about to spin some yarn about them looking for something lost off a boat. But Kronziac decided to answer Crandal directly once she'd she regained her breath.

'Mr Crandal, we have reason to believe that a missing woman from Las Vegas may have been dumped in the lake here.'

Crandal's eyes narrowed, an expression of incredulity on his face. 'You're looking for a body?'

'Yes,' said Kronziac. 'There's a big chance we won't find anything at all, but we have to try.'

Crandal retreated a couple of steps. 'You're shitting me.'

'No shit,' Kronziac answered Crandal, shaking her head.

Ellstrom stood up, examining the water around them. 'Are we moving?'

'Yeah,' Crandal answered, unconcerned. 'A little.'

'Downstream, right?' Ellstrom figured.

'That's the way a river flows,' Crandal informed him, as if talking to an imbecile.

Quickly taking out one of his scraps of paper, Ellstrom searched the pockets of his trousers for something else. 'You got something to write with?' he asked Kronziac.

She too looked at him as if he was an imbecile. 'I've just come out of the water,' she said, still just dressed in her shorts and wet T-shirt.

Ellstrom turned to Crandal who threw his gaze up to heaven and produced a pencil from the breast pocket of his check shirt.

Placing the paper on the transom at the stern, Ellstrom began drawing a vertical line. 'Okay, we have a depth of eighty metres,' he announced. 'Now, Agent Kronziac, would a human body in the water be lying at the bottom or would it be floating?'

'Depends on how long it's been in there,' Kronziac retorted tartly, not fully appreciating Ellstrom's little exercise. 'But I reckon at this stage it would be floating on the surface.'

'Right,' Ellstrom nodded. 'Well, taking into consideration the forces of buoyancy and the water current the body should be resting in a position around here.' From the bottom point of the first line he began to draw another line of the same length at an angle.

'So if we vector this at forty-five degrees then she should be lying here.' He tapped the end point of the diagonal line with the top of the pencil. 'And since we know this line is also eighty metres and we know the angle, we can use Pythagoras's Theorem to find the length of the other side of the triangle and thus the distance from the *Iapetus*. We can also calculate the depth at which she lies.'

'How are we going to do that?' Crandal asked, intrigued.

But Ellstrom was already scribbling and mumbling figures to himself. 'Reduce to lowest factor . . . eight squared . . . sixty-four . . . other sides of equal length . . . therefore . . . two-X squared equals sixty-four . . . X squared equals thirty-two . . . square root of thirty-two . . .'

Kronziac was about to say something but Ellstrom put up his hand and closed his eyes to stop her as if he was listening to a favourite piece of classical music. He opened his eyes.

'Fifty-six point five metres,' he announced with hushed triumph, then closed his eyes for another little performance. 'And a depth of twenty-three point five,' he said and turned again to Crandal. 'You keep any charts?'

'Nope,' Crandal replied.

'Right,' Ellstrom nodded. 'You know the place like the back of your hand.'

'No, smartass,' Crandal rebutted and pointed at the Nav rack. 'Got a navigation computer, with distance measuring equipment an' all.'

Ellstrom smiled demurely. 'Excellent. Can you take us fifty-six metres downstream from the buoy, please?'

'I guess.' Crandal shrugged.

'Hold on.' Kronziac spoke up, having dried herself off and put her fleece on again. 'If she's, what, twenty-three metres down, then how—'

I can't dive,' Ellstrom interrupted, knowing what she was going to ask.

Kronziac turned to Crandal who moved swiftly to the navigation equipment.

'Sorry, honey, this ain't none of my business. And besides, I gave up blowing bubbles in the blue over ten years ago when the ol' ticker went US on me on a reef down in the Keys.' He started nodding to himself. 'I took Uncle Neptune's warning note and I've stayed dry-side since.'

'Fuck this.' Kronziac cursed under her breath and unzipped her fleece again.

'You certed?' Crandal asked.

'Basic open-water,' she confirmed.

'Okay.' Crandal moved fore to a locker under the bow. Stowed inside were three silver oxygen tanks and the black folds of some wetsuits. 'I've got an aluminium 80-tank with K valves, a ScubaMax RU-20 multi-stage reg, standard fins, mask and snorkel, full wet-skin and—' he held up a bright luminous vest '—a nice pink buoyancy jacket for the lady.' He smiled sweetly.

'Fine,' Kronziac said blankly and took the wetsuit from him.

'It's getting late,' Ellstrom observed as the launch chugged slowly downstream towards the dam. While the other side of the canyon still basked in a fiery wash of late-afternoon sun the near side was darkening under its own shadow.

'Water looks cold,' Kronziac remarked, tightening the straps for the air tank on her back.

'Shouldn't be any thermoclines,' Crandal advised her, watching the distance measurer counting down the metres. 'Here we are,' he declared. 'Fifty-five metres, directly downstream from our previous position.'

Ellstrom helped Kronziac to the taffrail on the rim of the boat where he pulled the moulded soles of the rubber fins onto her feet.

'You sure you want to do this?' he asked as Crandal hoisted the diving jack on the craft's small mast above the cabin.

'Yeah, I'm sure,' Kronziac replied.

Ellstrom handed her the mask. 'You want me to spit in it for good luck?' he joked.

'Don't be disgusting,' she chided him and squeezed a delicate glob of spit from her mouth into the mask, rubbing it in with her fingers.

'Be careful of the light,' Crandal warned. 'It's very dark under the cliffs here and it gets even darker as you go down.'

Kronziac nodded as she pulled her hair back and fitted the tight mask and snorkel over her face, the rubber seal sucking at her skin. She then clenched the mouthpiece of the regulator in her mouth and tested the air link from the tank, giving the okay signal.

'About twenty-five metres down,' Ellstrom reminded her, tapping the large dial of the diver's watch strapped to her wrist.

She plucked out the mouthpiece quickly. 'If you're wrong I'm gonna shove this air hose up your keister.'

This made Crandal laugh out loud and endeared Kronziac to the old man more than anything she had said or done all afternoon.

Ellstrom was a little shocked at her language. 'And what if I'm right?' he asked.

But Kronziac didn't answer. Putting her mouthpiece back in, she began breathing the oxygen from the tank and left herself fall backwards into the water.

The surface slapped her back as she broke through and after a flurry of bubbles she floated into the quiet stillness. Above her the shape of the dive launch wavered against the light blue sky and as she turned around the water appeared like a dark block to her left, brightening gradually to the right where the sun shot through water in the middle of the channel. Angling her body downwards, she drifted towards the blurred gloom below.

'She *is* a diver – a qualified diver – isn't she?' Crandal asked Ellstrom as they leaned over the side of the boat, looking into the twining ripples.

'I suppose so,' Ellstrom answered.

'Ain't you guys married?' the old man asked, turning to Ellstrom.

'No,' Ellstrom replied frankly.

'Boyfriend–girlfriend?'

'No.'

'Well, just friends?'

'Not really,' Ellstrom said vaguely. 'I've only known her two days.'

Crandal shook his head and turned back to the water. A small commotion of bubbles bristled on the surface where Kronziac had dived.

Descending slowly, the heavy cold water of the lake closing darkly around her, Kronziac checked the backlit read-out on her watch. The numbers indicated a depth of twenty-five metres. Looking up, she could still see the shimmering outline of the boat hull set against the watery backdrop of light blue. But now it was much smaller. Her breath gurgled and rose in a festival of bubbles, floating in little metallic-looking orbs towards the surface. All she could see beneath and to either side of her was the growing darkness in the canyon's shade, edging closer.

'What's that?' Ellstrom asked, squinting with concern as the sonar swept a fuzzy smear of green in the centre of the monitor.
Crandal leaned over the seat at the helm to take a closer look, tweaking the buttons to enhance the echo image.

Kronziac twisted around in the water, trying to peer into every corner of the thickening gloom. Something banged against her thigh, like a child impatiently tapping an adult's leg for attention. Another tapped the back of her head, nudging, then something slithered over her arm, her legs. A tail fluttered across her mask, waving. Little eyes shimmied by.
'Jesus!' she gasped.

'It's okay,' Crandal uttered, relieved. 'Striped bass, I'd say.'
'What?' Ellstrom cried, standing next to him.
'Take it easy, buddy,' Crandal turned to Ellstrom. 'It's just a shoal of fish . . .' His words tailed off as he focused on something in the distance, upstream, over Ellstrom's shoulder.
'Assholes,' he intoned angrily.

The air venting out her regulator fizzled loudly, filling Kronziac's field of vision with a miniature storm of churning bubbles. She watched the flotilla of fish glide in unison like a flight of arrows into the depths and closed her eyes, trying to calm her breathing. But she opened them quickly again as a faint and continuous roar, like the noise of a distant waterfall, assailed her ears. Instinctively she checked the depth.
Thirty-one metres.
She had descended nearly twenty feet when the shoal of fish had engulfed her.

Checking her regulator and hosing, she found that all the breathing apparatus was in good order. But the noise grew steadily nearer.

Ellstrom jumped up and down on the boat, rocking it from side to side.

'Diver down! Diver down!' he cried as a twin-engined fiery red Zodiac inflatable roared towards them, pulling a water-skier behind.

Crandal ran to the side of the boat and searched the water for any sign of Kronziac. 'Good,' he sighed. 'I can't see her – she's out of harm's way below.'

The red Zodiac peeled off as it neared the launch, banking high in the water, its male driver smiling at them, the female passenger holding up a beer bottle in salute.

Ellstrom gave them the finger as Crandal grabbed the baseball bat he kept under the seat at the helm. Watching the water-skier heading towards them, Crandal took up a batter's stance.

'I'll knock this fucker's head for a homer,' he shouted angrily as the skier swerved by them, not more than ten feet away, smiling through the shower of spray.

Kronziac thought it was quite beautiful. Floating there in calm silent suspension, she looked up as the rust-red belly of the speedboat glided across the liquid ceiling, the props twirling frantically in the water, opening the surface in a widening 'V' like a zipper. Then the two skis followed, just parallel thin rectangles, skipping above her. She watched them disappear across the roof of the lake, until another movement caught her eye.

From the edge of the canyon's dark shadow, just peeking out on the bright border of electric blue incandescence, about fifteen feet above her, a shape came bobbing into the light. Floating, flying, arms and legs splayed, hung with torn clothes, loose like those of a scarecrow, a chain around its waist, an outstretched ragged claw – a human hand, bony, with shredded flesh, three fingers and a thumb.

2434 ABRAMAR, PACIFIC PALISADES, CA

It was early.

Kronziac opened the door to bright morning sun and the serious faces of Agents Phillips and Ramirez.

'What, no bagels?' she asked sleepily.

'Sorry, not today,' Phillips said brusquely and came in. Maggie kissed Kronziac gently on the cheek, studying her with concern.

'You look tired.'

'Long day yesterday,' Kronziac explained, wrapping a light cardigan about herself. She was still dressed in a baggy pyjama bottom and one of her favourite tank tops.

'We know,' said Maggie, drawing a surprised look from Kronziac. 'Vegas PD were on first thing this morning.'

'What did they say?' Kronziac wanted to know as they followed Phillips into the living room. 'Have they made a positive ID on the body?'

'Not yet,' Maggie replied. 'But they were kinda pissed that you didn't let them know what you were doing out in the lake before you found the body.'

Kronziac fell onto the couch. 'Shit. Does Foley know?'

'It's Christmas Eve, Nance,' Maggie reminded her. 'Foley's gone off with the family to Aspen and won't be back till New Year.'

'How about Sedley?'

'Sedley's too busy keeping his ass clean,' said Phillips as he kneeled down and tapped at Hector's cage, trying to annoy the chameleon who was dozing on his perch.

'Still, he's probably gonna find out,' cautioned Maggie.

'We called the police as soon as we found the body.' Kronziac defended herself. 'If I'd gone to them sooner and told them I had this riddle that might help us to find a missing old woman they would have thought I was some sort of whacko. I had to be sure we weren't on a wild goose chase.'

'Well,' Phillips said, standing up. 'Maybe it's goose season.' He took out an envelope that had lain curled in the pocket of his coat.

Kronziac looked at him apprehensively.

'Number three, I think,' he said, handing her the envelope.

Maggie sat down beside her. 'It came in late yesterday,' she said. 'From Oregon this time.'

Inside the envelope Kronziac could see a single sheet of paper.

'Go on,' Phillips prompted her. 'It's just a copy.'

She carefully slipped the sheet out.

It was another Missing Persons notice, from Heppner Police Department, Morrow County, Oregon. On it was a grainy picture of a man in his forties.

'He's been missing for three weeks now,' Phillips said.

Kronziac just nodded and turned over the sheet. 'Oh, fuck,' she exhaled with quiet, deadly realization. 'Another code.'

'Looks like it,' Maggie remarked.

Shaking her head, Kronziac was unable to make any sense of the four lines of numbers and letters.

III I V B 21 24 20 KAD
KTQFV IDJWF SRAFM NUTWG QXRUW YQLKQ ZRFKB MLBSX
DQGTE ZCGXL GGKWS YZPWV EFKES IIRQG XRMBW WLZRZ
JKSMA XQVFO FSLQQ QDQKY VFOZF YDGXL UFANK RJCKT FYN

'Has Sedley or anyone else at the office seen this?'

Phillips shook his head. 'No,' he answered plainly. 'But maybe it's time they *should* know. This could be one for the SCU – it's the third one, right?'

'But only two bodies so far,' Kronziac said defiantly. 'And the one we found in the lake has not yet been positively identified.'

'Aw, come on, Kronziac,' Phillips cried. 'You're clutching at straws. We have three riddles for three missing persons, two of them have been found dead. We're talking a series of related crimes here.'

'He's right, Nance,' Maggie said softly. 'We should talk to Foley about it.'

'Foley's on vacation,' Kronziac reminded them and stood up. 'That gives us some time to work this one out.'

Phillips looked at Maggie, shaking his head, then back at Kronziac. 'Jesus!' he exclaimed. 'You're like a junkie.'

A calmer, unfamiliar voice broke the tension.

'Who's like a junkie?' Ellstrom asked, standing at the doorway from the bedrooms, laying his travel bag down by his feet.

'Miss your flight again?' Phillips asked, brightly.

'Hoping to get one this morning, Special Agent Phillips,' Ellstrom replied.

Maggie looked at him curiously. 'Maggie Ramirez,' she introduced herself and walked over with her hand out.

'How ya doing?' Ellstrom shook her hand.

'Nancy hasn't told me a thing about you,' Maggie said, smiling and glancing at Kronziac as she held on to Ellstrom's hand for a moment longer than was necessary.

He had to let go as Kronziac pushed the sheet of paper in front of him. 'Fancy spending Christmas in the sun?'

Ellstrom took it from her and looked at the rows of letters for a moment before turning it over. The MP notice described Peter Kelley as a well-loved local family man.

'Do you know how to make mince pies?' he asked Kronziac.

DEVONSHIRE COMMUNITY POLICE STATION, 10250 ETIWANDA AVE, NORTHRIDGE, CA

'Agent Kronziac here to see you, Sarge!' the young patrolman announced as he opened the door into the Tech Support Room.

Cunningham was sitting in front of a TV screen and a VCR, fast-forwarding through some video footage. His weighty midriff sank in a thick fold over his waist.

'Come on in,' he called, speaking over his shoulder as he concentrated on the screen, which flickered with shooting snakes of traffic in fast motion.

'Thanks.' Kronziac smiled at the patrolman as he held the door open for her. 'Hope I'm not keeping you from anything,' she said to Cunningham and grabbed a chair, pulling it up next to him.

Cunningham glanced at his watch and declared excitedly, 'I'm off duty in about thirty minutes, on a few days' Christmas vacation.' He pressed the pause button on the VCR and a single, grainy frame flickered on the TV. 'You usually work on Christmas Eve?' he asked, leaning around to her.

'I'm already on vacation,' she told him. 'Remember?'

'I hope Jerry appreciates the time you're putting in for him and his daughter,' Cunningham said and grabbed a case file from beneath the desk.

Actually, Kronziac hadn't seen Jerry Blaynes for a while. She wasn't exactly avoiding him but had no positive leads on the case for him.

'I'm sure he does,' she muttered and took out her own folder. 'So what have you got for me?'

Cunningham nodded at the screen. 'Well, we sifted through hours of footage from traffic and security cameras around Northridge that might help us fill in a couple of the gaps in Cherie's whereabouts that night.'

'Anything interesting?' Kronziac asked hopefully. Cunningham didn't seem too excited.

'We got this from a traffic camera on the intersection at

Devonshire and Tunney Avenue.' He pressed 'play' and the screen blinked to life with a bad-quality picture of cars flowing through a busy cross-roads.

'What time?' Kronziac asked, squinting at the white-blocked digits in the top right-hand corner of the screen.

'19.29,' Cunningham confirmed. 'And—' He waited with one hand raised in anticipation. 'Here she is!'

A blurred small light-coloured car drifted by. Stabbing the pause button again, Cunningham froze the car on screen, its edges fuzzy and bleeding colour in a hazy aura of red and blue.

'Not great quality,' he admitted. 'But it's her, all right.' He glanced at Kronziac, a hint of a smile tugging at his lips. 'Watch this.'

He pressed 'play' again and the little car proceeded to the intersection. The left indicator started to blink and she swung left.

'She's now heading north on Tunney towards Chatsworth Street and Porter Valley.'

As Cherie's car headed left up the road and disappeared off the frame Cunningham sat back in the chair.

Kronziac looked at him, waiting for more. 'Where is she going?' she asked.

'Well, she's not going towards Receda,' he answered, making her feel a little stupid.

'There's no more shots of her up on Tunney or Chatsworth?' she persisted.

Cunningham shook his head and pressed the fast-forward button, triggering frenetic movement on screen as the cars flicked by, stopping suddenly as the traffic lights changed, then moving off again like frantic ants chasing each other. The time block in the corner of the screen spun the minutes down like seconds. At 20.09 Cunningham punched the play button and the cars settled down to normal speed.

'Don't blink,' he warned. 'She rips through the intersection again fairly quick.' He paused the tape.

'There!'

Kronziac could see the Mazda speed down Tunney Avenue and hang left, swinging on to Devonshire just as the lights changed to red. It disappeared into the distance. Cunningham pressed stop and the screen turned a blank blue.

'So we've no idea where she was for—' Kronziac did a quick calculation '—for nearly forty minutes.'

The detective shook his head and ran his hand through the dark strands of his thinning hair. 'No . . . none,' he confessed. 'Not many cameras up around where she went.'

He pressed 'eject' and the machine whirred, clunked and regurgitated the video tape. Cunningham took it out and pushed in another one in its place. 'Next time we see her she is pulling into the parking lot at the mall at twenty-four after eight.'

Kronziac could make out Cherie's car turning into the car park and slotting itself into a space between two other cars. After thirty seconds or so they could see the figure of Cherie Blaynes in her red sweater and light blue jeans emerge from behind the car and walk quickly towards them, her blonde hair caught brightly in a crimson band of sunlight. She stopped and put her hand on her shoulder bag, but then carried on, increasing her pace until she exited the frame, going out to the sidewalk on Receda.

'Didn't seem to be anyone suspicious around her or following her,' Kronziac concluded as Cunningham swapped another tape.

'This is from the bank ATM,' he told her, shuttling through the footage taken from a point above the ATM. The car park grew darker and quieter until the big lamps came on, bathing the area in a dim wash of light. Cherie's car was the only one left. The emptiness was broken as the face of Donnie Claterios came into view, a few feet below the eye of the security camera. As he slotted his card into the machine and tapped at the buttons they could see Cherie walking away from them towards her car. They watched closely as Donnie stayed at the machine, glancing over his shoulder as Cherie disappeared into her car. After about forty seconds – Donnie had to re-enter his PIN in the machine – the lights came on in the car and it slowly moved away, turning onto the street and disappearing.

Below the camera Donnie retrieved his cash and walked out of frame.

'I didn't see anyone else around there, either,' Kronziac

commented, disappointed that none of the videos were yielding any clues. 'Is that the last one?'

'One more,' Cunningham answered swiftly and put the first tape back in the VCR again. 'It's a long-play copy,' he said. 'Covers six hours.'

He pressed the fast-forward button and, as the tape spun on its reels, whirring like crazy, Kronziac looked through her folder until she found the itinerary of Cherie's movements that night that Jerry Blaynes had given her.

'What time was it again we first saw her at the intersection?'

'Er – 19.29 hours,' Cunningham answered. Kronziac wrote it down.

'And the next time was about ten minutes after eight, right?'

Cunningham nodded as he pressed 'stop' and the VCR halted. 'Okay, this is from the same camera at the Devonshire-Tunney intersection at—' he looked at the time block to make sure '— At 11.35 – fifteen minutes after she left the car park.'

He pressed 'play' and after a moment he pointed at the familiar small car, this time coming towards them, the car lights blazing through the screen.

'Watch,' he whispered.

The Mazda slowed down as it came to the intersection, its right indicator blinking brightly in the dim street light. Other cars drifted by, their lights trailing up the screen into the gloom. As the traffic lights changed the Mazda swerved right and headed north once more on Tunney.

'It's going back up the same way it did nearly four hours ago,' Kronziac realized.

'Remember, the car was found up by the Porter Valley Country Club,' Cunningham reminded her.

'Is that the last we see of her?' Kronziac asked, wondering if Cherie's little Mazda car had been caught on any other surveillance cameras.

Cunningham nodded solemnly and jogged the tape back on play mode. The car reversed back around the corner of the intersection so that it was facing them again. 'That's the last time we see Cherie alive,' he said stoically and stared at the black rectangle of the windshield.

'Why would she be going up there twice that night – and without telling anyone?' Kronziac wondered aloud as some officers bundled two drunken college kids down the hall, singing 'Jingle Bells' all the way to the holding cells.

'Short cut home?' she offered offhand.

Cunningham seemed very doubtful. 'Nah – It's a longer route.'

Kronziac began throwing out whatever she could think of in the hope of sparking some lead. 'Was she going to pick something up? To meet someone? You talked to all her friends at school, right?'

Looking at his watch, Cunningham began stretching his long arms and raking his hair back once more with his hand. 'Yes,' he confirmed. 'I talked to them all or as many as I could. Nobody knew anything about her little excursions.'

Kronziac studied her notes, something nagging at her mind. 'Before she left home,' she began vaguely. 'Em – there was a phone call at about ten before seven—'

'Yeah,' Cunningham interrupted. 'It was the boyfriend, Donnie.'

'I had a talk with him the other day,' Kronziac went on, 'and he said that a few minutes after he called she had to go because there was another call.'

Cunningham thought seriously about it for a moment. 'Jerry never mentioned that they heard another call,' he said and began rifling through his file for the witness statements.

'No, the rest of the family wouldn't have heard the phone ringing as it was a call-waiting – only Cherie would have heard the beep on the line.'

Shaking his head with vague annoyance, the detective scanned through his statements. 'None of her friends said that they called her about that time.'

'Might be worth talking to them again,' Kronziac suggested cautiously, not wanting to appear to be telling him how to do his job.

'Mmm . . .' he grumbled. 'Oh, and I suppose you'll want to see this,' he said, coming across a police forensics report and passing it to her. 'The car,' he said simply.

Kronziac grabbed it and quickly read over it, picking out the salient comments. 'Tailgate lock shows some signs of forced entry . . . no items missing . . . no unidentified latent prints.' She sighed. Not much here either.

Looking down the page she found the trace-evidence paragraph. 'Some diatomaceous soil . . . fibres on pedals – yet to be matched . . . that might be something,' she remarked and continued. 'No blood under Luminol and UV test.' She shook her head again. Not much: pretty run-of-the-mill traces that could be found in any car. 'Where is it?'

'What?' Cunningham asked, yawning.

'The car.'

'Over at SID.'

Kronziac nodded. She knew the LAPD Scientific Investigative Division facility over on Ramirez and some of the people there.

She held up the report. 'Can I?'

'Sure.' He waved it off. 'Keep it.' One of Cunningham's colleagues stuck his head round the door, already in festive mood. 'Come on, Sam, get your skates on! We're planning a serious 11-83 with a keg of Warsteiner in Toledo's!'

'Gimme five,' Cunningham shouted back. The other detective nodded and went off down the corridor. Cunningham began gathering up his things, obviously anxious to begin his Christmas holiday.

'Anything else, Agent Kronziac?' he asked briskly, conveying an unspoken hope that she would say no – off you go – Happy Holidays!.

'Just one thing,' she said quietly, knowing she was pissing him off. 'Did Bob Vesoles get back to you about the marking on the head?'

As he put a jacket on Cunningham seemed to struggle with his memory, not quite sure what detail she was on about. 'Er – mark on the head?'

Kronziac turned to the LA County Coroner's Report in the file. 'Marking on frontal skull bone – glabella . . . the forehead.'

'No. I haven't heard from him,' Cunningham admitted, picking up the videotapes.

'Do you mind if I ring him?' she asked, still wanting to stay on side with Cunningham.

'Go ahead.' He laughed. 'But you'll be lucky to find him until after the holidays.'

'I'll try anyway.' Kronziac smiled sweetly but she knew Vesoles would be at work, like he was every day, Christmas Eve or not.

As she picked up the phone on the desk next to the TV Cunningham stopped before going out the door. He was smiling and shaking his head. 'Don't you have a husband or a boyfriend or some family to go home to?' Then he turned and left, not expecting an answer.

As the phone hummed at the other end Kronziac thought about Cunningham's question and had to wonder, rather sadly, if a terminally depressed lizard and a crazy math professor whom she hardly knew counted.

LA COUNTY CORONER, USC MEDICAL CENTER, 1200 NORTH STATE

Dr Robert Vesoles's office at the back of the building was stark and sparsely decorated but was mercifully warm. Kronziac followed the pathologist from the cold corridor of the morgue and could feel a pleasant blanket of warm air cover her goose-pimpled skin.

'How have you been, anyway, Nancy?' Vesoles asked, taking out a large file from a cabinet.

'Oh, not too bad,' she said, not giving much away.

He sat down behind the desk and, unhitching a small clipboard from his waist, he opened the file. 'Well, it's nice to see you, anyway,' he smiled.

Kronziac had always liked Vesoles. Despite his cool silky voice and debonair manner he never affected the dry crass humour many pathologists indulged in, especially when they had an audience – telling a bad joke about defence lawyers while they plonked someone's liver on the scales, for instance. In his early fifties, Vesoles was a handsome man with dark eyes and dark hair, streaked with steely strands of silver.

'Cherie Margaret Blaynes,' he read out, going through his own autopsy. 'Trauma to the head.'

'Yeah,' Kronziac confirmed. 'You mentioned an indeterminate marking on the forehead.'

'Yes, I remember now.' He nodded, retrieving some colour photographs from a plastic sleeve. 'You want to see?' he asked, looking up at her.

Kronziac took a deep breath. 'I don't *want* to,' she smiled nervously. 'But I'd better.'

The first shot was a close-up of the head.

'A lot of deterioration – as you will see,' Vesoles said, preparing her.

Kronziac could hardly recognize the oval-shaped mess of black skin, collapsed on one side, a jagged horn of bone protruding from it. Only the lank streaks of light-coloured hair gave any indication of the girl's former appearance.

'It's quite difficult to make out,' Vesoles went on. 'But you'll notice a slight crease in the epidermis on the forehead, roughly circular in shape.'

Kronziac looked closer and could only see a round trail of bunched scar tissue on the forehead.

'I removed the skin flap to reveal the front cranial bones.' He described the procedure as he handed her another close-up that showed the cream-white bone of Cherie's skull. 'Her right side, of course, is crushed in the orbital and parietal due to the blow,' Vesoles continued. 'But we see some form of scraping on the glabella itself. You'll see it better in this one.'

Passing her a third picture, he ran his finger around a red shape gouged in the middle of the skull bone of the forehead.

'Jesus,' Kronziac quietly gasped.

'I poured some red food dye in,' he explained, 'and carefully cleaned around it to make the mark more visible.'

Kronziac looked up in amazement. 'Could this have been caused by the blow to the head?'

Vesoles thought about it for a moment, staring at the pictures. 'I don't think so, really. It's not a shock fracture. It's more of a scraping – a gouging wound.'

'Post-mortem?' she asked.

But Vesoles shook his head. 'That's hard to call, given the decay of the epidermis and the blood vessels.'

Kronziac took the photo from the desk and examined it very closely. On the smooth yellowy surface of the skull bone, as if scraped by a sharp tool, was a familiar-looking shape and a small squiggle above it.

She looked up at Vesoles again. 'What do you think it is?' she asked.

The pathologist smiled. He wasn't going to be the one to say it. Years of expert-witness testimony had taught him never to stray into the dangerous area of conjecture. 'What do *you* think it is?' he responded, smiling.

She stared at the picture, the shape streaked in red dye,

running through the alabaster bone. 'It looks like a six – the number six,' she said finally, quietly astonished at her own words. 'With some other little mark over it.'

'That's what I kinda thought,' said Vesoles. 'It might mean nothing or—'

'Or?' She held his gaze.

'Or . . . you might have a ritual-type perp or a message killer on your hands.'

2434 ABRAMAR, PACIFIC PALISADES, CA

Kronziac found Ellstrom asleep on the couch, still dressed but for his shoes, which lay discarded on the floor. He had been working on the Peter Kelley cryptogram when she went to bed at about two a.m. Hell of a way to spend Christmas Eve, he'd complained but had refused to give up. Around him lay crumpled balls of notepaper with letters and numbers pencilled on them in hundreds of combinations. On the computer the screen-saver flashed its daily saying – this time it was a Christmas quote from Longfellow: *Of peace on Earth, and good will to men*. A vivid red Santa jumped across the monitor like a demented dwarf, throwing out a comet tail of brightly parcelled presents.

Kronziac gave Hector a Christmas-morning treat of some juicy mealworm and squashed cricket and turned on his basking light.

It was a grey overcast day as heavy rolls of cloud unfurled themselves over a quiet sea. Opening the patio doors, she walked barefoot out onto the veranda.

'Might have rain!' a voice shouted at her, as if it had been waiting all morning to say it.

Kronziac turned around. 'Morning, Mrs Peters!'

'Merry Christmas, Nancy!' the old woman called from her bedroom window. 'A nice quiet day for you, I suppose,' she added.

'I suppose,' Kronziac agreed and checked some of the plants.

'Got a visitor at the moment?' Mrs Peters probed, trying to get some information from Kronziac on the strange man staying with her.

Kronziac smiled to herself. 'Yeah,' she shouted back. 'A friend.'

Mrs Peters took a drag on her cigarette and her eyes seemed to twinkle as she exhaled. 'A nice friend,' she purred hoarsely.

Kronziac just smiled back and plucked a dead leaf from one of her yuccas. 'Well, happy Christmas, Mrs Peters,' she said and headed back into the house.

'You too!' the old woman shouted back, stubbing her cigarette out on the sill and closing the window.

Ellstrom creaked to life, yawning and stretching, slightly puzzled to find himself hunched uncomfortably on the couch.

'Good morning,' Kronziac greeted him, clearing up some of his discarded papers. 'Long night?'

As he hauled himself up he answered with a non-committal grunt, still half asleep and rubbing a sore neck.

Kronziac continued to clean up around the room. 'Not really a morning person, are you?'

Ellstrom was watching Hector as he crunched happily on some cricket legs. 'What time is it?' he asked, grimacing.

'Nearly midday,' Kronziac replied as she went into the kitchen.

Getting up, Ellstrom looked around him as if sensing something was missing. 'It *is* Christmas Day, right?' he asked. 'I mean, don't you put up a tree, decorations or something? I thought America was the land of Yuletide overkill.'

She shouted back something from the kitchen but his brain, still woolly, couldn't quite understand what she said.

'What?' he croaked, his mouth dry and sticky.

Kronziac popped her head over the counter of the Hawaiian bar. 'I'm Jewish,' she smiled.

'Oh – I didn't know . . . sorry' he stuttered, beginning to wake at last.

'No need to apologize. I'm not exactly the religious type, don't really observe the faith,' she said as she placed a cup of smoky black coffee on the counter. 'Obviously Christmas isn't that big a deal for me but how about we go up to the Country Club and I'll treat you to Christmas lunch? Least I can do.'

'Okay.' Ellstrom shrugged and picked up his cup.

'So, any luck with the crypto?' Kronziac asked, fluffing the pillows on the couch. She had to wait for an answer as Ellstrom took a slow drink of the piping hot coffee.

'Yeah,' he answered finally.

Kronziac dropped one of the cushions. 'You worked it out?' She blinked, amazed.

Ellstrom walked over and stood by the patio doors, coffee in hand, shaking his head as if annoyed with himself. 'I can't believe it took me so long to spot it.'

'Spot what?' she asked excitedly.

'Those digits and letters in the first line,' he reminded her. Kronziac nodded.

'Well, they weren't codes *per se*,' he explained.

'What were they?'

Ellstrom moved swiftly across the room to the computer. As he touched the mouse the Santa disappeared and a graphic blinked into view.

'What were they?' Kronziac asked again anxiously, wishing he'd just tell her.

Ellstrom seemed still annoyed at himself for some reason. 'They're settings,' he said simply.

'For what?'

He nodded at the screen. 'This.'

Moving closer, Kronziac wondered what it was. It looked like a small typewriter with two sets of alphabetic keys.

'Enigma,' Ellstrom whispered, marvelling at the picture of the machine on the monitor. 'This is an Enigma emulator I downloaded from the net.'

It began to dawn on Kronziac that what she was looking at was a simulation of some sort of code machine. 'They used it during World War Two, didn't they?' she asked, vaguely remembering a documentary on the Discovery Channel about it.

'The Germans used it, primarily for sending intel signals to the U-Boat fleets in the North Atlantic.' He began shaking his head again. 'I'm so stupid – I can't believe it took me so long to figure it out.'

'No one else would have spotted it.' Kronziac tried to reassure him. 'I certainly didn't.'

This did nothing to assuage his annoyance. Of course *she* wouldn't have spotted it.

'You don't understand,' he said. 'My grandmother worked at Bletchley Park during the war as a cryptanalyst. She helped Turing break Enigma.'

Kronziac was surprised at the strength of his emotion about

it. 'Well, the important thing is you cracked it – you did, didn't you, break the Peter Kelley code?'

'Yes,' he replied tersely. 'The Enigma is made up of a fiendishly complicated arrangement of circuit boards and scramblers. But once you have the rotor numbers, reflector, ring settings and the positions – then you're away with it.'

He picked up the cryptogram and typed in the first letter on a long narrow box marked *Input*. As he did this a letter appeared on another box below marked *Output* – the letter T.

Ellstrom began to smile. 'Actually, Enigma allows for about a thousand trillion letter combinations – that's a lot of options for encryption,' he added, infatuated with the old machine.

'You can tell me all about it some day,' Kronziac said impatiently. 'But for now I just want to see the plaintext.'

Ellstrom tore himself away from the screen and handed her a piece of paper with three lines scribbled on it.

take forty-six from one-nine-nine from the ggge fffd to find him cast into the underworld from which the river styx flows through the belly of the whale

It was the riddle about how to find the body of Peter Kelley.

DOMINGO'S, RIVIERA COUNTRY CLUB, PACIFIC PALISADES

Trying not to call attention to his scuffed loafers, Ellstrom trod lightly across the dark oakwood floor. The dining room hummed with the low, discreet chatter of its well-to-do patrons – mostly families and older couples enjoying the expensive Christmas-lunch buffet. A pianist in the corner lightly tinkled out some Christmas favourites between Bacharach and Cole Porter numbers on a baby grand.

Ellstrom found the restaurant, an odd assortment of Mediterranean-style rough plaster walls mixed with Gothic wood carvings and a ceiling of fanned cane, absurdly charming. Though it was a dull day, one side of the dining room bloomed under a bank of light from the Conservatory, which looked out on the club's eighteen-hole championship golf course. The golf theme was further enhanced by a series of long thin pastel etchings of golf greats in various stages of swing arranged along the walls. Over some of the larger tables and the salad bar in the centre of the room deep emerald-green canvas canopies hung like over-sized parasols and gave each table a further illusion of privacy and novelty. Their own small four-seat table was situated on the darker side along the back wall where an earthy clay ledge was lined with fat white church candles that winked in the draughts of air.

Kronziac was looking distractedly over the menu. It was the first time Ellstrom had seen her wear more make-up than the usual light touches of mascara and lipstick. She wore an above-the-knee flame-red cupro dress with two narrow straps and high-heeled slingbacks which brought her height up to about five-nine – maybe five-ten. Her long dark hair, combed straight, lay swept behind one ear while on the other side it fell softly on her bare shoulder.

'You find the restrooms all right?' she whispered as Ellstrom took his seat.

'Yeah, they were as luxurious as this place,' he answered,

very impressed with the opulent settings of the Country Club.

'I wasn't sure if I gave you the right directions,' she said. 'The whole place has changed just recently,' she remarked, looking around. 'Though I think the designer was on acid,' she added with an impish smile.

'I feel a little underdressed,' Ellstrom admitted, settling into his chair and trying to straighten the sleeves of his blazer.

'Don't worry,' Kronziac assured him. 'You're an academic. Most of the people around here are either movie producers, lawyers or property developers. They would be very impressed if they knew you were a professor from Harvard.'

'Really?' he asked brightly, looking around to see if anyone was checking him out.

'Sure,' she answered. 'The only reason I got membership is that I inherited it from my aunt and for some reason the committee likes the idea of an FBI agent on the books, makes them look – I dunno – eclectic. Anyway, what'll you have?' she asked, passing him the menu. 'I don't know if they do mince pies but I hear they have a killer traditional turkey dinner.'

Ellstrom's expression grew slightly pained as he opened the menu and scanned down the wide range of cuisine from French to exotic South Pacific seafood dishes. 'Prices match the decor,' he said, spotting a lot of digits.

Kronziac turned her palms up in a shrugging gesture. 'Have whatever you want,' she urged. 'It's the least I can do for ruining your Christmas.'

'Oh, I wouldn't have been doing much back east,' he said, taking a delicate sip of water as if it was an expensive Chablis.

'You like teaching?' Kronziac asked.

'I suppose,' he replied, still looking over the menu. 'Though most of the senior students are a lot smarter than me.'

'Yeah, right,' Kronziac smiled, not believing him.

'No, really. Mathematicians are at their best in their late teens or early twenties. Look at Ramanujan, Galois, Turing!'

Kronziac just smiled and nodded as if she knew who or what he was on about. She looked around for a waiter.

'If you haven't made it by twenty-five you can forget it,' he maintained.

'A bit like fashion models, then,' Kronziac remarked, drawing a sly smile from her companion.

'I like being at a university,' Ellstrom went on. 'But more for the research than the teaching. I suppose I could go and work for AT&T or go into banking or insurance – but where's the fun in that?'

'Beats me.' Kronziac shook her head. 'The thing about math is either you get it or you don't – the answer is right or wrong – there's no room for ambiguity.'

'You're right,' he agreed reluctantly. 'To a large extent. But maths – well, there's a thin line between pure mathematics and philosophy . . . an abstract expression of the underlying principles of nature and creation,' he said, glowing with the idea.

'You make it sound like a religion,' Kronziac remarked, never having seen the subject in quite the same way as he described it.

'*Faith in numbers.*' He nodded, happy with the metaphor.

'You're a bit of a pagan or a – what do you call it? – a numerologist?'

'Anglican, actually,' he retorted. 'But faith in Christianity will die out in about another 1000 years, give or take a century,' he said.

'How did you come up with that figure?' she asked.

'Well,' he began, adopting his annoying scholarly pose. 'Based on Newtonian physics, which posits that the diminution of magnetic force between two bodies is in proportion to the increase in distance between them, one can deduce that the strength of faith similarly declines the further we travel in time from the original faith-inspiring event. Therefore, some mathematicians believe that by the fourth millennium faith in Christ will have decreased to zero since three thousand years will have elapsed since his crucifixion and he will again have to make an appearance.'

'Hey.' Kronziac put up her arms. '*We*'ve been waiting for him already for thousands of years!'

'I thought you said you weren't a very devout Jew,' he reminded her.

Kronziac put her hands down. 'I'm not. Let's eat.'

She looked around for one of the waiters but they were rushing in and out of the kitchen swing-doors bearing plates of varying foods for the Christmas Day diners.

'I could tell you your age,' Ellstrom declared confidently. 'If you gave me the first digit.'

'Well, then I won't, will I?' Kronziac returned defiantly.

'Did you know that the thirteenth of the month is more likely to fall on a Friday than on any other day?' he asked. 'There are 293 ways to make change from a dollar,' he continued. 'Pick a three-digit whole number,' he told her and took out a tiny pocket calculator.

'What?'

'Pick a whole number – you know, no fractions,' he repeated. 'Go on,' he urged her and pressed the calculator into her hand.

'Okay,' Kronziac said wearily and thought of 153.

'Repeat the digits' he said.

She tapped the tiny keys.

153, 153.

'Now divide by seven.'

21, 879.

Divide by eleven.'

1989.

'And finally divide by thirteen,' he said.

She pressed the keys.

153.

'Back at the same number, aren't you?' He grinned.

'Yes . . . that's quite scary,' Kronziac said, decidedly unimpressed. 'Though not as scary as the fact that you carry a calculator with you when you go to lunch.'

'No, it's just beautiful,' he said. 'If a solution is beautiful then it's gotta be true.'

Kronziac handed back the calculator and craned her head to somehow try and attract the attention of one of the waiting staff, before Ellstrom could drive her nuts with his ideas of math and beauty.

'Do you know what the best numbers are for winning the most money in the lottery?' Ellstrom asked teasingly.

Kronziac looked at him. 'Go on, then . . .'

'26, 34, 44, 46, 47 and 49,' he answered proudly.

Kronziac was going to reach into her purse and write down the numbers but stopped. 'Is that because they are the ones most likely to come up?' she asked suspiciously.

'No,' he admitted proudly. 'They have the same chance as any other numbers. It's just that – generally – people pick these numbers less frequently – thus increasing your share of the winnings if, by some miracle, those numbers actually came up.'

She left her purse alone. 'I should take you with me next time I go to Vegas,' she said, playfully sarcastic.

'I'm just trying to show you that numbers can be fun,' said Ellstrom.

'Have you always been like this?' Kronziac asked.

He smiled. 'Like what?'

She was tempted to say like those geeky little shits she'd encountered at his lecture at Harvard, the same geeky little shits who would some day rule the world with their software empires.

'In love with math . . . numbers,' she said.

Ellstrom nodded thoughtfully. 'When I was six or seven I used to help my father with the football pools, calculate the cost of my mother's weekly shopping before we even reached the checkout.'

Kronziac began laughing. 'While other kids were dreaming about being firemen, soldiers and astronauts . . . you were dreaming about being a math professor.'

'You're right,' he said. 'I had a dream, the earliest I can remember. A landscape of numbers, primes growing randomly like weeds among the clusters of rationals, perfect numbers sprouting like orchids . . .'

'The Martin Luther King of the math world, eh?' Kronziac joked.

'I was actually paraphrasing someone, can't remember who, but I dreamed the same dream. I know what he meant,' he said.

'I think I know what he meant, too,' Kronziac said, nodding appreciatively. 'Only I see music,' she added shyly.

'You see music?' Ellstrom blurted out, intrigued.

'Yeah – kinda. I mean the flowers in the garden; the dark

bass notes of the earth, the greens climbing like a chorus, the ivies strings, long and thin, the reds like violins, the large bushes like the brass section, big fat notes. Like you see numbers, I see musical notes in the colours.'

Ellstrom said nothing, as if struck dumb.

A polite, chirpy little cough interrupted Kronziac's own reverie. 'Excuse me, madam, may I take your order?'

A small, bald waiter, nattily dressed in a black uniform, with the club's crest on the breast pocket, stooped over the table, smiling with polite anticipation.

'Oh, I'm sorry,' Kronziac babbled and reached for the menu. 'I'll start with the Fresh Fish Ceviche – what's the marinade on that?'

'Lime juice, tomatoes, onions and jalapeno peppers,' the waiter courteously advised her.

She nodded. 'And for the main course I'll try the Cioppino, but without the spicy tomato, I think.' Kronziac closed the menu.

The waiter turned to Ellstrom who was frantically searching the pockets of his blazer and light canvas trousers.

'Can I take your order now, sir?' he asked softly.

Ellstrom finally found what he was looking for, pulling out a scrap of paper from his back pocket.

The waiter watched him, bemused by the spectacle.

'Er . . . James, what are you doing?' Kronziac asked, keeping her voice low, faintly embarrassed by his behaviour.

'Musical notes,' he stuttered. 'In the riddle.'

The waiter glanced inquisitively at Kronziac, who just shrugged.

Ellstrom got up from the table abruptly, knocking over the menu, and hurried to the piano in the corner where the pianist was tickling out the last chords of *Memories*. His expression grew more concerned as he caught sight of Ellstrom's tall frame approaching. A prim older couple at the table nearest the piano looked up in surprised shock as Ellstrom bounded past, his purposeful stride alarming amidst the quiet decorum of the restaurant.

'Excuse me!' Ellstrom said loudly to the piano player. 'I'm terribly sorry, but could you play these notes?' He held in his hand the scribbled plaintext of the Peter Kelley cryptogram.

The piano player, another delicate-looking man with slender white fingers, stared at Ellstrom for a moment, then nodded. Anything to break the monotony. He always tried to accommodate people's requests and Ellstrom appeared to be like one of those eccentric British film directors who either gave you a 100-dollar tip or apologized for not having any American money and gave nothing but a crooked smile.

'I'll call them out,' Ellstrom said, reading the letters at the end of the first line: *G – G – G – E . . . F – F – F – D.*

The pianist obliged by pressing the corresponding keys on the piano.

Kronziac had joined them and was asking what was going on.

'Can you play them all together?' Ellstrom asked restively. 'If I call them out faster.'

But the pianist just smiled. 'No need,' he replied and played the notes again, this time quicker.

Da da da daaaaaa . . . da da da daaaaaa.

'I know that,' Ellstrom cried, trying to think what it was. A tune everyone had heard but few could put a name to.

'So do I,' Kronziac echoed, getting caught up.

The pianist's smile broadened as his lean fingers worked the keys. 'One of the most famous pieces of music,' he said. 'Beethoven – Symphony Number 5.'

Ellstrom turned to Kronziac, a smile breaking out on his face. 'Five,' he said quietly.

The couple in the nearby table were staring, the man admiring Kronziac's slender legs, his wife noticing Ellstrom's shabby shoes.

17558 MIZETTE ST, EAST PALO ALTO, SAN FRANCISCO

The neighbourhood appeared deserted with its rows of seem-ingly empty houses. Some families were still away on holiday, others were back at work, either glued to their workstations at Hewlett Packard or in their labs at Stanford.

Shayla Wilson felt like the only person left on the planet as she watched the mailman disappear around the top of the street to begin his round on Collingwood. Between the houses across the road she could see the grey line of water in the Bay bright-ening as the sun shone through the early-morning mist like candlelight through tracing paper.

She let the net curtains swing softly back into place, silent like the closing wings of a butterfly. Turning around, she sighed at the mess, the Christmas tree beginning to shed its tinsel decorations, the balloons half-deflated bladders, shreds of wrap-ping paper in every corner and down the back of the couch. She would start with the kitchen, then make her way into the den and gather up the mess of new toys and books left by the kids and that monstrous half-built model battleship her husband had abandoned the day after Christmas. She was glad he had taken himself and the kids off early to see his parents. It gave her the space and the time to get the house back in order after the holidays. In the corner of the room the TV thumped with an early-morning workout programme while the rest of the house lay still and free from sound. Walking into the kitchen, she could hear the windows ticking as a breeze swirled around the back yard. Shaking her head, she wondered how two chil-dren and one grown man could make such a mess and leave it exactly where they created it. The breakfast table was strewn with boxes of cookies, cups, bowls of milk and cereal slush. A dappled path of orange juice led from the refrigerator, becoming gummy underfoot on the tiles. The sink was a pit of clouded glasses and plates in a backed-up pool of dark brown water – the drain was plugged with a clot of wet tea bags. Beside the sink, against the walnut units, lay the fat black worm of a bin bag, bulging with crammed-in refuse. They lived in a half-million-dollar house and her husband earned nearly 200K a year to supervise the development of relational databases for UNIX-based computer network servers. She'd had to rehearse that one when he got the promotion.

'What do you do again?' she'd asked for weeks after. Systems Analyst simply wasn't good enough any more. She tipped the tea bags into the garbage and the drain sucked with a guttural groan at the soupy mess of crockery in the sink. Dragging the bin bag to the back door, she twisted the key and the door pushed open, nudged by a rush of wind that shook the line of trees at the end of the garden and licked up a commotion of dust in the backyard by the trash cans.

With the effort of a weightlifter, Shayla swung the bag up and over into an empty can. Wiping her hands, she cursed as she noticed yellow blotches of OJ soaking into the white fabric of her sweatsuit. She rushed inside, slamming the door behind her, and went upstairs.

Their bedroom was a mess, too, the bed unmade, with the duvet dragged from the mattress and clothes heaped in the corners waiting for their turn in the laundry. Kicking off her trainers, she wriggled out of her top and noticed two large yellow blots on her pants also. She pulled them off, too, and added them to the pile of unwashed clothes.

She was about to open the wardrobe to retrieve a fresh pair of jeans and a top when she stopped to look at herself in the full-length mirror on the door. She stood there in her underwear and white sport socks. Forty years old, she was still in good shape. Her figure had always been her best feature – her face, though not unattractive, was not remarkable: dim blue eyes, pale skin, low cheekbones, hair mousy and cut roughly in a bob. All her boyfriends in school and college had assured her readily that she had a good body when she asked them how attractive she was. It was almost like saying someone had a great personality when they really couldn't think of anything good to say about their looks. Blessed with an efficient metabolism, her husband would say, dismissing any suggestion by her that she was putting on a bit of weight.

She twisted her hips around and looked at her rear view in the mirror. The cheeks of her butt peeked out from the sides of her underwear in the soft marbled texture of cellulite that continued down the back of her thighs. From a distance she could still look good but closer inspection would reveal her age. She resolved there, confronted by the evidence of the mirror, to try the early-morning workouts on KPIX-5 in the New Year. She stood up straight so the orbits of her knees touched and held her arms up like a gymnast about to start a routine. She stretched them in an arc, out and down, to touch her toes but found that she couldn't. She stayed there for a moment, dangling her arms and shoulders in front of her torso until she felt the tingling swell of blood pulsing in her head. She drew up quickly, exhaling. She felt dizzy as she blinked her eyes – and then her heart stopped.

Reflected in the mirror, standing in the doorway, was a man, watching her.

She turned to scream but he moved quickly and stung her in the neck with a needle. Suddenly her head filled with darkness.

CRAPS

Something was juddering across the floor.

The grinding metallic scream of table legs.

She woke to find herself looking into the black hole of a trash can. Then the table surface moved over it like a trapdoor.

In a hazy momentary pause like that when the world blinks at dawn and the remnants of dreams retreat like bowing courtesans, Shayla Wilson thought she would get up and stick a mental post-it to her brain: *Don't try touching your toes so quickly again.*

But then she realized that her body was held in a kneeling position, her bare knees against the floor, toes curled painfully under her feet. Trying to move her head, her neck bucked against a hard edge of wood. She reached up to touch her face but her knuckles cracked against the wood that surrounded her neck like a collar that clamped her in place. Feeling up further, she could feel two uprights, again made of wood but rougher, with grooves dug in the centre, the gritty rub of dirty oil in them. Below, her field of vision was filled by the surface of the table, marked and scratched but sheened with a gloss of fresh varnish.

Someone or something brushed up against the goose-bumped flesh of her buttocks. She was still dressed only in her underwear and was bitterly cold.

'Hello . . . hello . . . who's there?' she called, trembling.

No one answered but a man's hand placed a large, curved piece of plywood on the table directly below her head and pushed it further in under her throat, like a bowl pressed under the nose of a dog. The inner side of the wooden semicircle was coated with a thick strip of black foam, dimpled like an egg carton. She could smell his musty breath and his skin, the unctuous tincture of a medical balm.

'Pleeeese – where am I?' she pleaded.

A glint of silver flashed in front of her eyes and she had to squint to see the point of the knife staring at her. She flinched but couldn't move back, the wood frame about her rattling, trapping her.

A voice wheezed in her right ear with hot gassy breath. 'Make a sound an' I'll fucking drive this through your neck before its bigger brother gets the chance.'

Her own breath panted on the blade, clouding its silver hilt for a second.

Two sets of primal instincts now fought within her – one to scream for help, one to reason with her captor, whoever he was. The battle left her body shaking with fear as she pleaded in a high-pitched but hushed voice.

'Pleeeese – I beg you . . . let me go . . . let me go . . .'. Shayla shook the wooden bridle about her throat but nothing budged. There was only the knocking of a fat padlock against the timbers that she fingered desperately to open.

'It's no use.' He mocked her, his voice moving around in front of her about five or six feet away. 'I suppose I should explain the rules,' he said and she heard the thump of a stool being set in place.

'Though I'm sure you know them well – you watched us often enough,' he hissed, his tone loaded with hatred.

'You're buying in with three chances to win – and three chances to lose!' he said. 'We'll make it real easy, just Pass Line bets with the house edge of just over one per cent, best odds on the floor.'

He moved around the table, to Shayla's left. Her eyes hurt as she tried to follow the movement but she could only just make out a strip of black and the edge of his denims, dull with grime. She could also just see the tip of a handle, brass, shining in the dim light.

'This is the handle – or *declic* . . .' he amended, with a flourish. 'It has four settings – *interesting*, *very interesting*, *up shit creek* and *don't have to worry about hats no more*,' he hooted. It sounded like he was slapping his thighs in his mirth.

Shayla began sobbing, her tears blatting off the table like rain falling on a lily pad.

'Hoping to influence the fall?' he said, moving back to his stool again. 'Okay, seven or eleven on the "come-out roll" and

you win. Two, three and twelve – you lose. The other numbers
go point, which shooter rolls for, winning on it or busting on
seven. Like I said, Pass Line bets only. Three strikes you're out
. . . three wins and – Now, don't go losing your head,' he
added, cackling like a giddy child. 'Ready?'

Closing her eyes, she cleared her throat painfully and raised
her knees to relieve them of the numbing pain. But she had to
put them down again and her kneecaps stung.

'I'm begging you . . .' she groaned.

But he ignored her.

The game started.

'Shooter rolls!'

The dancing tap of the dice, bobbing up the table, bouncing
against the foam and falling in front of her eyes.

'Six – money is right!' he shouted and leaned over to retrieve
the dice. 'Now you've gotta throw a six before a seven,' he warned.

Her sobs thickened to a shuddering whimper, dripping more
tears on the table.

'Come on, that's not fair,' he complained but scattered the
dice down the table again.

'Nine!' He gave the surface a quick wipe with his black shirt
sleeve.

'Cry, bitch!' he spat. 'Now you know what it's like.' Rattling
the dice in his cupped hands, he whispered to them.

'Come on, seven.'

They rolled, jumping down the table, bouncing against the
foam back.

'Five and snake eyes!' he shouted, thrilled, and jumped up
from the table.

He moved the brass handle one notch and Shayla could hear
something heavy shifting above her, clunking into place.

He sat down again.

'One chance down . . .' he said with calm delight, excitement swelling below.

The dice rumbled over the wood again, chasing each other,
knocking themselves out against the foam dam.

'Five . . . money's right,' he grumbled and picked up the
dice again.

As if trying to get to the end of the game quicker he now began firing the dice rapidly, snatching them up in front of her to throw again.

Struggling in her harness, Shayla fought the numbing paralysis of fear, trying somehow to think what she could do. Each time she cried or moaned too loud he roared at her to shut up and threatened her with the knife or warned that he'd pull the handle the whole way and it would be all over.

'Seven!' he announced gleefully as the dice rolled to a stop. He jumped up, lowering the lever another notch. The whole wooden structure vibrated around her as the weight high up clinked heavily again – like a rifle cocking or a beam creaking under a weight of rubble.

'Dear God!' Shayla prayed loudly. 'Please let me out of here!'

'Lady Luck's the one you should be praying to,' he snapped, firing the little white-spotted red blocks across the wood again.

'Eight! Roll 'em again!'

He picked up the dice, blowing them in his hands as Shayla's tears dried on the table.

'Eight's the point,' he shouted and launched the nuggets again.

She opened her eyes.

A six and a one.

'Come on, baby!' he shouted in triumph, leaping up to the handle. 'You're up shit creek,' he sneered, laughing as he pulled the handle to the last notch. 'Next throw and it could be goodbye to neck scarves!'

Shayla hoped she would lose consciousness and wake up in a different place and a different time as he plucked the dice up once more.

It wasn't long before they came tapping over the wood again, sliding up to the foam.

A ten.

'Money is right,' he said, disappointed, and grabbed them again.

'If you don't let me go I'm gonna scream. Someone'll hear,' Shayla said as calmly as she could. But her voice was shaky and hoarse. Her whole body was trembling and she thought she might throw up on the table. At least that might stop his cruel stupid game.

He ignored her, muttering odds to himself.

The dice rolled again, tumbling on the varnished surface. She loathed that sound.

The tapping stopped. He remained silent.

Another ten.

'You won,' he intoned dolefully and slowly got up from the stool.

'Just let me go!' she roared, her body quaking.

Pulling at the handle, he unhitched it from the final notch – and began to curse under his breath as he struggled to push it back to the previous point.

'What – what is it?' she screamed, wrenching her head to the side to see.

He was grunting, his hands white with the pressure of pushing the handle.

'Let me go! . . . Let me go!' She was roaring hysterically.

Suddenly he jumped back from the handle as it sprung from his grasp like an escaping animal.

As if by instinct he pulled the table back and the black well of the trash can now reappeared beneath her.

She was clutching the wooden harness about her neck, trying to free herself, when the whole frame jerked. She heard the weight spring out of position and descend on her rapidly, whooshing like a sled shooting over wood, a bolt snapping shut . . . slicing itself into silence.

He jumped back in surprise as the head bounced in the trash can.

The body collapsed behind the guillotine, fell back on its heels as if to give thanks for its release then swayed sideways onto the floor, her – literally – cut-off scream just breath venting from the severed gullet, the aorta spurting like a water pistol.

He ran to the can to look in.

Shayla Wilson's eyes were moving, flickering side to side, as if surprised by a sudden change in surroundings. In the last synaptic twitchings of her amputated head, in that last split second between life and death, she wondered if she was back in the yard at home and had, for some reason, fallen into the can with all the other garbage.

The mouth fell open, the lips rounded in an 'O'.

STATE HIGHWAY 46, OREGON CAVES NATIONAL MONUMENT, SOUTHERN OREGON

The narrow road meandered through the tree-lined slopes of the Siskiyou Mountains where marble outcrops jutted from beneath the tall stands of Douglas fir and cedar. The tree branches hung heavily under thick pillows of snow and above the peaks white clouds grew like puffing folds of wool, trying to close out the squares of blue sky. On the lower reaches pines grew amid the broadleafs like the orange-barked Pacific Madrone, canyon live oak and golden chinkapin. At the edges of the road purple brush-heads of manzanita wore a powdery dusting of snow, like icing sugar tipped from the sky.

They hadn't seen anyone since Cave Junction, nearly twenty miles back.

'Okay,' muttered Ellstrom, stretching stiffly in the passenger seat of the Explorer as it neared the end of its slow 4,000-foot climb into the mountains. 'We've taken State Highway 46 from Highway 199 from the Interstate 5 – now what?'

'That's what,' Kronziac answered, flicking her finger at a sign for the Oregon Caves. She waited to take off her sunglasses until the car had squeezed around a tight bend, the back tyres throwing up a spray of dirty snow. The clouds had won, moving in over the mountains as small flakes of snow fell like scraps of paper.

Though they had been up nearly three hours they both still felt tired after an uncomfortable night in a motel near Shasta Lake. Kronziac had driven nearly ten hours the previous day, following the I-5 all the way up from LA until they'd decided to stop for the night. They had got up at seven and after a greasy breakfast of bacon, sausage and waffles they had continued north into Oregon, turning off the interstate at Grant's Pass and heading south-west towards the Siskiyou mountain range. At Cave Junction they'd turned east to the Oregon Caves National Monument.

The road widened at the car park, which was empty except

for one car and a camper at the other end. A dark earthy brown building came into view, nestled into the side of the mountain and surrounded by a glade of trees and the bubbling rush of a waterfall.

Oregon Caves Chateau, read the sign outside the 1930s-style six-storey building. Another sign, clipped on beneath, told visitors that it was closed for the winter.

'At least there are some people around,' Kronziac observed with relief as she spied some movement in front of another building further up the road.

A Swiss-type chalet, the building looked like a large barn with long narrow windows and rusty brown bark-sided walls, crouched under a towering crescent of trees that dripped melting snow onto the roof.

A man and a young woman were walking up and down the steps at the side of the chalet, loading boxes into a pick-up.

The man stopped and watched as they drove up towards him. Kronziac gave a friendly wave as she got out of the car and for the first time in over three hours felt the bracing bite of the frigid mountain air. Ellstrom zipped up his large blue Gore-Tex hiking coat that he had purchased at Shasta Lake and a white plume of smoky air shot from his mouth as he rubbed his hands to warm them.

'Good morning!' Kronziac shouted, walking up the steps.

'Morning,' the man replied, nodding without much expression.

Tallish, with a thick curly thatch of ashen hair and a moustache, he wore a ski jacket with a small crest on it bearing the words *Oregon National Monument Tour Co.* Kronziac also noticed that the doors of the pick-up sported the same emblem.

'Beautiful day.' Ellstrom smiled, shivering. But the man remained unresponsive.

Obviously not one for small talk. Kronziac came out with it and asked directions to the nearest Ranger Station. He shook his head scornfully.

'Nearest station's at Cave Junction,' he informed them. 'You passed through it already.'

'Oh, right.' Kronziac nodded, feeling stupid. 'Are the caves open?'

He almost smiled. 'No. closed till second week in March.'

Kronziac looked around for a moment, figuring what next to say. She felt like a trespasser. 'Is there anyone we could talk to that might let us in?'

'You're talking to him, I guess.' The man grinned, smiling openly now, having waited for his chance to say those words.

Realizing she had two options, Kronziac debated whether she should flash her ID or show some dollar notes – get into further trouble with Foley or risk getting a jail sentence for attempted bribery.

She was about to opt for the latter when a female voice called from inside the large open doors of the chalet store.

'Ken! Can you take care of this?' A young blonde woman shuffled out from the store, nudging a heavy box along the ground with her feet.

'Oh – hi.' She smiled, seeing the visitors. 'Ken, can you take this, please?' she said again. Kronziac and Ellstrom couldn't keep themselves from smiling as the surly character had to get down on his haunches and pick up the box to transport it down the steps to the truck.

'There are about seven more,' the young woman told him, which prompted him to utter some unheard profanity under his breath as he struggled with the weight of the box.

'A lovely day, isn't it?' she said brightly, turning to Kronziac and Ellstrom. In her late teens or early twenties, the girl was small in build with short black hair tucked under a ski hat. With her dark eyes and bouncy manner she reminded Kronziac a lot of Maggie.

'Going hiking?' she asked.

'Well, we were hoping to get into the caves,' Kronziac said.

'But Curly there,' Ellstrom butted in, 'said they were closed.'

The young woman gave a girlish laugh. 'Oh, you met Ken,' she giggled. 'Don't mind him, he's just a little grumpy in the mornings.'

Ken knew they were talking about him but remained silent as he mounted the steps again to get another box.

'So there's no chance of us getting in?' Kronziac asked, fixing the young woman with a plaintive stare.

'The cave tours are closed to the general public from December to March,' she replied. 'Sorry.'

'The general public?' Ellstrom said, picking up on the words.

'Yeah, you know – day trippers, tourists, hikers.'

'Do you have other tours?' Kronziac asked. 'During the winter?'

'We have the odd college tour, undergrads or researchers. I go in myself a lot,' she added grandly. 'I'm a sophomore at Oregon State, studying geology, so being a tour guide here gives me a lot of opportunity to observe at first hand the geologic action of groundwater.'

'A geologist!' Ellstrom exclaimed.

'Hope to be,' the young woman beamed.

'Very cool.' He nodded approvingly, making Kronziac glance in his direction.

'I'm a mathematics professor at Harvard,' he continued. 'And this is my research assistant Nancy.'

Of course, this prompted Kronziac to shoot him an even more vicious look.

The young woman smiled and studied Ellstrom for a moment, not really convinced that this guy looked like a math professor.

Ellstrom read her mind and produced from his wallet his faculty ID. 'Professor James Ellstrom.' He introduced himself and presented her with the laminated card.

'We're doing some research on geometric growth patterns in geologic forms,' he said and smiled. 'Numbers, like rocks, have been around a long time.'

The girl's face opened in a broad beam as she examined his ID. She had thin lips and slightly crooked teeth, like these of a child needing braces.

Kronziac sighed to herself. For some reason Ellstrom was annoyingly charming to just about every woman he met, young or old.

Still smiling, the young woman handed him back the card. 'You can cut the shit, Professor,' she said and looked at them both. 'You guys just wanna see the caves, don't you?'

244

Ellstrom's mouth fell open slightly, as if he had some words but had somehow lost them.

Kronziac laughed. She liked the girl. 'Yes, we just want to see the caves.'

The young woman nodded. 'My name is Petra and I'll be your guide.'

In the three-minute walk down the path to the cave entrance Ellstrom loitered a couple of strides behind, like a scolded child, while the two women chatted. Petra had given them each a yellow hard hat, complete with a caver's lamp perched above the peak, and she herself hooked a large rubber sealed torch to her belt.

'It really is beautiful here,' Kronziac remarked as a cool wind blew through the trees, the narrow stands of fir, heavy with snow, creaking like masts on a giant schooner. Among the marble outcrops swordfern sprouted in wide green blades amid the prickly leaves of Oregon Grape. Chipmunks scattered through the undergrowth at their approaching steps while ground squirrels stood on their hind legs, nosing the air.

'I love it at this time of year,' said Petra, taking a deep breath, inhaling the cool air spiced with cedar and pine. 'Any special reason why you want to see the caves?'

Kronziac stared at the ground as they walked, burying her hands deep in the pockets of her fleece-lined anorak. 'We'll tell you if we find it,' she answered as they neared the guide shack. A small wooden rotunda, its windows were shuttered and displayed a sign listing park regulations underneath a map of the cave complex.

'No small children,' Petra laughed, looking around as Ellstrom caught up. 'It's not the most pleasant place in the world if you're claustrophobic,' she added with a note of seriousness, not lost on Ellstrom.

'Is it very cold in there?' he asked.

'A constant forty-one degrees all year round,' Petra replied.

'About five degrees Celsius,' Kronziac translated for him.

'It can be quite slippery, so be very careful,' Petra warned.

Kronziac examined the map on the wall of the guide shack.

It reminded her of kindergarten, when they used to pour ink on a sheet of paper and then blow the blobs of ink all over the page, making a spidery black tracery.

'Is there a lot of water in there?' she asked.

'We have a small river running through parts of the cave,' Petra confirmed. 'It's called the River Styx,' she added jovially. 'Welcome to the underworld.' She gave a wry smile.

'River Styx,' Kronziac whispered to Ellstrom who was also staring at the diagram. He was running his finger around the various names marked on the cave network: *Paradise Lost* . . . *Miller's Chapel* . . . *Niagara Falls*. He glanced at Kronziac, his finger tapping another name – *Whale's Belly*.

'What are they?' he asked their guide.

'Names for the larger cave rooms,' Petra explained. 'Some of them are descriptive. *Niagara Falls*, for instance, exhibits frozen cascades of flowstone and *Grand Column* has a beautiful pillar of dripstone.'

'And *Whale's Belly*?' asked Kronziac.

'You'll see.' The young woman smiled mischievously and tightened the strap on her helmet. 'Ready?'

Kronziac nodded and followed Petra into the cave.

Ellstrom paused.

A corner of sky had opened up and sunlight, like a beaching wave, fanned across the trees sparkling with snow drops. The hushed silence of the forest was broken only by the distant noise of waterfalls, chirping jays and the intermittent clocking tap of a woodpecker on the fir trunks. He turned to the cave entrance, its dark aperture clad in a dun green suede of moss and alum root, the gaping mouth sighing, a waiting giant's breath.

Petra had turned on only the emergency lights in the caves, which gave just enough illumination to see where they were going as they climbed the steep steps and crept over the rough floors of stone. Some of the ceilings were very low and dripped water that tapped resonantly on their hard hats. Passages were very narrow in places, their slimy walls squeezing tight around the walkers. In the larger rooms the dim acid-yellow light did not reach the dark recesses. Only the concentrated beams of their miners' lamps zigzagged across the black walls.

'They were discovered in 1870 by a young hunter called Elijah Davidson,' Petra explained, 'who followed his dog Bruno, who was chasing a bear, into the caves. He only found his way out by crawling through the dark, following the running water.'

'Where is the water?' Kronziac asked, squinting around in the semi-dark. 'I can hear it but I can't see it.'

'All around you,' Petra replied. 'There's water percolating through the whole marble bedrock, in drips and in streams. The caves were formed when the Siskiyou Mountains were pushed up from the Pacific seabed 190 million years ago and the draining water dissolved the marble and formed the caves.'

As they entered a wide passageway, Petra stopped and pointed at the ground where small rough circular nodules of stone grew.

'Cave Popcorn, number seven in the cave tour,' Petra explained. 'Formed by evaporation as air flows through. If you follow it you could find your way out since it follows the airways – in theory, anyway,' she added and then pointed to a cheesy residue of white calcite growing like a moss on the rock.

'Moonmilk,' she said. 'It's supposed to have medicinal uses.'

'Are we near the Whale's Belly?' Ellstrom asked, puffing, as if finding it hard to breathe.

Kronziac looked at him.

'Next room,' Petra confirmed. 'Number eight.'

As they continued through the passageway, Petra pointed out a pattern of small interconnected rivulets on the grey stone, like the frozen surface of a lagoon. 'Rimstone Dams,' she called them.

The passageway finally widened out into a large cavern. The floodlights spread a milky blanket of light over the floor from which columns of stone rose like ice-cream whips, with whirls of frozen grey-white rock reaching for the ceiling.

'Stalagmites or stalactites?' Kronziac wondered, never able to remember which was which.

'Stalagmites,' Petra smiled. 'It takes about 4,000 years and eighty million drops of water per year to deposit enough calcite to form one of these two metres long.'

She took out the large torch and directed its cone of light at the ceiling. 'And them's the stalactites,' she announced, illuminating a citrine-coloured blunt spear of rock that jutted from the ceiling. 'The other pendants are called soda straws.' She panned the light across the ceiling, glazed with crusted icicles of rock.

'Well, this is it,' Petra said. 'The *Belly of the Whale* – so called because of the giant ribs of flowstone,' she enthused, marvelling at the banded draperies of rock that circled the walls. She angled the torch so the light climbed the walls until the beam disappeared into a curtain of darkness above them.

'I hear water,' Kronziac remarked.

'There's a river pool up there, I think,' observed Petra. 'Shall we move on?'

'The River Styx?' Kronziac asked, not budging.

Petra stopped in her tracks. 'Yes,' she responded, a little surprised at Kronziac's interest.

'Can we get up to have a look?'

'It's a bit of a climb,' Petra told her. 'It would be easier, maybe, to get at it from the outside.'

Ellstrom came close. 'What do you mean?'

'Well, if I remember correctly there's an opening to the outside up there, on to the cliff trail to Phoebe's Perch, a crop of cedars.'

'How long would it take to get out there?' Kronziac wanted to know.

'We'd have to find our way out and then follow the trail,' Petra answered. 'I'm not sure – an hour, hour and a half.'

Kronziac went over to the smooth ribbed limestone wall. She stretched and tried to reach one of the rills of rock to get a grip but fell back, unable to reach it.

'I'll go,' Ellstrom sighed, watching Kronziac attempting it vainly one more time.

Petra was getting increasingly concerned by their interest in the hidden ledge above them. 'What's going on here?' she asked finally as Ellstrom reached up, standing on his toes, and gripped one of the narrow bands of rock.

'Can you make it?' Kronziac shouted as she watched Ellstrom

pull himself up, his breath visible as white puffs of air in the light of his helmet lamp.

'Just about,' he grunted, hauling himself up the wall to the next rill, the toes of his shoes scraping the rock face. He finally dragged himself onto the ledge. He was barely able to stand up since his hard hat banged against the low ceiling.

'I'll need the torch,' he shouted down, peering into the blackness ahead of him which lightened in the distance where a small plume of light wavered like a phantasm. He could also hear the low murmuring of deep, fast-flowing water.

Kronziac turned to Petra who stood back defensively.

'Please, Petra, can we have the torch?' she asked.

But the young woman shook her head. 'If you don't tell me what you two are up to right now I'm gonna call the police,' she warned, stepping back further.

Ellstrom was calling from the ledge again.

Shaking her head, Kronziac reluctantly reached into the pocket of her coat and took out her black ID wallet. Flipping it open she showed it to Petra.

Petra looked up at Kronziac. 'FBI?' she asked, shocked.

Kronziac nodded. 'Please – the torch.'

'Shit, why didn't you tell me?' Petra cursed and handed over the lamp.

'I know I should have,' Kronziac apologized and then carefully threw the torch up to Ellstrom waiting on the ledge. 'You sure you want to do this?' she asked.

He nodded but Kronziac noticed the torch trembling in his hands.

After a moment's deep breathing to steady himself, Ellstrom slowly inched his way along the ledge, the cave ceiling pressing down on him the further he went. By the time he reached an opening at the other end of the ledge he was nearly crawling on his knees. Water ran beneath him, like a storm river in spate. He could just hear Kronziac's voice calling but she sounded as if she was on the other side of a wall.

As he squeezed through the fissure he explored the new ground beneath his feet carefully. He could feel something slimy and he reached out with his free hand to keep his balance, holding on to the ledge wall. Steady for the moment, he pointed the torch up the sides of the chasm where puffed ribs of marble grew up the flanks like gas-filled bags or parachutes, rising towards a small hole in the ceiling about a hundred feet up. A small cone of light entered the hole, pouring a dim ray on the winding green stream of water below. He tracked the torch's beam across the twisted folds of rock that now resembled large intestines – this cathedral of stone had turned into a giant's stomach.

His nose was spiked by a sharp stringent odour of ammonia. He stopped moving the torch and held himself steady. A feeling grew, tightening in his chest as his eyes adjusted to the light and his ears got used to to the roar of the underworld river. His senses were now aware of something close, something very large, something alive, the low heartbeat of a presence. He settled his feet into the slimy cream below him, from which, he now realized, the sickening stench radiated, and craned his head, following the torch beam as he moved it up, playing it over the cave ceiling directly above and behind him.

At first he was puzzled.

The ceiling was black, feathery, like flakes of hanging dry plaster. He moved the torch again and ten thousand red eyes opened above him. The ceiling heaved with a blizzard of snapping, screaming wings that shattered the still, vapid air and descended on him in a black cloud of screeching claws and teeth.

Ellstrom screamed and slipped off the wet slick of bat guano. He could hear Kronziac's muffled voice in the distance as he reeled headlong into the thundering water. He fought the thick black cold liquid flood for what seemed an eternity until somehow he burst to the surface. The deafening swarm of bats drained out the hole in the ceiling like black water siphoned through a sink hole. In darkness he thrashed across the river, his body growing numb, his limbs stiffening. But he could feel the hard wet flanks of rock on the other side and manoeuvred himself along the stone bank into the shaft of light that poured in from the hole in the ceiling. The bats were all gone, screaming into the distance. But he knew the bright outside world would turn them back and they would return. He had to get himself out quickly. This thought surged across his mind as he reached for a small island of rock. He stretched out and clawed himself around it to the lower side to pull himself up. But there was something on it, a broken, twisted shape.

Beached on the rock was a half-eaten face, turned in Ellstrom's direction, staring with burnt eyeballs, its flesh bloated and scorched. The body of Peter Kelley sat on the jagged rock – one arm dangled over the other side, finger bones trailing in the water – lounging on a throne of marble.

California State Lotteries

MegaLotto

RESULT

Wed 9th January

38   7   11   29   47   5

10796, BUCKMAN SPRINGS ROAD, CAMPO, CA

Phil Chavez had good reason to be happy with himself. He shook his head, still laughing at the corny slogan, reciting it once more to himself as he swerved the car into the driveway: *Ask not what you can do for your currency, but what your currency can do for you.*

A late-night creative meeting in the agency had kept him in the office on Fourth Street until 10.45 p.m., so it was well after midnight by the time he'd driven the sixty-five miles from San Diego. But the effort had been worth it. When they rang the CEO of Presidential Investments and pitched him the ad campaign for his company's new line of foreign capital venture portfolios, this difficult man with a reputation for steely conservatism told them quietly that they had won the 300,000-dollar account. Phil couldn't believe it but for his part he had landed a ten per cent pay rise and two weeks in the agency's condo in Tijuana.

He grabbed the bunch of flowers from the passenger seat, a wobbly bunch of Kingsblood tulips that he'd bought at the gas station to accompany the good news for his wife. The lights were all out on the street – everyone was in bed – as he walked up to the front door, balancing briefcase and flowers.

The taut squeal of a car alarm wailed somewhere across the neighbourhood and the flowerheads crackled beneath him as he fell to the ground. He wrenched his head to and fro against the gloved hand that clamped over his mouth and nose until the sharp pain driving into his neck dulled with a spreading numbness into black oblivion.

KENO

The ground beneath thrummed with the idle mumble of an engine. A coat of grease on the visor made the light diffuse and softened the appearance of everything beyond. Including that of the man at the valves.

It is hard to summon strength to shout when your face is confined in an oxygen mask. Philip Chavez's breath was being fed to him through a narrow hose and came hissing under pressure from its tank.

He could see that the young man was checking another long length of thick rubber hosing that led from somewhere outside the sphere of misty light.

Phil struggled in the harness, his own limbs tied with electrical cable to the arms and legs of the chair.

'Bobby boy! Glad you could make it!' his captor cried and sat down at the table in front of Phil, carrying a box. 'You liked it when we played Keno. He used to let you pick out the balls and you laughed and watched when he took his winnings.'

From the box he took out a plastic-framed drum on an axle. Inside it was a heap of small black balls with numbers on them, shiny as a scoop of caviar. On the table he placed a card with a grid of little squares, each numbered from one to eighty.

Phil had the distinct feeling of detachment of a helpless spectator, not a participant but still somehow the prey, watching from the suffocating cubicle of his mask.

'I'll give you six numbers and pick out ten balls,' the young man said, his voice woolly and distant though he sat no more than four feet away. 'If you get a match on three, then we'll leave the O-two on. Under three,' he warned, 'and you're suckin' tailpipe. Since you're tied up I'll pick your numbers.'

The young man took up a small pencil and marked six Xs randomly on the card. 'Shall we begin?' he asked.

Phil shouted at his captor but his voice only resounded thinly in the sealed rubber of his respirator.

The plastic drum rotated at the tap of a button, a child's toy turned by a little electric motor, the black balls falling over each other. When the drum stopped, one of the balls dropped into a plastic tray underneath, rolled out on a little chute and came to a stop. 'Number sixty-two!' the young man cried and craned his head over the game card. 'Sorry,' he muttered with fake regret – and quickly set the drum tumbling again.

Phil was thinking that his wife would be worried by now, would see his car in the drive, spot the crushed tulip heads – but his tormentor intruded into his field of vision, skittish, as excited as the boy who spots another caught under the teacher's looming shadow.

'Only two matches out of ten balls.' He grinned. 'Time for a hit of CO.'

He moved off to the oxygen tank and twisted the valve shut. Panicking, Phil began screaming muffled entreaties at his captor who moved to the thicker hose on the floor and opened another wing-valve on a T-junction.

'How long can you hold your breath, Bobby boy?' He smiled.

Phil stopped screaming as the acrid fumes spiked his nose. He could hear the vibrating mutter of a car exhaust piping carbon monoxide into his respirator from outside. His chest began to swell with the tight pain of asphyxia as the mask filled with hot pumping smoke.

The face outside was laughing, its owner dancing under the molten light.

ADIC'S OFFICE, FEDERAL BUILDING, WILSHIRE BLVD

Foley took a moment to savour his first Latte of the day, nodding appreciatively at his secretary Miranda who left them to business. Maggie, Sedley and Kronziac sat in a small semicircle in front of Foley's large desk while Phillips loitered in his usual place by the bookcases. Even Hoover seemed to be waiting.

Sedley leaned close to Kronziac. 'How's the wrist these days?'

'Good enough to fire a gun,' she replied.

'Right,' said Foley, smacking his lips, satisfied with the temperature and flavour of his coffee, and settled the cup back in its saucer. 'First, let me say I hope everyone had a nice Christmas and I'd like to wish you all a prosperous New Year.'

'Thank you, sir,' they all chorused in varying tones of appreciation, Sedley and Maggie the most enthusiastic.

'I would also like to say,' he went on, 'how nice it is to see our colleague Nancy back in the office – even in an unofficial capacity.' He qualified his welcome, making sure she still knew her place.

Kronziac smiled awkwardly as they all welcomed her back. She had the feeling it was like an AA meeting: she fully expected to be asked to stand up and tell the group how she was coping with staying away from her job for so long.

'Though she seems to have kept herself busy,' Foley said, not entirely approvingly. 'Nancy?' He gestured for her to begin.

'Thank you, sir.' She stirred, sitting up straight in her chair. 'I haven't had time to write anything down but I'll give you a verbal report.'

Foley nodded and put on his gold-framed reading glasses while the rest of them opened their notepads and poised their pens for Kronziac's report.

'Over the past three months a number of Missing Persons notices have been posted to police stations in Los Angeles, Las Vegas and Oregon. The notices have been printed out from police websites. On the reverse sides of the printouts cryptograms or codes, usually about three or four lines long, have been printed. With the help of a mathematician – a professor and expert number theorist from Harvard University—' Kronziac added, hoping to make the whole thing sound more credible '—we deciphered the codes and set about solving the plain-text riddles.'

'Riddles?' Sedley murmured.

'Yes. Directions in the form of cryptic clues, using mathematics, music or mythological figures.'

Sedley nodded, somehow indicating only the most provisional acceptance.

'Go on,' Foley urged. 'These directions?'

'To the bodies,' Kronziac clarified. 'We found three in all. The first was Cherie Blaynes, a sixteen-year-old schoolgirl from the Valley – we found her corpse at the Hyperion plant. The second was Ellen Holby, a sixty-six-year-old senior citizen from Vegas – we found her out by the Hoover Dam. The latest one, Peter Kelley, we found in the Oregon Caves. He was from the town of Heppner, upstate Oregon.'

'So all these riddles led you to these bodies?' Sedley enquired, rubbing his strong jaw.

'Yes.'

'Anything on cause of death, Nance?' Maggie asked delicately, sensing that her friend was again under the spotlight.

'The only autopsy I've seen has been the one for Cherie Blaynes,' Kronziac replied. 'The ME stated that she was tied up for some time before being killed by a severe-force trauma to the head.'

'Any sexual element or extraordinary characteristics that might point to an MO?' Sedley asked.

'Well, like I said, I've only seen Cherie's autopsy and talked to Bob Vesoles over at the county morgue. The girl may have had sexual intercourse around the time of the abduction but it may have been consensual and nothing to do with her murder. As regards any special features . . .' Kronziac was reluctant to say anything further. 'Dr Vesoles did discover a mark on the victim's forehead, seemingly scratched into the skull bone.'

'What was the mark?' Phillips asked, his interest piqued.

'It looked like the number six,' Kronziac stated flatly.

They all nodded, thinking the same thing.

'Ritual killer?' Maggie articulated the collective opinion.

'Could be,' Kronziac replied.

'I hear you're especially involved in the girl's case,' Foley remarked, glancing at his notes. 'Cherie Blaynes.'

'That's how I got involved in the whole thing,' Kronziac explained. 'Cherie's parents asked me to be their Victim's Investigation Liaison Representative.'

'What exactly does that mean?' Foley asked, slightly annoyed that he'd never heard of it and wasn't sure how seriously he should take it.

'Part of the Attorney-General's new guidelines for Victim and Witness Assistance.' Kronziac was happy to fill him in. 'Basically I can monitor the police investigation of their daughter's murder and keep them informed of its progress and findings.'

'But not actually participate in the investigation?' Sedley put in.

'No,' she replied icily, picking up his subtle reminder that she was still a spectator.

'And this math professor,' Foley asked 'he's been helping you crack these codes?'

'Yeah, he's a bit of a cryptography expert. His grandmother worked for the British Secret Service during the war and helped break the German codes.'

Maggie smiled at her and Kronziac knew this extra information wasn't really impressing anyone. Perhaps it only made them more leery of the whole concept.

'And you took him with you on your expeditions to find the bodies?' Sedley asked, smiling thinly.

'Of course. He was able to use his expertise to solve the math and locate the bodies.'

The two men exchanged knowing glances.

'As far as I'm aware, Nancy, math professors are not law enforcement agents,' Foley observed. 'He really shouldn't be running around the country helping you find dead victims.'

'I don't see anyone else helping,' Kronziac commented from the side of her mouth and looked out the window.

The Assistant Director ignored her petulant remark, not just because he didn't want to get into a fight with her today but because part of him might concede she was right.

'Okay,' he said with an air of decision. 'We have three victims in three states connected by these—' He looked over his glasses at Kronziac '—cryptograms?'

'Or ciphers,' she added.

He continued. 'So Nathan here, as case coordinator, will set up a task force to liaise with the relevant police departments and—' he glanced at Phillips and Maggie '—assign you guys to the case since the DTU is kinda quiet at the moment.'

Phillips watched Kronziac to see what her reaction was to Foley sidelining her again and handing the case over to Sedley.

Kronziac remained impassive in her chair.

'Thank you, sir,' Sedley said, shifting his broad frame. 'I'd just like to begin by thanking Nancy for her ingenuity and hard work in the case so far, especially given the pressures on her regarding the Bitteroot situation.'

As he talked, Kronziac wondered how much his pristine grey cotton suit cost as he flipped through the precise notes that he had taken down.

'As Assistant Director Foley said, I will begin flagging the case with the PDs and Sheriffs' Departments in LA, Vegas and up in Oregon as well as with the different coroners. We've got to let everyone know we're all on the same side,' he added forcefully.

Phillips, behind, cast his gaze up, understanding how Sedley had been handed the job of a DAD so quickly. Management-speak went down well in DC.

'Obviously we don't know anything about the perpetrator yet but we can be in contact with the Behavioural Science Unit to help profiling. But for the time being I think we should concentrate on the forensics studies and autopsy reports.'

Foley nodded in full support of his deputy's proposal on how to proceed.

'So.' Sedley turned around to Phillips. 'If you can take care of forensics and police reports, starting on a background check, running through VICAP for any similar MOs of guys sending this type of clue. Try all federal and state offender registries and the other criminal background information programmes.'

Phillips nodded. 'That's a pretty wide reach,' he said, not looking forward to sifting through the FBI databases of serial offenders.

'Well, we've got to start somewhere.' Sedley smiled and turned to Maggie, who was waiting eagerly with her pen poised over a blank page in her notebook.

A knock on the door prevented Sedley from beginning. Miranda came in.

'Excuse me, but there's a call for Agent Phillips,' she said in her usual calm, slightly diffident voice.

Phillips looked at Foley for permission to leave the meeting and his boss duly nodded.

As Phillips followed the secretary out Sedley continued. 'Maggie, can you get all the ME reports together and join Phillips in running a search for any patterns with any known offenders or similar crimes.'

'Yes, sir.' Maggie obliged, duly scribbling *ME Reps* on her pad.

Sedley turned finally to Kronziac. 'Nancy, if you can give us all your notes on the case, that would be great.'

She looked at him suspiciously. 'Yes, of course,' she replied. 'But I'll still be involved, right?'

Sedley stared at her with a blank expression that slowly softened to a smile.

Foley stood up. 'Can you get cracking?' he said to Maggie, who got up slowly, trying to give Kronziac a quick nod as if to imply support for her. It was obvious they had decided she should take no further part in the case, the one she herself had brought in.

Foley went to the window and looked out at the city as it lay beneath a warm sun, glazed by a thin gauze of cloud.

'I've talked with Internal in DC,' he said gravely and without turning around. 'They want to hold a disciplinary hearing sometime towards the end of February.'

Kronziac had been preparing for this but now that a date had actually been set it seemed to make it suddenly more serious, more real. She couldn't believe she'd done anything wrong when she'd shot the Crebbs boy. It was purely self-defence. She had run it over and over in her mind the past three months and all she could see was the close, deadly black muzzle of his gun pointing in her face.

So I'm still on leave?' she asked, her voice unsteady.

Foley turned around and walked back to his desk, where he started to rub at an old stain on the veneer with his thumb.

'I'm sorry, but I'm afraid you are, and that's why you can't be officially a part of the triple-murder investigation. Not only has it nothing to do with your Unit − nor is it in your area of expertise − but you are still subject to a line suspension.'

'Can she still work on it in a non-official capacity?' Sedley asked, startling them both with his question.

'Well.' Foley seemed doubtful. 'That's up to you, I suppose. It would be wrong of us not to use her help but she still has to stay in the background.'

Kronziac felt like a naughty child whose parents were debating her punishment. But at least Sedley seemed to be going in to bat for her.

'She seems pretty close to the Blaynes case and is empowered anyway by the victim's family to be privy to the police investigation, regardless of her status here at the Bureau. Why not let her continue in that capacity?' Sedley suggested. 'If she wants to.'

About two minutes ago Kronziac had felt like telling Foley to take a running jump out that window and informing Sedley that he could have her case file but with the added suggestion that he should shove it up his ass.

They were looking at her, waiting for an answer, when Phillips burst through the door. He held two sheets of paper in his hand.

'What is it, Phillips?' Foley barked, irked by the sudden intrusion.

'Just got a call from Palo Alto Police Department, up in San Francisco. They received this yesterday and copied it to me on HINT just this second.'

Phillips handed Foley the first sheet. It was another Missing Persons notice and showed a bland colour photo of a woman with dull blonde hair. The notice named her as Shayla Wilson, last seen just over a week ago in her own house on Mizette Street, Palo Alto.

'This was on the back,' Phillips said, nervously excited, and handed his boss the other sheet.

Foley looked at it. Shaking his head, he was about to hand it to Kronziac but instead gave it to Sedley who examined it closely for a moment.

'Your mathematician friend,' he muttered, not looking up from the paper. 'Is he still with you?'

2434 ABRAMAR, PACIFIC PALISADES, CA

Ellstrom seemed to have recovered well from his ordeal in the caves, Kronziac thought to herself as she wound the car around the tight bends of Abramar, the view of the blue steely sea jumping in and out of the hedges on the bluffs. She'd been worried about him for the first couple of days and had insisted that he get a check-up at the hospital. He was a civilian, after all, and finding a dead body in a condition like Peter Kelley's would be enough to traumatize most people for weeks. She'd told him to go back to Harvard to be with friends and try and get his life back to some sort of normality. But he'd resisted and stayed on in the house – it would be a couple of weeks before he had to resume classes.

To keep his mind off things Kronziac took Ellstrom to all the major sights – the Tar Pits, Hollywood Boulevard, the *Queen Mary* in Long Beach, even Magic Mountain. It was like entertaining one of her sister's kids on their first trip to see Auntie Nancy in sinful LA. But she had to admit, despite herself, that she was enjoying his company and even slept better at night knowing there was someone else in the house. Though she figured his only defence against intruders might be to distract them by reciting theorems or boring them into unconsciousness with a tirade on the beauty of recurring modular forms.

Kronziac found Ellstrom on his hands and knees, going through her collection of DVDs, CDs and vinyl under the television cabinet. Hector was watching him with his usual fixed stare.

'Jeez, Kronziac, your taste in music sucks!'

Sometimes it was hard to believe he was an Englishman.

'Haven't you got any jazz?'

Kronziac hung up her coat, taking out a copy of the cryptogram from Palo Alto.

'Oh, no,' she replied. 'No jazz, no Big Willie Whiner from Crud Creek singing the blues. Jazz is miserable overrated crap,' she asserted, having endured years of her father playing Miles

Davis and Duke Ellington on their old record player at home.

'And this isn't crap?' Ellstrom held up an old Duran Duran record from the eighties.

'I was a New Romantic,' Kronziac admitted as if it was something beyond her control, as if she'd been taken in by some sinister sect. 'I was young.'

But Ellstrom was looking at the folded piece of paper in her hand. He put the record down and stood up.

'Another one?' he asked gravely.

Kronziac nodded and held the paper out to him.

'Christ, is someone else dead?' She said nothing as he took it from her, sank onto the couch and opened it.

'Someone called for you while you were out,' he said distantly, staring at the column of numbers now in front of him.

'Who was it?'

'A . . . a Detective Cunningham from . . . someplace – sounded like a place in England, actually.'

'Devonshire?'

'Yes, that's it. He said to give him a call as soon as you can.'

Kronziac thanked him but he didn't hear.

The numbers in front of him were weaving their shapes of mystery.

Cunningham was becoming a pro at working the VCR.

He smiled to himself as he edited two pieces of footage from the traffic cameras at the intersection of Tunney Avenue and Devonshire from the night Cherie Blaynes had disappeared.

Kronziac sat next to him. By his excitement on the phone she was sure he had solved the whole case.

He pressed 'play' and the small yellow car entered the frame from the left, slowly driving up Devonshire.

'Right, this is her at 19.29,' he announced.

'You already showed me that tape,' Kronziac reminded him. They watched as Cherie's car indicated and turned left, driving north on Tunney.

'Right.' Cunningham smiled again, as if he had been storing up the punchline. 'If we move forward five minutes—'

He pressed the shuttle jog button and the screen filled with fast-moving cars.

'—At 19.34—' he pointed at the time block in the corner of the screen '—this car enters the scene.' The sharp nose of a dark-coloured car slowed to a halt at the lights.

The detective turned to Kronziac. 'Remember it,' he told her and pressed the fast-forward button, sending the footage into a frenzy of movement once again until the screen went blank, filling up with a fuzzy blue for a few moments. Then the footage returned.

'I've cut this in, a piece from the same camera at the same intersection forty-five minutes later.' He let the video run at normal speed.

'Here she comes again,' he said, obviously having now watched the footage many times over. Cherie's Mazda sped down Tunney Avenue and turned left back onto Devonshire to continue in an easterly direction.

'All right,' Kronziac said. 'I've also seen this before.'

'Look!' Cunningham cried, jerking out his elbow to nudge her.

267

She watched closely to see if there was anything out of place but could only see a monotonous procession of cars being fed through the crossroads by the changing lights.

'See it?' Cunningham asked excitedly.

'See what?' Kronziac screwed up her eyes at the screen.

The detective leaned forward from his seat and tapped the screen. 'Dark car again,' he said.

The sports car, which they had seen over forty-five minutes ago go up Tunney, now came down again, and also headed east on Devonshire just a minute or so after Cherie's car.

The detective punched the pause button and the screen juddered in a frozen frame, showing the rear of the dark car just before it disappeared.

'You sure it's the same car?' Kronziac asked.

Opening a small folder, Cunningham read the registration details from the DMV. 'A 1994 Ford Thunderbird Super Coupe,' he recited.

Kronziac nodded. 'Could be anyone just travelling the same route as Cherie,' she remarked, not yet sharing Cunningham's excitement.

He read from the file again, expecting her to be cynical. He'd known she was that type from the first day they'd met. 'The car's registered to a Mrs Lucinda Macapelli.'

Kronziac furrowed her brow. She recognized the surname.

Cunningham handed her the file. 'Check out the address,' he directed her, being purposefully economical with his words.

'610 Locusta Street.' Kronziac read it out. 'About four blocks from the Blayneses?'

He nodded silently, waiting for her to figure it out for herself.

'I know the name,' she said.

'Sure you do,' he smiled. 'It's Jared Macapelli's mom.'

'Of course – Donnie's buddy.' Kronziac smiled.

'He was using his mother's car that night,' Cunningham went on.

Kronziac put the brakes on his speculation again. 'It could be a coincidence that he was travelling the same way – they do both live on the same street.'

'But why take the same unnecessary detour up towards Porter

Valley? And why not mention it in his statement? He just said he drove straight to the shopping mall from home, no stops, no errands, no detours.'

'I guess you'll be wanting to talk to him again,' Kronziac concluded.

'I guess I will,' Cunningham smiled. 'And I guess you'd like to come along,' he added, answering her unspoken question.

610 LOCUSTA ST, NORTHRIDGE

The unmarked police car drew up in front of the house. Kronziac and Cunningham immediately spotted the dark blue T-bird parked in front of a Hyundai station wagon in the driveway.

'Have you talked with Jerry Blaynes lately?' Cunningham asked as they got out.

'Just on the phone a couple of days ago,' Kronziac replied. 'He seems to be getting more and more depressed about the case.'

'It's to be expected, I suppose,' Cunningham said as they walked up to the front porch of the timber-frame house.

Kronziac noticed a lot of boxes in the back of the station wagon, blue lettering on their sides.

The doorbell chimed and a figure moved behind the frosted glass panels at each side of the door.

A lean woman in her late thirties opened the door, holding a small red plastic dish in her hand, a bland brown paste of baby food in it. She seemed rushed and flustered as she swung the door open.

She seemed to recognize Cunningham in his wrinkled suit, but she couldn't quite make out if Kronziac in her jeans, white shirt and long raincoat was a cop too.

'Morning, Mrs Macapelli!' Cunningham said politely. 'May we come in?'

'Yes, of course.' The flustered woman stepped back from the open door. She was a handsome woman with dark hair and brown eyes, but her heavy make-up, hastily applied, only served to accentuate her deepening wrinkles around the eyes and mouth. She had the hurried, distracted manner of an overburdened mother.

'You'll have to excuse me,' she said, 'but I'm just feeding the baby.'

She backed into the front room on the right side of the hallway where a television was playing some raucous cartoons loudly to an audience of children comprising the baby crying in its high chair, his mouth caked with dried food, and three other kids whose ages ranged from five to eleven.

Mrs Macapelli kept glancing at Kronziac, still trying to figure her out, and Kronziac in turn kept hoping Cunningham wasn't going to mention she was from the FBI. Maybe she could just pass herself off as a female detective.

'I'm sorry, but I have to give her her food before it gets cold,' the woman apologized as the baby wailed with impatience.

'Sure,' Cunningham said. 'It's Jared we've come to see.'

The woman screamed upstairs for her son to come down and then pointed at the closed door at the other side of the hall.

'You can use the good room.' She smiled weakly. 'Just turn the key. I have to keep it locked to keep the younger ones out,' she explained.

Cunningham and Kronziac thanked her and opened the door into a large bright room that looked much neater than the rest of the house. China ornaments lined the redwood shelves and a group of family photos crowded on the mantelpiece over a black iron fireplace as if the pictures themselves were lined up for a group shot.

Behind the large beige velvet couch Kronziac noticed more brown boxes like those in the car. This time she could read the large blue letters of the labels.

'The name ring a bell?' she asked Cunningham who was peeking at some trophies in a glass cabinet.

He turned and Kronziac pointed at the boxes.

'Harmonex Healthcare Products,' he read out and then looked at Kronziac blankly for a moment.

'Makers of the FemiForm cervical cap,' she said, reminding him of the contraceptive device found in Cherie's body.

Before he could say anything the door opened to let in the rasping sounds of a baby's colicky cries from the other room competing with the boxed rancour of a TV sitcom.

Jared closed the door behind him. His tousled dark hair hung lankly, as if he'd just arisen from bed. He looked sheepish and regarded them both nervously before forcing a watery smile.

'Hi,' he said.

'Hello, Jared,' Cunningham said.

'Hi.' Kronziac smiled, not sure if he knew her, though they had met one day at the Blayneses'.

'Hi, Miss Kronziac.' He nodded at her and then turned to Cunningham.

'Is everything all right?' he asked, pushing his hands into his voluminously baggy trousers that barely held up on his bony hips.

'Sit down, please, Jared,' Cunningham said nicely. 'We'd just like to go over a few things again.'

The teenager hesitated, letting himself down onto the couch slowly. 'Have you found out what happened to Cherie?' he asked.

'Well, that's why we're here to see you,' Cunningham stated, his slow drawl making the kid even more nervous.

Cunningham took out his tiny notebook as Kronziac wandered around the room, casually looking at the ornaments and pictures. Though the room was quiet they could occasionally hear Jared's baby sister crying or one of the other kids shouting at the TV.

'In your previous statement you said you left home at about eight o'clock on the night Cherie disappeared and met the others at the mall just after eight-thirty,' Cunningham read from his notes.

'Yes, sir,' Jared replied tightly.

'And you didn't see Cherie until then – until you saw her at the mall outside the movie theatre?'

'That was the first time I saw her that day.'

'And the last time you saw her was after the movie?'

'Yeah. We all said goodbye on the street outside the mall and we – me and Rhiannon – went up the other way to my car. Joanne was parked across the road on Receda. Donnie and Cherie went towards the parking lot and that was it – the last we saw of her.'

'What car were you driving?' Cunningham asked, knowing full well that Jared had already stated in his initial deposition that it was his mother's car.

The kid hesitated. He glanced up at Kronziac who stopped

browsing through the photos and stared at him, waiting for the answer.

'My mom's,' he said, slightly hoarse.

'A '94 T-bird SC?' Cunningham probed. 'The car outside?'

Jared nodded. 'Yeah,' he said quietly.

Cunningham stared at him, which unsettled the teenager, making him shift uncomfortably in the couch.

'You've no more you'd like to tell us?' Cunningham tempted him.

'About what?' Jared asked, the strain beginning to make his lips quiver and a hot flux of blood run to his face.

Cunningham spread his hands in a gesture of openness. 'Anything – anything at all. Maybe your relationship with Cherie?'

Kronziac could see the kid seizing up with fear, his eyes darting between his inquisitors, a pained expression tightening his forehead.

'She was my friend.' Jared shrugged. 'She was my best friend's girlfriend and Rhiannon's friend – we were all like . . . good friends.'

The detective lowered his gaze to his notebook but raised it again quickly to Jared, as if expecting more.

'What does your mom do?' Kronziac asked loudly, moving around behind the couch to the boxes.

'She's a rep with a medical supplies company,' Jared answered, having to look over his shoulder at her.

'Must be tough taking care of a family too,' she remarked, looking closely at the boxes. 'What sort of medical supplies?' she asked, suddenly bringing her gaze to bear on him.

'Er – I dunno. Medicine stuff, I guess,' he stammered.

Cunningham glanced at Kronziac. The kid was scared shitless, they both knew that, but he still wasn't opening up.

Kronziac remarked that Jared was wearing a bracelet made of two thin straps of leather looped together. She remembered that she had seen another wrist band, identical, among Cherie's private things that Jerry Blaynes had showed her.

'Yeah, made it myself,' Jared said nervously, tugging anxiously at the strips of leather on his bony wrist.

'Make one for anyone else?' she wondered.

Jared jerked his head up in surprise. His face glowed red with fear. His throat twitched as he swallowed hard.

Cunningham immediately stood up from his chair. 'Come on, you little shitbag!' he spat. 'We have footage of your car following Cherie's, a good half-hour before you said you left the house.'

The kid sat forward on the couch, his mind paralysed, his body trembling.

The door opened and Mrs Macapelli appeared, smiling, the baby slumped over her shoulder grizzling as she patted her back.

'Is everything okay?' she asked, sensing the silent tension in the room.

'Everything's fine,' Kronziac assured her.

'You all right, honey?' Mrs Macapelli asked her son. She could see that he was on the verge of tears and his hands were shaking.

He tried to smile. 'I'm okay, mom.'

'He's gonna be a great help,' said Cunningham, more for Jared's ears than his mother's.

'Can I get you coffee or tea?' Mrs Macapelli asked. The baby was now dozing quietly on her shoulder.

They all declined politely and she left them to it, closing the door quietly behind her.

Jared's head sank into his hands and he began sobbing quietly.

Cunningham sat down again.

'Please,' the kid pleaded, looking up at them, his eyes glazed with tears. 'I had nothing to do with her death – I swear to God!'

'It's okay – we know.' Kronziac tried to calm him down before his mother came in again and started screaming for a lawyer. 'Just tell us what you know,' she urged him gently and passed him a handkerchief to wipe his nose.

'It was just getting out of hand,' he sniffled. 'Donnie or Rhiannon were gonna find out sooner or later.'

'Find out what?' Cunningham asked, flipping open his notebook again.

Jared looked at him, still tearful. 'About me and Cherie.'

'Go on,' said Kronziac.

'We started messin' around,' Jared confessed. 'You know, nothing too heavy at first – then . . .'

His words trailed off and he blew his nose.

'Then?'

'Well, it got kinda intense.'

'The sex?' Cunningham asked.

Jared nodded, making throaty noises and drying his face. 'It became sort of a game. We'd try and do it wherever we could, whenever we could. It was exciting – pretty crazy.' He laughed nervously but then suddenly became serious again. 'Everyone liked Cherie, she was popular, good at school, didn't tick anyone off. But I knew a different Cherie. Shit, I don't think she knew herself at times. She was crazy for it.'

Again the uncontrolled anxious giggle as his voice shook.

'Sounds as if she wasn't the only one,' the detective remarked acidly.

'Look, I never hurt her,' the kid pleaded.

'All right.' Kronziac stepped in, trying to keep him calm again. 'Just take us through what happened that night. We're only interested in her abduction.' She gave Cunningham a look as if to remind him that this was their priority.

Jared wiped his nose once more and tried to pull himself together. 'I rang her at home, coming up to seven, and suggested we could meet up sometime before we were to see the others at the movies. We arranged to meet at The Ranges.'

'Up by Porter Valley?' Cunningham asked.

Jared nodded.

'It's a sort of make-out place for local kids,' Cunningham explained to Kronziac. 'A wooded hill up by the Porter Valley Country Club.'

'What then?' Kronziac turned to Jared again.

'So we met up at about 7.45 – did the business and left at about eight.'

Cunningham smiled snidely. 'Quick worker.'

'Then what happened?' Kronziac said forcefully, trying to keep Jared talking.

'I left a couple of minutes after her and followed her down Tunney on to Devonshire. But then I hung right and drove down Wilson so that I wouldn't arrive at the same time or from the same end of Receda as she did.'

'Was it you who got her the contraceptive device?' Cunningham asked.

'Yes,' Jared admitted bashfully. 'My mom works—' He gestured at the boxes.

'We know,' Kronziac said, saving him from having to explain.

'And that's it?' Cunningham said. 'You didn't see her any more that night, on your own?'

Jared shook his head. 'No. She was with Donnie and I was with Rhianon. I never saw her again after we left the mall.'

The detective looked at him sternly. 'No more to tell us?'

The kid shook his head again. 'That's it. I swear to God.'

Another worried look, a different one, appeared on his face. 'Do they have to know about this?'

'Who?' Cunningham asked.

'Donnie, Rhiannon – the Blayneses. Donnie told me Mr Blaynes attacked him on the street, saying he'd raped his daughter.'

It was a tough question.

'I don't know, son,' Cunningham replied and closed his notebook.

Jared threw Kronziac a begging look behind Cunningham's back but she couldn't offer any comfort either. They probably would have to tell the Blayneses about the reason why their daughter was up at The Ranges that night.

Mrs Macapelli watched them from the front door. The baby had been put in the cot and she now had more time for the other kids.

'You think he was telling us everything?' Cunningham asked, getting in the car.

'Yes,' Kronziac said. 'I think so.'

'Me too,' he agreed. 'It solves one mystery – but it brings us no nearer her killer.'

2434 ABRAMAR, PACIFIC PALISADES, CA

A cartilaginous click made Ellstrom stop rotating his head to try and ease the tension in his neck that had built up during the seven hours that he'd spent at the computer screen. To his right, by the mouse mat, sat the Shayla Wilson cryptogram – the alphanumeric lines still staring at him, grinning behind their impenetrable mask.

OE 6:21:32 OG 2:22:18 NJ 8:23:9 OG 6:11:1 OP 51:7:18
OI 22:18:11 NR 1:9:12 OG 6:11:9 NJ 1:11:29 NP 1:1:4
NE 1:2:13 OI 40:22:8 OJ 1:5:14 OZ 5:4:49 OE 22:30:19
NM 1:1:1 OD 7:22:14 ON 1:21:19 OG 1:3:1 NR 4:3:20
OR 1:1:6 NM 13:52:8

He had tried several methods of cryptanalysis, or *attacks* as they were called by code-breakers – statistical regularities, alphanumeric patterns, departures from randomness. Perhaps they were settings like the Peter Kelley code, for the Enigma or some other encryption engine. But this approach had yielded nothing – Ellstrom had tried all the well-known code-machine emulators on the web. If they were not settings, then perhaps they were some sort of co-ordinates – or even times, in hours, minutes and seconds. It was while working on this line of analysis that he began to see the alphanumeric combinations as reference points. He'd continued the *attack* with this conjecture in mind.

In the 1820s a prospector by the name of Thomas J. Beale disappeared without a trace but left in trust with a friend three ciphers detailing the contents and location of gold and silver treasure believed to be buried in Bedford County, Virginia. The ciphers were a jumble of seemingly random numbers. Random, that was, until an anonymous person solved the riddle of the Beale ciphers by simply recognizing that the numbers in fact represented words. But *what* words still remained a mystery – until this mysterious cryptanalyst discovered that the key text for the first cipher was the Declaration of Independence.

Applying this knowledge the code-breaker got the reference numbers to yield the plaintext and the cryptogram was solved.

Ellstrom decided to try and see if the Shayla Wilson cipher was a variation of the Beale method. However, after fruitlessly applying the numbers to some of the works of Shakespeare and to the poems of William Blake, he began to wonder about the only real departure from randomness in the cryptogram.

The first letter of each set of the two-letter combinations was either an O or an N. If this was a Beale cipher then the keytext might exist in a version of O and N.

Such a book has been a number-one bestseller for over two millennia – the Holy Bible and its Old and New Testaments. Rather simplistic, perhaps, but not that readily apparent.

Cryptography, his grandmother used to tell him with theatrical emphasis, was like snake-catching – once you see the first one your eyes become accustomed to their camouflage.

The second letter of the two-letter groupings, by deduction, could refer to the *books* of the Bible, such as Genesis and Numbers – G and N.

Following the reasoning further, the first number delineated by the colon could be the chapter, the second the verse and the last number the word.

With some degree of optimism, Ellstrom downloaded as many versions of the Bible as he could from the Net. But his excitement waned as the exhausting process of applying the system to both the Gideon and Webster Bibles resulted in nothing more than a senseless word-soup of plaintext as indecipherable as the crypto itself.

It was not until he tried the King James version that the pang of excitement someone feels on the threshold of discovery began to tug at his chest and zing in his ears.

Taking the first set **OE 6:21:32** it broke down thus:

O – Old Testament
E – Exodus or Ezra
6 – Chapter 6
21 – Verse 21
32 – Word 32

Fractions of Zero

Exodus proved useless since there were only ten words in the verse so Ellstrom tried the book of Ezra.

And[1] the[2] children[3], of[4] Israel[5], which[6] were[7] come[8] again[9] out[10] of[11] captivity[12], and[13] all[14] such[15] as[16] had[17] separated[18] themselves[19] unto[20] them[21] from[22] the[23] filthiness[24] of[25] the[26] heathen[27] of[28] the[29] land[30], to[31] seek[32] the[33] Lord[34] God[35] of[36] Israel[37], did[38] eat[39]

Using this attack **OE 6:21:32** deciphered as the word *seek*.

CLARK COUNTY CORONER'S OFFICE, 1704 PINTO LANE, LAS VEGAS

Luckily, Ellen Holby had not been buried yet. The coroner was waiting for the deceased's only relative, a niece, to fly in from Nebraska to claim the remains.

The assistant wheeled the sheet-covered corpse into the examination room, a cold, featureless place with stark lighting and beige stone-tile floors.

The ME strode in, moving with the urgency of a doctor catching up on her rounds. She flipped over the top of a clipboard. 'Morning,' she said in a haughty, clipped tone.

Dr Elizabeth Fulger was fifty-one, a slim silver-haired woman with the sharp manner of a lab-dweller who spent most of her day in the unresponsive company of dead human bodies. Her treatment of live people was equally clinical – at least, so it seemed to the casual acquaintance.

'Morning, Elizabeth,' Detective Mazzalo replied. From the Metro Missing Persons Unit, he'd hooked up with Maggie when she drove out from LA. His voice was muffled under a mint green surgical mask, his body short and squat in the scrubs that the ME always insisted visiting law enforcement officers wore if they entered the 'clean' areas of the morgue.

'This is Special Agent Ramirez from the FBI field office in Los Angeles,' he said and waved a gloved hand in Maggie's direction. She too was attired in scrubs and mask.

'Something big going down?' Fulger asked, a sudden smile lighting up her usually stern features.

'Possibly,' Maggie replied. 'I'm glad to meet you and I appreciate your assistance.'

Fulger looked at her for a moment, searching for any hint of sarcasm. She didn't like smartasses, especially young female ones, especially from the FBI. Kronziac had warned Maggie that this might happen from time to time.

Fulger muttered something non-committal and turned back to her clipboard.

'Sixty-six-year-old female with extensive tissue decay due to prolonged submersion in fresh water and marine predation. Cause of death was a single projectile gunshot to the left temporal lobe. Circular entry wound, inverted bevelling pattern on skullbone with attendant tattooing, singed hair and abrasion collar. Extensive destruction of cerebral matter and large exit wound, shattering a large area of right temporal, lower parietal and greater wing of sphenoid.'

She looked up from her board, satisfied with the listing of the symptoms and now happy to impart the diagnosis.

'This person was shot at close range, about two to three inches from the left temple and at a non-oblique angle.'

'Any GSR?' Maggie asked.

'Ballistics is not my area,' Fulger replied curtly.

Maggie glanced at Mazzalo for a little help but he was feigning interest in the police reports he carried with him.

'The body was in the water a long time,' Fulger continued, 'Gunshot residue would most likely be insufficient to aid ammunition or charge identification.'

'Does the cranial damage from the exit wound suggest an explosive effect such as would be produced by a soft-nosed or unjacketed bullet of large calibre?'

Fulger remained tight-lipped but before she could decline to answer the question on the grounds of it not being her area of expertise Mazzalo finally chimed in.

'Forensics reckon a 9mm,' he said quietly.

Continuing on through her autopsy notes, Fulger referred to her clipboard again. 'The only other extant injury was an amputation of the second digit of the right hand at the proximal phalanges.'

'Her index finger was cut off?' Maggie inquired, excited by the possibility of another lead on the killer's 'signature'.

'Yes, it would appear so,' the pathologist confirmed icily.

'With what?' Mazzalo asked, interested too.

'Well, the skin couldn't really give much of a clue as there isn't much of it left . . .' She gave the faintest smile, an awkward grin of someone unaccustomed to mirth. 'But the bone indicates a clean-cut contact with a snipping action, such as a . . . clippers or pincers.'

'Not an animal bite?' Maggie raised her eyebrows.

'I don't think so.'

The shortness of Fulger's answer led Maggie to move on to other areas of interest.

'Any tox screen irregularities?'

Though it wasn't obvious, Maggie knew the pathologist was smiling, somewhere, the corners of her eyes bunching a little.

'Agent Ramirez, the body was in the water for several weeks. A great deal of the blood and tissue was leeched out and as most of the proteins were broken down into amines we couldn't detect positively the presence of drugs or alcohol.'

'So no screen?' Maggie asked, to make sure – and to piss the ME off a little.

The answer came back quickly and sharply. 'No,' said Fulger, put down her clipboard on the stainless steel instrument table and unveiled the head of the victim on the trolley.

Snapping on her surgical gloves, she lightly touched the gnarled tissue of the forehead, like a surgeon checking the consistency of the skin before beginning an incision. Only its position on the ragged T-frame of shoulders would tell the lay observer that it was a head. The skull was no longer rounded in an oval but was a squashed rind of green-purple derma, covered oddly by a dry husk of grey hair.

'Just one moment, please,' Fulger said with an air of determination and left the room.

The ventilation system purred noisily in its steel housing overhead as Maggie moved closer to the body. Mazzalo stayed where he was.

Contrary to popular belief many detectives suffered the same revulsion anyone would when confronted with the sight of a putrefied body with a stoved-in head. Mazzalo was glad to carry his crime reports for distraction. 'A canvass of the neighbourhood gave us nothing,' he remarked suddenly.

Maggie, leaning close to the head, had no idea for a moment what he was talking about.

'Oh, her apartment building?'

'It ain't exactly Beverly Hills and the people there aren't the most cooperative citizens when it comes to police matters.'

'Any forensic leads?' she asked, standing back from the trolley.

'Nothing much.' Mazzalo shrugged. 'We sampled the carpets, the door and furniture – just some fibres.'

The heavy doors swung open and Fulger re-entered holding a beaker of maroon-coloured dye that looked like beetroot juice. Her assistant followed, carrying a kidney-shaped steel swab holder with a scalpel in it.

'This is the latest FBI weapon in bone-wound detection,' Fulger said acidly.

'I take it Dr Vesoles called you?' Maggie smiled beneath her mask.

'Gave me the recipe,' the pathologist said. 'Food dye,' she added disdainfully.

Kronziac had told Maggie to arrange with Vesoles to call the Vegas ME's office and tell them about his DIY bone-injury marker.

Fulger placed the beaker on the trolley next to the head and picked up the scalpel from her assistant. Every movement seemed to be punctuated by a metallic clank: all the fittings – the examination tables, dissection bowls, scales and receptacles – were forged from stainless steel. There was a slight crackle as she ripped through the mottled skin, cutting a five-inch line down the centre of the forehead.

'The skin is already broken up here,' she remarked, noticing a faint circular fissure dug in the epidermis.

'You think her forehead's been cut already?' Maggie wanted to know.

The pathologist did not answer as the scalpel rang against the steel, dropping into the tray.

Like ripping damp leather, she parted the sides of the incision, squeezing some brown juice from the skin. The gaping rift revealed the sullied yellow bone underneath. As Fulger let

283

go, the folds of parted tissue drifted slowly back as if slyly wanting to cover up the exposed glabella.

The assistant handed Fulger the beaker and she tipped the burgundy liquid into the wound. Fulger exchanged the beaker of dye for a petrie dish of water with a basting brush in it and, holding back the skin flap, began stroking the slick bone like a watercolourist streaking the wash.

'Mmm . . .' she mumbled.

Maggie peered in over her shoulder.

'Okay, Thomas,' Fulger said, putting the brush back in the dish, polluting it with smoky curls of dye.

Her assistant plucked a small digital camera from underneath his scrubs and, placing it to his eye, craned over the pathologist, aiming the lens at the forehead.

With her gloved hands, Fulger parted the flap once more. Examining the wet globe of skull, she twisted her own head from side to side, puzzling at the mark in the bone, scarlet-streaked.

'Looks like a cross,' she remarked, faintly amused, as the camera winked and flashed.

2434 ABRAMAR, PACIFIC PALISADES, CA

Ellstrom was still sitting at the computer screen when Kronziac came in.

The printer whirred, delivering a map.

'What's this?' she asked, picking it up.

'Sequoia National Park,' Ellstrom replied in a tired, hoarse voice. 'May I have it?'

She passed it to him. 'Is this to do with the Shayla Wilson crypto?'

'Hope so,' he answered and set to the map with a ruler and a pencil fixed to the short arm of a compass.

'The plaintext's there,' he mumbled, gesturing at a sheet of graph paper on the table next to the screen. It bore the clouded strokes of many corrections with an eraser.

'It's a Beale cipher, using the King James version of the Bible as the key,' he explained, carefully drawing a straight line between three points on the map, creating a triangle.

Kronziac read the riddle.

> seek her beneath the snowball in the core of the circle that timber
> gap the little five and rainbow inscribe

'What are they – the snowball, timber gap, little five and rainbow?' she asked.

'Timber Gap and Rainbow are mountain peaks and The Little Five is a set of lakes, all in Sequoia National Park. Don't know what the snowball refers to.'

Kronziac was straining her eyes at the riddle. '*In the core of the circle?*'

'The *centre* of the circle,' Ellstrom assumed as he carefully twisted the compass, inscribing an arc within the triangle.

'What are you doing now?' Kronziac asked.

Ellstrom felt like a father harangued by an inquisitive child. 'I'm drawing a circle inside the triangle made by the points on the map so that each side is tangential to the circuit within.'

'Wouldn't that have been easier to do on the computer?' she wondered. 'On one of the graphics programs?'

'Do *you* know how to use them?' he retorted indignantly.

'Well, no,' Kronziac admitted. 'I never use them.'

'Sometimes it's better and quicker to use a simple pencil and paper,' he maintained as he completed the circle with the compass. 'The centre is on the intersection of the bisectors, or half the diameter, of course.'

With a small ruler, Ellstrom measured the radius of the circle and established the centre.

Kronziac looked closely. The point he marked coincided with a mountain indicated on the map.

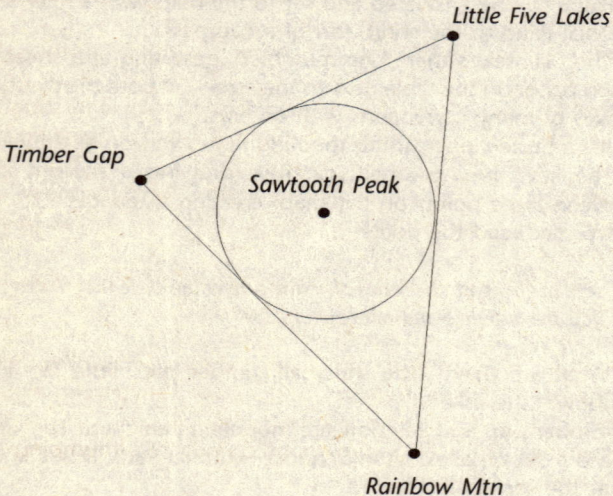

Little Five Lakes

Timber Gap

Sawtooth Peak

Rainbow Mtn

'Sawtooth . . . Sawtooth Pass!' she exclaimed excitedly.

Ellstrom scribbled QED on the map and got up from the desk, his legs creaking at the knees.

'Looks like we'll have to put on our hiking boots again,' Kronziac remarked, looking over the map that showed the details of the mountainous terrain of the Southern Sierra Nevadas.

HELIPAD, FEDERAL BUILDING, WILSHIRE BLVD

The large black Bell 430 helicopter landed on the roof of the building, the air swirling beneath its blades. Sedley and Kronziac turned away from the blizzard of dust as Ellstrom, shielding his eyes, watched with a mixture of excitement and fear as the large chopper sank on its skids and the whining rotors wound down. Sedley had been granted the use of the helicopter by the FBI HRT Air Support Unit from the Critical Incidents Response Group, Western Division.

Its meter ticked by the second and Sedley hoped Kronziac's Professor had got his math right.

'Where the hell is Phillips?' he shouted, the rotors still whooping above their heads.

Kronziac was trying to keep her hair in place and shouted back. 'Someone in the office called him just as we came up the stairs.'

Ellstrom beside her was smiling nervously, like someone windy at the thought of getting on one of the big rides at Magic Mountain.

The pilot was holding his hands up, wondering what the delay was.

'We'd better get on board,' Ellstrom said.

Kronziac was about to move when she saw Phillips running up the steps from the roof escape-door. He was carrying a sheet of paper that flapped wildly in his grasp.

'Come on, Phillips!' Sedley shouted under the thumping air. 'This bird's costing me big.'

'Sorry, sir,' replied Phillips, a little out of breath, instinctively lowering his head under the helicopter blades. He handed Sedley the sheet. 'This came in from Campo Police Department in San Diego.'

'Another one?' Kronziac asked.

Phillips nodded. 'A Philip Chavez. Been missing for almost a week.'

After reading it, Sedley turned to Ellstrom. 'We can provide

you with any technical assistance you need,' he promised,
thrusting the sheet into Ellstrom's hands. 'Computers, personnel
– whatever the Bureau can provide.'

Ellstrom looked at it, shaking his head at the line of cryptic
symbols on the paper. 'I'm not sure if I know where to start
with this one . . .'

'Well, please try,' Sedley implored him, glancing anxiously at
the waiting helicopter.

'Here, take these,' said Kronziac, holding out her car keys to
Ellstrom.

Ellstrom took them reluctantly.

'Let's go!' Sedley shouted. Followed by Kronziac and Phillips,
he ran across the pad to the open door of the helicopter.

Ellstrom watched as the engines got up to speed. The aircraft
gently rose, hovered for a moment, then swung out over the
city, heading north for the Sierras.

MINERAL KING RANGER STATION, SEQUOIA NATIONAL PARK, CA

Following the snaking line of Highway 198 at an altitude of 8,000 feet the FBI chopper passed by the Tehachapi Mountains and Bakersfield, over the San Joaquin Valley and its endless citrus groves. The south-west edge of the Sierras presented themselves like the forward runs of a lava flow, smooth spills of rock covered with grass and upland prairie. The terrain grew higher and rougher as they followed the Kaweah River, its tributaries forking east into the Great Western Divide and the white ranges of Sequoia National Park. The East Fork Canyon, still sporting brown gashes of flood damage along the banks, guided the helicopter into a clearing in the snow-coated pines where the Mineral King Ranger Station helipad was located.

While Sedley cleared details with the head Ranger in the station, Kronziac and Phillips transferred from the FBI copter to the yellow-and-red Medevac Bell 412 of the National Park Service Search and Rescue Unit.

The pilot provided them with bright orange-coated nylon parkas, alpine boots, cold-weather mittens and headsets for communication.

Phillips had to sit in the stretcher platform as Sedley climbed aboard with the Park Ranger to take the available seats amid the compact racks of emergency medical equipment.

'This is Ted Quin, National Park Service.' Sedley introduced him to his agents.

A large powerful man with spadelike hands, Quin exchanged salutation nods with Kronziac and Phillips.

'Do you know where we're going?' Kronziac shouted as the engines began whining into life and the blades started to whirl.

'Tethys Rock!' Quin shouted back and attached his headset so they all could hear. 'Known to climbers as the Snowball, a glacial erratic scooped from the peak about ten thousand years ago and deposited at the base in the pass.'

The Ranger leaned over and, retrieving a folded map of the area from his parka, he pointed at the location.

Kronziac nodded as the helicopter ascended above the log roof of the Ranger station and set its course towards the white peaks in the distance.

2434 ABRAMAR, PACIFIC PALISADES, CA

The Missing Persons Notice named the victim as Philip Chavez, a resident of Campo, San Diego.

He was twenty-six years of age.

Ellstrom shook his head, turned over the page and examined the mysterious characters for about the twentieth time.

᛫ᛋ᛫ᛘ᛫ᚷᛋ ᛝᛒ ᚷᚦᛈᛝ ᚳᛝᛋᛝ ᚨᛋᚷᚷᛘᛙ ᛝᛝᛈᛝᛒᚳ ᛋᛝᚹᛒᚷᚷ ᛝᛒ
ᛋᛝᚷᚷᚦᛝᚷ ᛝᛝᛝᛈᛈᛋ ᛈᚷᚷᛒ ᛝᛝᛈᛈ ᛈᚦ ᚳᛋᚦ ᛝᚦᛝᛝ ᛈᛝᚦ
ᚷᛈᛝᛝ ᚷᚻᛈᛈᚳᛋ ᛁᚦ ᛋᛝᛒᛏᚷᚳᛈ ᚷᛏᚷᛝᚦᚦᛁ
ᚷᛈᚷᛝᚳᛝ ᛝᛈᚷᚷᛈ

He knew they were some sort of hieroglyphic but of what tradition he couldn't tell.

Though he was expecting the return call it nevertheless startled him when the phone bleeped. It was Professor Clark from the Department of Classics at Harvard, a casual acquaintance of Ellstrom's on campus. He'd phoned back with the name of a classicist at UCLA who might help.

Ellstrom surprised himself by not responding excitedly that he was helping the FBI hunt a serial murderer to Clark's question about why he hadn't seen him around the University since before Christmas. Instead, he told him that he was just visiting friends in California and promised to buy him a brandy in the staff commissary when he returned.

After putting the phone down he looked at the name and wondered what someone called Theophile de Huesca would be like.

SAWTOOTH PASS, SEQUOIA NATIONAL PARK, CA

A vast rampart protecting the coastal cities of California, the Sierra Nevada mountain range extends from Honey Lake in the north to the hot desolation of the Mojave Desert in the south, reaching an elevation of just under 14,500 feet at Mount Whitney, the highest mountain in the forty-eight contiguous states of the USA.

Quin pointed at the mountain to the east, figuring his guests from Los Angeles might appreciate the view of its impressive bulk, black under a high sun.

To the west they could see another of the country's natural wonders. Growing at an elevation of about 5,000 feet, the towering giant Sequoia trees grew in a smoky red band on the flanks of the range, their rust-coloured trunks bearing with ease the weight of a fall of snow on their lofty branches. The ranger muttered something about the General Sherman tree, the largest living object in the world, but Kronziac found it hard to hear him as her ears began to pop with the altitude.

A gully in the mountains led the helicopter across the white-veiled crags of marble and shale, stitched with pine and sage-brush. They ascended through a low cloud bank that floated past like the dispersing wake of a steam train and then sunlight flickered in the cabin through the hacking blades overhead.

The pilot's voice patched in, crackling in their earphones, and announced that Sawtooth Peak was up ahead.

Nudging Sedley, Quin pointed at the granite slope, piercing a blue haze of sky.

'We don't have to go up that far, do we?' Phillips shouted at the Ranger.

'No, the Snowball's in the pass, lower down at the trailhead,' Quin assured him.

They could now just about see two lakes, one higher than the other like drop pools, beyond the shoulder of the pass, their surfaces caked with slabs of frozen ice and snow. A collar of red fir fringed the foothills in a crescent, turning up a shallow ravine that Quin called the Chihuahua Bowl, an avalanche-scoured basin named optimistically after the rich mines of northern Mexico.

'The Snowball!' the pilot exclaimed like a busman announcing the terminus.

About fifty feet in diameter, the circular lump of granite lay at the foot of the mountain, capped with a coating of thick snow. Gouged from the higher peaks, the rock had been carried in the arms of a crawling glacier and beached on a bed of scree when the ice caps retreated, its edges smoothed by millennia of wind and rain.

'Can we circle it?' Sedley asked, tilting his head and holding his microphone closer.

'Sure,' the pilot confirmed.

Deftly tilting the cyclic control, the pilot pivoted the helicopter in a circle, keeping the nose pointing at the rock below. Some of the loose fresher snow blew away like chalk dust beneath the orbiting machine. As they flew round the rock Kronziac noticed tracks in the snowfield around it.

'Bear, or possibly cougar,' Quin guessed.

He directed the pilot to flick on the thirty-million candle-power Nitesun searchlight to illuminate the dark recesses under the rock. But they couldn't see anything as the yellow disc of light shivered over the grey flints of scree, unable to penetrate the blacker corners beneath.

'I can't get right under,' the pilot uttered, a note of exasperation in his voice.

Sedley turned to the Ranger. 'Can we take her down?'

Quin glanced out the window to assess the conditions. But the pilot himself answered, overhearing the FBI agent's request.

'I can land her by the lake,' he said, lifting the chopper away.

'Okay.' The Ranger reached under Phillips's seat to the rifle locker.

They set down on a wind-cleared sandy lip above the lakes. Quin led the way, prodding the powdery snow with a ski pole as they traversed the pass. Kronziac followed just behind. For some reason she found the sight of the .22 hunting rifle strapped to the Ranger's back reassuring. For the first time in months she felt as though she was working with law enforcement people again.

She felt in some way rehabilitated.

'How high is the peak?' shouted Phillips, his voice flat in the still mountain air.

'The Sawtooth's over 12,000,' the pilot informed him. Phillips blinked at the peak looming above them, its summit blinding in a bright halo of sun.

The air smelled clean, sterile clean, as if filtered by the dry snow, almost metallic, with a strong element of pine. For the FBI agents it was hard going, their alpine boots soughing through the snow, their ribcages feeling tight in the rarefied air.

The Snowball seemed much larger now as they approached it from the ground.

'You get hikers up this time of the year?' Kronziac asked, breathing heavily.

'This part of the park is closed now and won't open again until Memorial Day,' Quin told her.

'But people can still get up here, without a chopper?' Sedley wanted to know.

'Mineral King Road is closed, but yeah – people could get here if they really wanted to,' the Ranger said. 'Officially it's a Class 2 hike, but most people figure it's harder, more like Class 3, almost Mountaineer category.'

As they reached the Snowball they paused to rest, panting out white jets of breath.

'Okay,' Sedley puffed after a few moments. 'Let's split up and circle it.'

Kronziac found it even colder on the other side under the rock where an icy wind coiled in the shade. She peered into the dark but could see nothing except a strewn litter of grey shale. She heard Phillips exclaim as if he'd stood on something unpleasant and she rushed to his side of the rock. When she found him he was sitting on his heels, about five feet under the overhang, his palm pressed to his mouth. He was looking at a near-naked female body wrapped in a large clear polythene bag, packaged like vacuum-packed meat. The dead woman was squatting rigidly, her knees drawn to her chest as though she was taking a piggy-back.

Sedley and the others joined them.

'Jesus!' Quin blurted. 'There's no head.'

The pilot did not come close, allowing himself only furtive glances, as if the sight would pain his eyes.

Sedley, cooler, leaned down next to Phillips and Kronziac. 'Holy Christ,' he gasped.

They could see the arms cradling the blood-caked head, holding it close to the breast as though nursing a child. The face was turned out, peering from the dark with dull, half-closed eyes. As the others whispered exclamations of disgust and horror, Kronziac was looking at the blood-streaked gash cut into the forehead.

ROOM 1137, DODD HALL, UNIVERSITY OF CALIFORNIA LOS ANGELES

The afternoon sun sank like a melting sweet over the campus, flooding the room with a crimson wash that illuminated the Attic *krater* Ellstrom held in his hand, depicting Aegisthus as he stabbed the king of Argos reeling in the web of Clytemnestra.

'Nice pot,' he remarked.

De Huesca's shoulders shook with laughter as he kept the glass lollipop eye of the magnifier to the document while he sat at his large desk.

'Got it in Paros for one hundred drachma,' he replied proudly.

Ellstrom felt at home amidst the shelves cluttered with ancient texts from Aeschylus to Plato and the Homeric tales with their titles embossed in gold leaf. The walls were hung with photographs of excavation sites, oil paintings of Corinthian glades and lithographs of the toppled columns of Rhodes. There were pictures of the Arcadian frieze with the Lapiths battling the Centaurs, the Artemisian slaughter of the Niobids and consultations at the Delphic Oracle.

Above the shelves, leaning against the wall, was a large terracotta plate of Aphrodite's flight, in a chariot driven by the winged Eros and Psyche. On each side, on amphorae, the blinding of Polyphemus and the frolics of a satyr play. Ellstrom sat down in the corner of the room beneath a black-figure plate from Laconia showing the bound Prometheus, blood pouring from his breast as the Eagle of Zeus pecked at his liver and his brother Titan looked dispassionately on.

Above all, Ellstrom felt comfortable in the hushed corridors of academia while he now waited in the sun, its light swarming with book dust, as he watched the Venezuelan classicist pore over the mysterious characters of the Philip Chavez cryptogram.

He'd liked him the minute they met. When he'd introduced himself De Huesca had declared they were already brothers, united by the love that mathematicians and classicists share for

296

the Hellenic tradition. Ellstrom kept to himself that his preferred language was Latin.

A corpulent man in his forties, De Huesca sported a thick dark beard, scorched red in patches as if he frequently stooped too close to the glowing incendiary of his panatella that was wedged lazily in the corner of his mouth. With an ochreous tan he had the bearing of a well-travelled man, starting at the UNIMet in Caracas, then on to the Catholic University of America for an MA, a year's fellowship in the American School, Athens and finally to UCLA, with endless excursions to the classical sites of southern Europe in between.

'Seems a crude use,' De Huesca murmured, the plosive whisper of a confessor.

'Of what?' Ellstrom inquired.

Lowering his magnifying glass, De Huesca turned around and smiled broadly around his slim cigar.

'Linear B.'

Ellstrom squinted in thought. 'Sounds familiar.'

'Sounds mathematical, I grant you,' De Huesca said and turned back to his desk.

'Is it a language?' Ellstrom asked.

'Sort of,' De Huesca answered vaguely, reaching for a copy of Chadwick and Ventris's *Documents in Mycenaean Greek* among a collapsed stack of lexicons.

'At first thought to be Minoan but now accepted as Mycenaean,' he went on.

Ellstrom stood up to peer over the Greek scholar's shoulder, the hieroglyphs distorted under the convex magnifier.

'Are they letters?' he asked, reverently, as if they were peering at the cryptic jottings of Pythagoras himself.

'Linear B is an inflective or syllabic system rather than alphabetic. Each character represents a consonant-vowel pairing and reads left to right, with ninety known figures. It was first seen on tablets in the ruins of the Minoan Palace at Knossos.'

De Huesca looked up, his head moving side to side as if following a fish darting in a pond.

'Ah!' he announced and tugged a pamphlet from beneath a

pizza box, frescoed with dry tomato bits and looking oddly at home among the ancient papyri.

He handed Ellstrom the pamphlet, which explained the history of the decipherment of Linear B from Evans to Kober. On the front cover, in marble weave, was a drawing of the Temple of Athena, the Parthenon.

'This seems to be a mixture of ancient and modern Greek,' De Huesca mumbled as he began his translation. 'Who the hell wrote it?' he asked, irked as a fleck of ash crumbled from his tapering cigar and fell on the page. Ellstrom retreated to the back of the room, pondering the same question himself.

The sun slid over the building and the room cooled as he sat under the Laconian plate, with its images of Promethean blood, the feasting eagle and the slack eye of Titan.

JEFFERSON COUNTY CORONER'S OFFICE, MEDFORD, OR

The American MD-11 bumped its way on a roller coaster of turbulence into Portland, Oregon and left Maggie light-stomached. She hated flying.

Doug Thornley, an agent from the Portland Field Office, drove her the two hundred miles or so to Medford. Still giddy from the flight, she droned on about the pros and cons of living and working in Los Angeles and how nice it must be to live in such a green state.

To shut Maggie up Thornley tossed her a copy of the Heppner PD crime scene report on Peter Kelley's disappearance from Umatila Forrest.

Signs of a struggle but no definite trace evidence around his abandoned cab . . . some tyre tracks around the clearing . . . casts sent to National Automobile Standards Bureau in Syracuse . . . clothes of the victim swept for fibres and second party hairs . . . some soils, fibres and a resinous substance, alkyd.

Now, in the frigid starkness of the morgue, she and Thornley waited next to the shrouded shape of Kelley. Oregon State Police pathologist Dr George Riecker entered the room in a suit and a plastic vest tied at the back with apron strings. He carried an old leather satchel and a cup of mint tea. In his sixties at least, he had the off-beam demeanour of a scatty academic, complete with a hesitant and shaky voice.

'Morning.' He smiled pleasantly, a wide grin of large yellowed teeth.

'It's Doug, isn't it?' he asked, holding his smile.

'Good morning, Dr Riecker,' Thornley replied and turned to Maggie.

'This is Special Agent Ramirez from Los Angeles.'

She held out her hand. 'Maggie,' she said.

'Delighted to meet you, m'dear.' Riecker bowed ever so slightly and she was sure he was about to kiss her knuckles.

'Yes,' he went on and laid his dark emerald-coloured tea on

the steel table that held the body. 'I got a call from a Doctor
. . . Doctor . . .'

'Vesoles?' Maggie prompted him.

'Yes – so here we go.'

Maggie had the vague impression that the pathologist still
had no idea who they were.

He rounded his shoulders and tugged at the sides of his vest
before lifting the sheet up to reveal the scorched head.

'Thirty-nine-year old male,' he began, without the aid of
notes. 'Positively identified from clothing and personal items.
Extensive crocodiling of the skin with collapsed blistering, keratin
nodules and pitting. Also parts of the skin arborescent in a fern-
like pattern. Many of the bones are fractured and internal organs
mottled and burnt.'

He looked up at Maggie, grinning gently. 'I've never seen
this before. It is obvious, though—' his eyes moved sideways
to Thornley '—that this man was *fried* – subjected to a massive
electrical charge – and it's hard to say what killed him first. The
whole ruddy thing, I suppose.'

On the crown of the blackened head he pointed at a shaved
rim of stubble like a skullcap. 'There was an electrode here and
on the calf of the right leg. See?'

Indicating the marks concerned with discreet pointing
gestures, he invited them to take a closer look at the scorched
patch on the head.

Thornley stayed where he was, declining the pathologist's
invitation. 'I'll take your word for it.'

Maggie heard herself say, 'So he was electrocuted?' in a strangled tone as her throat tightened with revulsion at the sight
and smell of the burnt corpse.

Riecker couldn't hold back his laughter. 'Yes, I think we can
safely say he's been zapped well and good.'

Standing back, Maggie straightened her shoulders. Riecker
looked at Thornley, obviously hoping he'd join in the laughter
but the FBI agent only smiled thinly and looked away. Kronziac
had told Maggie that the body was in bad shape when the
police dragged it out of the Oregon Caves but that still hadn't
prepared her for the sight.

'I suppose you might want to see the tox screen?' Thornley asked quietly, sensing she was a little out of kilter.

'Yes, yes – Dr Riecker, was there anything unusual in the serology?'

The pathologist retrieved a file from his satchel and took a slurp from his mint tea, now as cold as the body it sat next to.

His finger ran down the test sheet of mostly empty boxes. 'Blood ethanol negative, heavy metals negative – some traces of non-volatile organic compound. Blood, tissue and urine samples tested for scheduled drugs by thin layer and gas chromatography – all negative.'

'Those non-volatile compounds – any idea what they were?' she asked.

'I'm sorry, Agent . . .'

'Ramirez.'

'Agent Ramirez.' He bowed again in apology. 'This is just a county coroner's office. We don't have the equipment or the expertise for extensive analytic toxicology.'

'Do you still have the samples?'

'Of course.'

'Good.' She smiled. 'We might need them.'

'Will that be all, Agent . . .? I have an auto-accident appearance in twenty minutes at the courthouse.'

'Not quite.' Maggie stalled him. 'The test Dr Vesoles advised you on.'

'Of course!' he cried. He reached once more into the gaping jaws of his satchel and took out a large envelope. 'Intriguing,' he muttered and handed her the envelope.

Inside were two large-format colour photographs of Peter Kelley's forehead, the charred skin parted like an open purse to reveal the ivory bone beneath.

'Now, if you'll excuse me,' Riecker said and tossed the white sheet back over the head.

'Thank you, Doctor,' Maggie said loudly as he loped out through the doors.

Maggie and Thornley examined the photos closely without saying anything for quite a while.

'It looks like it's been carved,' Thornley remarked, deep in concentration.

'Mmm . . . but what is it?' she asked, wondering at the red dye-streaked marking dug into the bone.

Thornley huffed a little snort of surprise. 'Maybe I'm seeing things but it looks like an "a".'

NORTH AMERICAN BANK FIRST & UNION, 19302A
RINALDI ST, NORTHRIDGE, CA

The Super's starched pants rustled, almost sparking, as he led them into the Security Control Center on the top floor of the building. A long narrow room with tinted windows, it served as the bank's surveillance nerve centre. Long maple desks supported banks of VDUs, blinking with live footage from the cameras inside and outside the bank.

Kronziac barely had time to draw breath when she got back from Sequoia National Park before Ellstrom, preoccupied with the Phil Chavez riddle translation, mentioned that Cunningham was looking for her again.

That's Jack Shea.' The supervisor nodded in the direction of a heavy-set security man, sitting at one of the screens near the door. He nodded back, winking an eye red with conjunctivitis. 'And this is Josh Greene.'

He led them to the far end of the room and another security officer.

'Detective Sergeant Cunningham, Devonshire PD and Agent Kronziac, FBI.' The supervisor introduced them.

A rangy, thin African-American, Josh stood up from his screen and offered his hand, a broad smile on his face. His blue uniform hung loosely on his pole-like limbs.

'Josh, they want to take a look at the archives for the evening of September third last. The manager's okayed it. Can you key it up?'

'Sure.' Josh nodded and sat down again, grateful for something new to break the plain white boredom of the day shift.

The supervisor pulled over two swivel chairs and excused himself. The walkie-talkie on his hip warbled for his attention as he went out the door.

'Okay, folks, September third,' Josh said. 'Can you give me a time?'

'From about seven-thirty in the evening,' Cunningham suggested.

'Any particular side?'

The detective glanced at Kronziac. 'Any pointing towards the country club?' he asked hopefully.

'Porter Valley?' Josh asked.

'Please,'

Josh nodded. 'We got all angles covered,' he boasted.

Kronziac looked around the room. It was clean as a morgue: no paper, no pens, nothing other than the computer screens and a long dull blue cabinet housing the huge disk drives, green LEDs winking to show retrieval activity.

'Pretty swish set-up you got,' she remarked and smiled at the other security guard who was watching from the other end of the room, pretending to be busy at his keypad.

Josh's fingers were tweaking what looked like a white cue ball in a black socket, which made the cursor dance over the various icons on the screen.

'Yeah, this is the bank's latest Image Capture System. There are no more videotapes. All the images from the security cameras are digitized and stored in the servers behind.' He threw a thumb over his shoulder, indicating the cabinets, their fans humming beneath.

'We don't get any degradation that way, like you do on mag tape. It's a first-gen image, high res every time and easily retrieved through the bespoke archive program.'

'Should have one of these over at the station,' Cunningham wished.

'Yeah, tape's history,' Josh chanted. 'Though this particular system will relieve you of about two million bucks turn-key and will need about twenty grand maintenance a quarter . . . Right, here we go!'

He rolled the cursor ball and clicked on a folder marked '09'. The screen opened up, listing thirty sub-folders and he clicked on the top one. This in turn produced thirty-five files.

'Right, we got four cameras of the thirty-five covering the northern perimeter over the car park with the country club behind.'

'We're specifically looking for a shot of the . . .' Kronziac tried to remember.

'The Ranges,' Cunningham said for her.

Josh turned around to them, his hand stationary on the cursor ball.

'The Ranges?'

'Yes,' Cunningham confirmed. 'A bank in the trees below the course.'

'Yeah, I know,' the security guard said and turned back to the screen again. 'Around seven-thirty, you say.'

'Seven-thirty, seven-forty-five,' said Kronziac.

'We've three cameras on which you can pick up that area,' Josh said quietly and three pictures appeared along the top of the screen like postcards.

The frames made up a wide panorama of the car park behind the bank and the wooded hill of the country club in the background.

'Can you zoom in?' she asked.

'Well, it's not exactly zooming in the camera lens,' Josh said. 'But I can magnify the image at whatever part of the frame you want. We lose some res, of course.'

'How about up there?' Cunningham suggested, touching the screen with his finger on the first frame. 'The wall under the trees.'

'Please don't touch the screen,' Josh scolded him, a large grin on his face which was somehow worse than if he'd looked angry.

He clicked on the cursor palette and the first camera shot jumped in, widening the view of the trees in the background that hung over a graffiti-etched wall. The quality was slightly worse than the other picture boxes, more pixelated.

'What time are these shots at?' Kronziac asked and Josh punched a button on the small keypad next to the cursor ball.

'1800 hours,' he said as the time block appeared beneath the frames.

'Can we fast-forward to about 19.40?' Cunningham said.

The security guard nodded, clicked the keypad again and a rectangle appeared on screen. Like the console of a VCR the panel had play, fast-forward and rewind buttons as well as other controls.

Touching the screen on the play button made the three frames jump, quiver and settle again. On the wide-angle shots cars moved in and out of the bank's parking lot in the foreground while the trees on the hill-line behind remained motionless.

'What are we looking for here?' Josh asked.

Kronziac moved forward suddenly, squinting at the monitor. 'That!' she answered. 'I think.'

On the third camera a small light-coloured car slid through the trees and disappeared. As if travelling across the monitor screen itself the car re-emerged on the second camera, coming to a stop, the front pointing directly towards them.

'Can we magnify number two?' Cunningham asked excitedly.

Josh tapped the keys and the second frame moved in to a close-up of the yellow car.

'Fuck,' Cunningham said. 'It's her car, all right.'

They watched for about a minute while the small blonde figure got out of the car and walked under the trees, disappearing out of shot but reappearing, larger now, in the first frame. A red sweater, the gold strand of her necklace twinkling.

'Nice girl,' Josh remarked, watching as Cherie paced nervously up and down under the dark canopy of trees. 'Waiting for the boyfriend?' he asked, smiling.

The others remained silent. Kronziac's attention was on the third camera. A dark car was moving through the trees. It stopped next to Cherie's Mazda in the second frame and they could all see the figure of Jared Macapelli get out. They waited for him to appear in the first picture frame.

Cherie turned around, her arms open as he arrived, coming from the right. They embraced and began kissing passionately, which seemed to thrill Josh further.

'It's a real make-out place, a'right,' he cackled.

As he said this the three frames suddenly went blank, the pictures gone, blinking only in an electric blue.

'Shit!' Josh cursed.

'What the—?' Cunningham exclaimed angrily. 'Is it some sort of breakdown?'

Josh seemed to freeze, the reason for the interruption suddenly clear to him. He worked aimlessly over the keypad, pretending to be unperturbed. Casually glancing over his shoulder, he called to his colleague down the room.

'Hey, Jack, can you do me a favour and grab us some coffees?'

Shea's bulbous eyes stared at them as if he was detecting the palpable scents of conspiracy.

'Er – yeah, sure . . . you guys take milk and sugar?' he asked, getting up from his perch at the desk.

Kronziac and Cunningham gave vague preferences, bewildered by Josh's sudden concern for a coffee break. He glanced up at Shea as the older man left the room. 'Thanks, man.'

The door shut softly. A sigh of relief came from Josh.

'Okay,' he said hurriedly. 'Look, you gotta understand, Jack's officially my superior an' I don't wanna get him in trouble.'

'All right.' Kronziac went along with him, allowing him to explain.

Josh turned to the screen again and, with the dexterity of a concert pianist, he scrolled and clicked through a hierarchy of folders as they reeled down the monitor.

'The footage isn't missing,' he explained. 'It's just probably been . . . appropriated to Jack's private collection.'

'Collection?' Cunningham asked.

'Live porn,' Josh said as he tapped in a password. 'He doesn't know I have this. Silly fuck uses his dog's name.'

He accessed a folder labelled ADMIN and ran through the sub-folders until he recognized the date and time code.

'Here's the cut,' he announced and double-clicked the item. The three picture boxes blinked to life again. Magnifying the image on the first shot, they could see Cherie and Jared embracing, kissing passionately against the wall under the cover of the trees. On the second frame their cars were parked side by side and the road was quiet on the third screen.

Kronziac had to remind herself that what they were watching wasn't live – that Cherie would just walk away, go the movies with her friends and go home to her family. It was hard to keep in mind this had all happened nearly five months previously.

'The kids around here use the place a lot for their . . .

rendezvous.' Josh grinned, exaggerating the French word for effect. 'Who the hell needs the Net?' he added, chuckling. He quickly stifled his mirth, remembering he was in the presence of a cop and an FBI agent.

But Cunningham was watching the first frame closely. Jared had his back to the camera and let go of Cherie, who was against the wall. He reached down in front, between his legs. Cherie's hands moved around over his back and slid down beneath his jeans as he began thrusting into her.

Kronziac's eyes narrowed. 'Look at number two,' she whispered and the other two shifted their attention from the lovers under the trees. 'The trunk of Cherie's car just closed,' she said.

'What?' Cunningham cried.

'Can you freeze it and go back?' Kronziac asked and Josh worked his magic with the touch-screen console.

They all watched closely as the trunk of Cherie's car appeared to lift, its image fuzzy through the windshield. The car shook slightly and the tailgate snapped shut.

'What the fuck was that all about?' Cunningham ranted and glanced back to see Jared pumping away at Cherie.

'Someone else just opened the trunk,' Kronziac concluded.

'Well, maybe that's our answer,' Josh suggested, pointing at the third frame.

A shape, regular, the straight lines of a box, parked amongst the soft mosaic of leaves.

'Looks like the top of a truck or van,' Josh said.

'Yeah,' agreed Kronziac, peering closely at the dark shape. 'Can't see too much of it but I think you're right. A van. Kinda brown.'

Cunningham was shaking his head. 'Can't see the goddamned plates.'

The first frame again only showed the wall, grey under the overhang of trees. Cherie and Jared were getting into their cars and driving off.

'Well, that *was* a quickie,' Josh remarked. But Kronziac was still watching the dark shape of the van top.

'It's staying put,' she observed and turned to Cunningham. 'You thinking what I'm thinking?'

'Her car was a hatchback,' he said.

Kronziac nodded.

'In theory, you could crawl from the trunk through the back seats into the car. Right?'

'Yeah – in theory,' the detective agreed.

DEPUTY ASSISTANT DIRECTOR'S OFFICE, FEDERAL BUILDING, WILSHIRE BLVD

Kronziac was the last to arrive. She left Ellstrom outside, with the secretaries clearing room for him on the waiting lounge table for his maps and drawing instruments.

The office was not as big as Foley's. The windows faced north and you could see the Hollywood sign on the hills before the city dipped into the Valley beyond. From outside the thick windows you could still hear the hum of Wilshire traffic and the faint machine-gun stutter of a jackhammer gnawing at the pavement.

Sedley sat behind his redwood desk, under a picture of some yachts on Lake Michigan. He was indulging in small talk with Phillips and Maggie who were politely laughing at all the right places. They held on their laps thick folders and notebooks. Detesting clutter, Sedley had on his desk only a banker's lamp, a blotting pad, the open glowing screen of the latest palm-top computer and an oval-shaped photo of his wife and kids, framed in braided silver.

'You don't have to be here,' he scolded Kronziac. She was late and still felt flustered from the rush through the early morning snarl of cars.

'Sorry. I do appreciate you letting me sit in,' she said, acknowledging Sedley's last-minute invitation to join them for a progress meeting on the Cryptogram Murders, as they were now calling them. She wore one of her grey trouser suits and had her hair pulled back in a tail. She felt part of the office again, if only for a morning.

'Let's get at it,' Sedley said, opening a leather-bound notebook on his desk and tapping at the compact computer. 'Unless anyone wants a tea or coffee?'

He looked up at them to see who would dare.

They all declined.

'Great, let's motor.'

Kronziac was stunned by how easily he had assumed Foley's

terse dictatorial style. She wondered for a second, as she fumbled about in her case-file, how long it would be before Foley would retire and Sedley would inherit the oak desk, the sunny southern view and the brooding Hoover portrait.

'Let's start with Ellen Holby, shall we,' said Sedley. 'We'll come to Nancy to update us on the Cherie Blaynes case. Okay, Phillips, anything in the victimology?'

Phillips cleared his throat and ran a hand through his streaked blond hair as if to clear his head.

'Sixty-six-year-old female, white, senior citizen, lived in a run-down apartment building in Las Vegas. No family to speak of. Played the slots at the casinos but never ran up a debt. No record with the PD of any complaints made by her against anyone.'

He looked at Sedley and shrugged. 'That's it.'

'Okay.' Sedley nodded. 'Who's next?'

'Peter Kelley,' Phillips went on. Thirty-nine-year-old taxi driver. His own business. Just started out, so not rich by any means. White. Lived in rural Oregon. A family man. No reports of disputes with anyone.'

Sedley nodded as he jotted down his notes. 'Go on.'

'Shayla Wilson. Forty-year-old housewife from Palo Alto. Mother of two small kids. Happily married, according to the husband. And that's it on her, I'm afraid.'

Shaking his head, Sedley was taking fewer and fewer notes. 'And the last one?'

'Phillip Chavez. Twenty-six-year-old from Campo, Southern California. A junior advertising executive with a firm in San Diego. Recently married. No problems with anyone reported.'

Phillips looked up from his file. 'Pretty mixed bunch of pretty ordinary people,' he concluded.

Turning to Maggie, Sedley hoped for something of a lead, anything. 'Please. Forensics and autopsies have to yield something.'

Maggie didn't seem too sure about it but began eagerly. 'Technicians in Vegas swept the floors of Ellen Holby's apartment but came up with the usual traces of soil, dust, hair and clothes fibres – all relating to the occupant. Though some fibres found in the hall are yet to be identified. There were no prints on the door handles or furniture and no signs of forced entry. The door was found open.'

'She let him in?' Sedley asked quietly.

'Possibly,' Maggie said, her rhythm temporarily upset. 'The autopsy revealed that she was killed by a close-range gunshot to the head and a mark was cut into the skull bone, a cross we think. Her corpse was submerged in Lake Meade for about three weeks.'

'She was weighed down by a rope around her waist and tied to a concrete block,' Kronziac explained.

'Any traces on her?' Sedley asked.

Maggie shook her head. 'Submerged in the water that long,' she reflected. 'Not that much left to go on that wasn't destroyed or contaminated. No serology, no tox screens.'

'Any signs of sexual interference?' Phillips asked.

'No – none that could be found. She was quite possibly tortured, though.'

Sedley looked up from his notes.

'The forefinger of her left hand had been neatly severed,' she explained

'Any other mutilation?' Sedley asked.

'None that could be detected in the skeletal system.'

Sedley jotted down something. 'Next. Peter Kelley, I think.'

Maggie's answer came tumbling out almost in one breath. 'Crime scene yielded little. Some signs of a struggle with disturbed grass markings but no shoe impressions. Some tyre tracks were found nearby. A lot of hunters use the forest,' she added, not to get their hopes too high. 'The casts have been examined by the National Auto Standards Bureau in Syracuse and the tyres that made the tracks were identified as sixteen-by-six-and-a-half-inch radials, a general tyre for small trucks and vans.'

'What about the autopsy?' Sedley asked, becoming impatient.

'Cause of death – electrocution,' Maggie said sharply. 'Extensive burning of the body, both inside and out.' Though they had heard about it, the others in the room winced as she detailed the injuries.

'He was bound by the wrists – scrapings suggest an electrical

312

cord. His mouth was taped: some fragments of adhesive were found on the lips.'

She paused as if somewhat unsure about the only other detail she had from the post-mortem.

'The forehead displays . . . the skullbone had been gouged in what appears to be the letter A.'

'Is this guy trying to write someone's name or send a message? I mean, Western Union would be a lot less hassle,' Phillips chuckled, unnerved by the absurdity of it.

Sedley shot him a reproachful look.

'Quite possibly,' Kronziac reflected.

'Did any of the pathologists give any indication how these marks were made?' Sedley wanted to know.

'Not particularly,' Maggie replied, embarrassed at the paucity of information. 'They don't see a lot of this sort of thing.'

'Vesoles thought Cherie's mark might, and I stress *might*, have been made with a power tool, a small grinder bit.'

'Okay, we'll come to the Blaynes case soon,' said Sedley and turned back to Maggie. 'Anything else on Kelley?'

'No hard evidence, but some fibres on the combings of his clothes, no prints and no incidental hairs from a second party.'

'Great!' Sedley snorted. 'What about the fourth victim, Shayla Wilson?'

'Right,' Maggie began brightly. 'Palo Alto forensics carefully swept her home and again found some unidentified fibres in the carpet in her bedroom. They also found some traces on the duvet.'

'Traces of what?' Kronziac wondered.

Maggie shook her head. 'They don't know, that's why they mentioned it. Stood out because they could only identify it as some sort of—' she read from her reports '—alkyd resin, a generic cream constituent. Doesn't mean it's anything significant to the case but—'

'But it's worth checking out. Get it to Westwood,' said Sedley. 'Do we have anything on her post-mortem yet?'

Kronziac fielded that one. 'She was taken to LA County when we brought her back. I asked Bob Vesoles to do the exam. We should have a report by tomorrow.'

Sedley nodded. 'Okay. Seeing as you're talking, you might as well fill us in on the Blaynes girl.'

Kronziac began quickly, rattling off the main details of the case. 'White female, sixteen, from Northridge. Happy family background. No problems at school. All the activities of a normal teenager. Abducted at night,' she added finally, deflated that after four months she had little else to say on the case.

'Forensics?' Sedley asked, popping his head up from the glow of his palm-top.

'It was an old-model Mazda and the trunk lock was tampered with. SID found some soil traces and unidentified fibres in her car, in the boot and on the pedals.'

'You think her abductor drove the car?' Maggie asked.

'You think he got in through the trunk?' Phillips joined in.

'Maybe both,' Kronziac replied.

Unable to help himself, Phillips gave a jittery gasp that sounded like a dismissive laugh and riled Kronziac a bit. 'He hid in the trunk!'

'I think he might have!' she retorted. 'We have footage of Cherie up near Porter Valley Country Club the night she went missing.'

'When?' Maggie asked, puzzled by the new development. 'What time?'

'About seven-forty-five, a few hours before she disappeared.'

'Go on,' Sedley said in his judicial tone.

Slightly chastened, Kronziac explained in a calmer voice. 'Well, she was meeting someone there and while she was occupied you can see on a surveillance camera from a nearby bank a dark-coloured van draw up. It's not very clear, a lot of trees are in the way and you can't see the plates or the driver. After a couple of minutes you can see on another angle the tailgate of Cherie's car opening and quickly closing again.'

'What exactly is your thinking on this?' Sedley asked, testing the water with her.

'I know it sounds a little out there, but maybe her captor got into the trunk of the car, stayed there until later when she left her friends and boyfriend in the car park and made his way into the car through the back seats.'

'What is he? A freakin' ghost?' Phillips exclaimed.

'It's a hatchback, Phillips, it's possible,' Maggie said in defence of Kronziac.

'And?' Sedley contiued to probe her.

'And he subdued the girl, drove the car back to Porter Valley and transferred her to the van.'

'The cameras pick it up?' Phillips asked.

'Too dark,' Kronziac said quietly. 'But they do show the van stayed put long after Cherie left. And her own car was found abandoned up near there,' she added, placing the fact in front of Sedley like an appetizer.

'Okay,' he mumbled, ruminating on it. 'Interesting theory. Can we get a positive ID on the van? Make and model?'

'We only got a shot of the top of it,' Kronziac confessed.

'Well, we'll mark it as a possible lead,' Sedley said as he noted it down. 'What about her autopsy? What did he do to her?'

The direct question seemed to invite a direct answer. 'Cut her eyeball out and broke her skull so hard she bled out through the head injury. He cut what looks like a figure six into the glabella, the front skull bone, and dumped her in a sewage tank out at the Hyperion plant.'

Phillips shook his head as if suffering mild concussion and Kronziac felt a cold zing in her back which made her wriggle in her seat – not because of the graphic nature of the violence but the way she could just reel it off.

'I assume not much traces on the body?' Sedley asked.

'The sewage ate it all,' Kronziac replied quickly, regretting it immediately. 'No, nothing,' she added.

'Well, that seems to sum it up,' Sedley concluded as he looked over his notes. 'Victimology doesn't really give us anything – does it?' He opened it up to the floor.

Maggie shook her head. 'The victims are spread out from San Diego to Oregon and Nevada to LA.'

'All ages,' Phillips added. 'All backgrounds.'

'They're all white,' Sedley suggested.

'That narrows it,' Phillips mumbled low enough for Sedley not to take him up on it.

'Phil Chavez was Native American,' Kronziac reminded them.

'Forensics aren't much better,' Sedley continued, looking at his paltry few notes. 'No hairs, no saliva, no semen, no blood transfer – that's DNA out. These unidentified fibres? Any idea? Are they unidentified clothing fibres? If they are – well, that wouldn't give us much either.'

'Some of them might be synthetic clothing fibres,' Maggie tendered. 'The forensic boys in Oregon reckon some of them are possibly talcum powder.'

That didn't seem to satisfy Sedley. 'I want all samples shipped under appropriate protocols and containers to Westwood. See if the whitecoats over there can help us.'

He moved on quickly. 'As regards a profile. Well, the figures cut in the head seem an obvious signature. So, Phillips, continue running it through VICAP and the other boards for any matches.'

Phillips nodded.

'Anyone want to try their hand at profiling or do we want to hand it over to Serial Crimes or Quantico BSU?'

Kronziac stirred as if wanting to voice dissent.

'Nancy?' Sedley raised his eyebrows. 'You're not officially on board.'

'I know,' she replied. 'I wasn't volunteering but I was gonna suggest Fred Stranski would be good, best in the country in my estimation at understanding the human mind, especially the deviant one.'

'Fred's a good guy,' Phillips echoed.

'Stranski?' Sedley asked, frowning as he tried to recognize the name.

'He's with the FAA,' Kronziac informed him.

'How the fuck . . .' He paused to rein in his surprise. 'How would someone from the Federal Aviation Administration know about profiling a violent serial criminal?'

'He's ex-Bureau,' Kronziac explained.

'*Ex*-Bureau!' Sedley said, as if the 'ex' was worse than *never*-FBI.

'Taught Criminal Investigative Analysis at the Academy,' she explained further.

'At Quantico? Must have been before my time,' he said.

'Actually, after your time.' Kronziac volleyed it back without sounding too much of a smartass.

Sedley bowed his head, in partial and reluctant admission that he'd been outmanoeuvred. 'Well, we might be lucky to get anyone at all. Like you guys, Serial Crimes are being down-graded at the DTU. It seems cyber-crime is the flavour of the new century. The Bureau is putting more and more resources down that particular bottomless well.'

It was obvious that they were all getting tired in the room.

'Give him a call. It can't do any harm. If he's ex-Bureau at least he oughta know how to keep his mouth shut. Now, speaking of outsiders. Does your professor friend have anything on the cipher for Philip Chavez?'

'He's outside,' Kronziac said eagerly. 'He can tell you himself.'

As she went out they continued to exhaust all the angles on the case.

'Phillips, have Questioned Documents run through all the original Missing Persons Notices sent to the various police stations?'

The way Phillips said yes didn't fill his boss with much hope of a lead there either.

'Q-Docs confirm the type is laser-printed, no latent prints, no epithelial cell from saliva on the stamps for DNA typing.'

'Zip codes?' Maggie asked.

'Postal districts from San Francisco to LA,' Phillips answered.

Kronziac returned to the room, Ellstrom following her, his maps and papers bundled hurriedly in his arms.

Sedley stood up. 'Good to see you again, Professor Ellstrom.'

'Thank you.' Ellstrom smiled.

They were all smiling, trying to allay Ellstrom's nervousness.

'I think James may have cracked the Chavez riddle,' Kronziac announced, turning to Ellstrom. 'Haven't you?'

He shrugged and dumped his stuff on Sedley's tidy desk, knocking over the family photo.

'Sorry.' He blushed.

'No problem.' Sedley smiled and quickly moved the picture to a bookcase.

'Well, I think this one is all about projectiles,' Ellstrom began as he flattened a National Geographic map of the western states on the desk.

He picked up the translation from the Linear B cryptogram and read it out for their benefit.

> *shot from home according to the sum and produce of the*
> *third column in the square of sorrow to lie beneath a bed of*
> *stars by a sweet water*

'Of course, it took a while and a few more phone calls to the translator regarding the word *sorrow*. He felt it should really mean *melancholia*. And this gave me the breakthrough.'

'What's the difference?' Phillips asked.

Ellstrom took out another sheet of paper, a printout from an art website. It showed a dark engraving of a winged angel in thought surrounded by geometrical figures, a seascape and a sleeping lamb.

'It's called *Melancholia* and it's by Durer, a sixteenth-century artist and mathematician.'

He passed the sheet to Sedley and the others gathered around the desk to see.

'In the top right-hand corner, under the bell, you will notice a square of numbers. This is called a *Magic Square*.'

'We did those in school.' Maggie sounded as keen as if she was back there.

16	3	2	13
5	10	11	8
9	6	7	12
4	15	14	1

'Each line of numbers in the square, whether horizontal, vertical or diagonal, adds up to the same total. In this case thirty-four. That's the magic part.'

Sedley and Phillips were looking at him strangely.

Ellstrom referred to De Huesca's translation once more.

'*Shot from home according to the sum and produce of the third column in the square of Melancholia.* Here I think he's giving us the parameters for a projectile.'

'*SHOT from home.*' Kronziac nodded.

'The sum of the third column in the square is thirty-four, like all the columns, and the produce or product is 2,156. Assuming he's writing in metric, then we can calculate the range by squaring the velocity: 2,156 metres per second, divide by the constant of acceleration due to gravity and multiply by the sine of twice the angle of shot, thirty-four degrees.'

Now they were all looking at him a little strangely.

'That works out the range at 439.8 km from his home – which gives us a circle, radiating from Campo, with a diameter of 440 km approximately.'

Sedley was staring dumbly at the sheet of calculations, trying to catch up. But Ellstrom moved to the map, which had a circle drawn in pencil, its centre marked as Campo, on the Mexican border – Phil Chavez's home town.

'I believe the body is somewhere on the line of the circumference.'

'Covers a lot of ground,' Maggie commented, her finger trailing the circle from mid-California through Nevada, Arizona and on to northern Mexico.

Ellstrom seemed prepared for this. 'The last words in the riddle translate as *"by a sweet sea."*'

He pointed at a small lake east of San Luis Obispo, just north-west of Los Angeles and on the circle. 'Soda Lake,' he said quietly.

'A *sweet lake*?' Kronziac asked. 'I suppose that could be it.'

'Well, the other waterways that intersect the circle don't come near to the word *sweet*,' Ellstrom said.

'What's the *bed of stars* all about?' Sedley asked.

Ellstrom shook his head. 'Might be apparent when you get there.'

They remained quiet, looking at the map, the riddle and the calculations, trying mostly just to absorb the concept of a killer sending such an elaborate clue to the whereabouts of one of his victims.

Sedley was deepest of them all in thought, putting his hands on his hips as if about to ask another question but instead reaching for the phone and asking to be put through to the chief of CIRG in Washington to request the helicopter again. He looked up at the mathematician as he talked.

'Nice work,' Kronziac whispered, nudging Ellstrom. 'If you're right.'

SODA LAKE, SAN LUIS OBISPO COUNTY, CA

The copper-band horizon lifted in the windows as the black FBI helicopter banked for the last time over the water. Phillips allowed himself a yawn and surprised himself by feeling almost glad that they might be going back empty-handed to tell Sedley and Kronziac that the math genius had got it wrong.

They had spent the day at the lake, he and Agent Morris from LA with some of the local sheriff's officers, searching the shoreline of Soda Lake. They had checked the shaft entrances of the old mineral mines that ringed the water and peered under just about every sodalite-crusted rock but had found no sign of Philip Chavez's body.

The pilot was registering concern about fuel and visibility as Phillips stared upwards through the flickering circle of the blades, the stars emerging from the violet ink of a dusking sky.

'Beautiful,' Morris remarked. Phillips turned around to agree but found the other agent looking directly below them.

On the southern fringe of the silver-plated lake a galaxy of winking emeralds had appeared in the sand. Under the dim cabin lights Phillips read the riddle one more time: *to lie beneath a bed of stars.* He had to shout over the beating whine of the rotors to tell the pilot to take them down.

2434 ABRAMAR, PACIFIC PALISADES, CA

Ellstrom was slowly turning Kronziac's living room into a West Coast version of his study at Harvard. The hexagonal commode table was piled with scribbled notes of decryption rough work, atlases and encyclopaedias, while the couch and computer desk were strewn with downloaded printouts. Only Hector's cage remained uncovered by material. An uneasy truce had prevailed between himself and the lizard since Ellstrom's arrival at the house but they kept their distances. Ellstrom always left the room and sauntered on the patio or in the garden during feeding time – the lizard sounded as if he were tucking into a crusty burrito as he munched on cricket legs and a side dish of waxworm.

On the mantelpiece over the fireplace Ellstrom had placed the National Geographic map of the western states, the locations of the bodies flagged with brightly coloured pins.

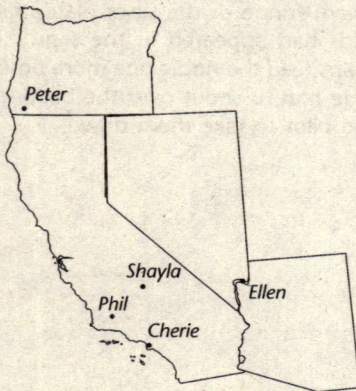

In front of the fireplace itself stood the blackboard from the Hawaiian bar, its menu of exotic cocktails erased and replaced by what he told Kronziac was a horizontal semantic table. On it he had chalked in the variables of the series of cryptograms and the locations of the bodies.

'Why don't you do that on the computer?' Kronziac asked, upset that her home was turning into a messy classroom with chalk dust atomizing in the sunlit air.

'I think better with a blackboard,' Ellstrom replied. 'Computers are fine for fast computation but they have no intuition. At college the Spanish Department has more PCs than we do.'

Kronziac glanced at her PC, forlornly streaming with the day's quote on the screensaver. Tennyson: *Knowledge comes, but wisdom lingers.*

Ellstrom hardly heard the knocking at the door and Kronziac running out to answer it. Standing back from the blackboard, he created some space between himself and the table to let the pattern of math and murder breathe and give the clues a chance to rear their heads out of the puzzle.

NAME	LOCATION	CRYPTO	RIDDLE	MARK
'Cherie'	Hyperion WWT	Caesar Shift	Keats – poem	6
'Ellen'	Lake Meade	Vignere	Mythology	+
'Peter'	Oregon Caves	Enigma	Beethoven – 5	a
'Shayla'	Sequoia Nat Park	Beale	Bible	
'Phil'	Soda Lake	Linear B	Durer	

Kronziac returned, herself preoccupied with reading the autopsy report on Shayla Wilson from LA County Coroner Bob Vesoles. Maggie had with her a stack of files cradled in her arms.

'Congrats, Professor,' she smiled. 'You were right again!'

Ellstrom turned. 'What?'

'They found the body of Philip Chavez buried on the beach at Soda Lake. He was in an air vent for one of the disused mine shafts, covered in phosphor-rich sand.'

'Really?' he said, brightening.

She nodded and retrieved a photograph of the burial site that Phillips had taken.

But Ellstrom didn't want to see it, turning instead back to the map and pinning in the location of Soda Lake, adding it to the other four points.

Maggie put the stack of files on the computer desk. 'Sedley wondered if you'd have a look through these.'

'What are they?'

'Information on the victims. Birth certs, addresses, vital stats, employment records . . .' She started to run out of steam. 'Everything we could get on them, really.'

'And what do *I* do with them?' he asked indignantly.

Maggie looked at him blankly.

Kronziac was still pacing the room, looking over the autopsy. 'Deputy Assistant Director Sedley hoped you might peruse this information to see if there was any sort of correlation with the cryptograms, the mathematical riddles and these people's lives.'

Ellstrom shook his head. 'Okay, just leave them there, please. I'll try.'

To get away from the noise of the others' conversation, Kronziac had retreated to the veranda and the silence of the sea. Maggie followed her out.

'What do you think?' she asked.

'Head severed . . . a clean cut . . . no signs of sexual assault . . . I don't know. It was like she was executed too.'

'Did you see the photos?'

'Not yet,' Kronziac said, still reeling at the thought of Shayla Wilson's decapitation.

'The ones of the forehead,' Maggie said. 'They're at the back.'

Kronziac flicked to the end of the report and found two colour prints of Shayla Wilson's exposed skull.

'It seems like just a line,' she observed, examining the gouged narrow channel in the bone.

'I think it's slanted, though,' Maggie said. 'Like a slash – you know, a back-slash. Toxes came up with a blood content of an alkylphenol.'

Kronziac looked up at her. 'Anaesthetic?'

'Propofol. Short-acting but quick. Puts you out like a light, according to Vesoles.'

Inside, Ellstrom was standing back from his exhibits once more, his mind connecting the invisible lines that ran between the points, drawing the shapeless network of the dead. He broke off, his head beginning to rattle, and turned to the files left on the computer desk to sort through the sheets of personal information with their endless lists of numbers, the statistics that govern all human lives.

MICROSCOPY LAB, MATERIALS & DEVICES UNIT, WESTWOOD PARK

A crucifix of spears in a field of crazed gold – sharp elongated splints of fibre braiding the yellow-shot light.

'Well, it ain't talcum powder,' Andrew Taggart sniffed as Kronziac drew back from the eyepiece of the microscope. 'Though under normal microscopy they would look similar.'

'You sure?' she asked, looking back at the 'scope, the light-infused image like a cat's eye in the black collar of the objective lens.

The young forensic scientist nodded firmly. 'Gross exam, phase polar exam and centre-stop dispersion gave the morphology and chemistry of the mineral growth habit. The fibres are monoclinic but anisotropic. The refractive index is 1.550 and the fibres soluble in hydrochloric.'

'So?' Kronziac urged Taggart, who seemed now to be just showing off.

'$Mg_3Si_2O_5 (OH_4)$,' he recited.

'Come on, Taggart, for fuck's sake, what is it?'

He began smiling, always enjoying the little thrill of stringing someone along when they needed his expertise. 'All the samples that were sent in, they're all the same,' he said. 'Asbestos, Kronziac, Chrysotile to be compositionally exact.'

'All of them?'

'Yep,' he confirmed, switching off the 100-watt illuminator under the scope. The image blinked out in the eyepiece.

'Chrysotile is the most common industrial asbestos form, found mainly in older buildings, used as insulation or sound-proofing. I'm sure you've heard the bad rap it's had over the past few decades. It's still around but not much in construction after the 1970s, not in this part of the world, anyway. The concentrations in these samples are low – more incidental or associative rather than a direct disturbance of the material mass. Still, it's nasty shit. I reckon all the samples were from a building with some asbestos insulation that's dislodging. Or the traces were left by someone working in the business of asbestos abatement.'

'Okay, thanks,' Kronziac said, pondering this information.

'A pleasure, as always,' he smiled. 'I thought they canned you for a while.'

'They did, still are – I've got a disciplinary hearing sometime soon.'

'Am I gonna get into trouble just talking to you?'

'Call DAD Sedley. I'm good, for now,' Kronziac assured him. 'Have you any results on the alkyd resin from the Shayla Wilson bedspread and Peter Kelley's clothes?'

'Oh, yeah.' He stirred, picking up a preliminary chemical analysis report from the counter. 'The techs in Palo Alto sent it in yesterday. Medford sent theirs the day before.'

He began reading the report. 'Analysis shows it to be some sort of organoclay, constituting de-ionized water and a high percentage of glycerin. We've a lot of petrolatum and other ingredients in smaller quantities.'

'Translation?'

'Some sort of cream.'

'Cosmetic? Could it have been the victim's?'

Taggart took a heavy breath. 'It's not just a moisturizer – it has some anti-inflammatory ingredients. More like a proprietary cream or emollient. But we'll have to run a cross-reference on the formulary to match the product and the manufacturer to find the exact purpose of it.'

'How long?'

'As quick as we can.' He smiled. 'So get outta here and let me get on with it.'

2434 ABRAMAR, PACIFIC PALISADES, CA

After her visit to the lab Kronziac called on the Blayneses. Though she had little for them she could at least assure them that everyone was still doing the best they could to track down the killer. She found the Blaynes household cold, Jerry and Cynthia quiet and uncommunicative, frozen in their still-raw grief, prolonged by not knowing why it happened or who did it.

Kronziac found it surprisingly comforting when she entered her own house and heard animated voices in the living room. Whereas before she'd always enjoyed the solitude and quiet of the place she now encouraged callers and secretly hoped that Ellstrom wouldn't be leaving soon. While there were people around the Woodsmen would stay away.

Fred Stranski was sitting on the couch, holding Ellstrom and Maggie in thrall with a story about an airline pilot who tried to climb out the cockpit side-window in an escape bid at 35,000 feet. The blue curl of Hector's green tail jutted from behind a large leaf; the lizard was shy of all the strangers.

Stranski got his lanky frame up off the couch and, after placing his cup of tea on the computer desk, held his long arms out to Kronziac.

'Nancy, Nancy,' he greeted her, his mouth wide in a toothy smile. 'Beautiful as ever.'

She hugged him and kissed him lightly on the cheek. 'Fred, so good to see you. How've you been?'

'Oh fine, fine,' he grinned, looking her over. 'How's your wrist?' he asked, suddenly concerned.

She flexed the digits of her right hand. 'Perfect now,' she declared.

'And how are *you*?' he asked.

'I'm fine, Fred,' she said in a firm way that reassured him. 'Shit, I could have picked you up from the airport. What time did your flight get in?'

'Flew into Van Nuys not more than two hours ago.'

'Van Nuys?'

'Yeah,' he answered proudly. 'Flew my new Cessna. Left National the day before yesterday. Spent the night near Wichita. I needed the hours to keep my rating.'

'Got a place to stay?' she asked, hoping he had, since her place was full up with herself and Ellstrom.

'Yeah, the Administration's got me a room at the Marriot.'

'The perks of federal service, eh?' Kronziac said. 'So you've met the gang.'

'Yes. It's good to see Ellstrom again. It's been a while.'

'Bet I can still whip your ass at snooker,' Ellstrom boasted.

Stranski leaned closer to Kronziac. 'He was more English than Noel Coward before he came here. Now he sounds like Jack Kennedy.'

He raised his voice so the others could hear. 'Agent Ramirez has been filling me in on the *cryptogram* case,' he continued, bemused at the strange description. 'Very intriguing.'

'Any ideas for us?' Kronziac asked.

The psychologist began laughing as he retrieved his cup of tea. 'I've only been here an hour and have had the briefest look at the salient points of the case,' Stranski said.

'Come on, Freddie, dazzle us with your incisive mind.' Ellstrom chuckled.

'Dr Stranski needs more time,' Maggie remarked. 'You can't just whip up a criminal profile like that.' She smiled.

'Thank you, Maggie.' Stranski bowed.

'Bullshit,' Kronziac shouted over her shoulder as she made her way to the Hawaiian bar. 'If I know Freddie he's already got some good ideas on the killer. Can I fix anyone a drink?'

'I'll have a dry one,' Ellstrom eagerly responded.

'I'm fine,' Maggie replied.

'Fred?'

'No. I'm fine, too,' he said distantly, pacing towards the French doors to look out on the ocean where the waves were tumbling lazily over themselves. 'I suppose all the classic indicators are there,' he began.

Kronziac winked at the others. She knew Stranski too well.

'Probably in his twenties, early thirties,' Stranski continued.

'Oh, and male, of course.' He smiled. 'Physically he might be quite strong as he is able to subdue his victims, even the male ones, quite easily. No overt signs of struggle.'

'Tox screens in one of the bodies show traces of a rapid-acting anaesthetic,' Maggie informed him.

'Someone in the medical profession?' Kronziac suggested as he handed Ellstrom his whisky.

Stranski continued. 'He's mobile, work takes him a long way, perhaps, out of state. He doesn't have to live by a nine-to-five schedule. Possibly a skilled or semi-skilled job. Limited contact with the public. Social interaction could be low, on the whole – conforming to the standard profile of this lone operator. A couple of friends but keeps to himself largely.'

'Traces of asbestos were found at the abduction sites and on some of the victims themselves,' Kronziac told them.

'The lab confirm?' asked Maggie.

'Yeah. Industrial chrysotile. We've gotta check out the asbestos-abatement industry,' said Kronziac.

Maggie wrote it down.

'Would he be married?' Ellstrom asked.

Stranski nodded his large balding head, the corners of his mouth downturned. 'Yes, possibly. But more probably a loner or a divorcee. Intimate relationships with this man would be difficult to sustain.'

Stranski began walking up and down. 'He might exhibit some pre-crime stress—'

'—Or post-crime,' Kronziac speculated, pouring herself a juice.

'He might betray himself by being careless in situations where he feels comfortable. Like a surgeon is careful in theatre but cuts himself slicing the tomatoes at home, so too might this fellow let himself go when not actually committing the crime.'

'Background troubled,' Kronziac mentioned. 'That's usually a given.'

'Oh yes,' Stanski agreed. 'Broken home, childhood characterized by physical and or mental abuse. Enuresis, fire-starter, animal torturer – all the preparatory psychosis of a junior demon. Probably got a rap sheet. A military discharge. Take your pick. Take the lot. All adds up.'

'I just don't get it,' Ellstrom protested. 'I mean, who would send these—' he gestured at his chalk scribblings on the blackboard '—cryptograms and riddles? It just doesn't make any sense.'

'Check the old case files,' Kronziac answered. 'Plenty of instances.'

'The Zodiac Killer in the seventies and eighties,' Stranski added. 'Sent cryptic messages to the police. Never caught, either. Was burying his victims according to some sort of geometric shape. A pentagram or something.'

Maggie was still pondering the present case. 'Would his ability to gain entrance to the house – I'm thinking specifically of the Shayla Wilson case – could it mean he is a practised burglar?'

'Yes, that's a fair assumption, Agent Ramirez,' Stranski said, pleased with the young agent. 'A police record might also reveal a history of substance abuse, petty crime, possibly a period of detention for violence.'

'Incarceration or institutionalized for mental illness?' Kronziac wondered.

'Yes.' Stranski agreed readily. 'The objectification of the victims is classically symptomatic of institutionalized behaviour or a product of such. He dumps them in specific places, uses them merely as messengers.'

'They are vehicles,' Kronziac said, 'their bodies only signposts on the trail of murder.'

'Right.' Stranski beamed, happy with his former student.

'But some of the victims were tied up before their execution,' Kronziac said. 'Cherie Blaynes and Ellen Holby had their fingers cut off. There seems to be an element of interaction here.'

'There are signs of a mixed behaviour.' The psychologist accepted the point and turned to Ellstrom. 'What intrigues me most is your work – or *his* work.' Stranski grinned but the comment made Ellstrom uneasy. 'The victimology,' he went on, moving over to the map on the mantelpiece, the blackboard beneath, its corners clouded with chalk. 'Most serial attackers initially operate within a geographically concentric area, the attacks radiating out from the criminal's hinterland. As he seeks fertile new areas of prey, he moves beyond the bounds of his own locale. But this case the victims show no geographic or social centralization.'

'Well, they're completely random,' Maggie stated.

'Exactly!' Stranski turned round abruptly. 'More correctly, they are *specifically* random.'

'Isn't that a paradox?' Ellstrom asked, slightly amused by the psychologist's excitement.

'It sounds like one,' Stranski admitted. 'But it's not, when you think in terms of the locations of the kidnappings and the burial sites.'

'Cherie was abducted and dumped in LA,' Ellstrom pointed out. 'The old woman from Vegas was submerged in Lake Meade, not too far away.'

'Peter Kelley came from Heppner, northern Oregon,' Maggie said. 'But he was dumped hundreds of miles away in the caves.'

'And Phil Chavez was taken nearly 400 kilometres, from near San Diego to Soda Lake,' added Kronziac. 'If he just picked people off the street, as it were,' she went on, joining Stranski at the map, 'then why not select them nearer the location where their bodies were found?'

Nodding, Stranski remained silent, giving Kronziac space to continue her train of thought, which was running parallel to his.

'The level of premeditation,' she continued, 'has the mark of a patient predator who has picked his victim and planned the abduction, execution and disposal according to a system. The trouble he takes and the distance he travels to get the victim means that he himself is subject to this system, the rules of the game – a throw of the dice, a pin in the map – whatever he has decided it to be.'

'An arbitrary selection system,' Stranski helped her.

'That selects someone specifically,' Kronziac added, glancing at her old teacher who was giving her an encouraging smile, just like he used to at the academy when he opened up the floor to the cadets, stimulating them, providing the oxygen for their thoughts.

'To identify a person uniquely,' she concluded quietly, a little dazed now with the excitement of thought.

'Yes,' said Stranski, matching her hushed tone. He glanced at the blackboard. 'And, given the mathematical nature of the cryptograms and riddles, the identifier would almost certainly be numerical.'

'Fuzzy logic,' Ellstrom said. They were talking in an abstract language that he couldn't quite grasp. His statement seemed to break the spell.

Kronziac broke off and walked back to clean up the cups. Stranski watched her go. It was easy to get carried away. He had to remind himself that criminal profiling was, is and would always be an imprecise art, allowing only a broad and mostly foggy image of a killer's mind – illuminating not the bottom but the depth of his dark soul.

Maggie seemed to be the only one upset that the party was over, still wanting to continue the fascinating, if complex, analysis.

'What system of selection would he use?' she asked. 'A mathematical system, you'd say?'

But Stranski shrugged, suddenly feeling the effects of his long flight across the country.

Ellstrom contemplated the amber dregs of whisky at the bottom of his tumbler. 'Some sort of a random-number generator, maybe,' he offered casually.

WILL ROGERS STATE BEACH, PACIFIC PALISADES, CA

Kronziac squeezed the wet grist of sand between her toes as she walked, leaving deep prints along the shore of the great Pacific. Stranski kept his distance, just beyond the reach of the waves as they crashed onto the beach and ran hissing up around their ankles.

'You had a good rest last night?' Kronziac shouted over the noise of the rollers.

'Out like a light.'

'I really appreciate you coming here.'

'The FAA office out here needed some supervision in their airman medical-procedure updates and it's nice to get out of DC, especially at this time of year.'

He glanced up, his eyes squinting under the bright corn-flower sky. 'How about you?'

'I slept fine,' she replied, smiling to herself. Stranski was always uncomfortable about personal questioning, no matter how informal. He would always turn it around. Ever the psychoan-alyst.

Phillips told me all about the Woodsmen thing,' he remarked, trying to steer her into discussion on the traumatic encounter. 'Sounds like it was a close thing – and then the informer and the alligators.'

Kronziac laughed out loud, her voice light on the wind. It sounded comical – *the informer and the alligators*.

'Well, at least you can laugh,' Stranski said.

'It's been a shitty few months, all right,' Kronziac admitted, stomping the fizzing water with her feet.

'And then the internal investigation,' he mentioned. 'Can't help matters.'

'Well, that's just a friggin' mystery!' she exclaimed. She stamped the water again. 'They're saying I killed Matthew Crebbs prematurely, didn't give him a chance to surrender his weapon or inform him I was a Federal agent. I mean, it's bull-shit!'

Stranski drew back a foot instinctively. 'Who are *they*?'

'Inspection Division in DC.'

'But wouldn't your section chief be the main point of contact?'

'I am a section chief – or was,' Kronziac said. 'Foley and Sedley are my direct superiors in the Western Division.'

'What's this guy Sedley like, anyway?' Stranski asked. 'Phillips thinks he's a brown-nose. But then Phillips thinks everyone is.'

'I don't know,' Kronziac replied, her eyes scanning the horizon beyond the restless waves. 'I don't know what to make of him, really. All I know is I've got to persuade them that Crebbs was gonna kill me. I thought the fact that he had a .357 Magnum no further than the length of a gnat's prick from my nose might've swung it.'

'Did he make any statement of intent to fire?'

'Jeezus, Fred, really. You think he was going to send me a written warning or say "Excuse me but if you don't mind I'm now stating for the benefit of your asshole DC suits that I'm about to liberate your head from your sorry ass!"'

Stranski turned away as a lone gull cawed overhead, wheeling up the cliffs to the highway. 'You should see someone about your language,' he said, trying to lighten her mood.

'Sorry,' she said, her legs beginning to goose-bump.

'Did he get an order from any of the other raiders?'

'To do what?'

'Kill you,' Stranski said simply.

She shook her head. 'Not that I can remember. There was a lot going down, you know. It's not easy to recollect everything that happened. Wish to fuck we'd been wired.'

Stranski suddenly stopped and turned to face Kronziac directly but she carried on a few paces before halting.

'What?' she asked.

'Come here,' he said.

'Why?'

'Just come here.'

She came back and stood in front of him.

'Keep your head steady and look at me,' he directed her.

'Dr Stranski, you're not propositioning me, I hope,' she joked. 'Older man falling for younger woman.'

'Just shut up for one moment, will you?'

Kronziac tried to stay still and played along.

'Now, without moving your head at all I want you to look up. Move your eyes up toward your eyebrows.'

'My sight's fine,' she informed him, still smirking.

'Just do it.'

Kronziac rolled her eyes up as far as she could, keeping her head still.

'Now try and close your eyelids slowly. But keep the eyes where they are!' he added quickly.

Kronziac's eyelids flickered slowly, like someone taking eyedrops.

'Okay, open them again,' Stranski said.

Her eyes opened. 'What was that all about?' she asked, blinking rapidly as the surface of her eyes stung.

'To see if we can help you remember. But you're not a particularly good subject, according to the eye-roll test.'

A wave crashed in and sizzled about their feet, soaking Stranski's trainers, as Kronziac's cell phone rang in the pocket of her shorts.

It was Ellstrom, excited by a discovery.

DEPUTY ASSISTANT DIRECTOR'S OFFICE, FEDERAL BUILDING, WILSHIRE BLVD

They caught Sedley just before he left the office. He had to ring his wife to tell her he'd be late for dinner. She gave him no end of shit. They were expecting guests.

Kronziac introduced Stranski to him and they were still shaking hands when Ellstrom spread his paperwork over the desk, once again toppling the family picture.

'What time is it?' he asked anxiously.

'Er – about seven forty-five,' Sedley answered, wondering what the rush was all about.

'You get K-CAL?' Kronziac asked, glancing at a small TV/VCR unit on the bookcase.

'Yes,' Sedley replied, even more puzzled. 'What's this all about?'

'I think Professor Ellstrom is the best person to explain,' she said.

'After you sent over the personal records of the victims,' Ellstrom began, 'I started to browse through their details. It was rather tedious but I got a feel for the basic things that we all have in common and the elements which are unique.'

He laid a single sheet of paper on the desk. On it was a list of the five victims, numbers written beside each name. 'After a discussion yesterday—' Ellstrom gestured at Kronziac and Stranski '—there was some conjecture on the possibility that the perp was selecting his victims according to some numerical mechanism and that each victim was specifically or uniquely identified. Since we all now agree that a number-based identifier is involved, I thought about the numbers that tag us as individuals.'

Sedley was already having difficulty following the mathematician but knew there was a point somewhere.

'I tried birthdays,' Ellstrom went on. 'I tried addresses, telephone numbers and other personal numbers and their various permutations. But I found really that these numbers do *not* identify us uniquely. People can share the same birth dates. An address only refers to a place. There really is only one number that is unique.'

'But one that is governed by a uniform system. One that everyone in the country has, other than children,' Kronziac said, feeling that it was important to add this point.

Sedley held his hands up. 'Okay, guys you got me. Now just tell me.'

Ellstrom stabbed his finger at the numbers on the sheet. 'Social Security numbers.'

'What?' Sedley cried, expecting something more dramatic. 'Social Security numbers? I mean . . .' He was lost for words. 'How do you know he's picking them by their . . .?' He didn't want to have to say it again.

Smiling, Ellstrom was ready for the question. Hoping for it. 'Do you play the lottery, Mr Sedley?'

'No. Personally I don't agree with gambling. Especially the lotteries. A waste of a lot of people's money.'

'Wise man,' Ellstrom said.

'You're not answering my question,' Sedley persisted, getting heated.

'Show him the results,' Kronziac urged Ellstrom. He took out another sheet of paper, a printout with lines of numbers on it.

'This is from a website run by probability freaks who monitor the lotteries to see if there are any patterns in winning-number frequencies.'

'And?' Sedley growled.

'They show the order in which the balls were drawn for the last six months.'

'Okay,' Sedley said in a hard voice that made even Ellstrom realize he had better get to the point.

'On Wednesday, eighth August last, the winning numbers in the California State Lottery were drawn as follows. 5, 7, 21, 28, 41 and the PowerBall, 17.'

'All right, Professor, this must be very interesting to someone but—'

Ellstrom continued quickly. 'Put the numbers together and you get 5721284117.'

Sedley just stared at him.

Ellstrom pointed to the number scribbled next to the first name on the other list. 'That's Cherie Blaynes's Social Security number,' he said. 'Conforming to the new ten-digit code introduced by the Social Security Administration.'

'Her number exactly?' Sedley asked, not sure about it.

Ellstrom handed him the sheet. 'Exactly.'

Sedley shook his head. 'It's probably just a coincidence,' he suggested.

'Could be,' Ellstrom agreed, glad to answer the challenge.

'On Saturday, October sixth, the result of the California State Lottery was in this order: 5, 30, 18, 39, 3 and the PowerBall, 24 – which gives us 5301839324.'

'Ellen Holby's Social Security sumber,' Kronziac said, straight out.

But Sedley was shaking his head again.

'Another coincidence?' Ellstrom asked, beginning to enjoy himself. He read from the results page again. 'Three weeks later the numbers were 5, 43, 11, 33, 22 and the PowerBall was 8.

'Let me guess,' Sedley said. 'Peter Kelley's number?'

Ellstrom and Kronziac nodded.

'And the others?' Sedley asked. 'Shayla Wilson and Phil Chavez, their numbers come up too?'

'Not quite,' Kronziac replied.

Ellstrom referred to the results table again. 'On Wednesday, nineteenth December the numbers drawn were 2, 20, 13, 25, 17 and the PowerBall this time was 6. This gives us 2201325176.'

'220 isn't a California SSN prefix,' Stranski explained.

'Or Nevada or Oregon,' added Kronziac.

Ellstrom began to explain. 'There is a change in the system here and it took me a while to see what he was doing.'

'What change?' Sedley asked eagerly. 'What did he do?'

'He used the PowerBall, much like anyone else who plays the lottery, as a sort of floating number, putting it in place of another. In this case he took the PowerBall 6 and swapped it with the first ball, the 2. This then gave him 6201325172.'

'Shayla Wilson's Social Security Number,' Kronziac confirmed.

'A couple of weeks later the draw pulled out 38, 7, 11, 29,

47 and PowerBall 5,' Ellstrom continued. 'This again does not give a California, Nevada or Oregon area prefix so, again, he swapped the 5 with the 38 to give us 5711294738 and Phil Chavez's number.'

Sedley, as if having to see the whole thing with his own eyes, picked up both sheets of paper. 'You sure these are correct and that the whole thing isn't just some sort of numbers coincidence or the product of an overactive imagination?'

'The chances of this occurring randomly are about as remote as winning the lottery itself,' Ellstrom said. 'It's just too beautiful not to be true.'

Kronziac wished he hadn't said that because Sedley looked at him with a pained expression, obviously struggling to believe the whole concept.

Stranski felt he should say something, for what it was worth. 'I think the fact the system has changed, with the use of the PowerBall in *two* instances as a mechanism to increase his chances of a match is . . . well, there's just too deep a level of correlation here for it to be merely serendipitous.'

Kronziac looked up in exasperation. *These fuckin' academics.* 'Sir,' she said. 'It's just too much of a coincidence. It also shows that he is having to change the system to suit another imperative.'

'And what's that?' Sedley asked, preparing himself for another barrage of numbers.

'Time,' she replied. 'He's running out of time, so by allowing a subtle change to the rules he increases his chances of matching but still keeps within the bounds of the game.'

'Which are important to him,' Stranski added. 'The rules of the game are what provides the thrill.'

'Five and six are the crucial numbers,' Ellstrom said. 'They are the first numbers for all the SSN-area prefixes in the three states of California, Nevada and Oregon.'

'Which seem to be his *terra operandi*,' Stranski put in.

'Shit! What time is it?' Ellstrom cried.

'Two minutes to eight,' Kronziac said and turned to the TV on the bookcase.

'It is Wednesday, right?' Ellstrom asked.

'Yes,' confirmed Sedley, confused by the fuss about the television.

Kronziac turned it on and quickly scanned through the channels until she got K-CAL and the midweek lottery draw.

'Remember, five and six are the important numbers here,' Ellstrom reminded them as they watched the balls tumbling in the jaded glitter of the lottery circus that was the biweekly live-TV lottery draw.

They breathed a sigh of relief when they saw that the first ball rolling down the chute was number 21.

'Now we have to wait for the last one, the PowerBall,' Ellstrom reminded them.

In the two minutes it took to draw the other balls Kronziac reflected on the irony that, while some people were at home marking off their numbers, a few getting excited as numbers matched, someone, somewhere, going about their life was about to have their death warrant sealed by the fall of the numbers.

'Thank God!' Sedley breathed in relief as the PowerBall came out as 27. He turned quickly to the rest. 'What are our options now?'

'We'll have to keep a close eye on the next draw on Saturday,' Kronziac replied. 'If a matchable number comes up, we've got to be ready. Either get to the person before he does or . . . rig the lottery.'

'The clock is running but what timescale it's on nobody but the killer knows,' said Ellstrom.

'The system he's used to select the victims is changing,' said Stranski. 'It allows him more combinations and the time between selection and abduction is coming down. There was only a week in the Chavez case. This guy's in a hurry. If he changes his system again, then we'll have to cover half the population of the western states.'

DEVONSHIRE COMMUNITY POLICE STATION, 10250
ETIWANDA AVE, NORTHRIDGE, CA

'Hey, Sam! You on for Toledo's?' the detective shouted from the doorway.

'Nah, you guys go ahead,' Cunningham replied, keeping his eyes glued to the screen.

His colleague shrugged in disappointment. Sam Cunningham missing a beer with the rest of the boys. Mrs C must be on his case. Or maybe it was all the time he was spending on his own in the Tech Support Room, watching hours of the same traffic-camera footage, again and again.

Cunningham had a band of pain running across his forehead as he decided to rewind over the shots of Cherie Blaynes's little car turning off Devonshire up towards Porter Valley and keep her illicit date with Jared Macapelli. He had seen the footage at least twenty times. Again her car indicated and turned left to disappear up Tunney, heading north. Again the same traffic pulling up to the lights after she had gone. Three cars in the left lane, three on the right, joined by the slowing hulk of an oil tanker, which concealed the other cars. The lights changing again. Between the cab of the tanker and its rig the cars in the left lane slipped by, only portions of their bodies blinking past – then a patch of brown, almost purple on the hazy screen – the high square frame of a small truck roof. He punched the pause button, rewound, stopped again and shuttled forward frame by frame. The van jerked through the gap between cab and rig of the huge oil tanker, the illuminated spot of its left indicator pulsing. Stop. Rewind a frame. He brought his head right up to the screen, could feel the heat on his taut forehead, the tingle of static.

Cunningham could just make out the misty white rectangle of a licence plate and its yellow squiggle of numbers.

FBI OFFICES, FEDERAL BUILDING, WILSHIRE BLVD

Seven fifty-five. Saturday night.

Phillips had set up a laptop on his desk in the open-plan 'squad' office and logged on to the Social Security Administration's Online Employee Verification Service with the full access codes from the SSA's Baltimore records HQ. They could now peruse the details of every Social Security Number holder on file with the federal system.

Ellstrom had switched on the large TV in the room and tuned into K-CAL while Maggie brought Kronziac, Stranski and Sedley up to speed on Phil Chavez's autopsy.

'Carbon monoxide poisoning accounted for large metabolic concentration in the body toxicology. The victim displays extensive pink hypostasis from the carboxyhaemoglobin. Smoke marks and carbonaceous traces were found on the face and in the windpipe and lungs, suggesting an extreme exposure to the exhaust gases of a motor vehicle. Again, some asbestos fibres were found in the clothing.'

'We're checking out the asbestos-abatement industry in the Los Angeles area, see if they run brown-coloured vans,' Phillips said.

'Any mark on the head on this one?' Sedley asked.

Maggie nodded wearily, passing around the pathologist's autopsy photographs.

'Looks like an "n",' she said.

'Any alkyl resin?' Kronziac asked, remembering the unknown cream found in Shayla Wilson's bedroom.

'None mentioned, no other definite associative evidence,' Maggie confirmed.

'Seems to be another execution-style killing,' said Sedley and turned to Stranski. 'Retribution? Punishment?'

'*Vehicles* for retribution,' Stranski agreed, making the subtle but important amendment.

After a quick intro on how lottery funds had just helped install and equip a new gymnasium for a high school in Encino, the television buzzed with the glitzy California State Lottery's Saturday-night MegaLotto draw.

Phillips waited at the laptop as the others crowded around the TV.

'You know, I do this every week,' Maggie confessed.

'Well, I hope you didn't pick a five or a six this week,' Ellstrom said.

The drum was tumbling, the forty-seven balls inside tossing in a revolving tumult until the first was sucked out.

'Thirty! Thank God!' said Stranski.

'Now we have to wait for the PowerBall at the end,' Ellstrom reminded them as the second ball was selected.

'Twenty-five,' Kronziac said.

'That might not be so good,' remarked Ellstrom, glancing at his list of California Social Security Number area prefixes.

'It's frightening to think he's out there watching this too,' said Maggie as the next ball, sixteen, rumbled through the gate.

'The next *victim* could be watching,' added Phillips. The fourth ball picked was twenty-eight.

'One to go, then the PowerBall,' Ellstrom announced, sucking air through his teeth.

'It's a two,' observed Stranski as the ball came to a halt at the end of the chute.

'Okay, guys.' Kronziac raised her voice as the excitement grew in the room, each offering their odds on a five or six.

'This is it!' Maggie announced nervously.

Sedley turned to Phillips. 'You ready? Just in case.'

Phillips nodded, his fingers poised over the laptop keyboard.

The drum continued its last rotation, mixing the balls that were hopping like popcorn.

'A five or six hasn't come up for weeks,' Maggie remarked.

'That really has no bearing on whether they will come up tonight,' Ellstrom told her but hadn't time to explain.

'Everyone shut up!' Sedley snapped. 'It's coming.'

Kronziac closed her eyes and prayed to whatever gods there were who controlled such things to give them anything but a five or six.

'Looks like a nine!' Maggie shouted as the ball was sucked out of the drum and rolled the chute.

'No, it's a six,' Stranski said, watching closely.

'Jesus,' Ellstrom whispered. 'I don't believe it.'

The emcee was congratulating the winners out there in TV land and announced the jackpot at over twenty-one million dollars. Quickly she recapped the winning numbers, which were flashed up on screen before they went off air: 30, 25, 16, 28, 2 and PowerBall 6.

Kronziac turned quickly to Ellstrom who was already scribbling out the permutations with a shaky hand.

'If he swaps the six with the thirty then we have 6251628230! A valid SSN for California.'

Kronziac snatched the scribbled number from Ellstrom and shoved it in front of Phillips. 'Can you read it?'

Phillips nodded and tapped in the numbers in the SSN database query box. Before he punched the enter button he checked the numbers one more time. '6251628230?'

'Yes, yes, that's it! Enter it!' Ellstrom shouted.

The screen blinked as Phillips stabbed the enter button and several information boxes opened up.

'We've got a hit,' Phillips said, seeing the name coming up. 'An assigned number.'

'John Harvey Rogers,' Kronziac read out the name. '53725 Burmount Avenue, Annaheim.'

Sedley was already on the phone to contact the local police department and ask them to send an unmarked car, if possible, to the address while the FBI set up a surveillance plan.

'It will take time for the killer to locate and plan the abduction,' said Stranski, trying to calm the room.

'Might be the best thing to have happened,' said Phillips, sitting back from the laptop. 'At least now we know where the bastard's going to strike next.'

'Only if he sticks to the system,' Kronziac warned.

Maggie was shaking her head in horrified realization. 'He's planning it right now, as we speak.'

California State Lotteries

Mega Lotto

RESULT

Sat 3rd February

30   25   16   28   2   6

DEVONSHIRE COMMUNITY POLICE STATION, 10250 ETIWANDA AVE NORTHRIDGE, CA

They found Detective Cunningham at the front desk. He was talking to an official-looking woman in her fifties. With white alabaster skin, a blooming bouffant and oriental features she looked like Imelda Marcos in a red Chanel skirt and jacket, and smelt of a muted sweet scent favoured by older women. With a briefcase and a heap of files under her arm she had the casual formality of a DA, and Kronziac thought she recognized her from county court.

'Hey, Kronziac!' Cunningham saluted her loudly.

'Detective Cunningham,' Kronziac replied, wondering why he seemed so pumped. She introduced Fred Stranski.

'FBI too?' Cunningham asked as he shook the psychologist's hand.

'FAA.' Stranski grinned as a hollow hoot of laughter, more social than truly amused, broke out between the four.

'This is Assistant District Attorney Mary Scholte,' said Cunningham. 'Nancy Kronziac, FBI, she's the Blaynes family's designated investigation liaison.'

'You're not here as official Bureau rep?' Scholte asked, somewhat surprised.

'No,' replied Kronziac. 'I'm not quite sure why I *am* here.'

'And what are you doing here?' the DA asked Stranski, her forthright manner intimidating.

He looked at Kronziac for a moment. 'Er – psych consult to the FBI Los Angeles field office,' he said, not able to think of any other title for himself.

'Drafting criminal profilers from the FAA now, eh?' Scholte said. 'Whatever next? Forensic scientists from NASA?'

After a polite smile, Kronziac turned to Cunningham. 'Your call sounded urgent. What's up?'

He pulled out a large envelope from beneath his arm and pulled a large photo-real printout from it. 'Got this off the traffic cameras that I've been looking at. About ten minutes after

Cherie drove up Tunney, a brown van, just like the one we saw on the bank's cameras, followed her route. The guys at the NLEC Technology Centre in El Segundo were able to do some enhancement and pull the licence plate out of the picture. Murky as hell, but you can make out the numbers. California plates.'

Kronziac and Stranski looked at the print – dim yellow digits on a white digitized field.

'Great,' Kronziac said, genuinely impressed with the detective's persistence with all the video footage. 'Get a match?'

'Oh yeah,' he replied enthusiastically. 'It's a Chevrolet Express Commercial Cutaway van. Registered to the DynoTech Construction Company, San Bernadino. The truck is used by one of their guys – an Emery Madsen, twenty-seven-year-old employee with an address in Pomona.'

'What sort work do they do?' Stranski asked.

'Environmental reconstruction,' said Cunningham. 'Specializing in asbestos abatement. They've an office in Petaluma too, near San Francisco. Work all over the state and beyond.'

'Asbestos?' Kronziac asked excitedly.

'That's what they said,' he replied.

'Our lab confirmed that the fibre traces from the trunk, back seats and pedals of Cherie's car were chrysotile asbestos,' said Kronziac. 'Have you talked to him yet, this Madsen?'

'Not yet,' the detective replied and looked at his watch. 'He's coming in any time now.'

'Here?' Kronziac exclaimed. 'He's coming in here?'

Cunningham nodded, smiling.

'That's why I'm here,' Scholte interrupted. 'Sam wants to interview him and I'm to observe to see if we can build a case. But from what he's shown me so far – some fuzzy camera footage and the presence of trace evidence that does not relate definitely to the subject – then I'm not even gonna wet the ink on this one.'

'This is just an informal interview.' Cunningham tried to allay Kronziac's fear of scaring the subject off. 'I've okayed it with my ON in Pomona and with Madsen's employers. The guy's coming in off his own bat.'

'*If* he comes in,' Kronziac remarked doubtfully.

'I'm warning you, Sam,' Scholte stated. 'If you're going to question him as a suspect and not as a witness then you'll have to tell him his rights.'

Cunningham was looking at his watch again. 'Come on,' he said and led them down the corridor to the interview rooms by the cell block.

'You two shouldn't speak to him,' Scholte warned Kronziac and Stranski as they walked, her heels clicking on the floor. 'Especially you, Miss Kronziac.'

'I know, I know,' Kronziac lamented.

They followed Cunningham into an observation booth, a space not much bigger than a linen closet. On one side was the large rectangular window of a one-way mirror, permitting them a view of the empty interview room next door. The interview room itself was just a large white box, no windows, illuminated by the stark white light of fluorescent tubes. In the centre sat a sturdy pine table with two seats on either side and a telephone. Next to the table stood a small black video camera on a tripod which Cunningham had set up for the interview. They could hear the phone ringing. Cunningham rushed out into the interview room, snatching the handset from its cradle.

In the cramped observation booth, Scholte found a place for her case and paperwork on one of the three stools lining the back wall.

'So what do you know about this man?' she asked Kronziac. For a split second Kronziac thought she was asking about Stranski or Cunningham.

'This Emery Madsen,' the DA clarified, noticing the lost expression on Kronziac's face.

'Absolutely nothing,' admitted Kronziac. 'All we know is that in a series of related abductions and homicides we have traces of asbestos and a brown van as common factors.'

In the interview room Cunningham put the phone down and, giving them the thumbs-up, through the mirror, he rushed out.

'I've never tried a serial before,' Scholte remarked quietly and looked through the plate of glass, its film of coated silver tinting the interior of the interview room.

'Have you had a chance to run any background on this man?' Stranski asked.

Scholte seemed mildly annoyed by the request as she turned to dig some paperwork from her case. 'Nothing too extensive, obviously,' she said and began reading from the various official-headed papers. 'Emery Linus Madsen, DOB twelfth of the fifth '74, Temecula. Given up for adoption at age nine. Series of foster homes and young offenders' correction facilities. Juvenile detention for misdemeanours. History of drug violations. Assault. Did a stint at County at age nineteen for serious assault. Almost killed a guy in a back-street game of cards. Rehab programme for gambling addiction . . .'

She seemed to grow weary of the details, numbed by her job of prosecuting the endless succession of similarly historied young men who revolved through the legal system.

'Went off the rails a bit. Barbiturate addiction and psychotic episodes led to a serious assault. Eventual committal to a low-security mental facility in Oakland where he was diagnosed with borderline personality disorder.'

'What did he do?' Kronziac asked.

'Violent attack on an employee of a casino in Reno. Didn't like the cards, I guess. He was transferred to the Grovehurst Institute in Livermore and discharged three years later.'

'Some record,' Kronziac remarked.

The DA smiled. 'Background fits the bill, don't you think, Dr Stranski?'

Stranski turned immediately to the DA. By his expression, it seemed as though some recollection was bothering him. 'Did you say Grovehurst?'

The DA looked over at her files. 'Yes,' she confirmed. 'The Grovehurst Institute in Livermore.'

'What is it?' Kronziac asked him.

Stranski seemed a little reluctant to answer. 'Well – Grovehurst is kinda famous or infamous in the psych trade.'

'Why?'

'In the forties and early fifties it was called the Fursting Primate

Laboratory, also known as the Monkey Asylum, where they carried out experiments on animals. In the late fifties, however . . . they moved on to humans. As part of the MK-Ultra programme the CIA were supposed to be running mind-control experiments on young psychiatric prisoners – you know, Cold War hypnotic couriers and assassins, that kind of thing.'

'I think I remember Ted Kennedy's Senate hearing on that,' Scholte remarked.

'They're not still doing experiments there, are they?' Kronziac asked. Stranski shook his head vigorously.

'They tore down the lab, but the main building serves as a psychiatric hospital still,' he said. He was about to ask Scholte for a copy of Madsen's record when they saw Cunningham re-enter the interview room. He turned around and gestured for someone to follow him in. He pulled out one of the chairs and waited for his guest.

In the observation room they watched intently as Madsen entered slowly, his hands casually sunk in the pockets of his jeans. Tall, over six foot, and broad in the chest, he had lean swimmer's shoulders. The scalp of his square head was visible through a tight fuzz of razor-cut hair. His gaze scanned the room, appraising its dimensions. Kronziac was reminded of the Komodo dragon in the pit at the zoo, expressing his power through slow heavy movement.

Cunningham flicked a switch on a panel mounted on the wall above the table and a concealed microphone in the other room allowed the observers to hear the conversation.

'Thank you for coming in,' said the detective as he motioned for Madsen to sit down.

'Sure, no problem,' Madsen answered, a thin reedy voice, younger than his size suggested.

As he sat down his gaze still roved around the room until he spotted the mirror. He looked away, back to Cunningham who was now sitting directly across from him over the table. Kronziac was sure he smiled.

'Give him his rights,' Scholte whispered through her teeth.

*   *   *

'Firstly, Mr Madsen, this is just an informal interview. We're investigating the disappearance of a sixteen-year-old girl in September last. You do not have to respond to any question and you are free to go at any time. Let me make that absolutely clear.'

Madsen smiled. 'Sounds as if I'm a suspect,' he said, unnerving the detective.

'Er – no, not at all. It's just you might be able to help us with our enquiries.'

'If I can.'

Madsen kept the smile on his face as his eyes panned sideways to the mirror. His head didn't move.

'This interview, like all interviews here at the station, will be taped,' advised Cunningham, nodding over his shoulder at the camera.

'So I see.' Madsen smiled. He now seemed the more relaxed of the two as Cunningham fiddled with the record button on the small video camera, its LCD screen extended like a square wing from the silver body.

'For the record, can you state your name and date of birth?'

'Emery Madsen, twelfth of the fifth, '74.'

'Do you work for the DynoTech Construction Company in San Bernadino?'

'Yes, sir.'

'In the course of your work for DynoTech, do you drive a brown Chevrolet Express Cutaway Van?'

'Yep, sure do. The Express is a good rig.'

'And may I ask what sort of work you do?'

'Demolition, light industrial and domestic. We specialize in asbestos removal and abatement; floor tiles and insulation. We do a bit of lead removal, too.'

'Does the work take you far distances?'

Madsen nodded. 'Yeah, sure. Throughout the state.'

'And further afield?' Cunningham asked, excited by the answers so far.

'Sometimes.' The young man shrugged.

Cunningham took out some of the photographs of Cherie that Jerry Blaynes had given him and spread them out over the table in a fan. 'Do you know this girl or have you ever seen her?'

'No,' replied Madsen. 'I don't think so.' He looked away from the photos, glancing at the mirror again.

'Have you ever heard the name "Cherie Blaynes" or can you recall ever meeting a Cherie Blaynes?'

Madsen pursed his lips. 'Not that I can recall,' he said flatly.

In the observation room Stranski leaned close to Kronziac, whispering.

'He's extremely calm. Shows no signs of surprise or curiosity.'

Cunningham continued his questions, noting some details as he went.

'Now, when I rang you yesterday, Mr Madsen, I asked you if you could remember anything of the evening of the second of September last. I know it's five months ago but if you can recall anything that would be great.'

Cunningham was already beginning to write something on his pad when Madsen asked him why. The detective looked up in surprise.

Madsen was staring at him, his small eyes narrowed in scrutiny.

Cunningham smiled. 'Why what?' He wondered if Madsen could detect the quiver in his voice. Those in the other room did.

Madsen suddenly smiled back. 'Why would it be great?'

In the observation room, on the speaker, they could hear Cunningham laughing, his voice breathy with relief. 'It would be very helpful to our inquiries. Help clear some things up for us.'

Madsen pushed the nail of his thumb sideways between a small gap in the middle of his lower teeth. 'Let me see. I tried to remember, Detective Cunningham, but it's a long time ago.'

'Did you have to work that evening?'

'Well, it was a Sunday,' Madsen said. 'I checked the calendar. I probably took it easy. Watched some TV. I dunno – just hung out, I guess.'

'You didn't go for a drive anywhere, did you?'

'The company checkin' up on the mileage?' Madsen asked. An intense smile, too intense to be sincere, parted his lips.

'No . . . no, nothing to do with your bosses, I assure you.'

The young man thought about it for a few seconds as Cunningham, avoiding eye contact, looked over his notes. 'I don't know. Might have gone to the store for some beer – or might not.'

'Did you – might you have gone anywhere in Northridge or anywhere else up around here?'

'Around here?'

'Well, specifically, up around Porter Valley.'

'Can't really say for sure if I did or didn't. I can't see what I'd be doin' up around there. I live in Pomona, as you know.'

'You know where it is?'

'Where?'

'Porter Valley.'

Madsen leaned back, shrugging. 'I know it's around here,' he said casually.

The detective pressed on. 'So you might have been at home, that night, perhaps all night, the night of the second of September?'

'What?' Madsen asked, leaning forward as if hard of hearing.

'I said, to your best recollection you might have been home the night of the second of September last.'

'Yes, I was at home. I was doing some work.'

Cunningham noticed the direct manner of his answer. 'What sort of work?'

'Had to fix one of our filtration pumps. Was up most of the night,' Madsen responded in a flat tone.

Stranski moved closer to the one-way mirror.

'Facial gestalt,' he muttered under his breath. Scholte stared over at him.

'What was wrong with it?' Cunningham asked, not very interested, but at least Madsen seemed to be talking freely. The more they talked, no matter what the subject, the better for Cunningham.

'The motor was US,' Madsen said, holding his head steady, his gaze not moving around the room as it had previously. 'I didn't know if it was an electrical fault, the sparks, a break in the hosing or what. I tried to get it to work but it wouldn't. I tried several times again but it wouldn't go. It was really pissing me off.'

'What did you do then?'

Madsen took a moment to answer, waiting for the words to come. 'I decided to cut one of the wires. Thought there might be a short. So I clipped it.'

'Still no good, huh?' Cunningham asked.

'Fucking thing just wouldn't cooperate,' Madsen hissed, his mouth thick with saliva.

Kronziac stepped closer to the glass, her nose almost pressed against it. 'Pretty intense, isn't he?' she whispered.

Scholte was glancing at her watch. 'Three-twenty. I'm gonna have to go soon. I'm in court.'

In the interview room, Madsen was staring silently over the detective's right shoulder.

'I usually get mad with these things,' Cunningham remarked. 'Tried to fix an outboard there a few weeks back. Ended up kicking the heck out of it. Almost broke a toe.' He laughed.

'Me too,' Madsen said, nearly smiling, his gaze slowly turning to Cunningham. 'I lost it a bit. Gave it a punch.'

'The filter?'

'Yeah.' Madsen smiled, a bashful, pained grin.

In the observation room the DA was beginning to gather up her files again.

'What do you think, Mrs Scholte?' Kronziac asked, still instinctively keeping her voice low.

'I think he's a weird little puppy,' the older woman replied. 'With his background, I suppose it's hardly surprising. But of course that's not grounds, not *legal* grounds for suspicion.'

'Maybe we could search the van,' Kronziac said.

'That would require a search warrant, Miss Kronziac, and there's no probable cause here, no demonstrable evidence that he was following this girl.'

'The van was seen by a witness, a mailman, near the location of another abduction in Palo Alto, and tyre casts were found in Oregon near another crime scene.'

'*His* van? His actual vehicle?' Scholte shot back, interrogating Kronziac like she would a hostile witness in court.

Stranski turned to shush them up as he listened to the interview over the speaker and watched Madsen's demeanour.

'Do these witness statements or this tyre evidence point directly to his vehicle?' Scholte asked, lowering her voice again.

'Well, no,' Kronziac said reluctantly.

Scholte picked up her case. 'No magistrate's going to cut you a warrant.'

With her case and files tucked under her arm the DA opened the door as quietly as she could. 'Good day, Dr Stranski.' But he continued to study the men in the interview room and said nothing back.

Before she left the DA turned briefly to Kronziac. 'You'd have to get the owner's consent,' she said and closed the door behind her, leaving a heady trail of perfume in her wake.

Kronziac tried to say thanks but Scholte was gone. 'Of course, Madsen didn't own the van. It belongs to DynoTech,' Kronziac realized. 'They would surely be willing to cooperate and let us search it,' she said.

But Stranski was still watching the interview as Cunningham wrapped it up.

'Can I go now?' Madsen asked, his expression indicating his relief.

'Of course,' Cunningham replied as he turned to switch off the camera. 'If you remember anything else about that night then please give me a call.'

'Sure thing, Detective,' the young man said obligingly as he stood up. He glanced once more at the mirror and Stranski was sure he flinched – no more than a flutter of an eyelash, almost a wink.

'Hope you didn't get into too much trouble with the company for breaking the filter,' Cunningham commented as he followed Madsen out the door.

* * *

'He seemed to have a pretty good memory,' Kronziac remarked, getting ready to leave but lingering long enough for Madsen to clear the station.

Stranski put his hands in his pocket. 'Well, it was very selective,' he said, staring distractedly at the interview room, now empty.

837 ORINDA AVE, LADERA HEIGHTS, LOS ANGELES

It was a late-morning Jerry Springer rerun. *Don John – My Husband Keeps Falling For Transsexual Prostitutes.*

Leo Pretaran laughed and sat back on the faux leather couch, in his underwear of shorts and white vest. Once a sprinter back home, champion of Ziguinchor district, the major sinews of his dark legs still caught the light like steel pistons. He spooned a breakfast cocktail of muesli, banana and guava cubes into his mouth.

He didn't understand what the guests were saying but loved it when the stage erupted as a shoeless fat woman with fringed big hair clawed a six-foot-five man in a green-sequinned minidress and a pink feather boa. All for the love of a sloe-eyed Appalachian hick with a sparse wire-bristled moustache and white socks.

Leo laughed the laugh of a child watching cartoons. He had learned the chant of the bleating crowd and punched his fist into the air in concert.

A knock rattled the door.

Loud.

He quickly turned the television down and moved to the blinds at the window to peer through and see the street outside.

A few cars were parked: a faded old Buick, jazzed Camaros, a big brown Chevy van. No neat official saloons. The knock at door came again.

He set the dish down on top of the TV. The transsexual's wig was now off and the dumpy wife held it up like a prized scalp to the baying crowd.

The door rattled once more.

Demanding.

'Okay, okay,' Leo muttered, '*Putain de merde . . .*'

He thought it was Pierre with news of a job.

BACK LOT, TOMASO APARTMENT BUILDING, POMONA, CA

Kronziac lectured Cunningham as they eased the rubber evidence-handling gloves onto their hands.

'DA says to disturb as little as possible. We see anything suspicious and you phone in a warrant request.'

'Yes, sir,' Cunningham smiled. 'And officially you're not here, right?'

'We don't want to fuck it up on procedure,' Kronziac insisted, trying to impress upon him the fact that they only had permission from Madsen's company to look around the van, not to collect evidence.

'Where is he, anyway?' she asked.

'Inside his apartment. I've got an officer with him.'

'Nothing too heavy?'

'No. Just talking to him friendly-like.'

'Okay,' said Kronziac, looking apprehensively up at the shutter door at the back of the van.

The Chevrolet Express Cutaway is a medium-sized van perfect for small-cargo haulage or light industrial equipment transport. The van that the DynoTech Company was using for their fleet was the 159-inch wheelbase variant with a custom-made seventy-square-foot storage cube on the back – which made the vehicle look like a large box on wheels, basically.

The shutters rattled up and the chassis swayed as Cunningham hopped on board. He flicked a single switch on the wall and a light at the front end of the rig came on. Kronziac took his outstretched hand and climbed up herself.

'A lot of stuff here,' she said as they looked around at the shelves crammed with ropes, tools and dusty equipment. 'Hope there aren't too many asbestos fibres floating around,' she remarked as they made their way forward, deeper into the storage cube.

The dark air smelt of rusted nails and damp canvas. 'You could put one of those on,' Cunningham said, pointing at a gas mask lying on its side on one of the shelves, a tracery of scratches dimly gleaming on the visor, its air hose looking like a small elephant's trunk. About three quarters of the way down the rig a tall obelisk-like structure, which Cunningham figured to be some sort of fan or radiator, stood in the centre of the floor, blocking the way forward. About as high as Kronziac herself, it cordoned off the front part of the van where the light bulb was.

'Looks heavy,' she said as Cunningham tried to heave it to the side.

'Sonuvabitch!' he grunted as he shifted it on one of its corners, allowing them to slip through.

Kronziac could now see the table, covered by a dark-patched green cloth, standing in the middle of the floor. 'Like a little office,' she said.

'What the fuck is that?' Cunningham exclaimed. 'A throne?'

Against the front wall of the van sat a large wooden chair: a crudely constructed frame of two-by-two timbers and a black stained plywood seat.

'I suppose this is like his little workshop,' Cunningham figured as he looked around at the walls of the van, stacked with shelving on one side and a large tool chest on the other. On the floor under the chair were strewn bits of wood, scraps of duct tape, foam and black pools of gummy oil, glossed by the dull light from the bulb.

'I'll try this side,' Cunningham suggested as he moved over to the tool chest, a red stack of pull-out drawers with steel handles, mounted on a dolly for mobility.

Kronziac turned to the shelves on the other side. The air was cold, her breath smoking in the creamy light. She peered into the ledged compartments, grimacing as she smelt a fruity musk of decay. Lying on a bed of wound electrical flex lay an oval-shaped lattice of leather strapping and steel tighteners. She moved her head in closer, leaning sideways to examine the odd harness that looked vaguely medieval in its crude contrivance. She asked herself what it was, but had no idea. The fact that it had the same outline as a human head scared her deeply.

Cunningham, on the other side, carefully slid out one of the drawers from the chest. He was envious of the variety of fine tools and their ordered arrangement. Like precious instruments of industry they lay gleaming on beds of beige chamois and foam. There were drill bits with the varying lengths and gauges of miniature organ pipes, stainless steel wrenches with tight jaws, ratchet sets and screwdrivers, Stanley knives and open-legged pincers. On one of the lower drawers was a tray of bolts and Rawlplugs with a sub-compartment for assorted nails. In the middle was a plastic box of electrical wire lengths of various bores. Cunningham picked up one of the nails and used it to poke around the array of screws, the new ones like glittering jewels among the rusted rest. He flicked through the Rawlplugs and bolts, the strands of wire, some gleaming copper, others shrouded in grey flex. Two pieces were thicker than the rest, and shorter.

'What is it?' Kronziac asked, peering over his shoulder.

'Looks like a shrivelled old cigar,' he replied and prodded a two-and-a-half-inch strip of black fibre amid the other bits until it fell over on its side.

'Christ!' he shouted, recoiling back in surprise. 'There are two of them!'

Kronziac looked closer, examining the nearest object.

A black prong of dried flesh, cored with a white circle of bone, the fingernail painted in glossy patches of purple.

DEPUTY ASSISTANT DIRECTOR'S OFFICE, FEDERAL BUILDING, WILSHIRE BLVD

Sedley had hoped it would be their last meeting before they handed over the case files on the Cryptogram Murders and Emery Madsen to the Department of Justice prosecutors. Now they all sat quietly around his desk, Phillips pacing the room as usual. On Sedley's clinically neat redwood desk sat two pieces of paper.

'Came in this morning,' he said.

'Here?' Kronziac asked, astonished.

'Front office,' he confirmed. 'Regular morning post.'

'He knew we were handling the case,' Stranski concluded.

Ellstrom stirred in his seat uncomfortably. 'What about the man with the Social Security number in Annaheim – no one came near him?'

Sedley shook his head. 'No one. We had agents and police on him twenty-four hours a day since the lottery draw.'

'Looks like you may have gotten it wrong this time,' Phillips remarked.

'Screw you, Phillips!' Ellstrom replied angrily, his face flaring red.

Phillips came closer, sticking out his chest in a display of aggression. 'Screw me? What's that phoney American accent all about?'

Kronziac intervened. 'Shut up, both of you!'

Sedley pitched in. 'Phillips, keep your goddamned mouth shut or I'll put you on suspension. Professor Ellstrom is not Bureau. He didn't have to help and he's taken a lot of time away from his job.'

Phillips retreated to the corner of the room to simmer and looked out the window at the city.

'As it happens,' Sedley continued calmly, 'he got it right.'

'How do you mean?' Ellstrom asked.

The Deputy Assistant Director picked up one of the sheets of paper in front of him. 'This is a copy of the original we got

364

this morning. It's a printout from a web page again – but not a Missing Persons notice from a police site. It's from the web page of a private company that publishes personal information on people. A few of these companies have been closed down and prosecuted under the Social Security on-line Privacy Protection Act but some are still surviving. There's quite a lucrative business in selling personal data on-line to marketing and advertising companies, as well as to private individuals.'

He passed the page to Kronziac. It had an inky black and white picture of a man on it. 'Leonhard Pretaran. Illegal West African immigrant,' Sedley went on.

Ellstrom found the Social Security number box.

6251628230.

'The same number as the guy in Annaheim!' he breathed.

'Yeah.' Sedley nodded gravely. 'He was using a fake number to get work, I suppose, and somehow his details wound up in this non-government database.'

'Madsen's been using this website to find his victims,' Maggie surmised.

'It is searchable by SSN,' Sedley confirmed. 'But it does not match the numbers with the Social Security Administration's databases, so number duplication does occur, it seems. As I said, it's not an official government site so security or accuracy is not paramount.'

'Have we checked him out?' Kronziac asked. 'This Leonhard Pretaran?' She read the name out.

'He was living in Ladera Heights. Seems he was missing for a couple of days but nobody would report it. Most of his friends are probably illegal immigrants themselves.'

'That's bad luck.' Kronziac shook her head.

Sedley agreed. 'You punch in that SSN and Leonhard Pretaran comes up before John Rogers – the man in Annaheim.'

Phillips joined them again. 'Shit, Madsen worked fast on that one. He took this West African guy just days after the numbers came up.'

Sedley had more information for them. 'Detectives questioned him this morning in prison and he denies knowing anything about Pretaran's disappearance of course.'

'So he's not going to help us find the body?' Kronziac said. 'Not gonna try and cut a deal with the DA? Presuming Pretaran is dead.'

Sedley turned to the other sheet on his desk. 'I think we can pretty much assume he's gone the way of the others. This is a photocopy of the cryptogram on the back of the original.'

He passed it to Ellstrom who had hoped he would never see another one of them again. He had already rung the faculty at Harvard to say he'd be back in a couple of days.

They all peered closely at the page that was entirely covered by numbers.

'Just ones and zeros,' Stranski observed.

Kronziac was waiting for Ellstrom to say something, to give some indication that he had any idea how to start the decryption attack.

'It's a binary code,' he began. 'That's the simplest part of it.'

'Do you think you can crack it?' Sedley asked.

But Ellstrom was just running his bottom lip against his teeth as he thought.

'We should just crack Madsen's head and get the answer straight from him about where he hid the body,' Phillips offered, not really caring that his attitude wasn't helping matters.

'I think it's ASCII,' Ellstrom decided.

'Computer code?' Kronziac said.

'I think so.' He wavered. 'But not straightforward.'

'ASCII?' Maggie said. 'I've heard of it but I'm not sure what it is.'

'American Standard Code for Information Interchange,' Ellstrom replied. 'Each character – a letter or symbol – is represented by a specific combination of eight ones and zeros.'

As he talked he was running a multiplication table on the rows and columns of digits on the page.

'Yeah, it's a multiple of eight. So I think we're on the right track with ASCII. Though, knowing his previous cryptograms, there's probably another level of encipherment.'

'How can you check?' Sedley asked.

'A computer should do,' Ellstrom said.

'Phillips, take the professor outside and organize whatever he needs, please,' said Sedley.

'Okay.' Phillips complied quietly. 'Come on, you can use the laptop on my desk.'

Kronziac watched them go out the door as Sedley turned to Maggie.

'The DOJ want to nail him on prima-facie evidence,' he began. 'What's the result on the vehicle search?'

'We can link Madsen forensically to three of the victims,' she reported. 'They found items belonging to Cherie Blaynes: her diary, her purse – as well as her finger, along with Ellen Holby's, in his tool chest. There were multiple blood traces on the floor of the van, on the tablecloth and on the pliers he used to amputate the fingers. He also owns a gun, which we believe was used to shoot Ellen Holby. DNA testing under PCR typed saliva traces on a gas mask with Philip Chavez.'

Sedley closed his eyes and rubbed his face until it flushed red. 'A mobile torture chamber,' he muttered.

'That's not all,' Maggie said. 'On his computer we found some video files.'

'Of what?' Stranski asked abruptly.

'Him,' Maggie replied, 'and his victims. I haven't seen them but the engineering guys at Westwood had a look at them – or *tried* to look at them.'

'Gruesome?' Kronziac asked.

Maggie nodded. 'You can see him actually murdering them after he plays games, usually card games, with them. Cherie Blaynes, Ellen Holby and Phil Chavez.'

'And he taped it all?'

'A webcam,' she confirmed.

'He was broadcasting on the Net?' Sedley exclaimed.

'No,' Maggie said. 'They seem to be saved video conferences.'

'He must have had someone watching him, even so,' Kronziac said.

'Anything of the other two victims?' Sedley wondered. 'Peter Kelley and Shayla Wilson?'

'No. The only things we can use to link them with Madsen

are the asbestos traces and the tyre casts in Oregon and a witness, a local mailman, who said he saw a brown van on the street behind Shayla Wilson's house the morning she disappeared.'

'Forensics didn't find any specialist creams in Madsen's house, did they?' Kronziac asked Maggie.

'I don't know,' she replied. 'We could search again, I guess.'

'Yeah do,' Kronziac said. Remembering herself, she looked at the Deputy Assistant Director. 'There were traces of an unknown alkyl resin, or cream, in Shayla Wilson's bedroom. Might be another link to Madsen.'

'Okay,' Sedley agreed. 'Get them to check out Madsen's house again,' he told Maggie. 'At least we can get him on three definites, though I'd like to nail him on the five.'

'Six,' Kronziac corrected him. 'With the West African.'

'Might not be that straightforward,' Maggie told them. 'His defence attorneys are going to submit an insanity plea.'

Kronziac shook her head. 'Surprise, surprise.'

'We all know he is a crazy son of a bitch,' Sedley said, almost shouting. 'But what angle are they gonna use to try and get him off on?'

'They're saying he has absolutely no memory of the crimes.'

'Of course! He doesn't *want* to remember,' Kronziac stated, matching Sedley's anger.

'How about polygraph?' Stranski asked Maggie.

'Inconclusive,' she shrugged.

Sedley turned quickly to the psychologist. 'Could this insanity plea hold water, Dr Stranski? From what you know so far?'

'Which isn't very much,' Stranski hastened to add. 'Grovehurst sent me some of his clinical reports and the DA gave us his police and state records.'

'And?' Sedley urged impatiently.

'It's a complex picture,' said Stranski, shifting restlessly in his seat. 'He was abandoned by an alcoholic mother at nine, taken into a foster home in Oakland, where, along with some other kids, he was at the centre of a child-abuse scandal. It seems the family and those who worked at the house were all involved. The boy was, without doubt, psychologically damaged and turned to substance abuse and the other activities of juvenile maladaption.'

'Was he clinically insane?' Sedley asked.

'Officially, yes. He was committed to Grovehurst with serious depression and schizoid episodes that graduated from neurotic to psychotic. He was compulsive and violent. Clinically, the diagnosis was bipolar disorder with dissociation.'

'What does that mean?' Kronziac asked, beginning to think the defence might have a case.

'DID,' Stranski said simply. 'Dissociative Identity Disorder.'

'Something like multiple personality?' Maggie wondered.

'Not that old chestnut!' Sedley cried. 'I suppose he heard voices. Marilyn Manson told him to do it.'

'Is it MPD?' Kronziac asked Sedley quietly.

The psychologist made a face as if he'd swallowed a bitter slice of lemon. 'In a way – it is similar in concept,' he reluctantly conceded. 'But MPD is old hat now, too Jekyll and Hyde, too . . . Hollywood. You won't even find it in the DS manual any more. Instead of multiple personalities within one there are different points of *view* – fragmented *alters* who are amnesiac for each other. Sufferers of DID exhibit the psychopathology of post-trauma stress with a specific etiology, usually severe childhood mental and or physical abuse.'

'Sorry, Fred.' Kronziac interrupted him. 'I think you're losing us a little.'

Stranski blinked his eyes as he forced himself to slow down. 'Of course. I'm sorry.' He gathered his thoughts for a moment.

'Okay.' He began again. 'Take a kid who suffers severe and regular sexual abuse. His mind will set up an escape mechanism to deal with the stress and trauma. The child tries to detach himself by creating what can be called an *alter* – an alternative point of view – to pretend that the abuse is happening to someone else, not to him. When the abusive episode passes, this *alter* the child has created passes back into the subconscious and the child has no conscious recollection of the abuse. Most sufferers exhibit memory gaps during the switching.'

'Sounds like MPD to me,' Sedley maintained.

'The phenomenology is, like I said, similar,' Stranski agreed.

'What about Madsen?' Kronziac asked. 'Did he – *does* he have this disorder?'

'That's impossible to tell without a clinical evaluation. The causology and maladaption are present in his background and . . .' He paused, puffing out his cheeks, mentally struggling with something that had been bothering him since seeing Madsen at the police station. 'I've looked at the interview over and over again. When Detective Cunningham asked him about what he was doing the night of the girl's disappearance, most of his memories were vague, as would be expected of anyone after that kind of time interval. But then he began to describe in detail some work he'd been doing on a piece of equipment.'

'So?' Sedley asked.

'It struck me as odd, the detail he was able to recall. And his delivery was not characteristic of experiential or episodic memory, more like learned or rehearsed memory, and he seemed to display the facial gestalt of an autonome.'

'He was just reciting a learned alibi?' Kronziac suggested.

'Perhaps,' Stranski said, but in a distant way that made it seem as though he was humouring her.

'Dr Stranski,' Sedley began seriously. 'If his counsel jump in with an insanity case the prosecution, I believe, has the right to run a psych test on the defendant. Would you be willing to head up the evaluation team?'

Stranski began laughing nervously. 'Mr Sedley, I should remind you that I'm no longer Bureau. I try to help airline pilots get over jet lag. I don't run psychometric tests on serial criminals. I'm flattered, of course, but . . . surely BSU at Quantico or the DA can come up with someone more suitable.'

Sedley was smiling graciously. He was about to tell Stranski that he understood and to thank him for his help so far when Kronziac said something.

'Why don't you think about it, Fred?' she suggested. Just as he had advised her to be patient with Ellstrom when first recruiting his help, saying that the temptation of a good test would eventually be too much to resist, so Stranski himself could be hooked if he was given enough time for the case to seize his imagination. She was glad Phillips wasn't in the room since he would doubtless chide her for such shameless manipulation.

'Well, think it over,' Sedley said as Stranski's facial expression slowly changed from loose-featured amusement to the tightened lines of serious thought.

'You'd have to run the structured clinical interviews and it would be good for the psychobiology to run some EEG tests or, better, an FMRI or PET scan under narco-hypnosis.' He turned towards Maggie. 'And the video evidence should be previewed,' he said as Phillips and Ellstrom came back through he door.

'Any luck?' Sedley asked them anxiously.

'It's locked through a keyword transposition,' Ellstrom lamented.

'You can't work through it?' Kronziac asked.

'Oh, I could get it,' Ellstrom replied. 'But it would take about two years, working around the clock – and you guys ain't paying me enough,' he added jokingly, to which no one responded.

'I'm beginning to agree with Phillips,' Sedley said. 'Maybe we should *persuade* Madsen until he tells us what he's done with the body.'

'He's not going to say a word,' Kronziac stated. 'Not even if you whack the shit out of him.'

'There could be another way,' Ellstrom said tentatively.

'Spit it out, Professor,' Sedley urged him.

'I have a few mates in the cryptology units at the NSA.'

'Fort Meade?' Kronziac wondered.

Ellstrom nodded. 'The Cray supercomputers they've got out there could crunch the numbers faster than shit through a—'

Sedley picked up the phone and turned swiftly to Phillips. 'Book Professor Ellstrom on the next red-eye to Baltimore and I'll see if I can smooth the way with our colleagues at Meade.'

They all began to shuffle slowly from the room. As his secretary was connecting him to the NSA station chief at Fort Meade Sedley called to Kronziac, 'Nancy, hold up.'

She stopped and told Ellstrom and Stranski to carry on. 'Yes, sir?' she asked, returning to the desk.

'Inspection Division wants to meet you Wednesday morning,' he told her, palming the mouthpiece of his phone. 'Director Foley asked me to sit in with you.'

'Is it a full hearing? Should I have a staff rep?' she asked, dreading it already.

He shook his head, dividing his attention between her and his secretary on the phone.

'Should get your story together, though,' he advised and turned away to talk.

2434 ABRAMAR, PACIFIC PALISADES, CA

Kronziac tended, like most people, to giggle when made to do something she found wholly ridiculous. Still in her baggy old pyjama bottoms and a black Bureau sweater, she was laid out on the couch with her bare feet elevated on one end by the cushions.

Stranski was next to the couch, sitting on the coffee table. 'Let's try something else,' he decided.

'Aw, come on Fred,' Kronziac protested. 'You know I don't really buy this crap. You said it yourself, you can't make someone be hypnotized if they don't want it.'

'I'm just trying to get you to relax,' said Stranski patiently. 'It could help you unclutter your mind, which is clouded by anger and frustration over the disciplinary hearing.'

'You're just trying to practise your hocus-pocus for Madsen's evaluation.'

'Maybe I am,' he admitted.

His confession seemed to leave Kronziac with nothing to argue about so she just lay there and closed her eyes.

'Loosen now, relax,' he said in a steady but soft tone. 'Let a deep and pleasant sensation spread across from the left side of your body to the right – like a warm wave. Every limb and muscle is growing lazy and heavy. Now, from your head to the tips of your toes another soft warm wave is washing down over your entire body and every fibre of you relaxes, loosening like a rag doll.'

Kronziac's eyes stayed closed.

'Now another wave,' Stranski continued, 'gently flowing over you from your head to your toes, kneading your muscles softly like dough – your breath rising and falling to match it so that you drift with the waves . . . calmly . . . relaxing more and more with each gentle wave . . . each soft breath. How do you feel?'

Her eyes fluttered open, squinting against the bright screen of the sunlit ceiling.

'Tired,' was all she would say.

'You have a good imagination, don't you?' he asked.

'Not really.'

'You've always been too hard on yourself.'

'Well, you kinda have to be,' Kronziac said, 'to keep going in this job.'

'I want you to imagine something for me. Can you do that?'

'I'll try,' she replied and settled her shoulders into a more comfortable position.

'We'll try to test how good your imagination is. I'll describe something to you and then will ask you to visualize it.'

She nodded and mumbled in agreement.

'I'm going to begin counting back from ten to one. When I say "ten" let your eyelids fall and you will begin to see yourself at the top of a set of white marble steps leading down into a light blue pool or lagoon or whatever you want to see. You love the water, so it should be easy for you. Okay?'

'All right.' Kronziac sighed, continuing to humour him.

'Good.' Stranski smiled. 'Number ten and you can feel the smooth steps warming under your bare feet . . . now let your eyes close. You're at the top of the steps, nice and relaxed. Nine, let yourself go down, walking slowly. Eight, descending the steps, sinking into a calm feeling, looking forward to the water below gently lapping. Seven . . . six, moving down the steps. Five, the white water warm, rising up from your toes, up your ankles. Four, you begin to slowly immerse yourself in the calm water, letting it hold you. Three . . . two, now wading fully into it, letting it carry you. One, now you are floating, your body relaxing in every muscle, supported by the warm white-blue water . . . How do you feel?'

Kronziac opened her eyes reluctantly. 'Still tired,' she said resignedly. But the causes of her fatigue were beginning to matter less.

'Close them again,' Stranski said gently and her eyelids lowered.

'Now, imagine you are standing in front of your car. Can you see it?'

She gave a gentle nod.

'Can you see it clearly?'

A more definite nod.

'What colour is it?'

'Blue . . . *Pacific azure*,'

'Open the door and get in behind the wheel – are you doing that? Just nod. Good. Now look straight ahead. Okay? What colour is the steering wheel?'

'Brown . . . Prairie tan,' Kronziac replied.

'Good. Is there anything on it?'

Kronziac's head moved a little from side to side. 'The oval Ford sign. The audio and climate control buttons on the hand rest.'

'Great,' said Stranski, as he would to encourage a child who had completed a simple task. 'You could see all that fine and clear?'

'Yes,' Kronziac replied. 'Of course.'

'Good. Now let's see if you can imagine in another way. Try to visualize yourself at a beach or by a pool, a lake or river. Imagine you are at that place. Can you see it?'

Kronziac nodded, a soft expression of contentment around her mouth and eyes.

'Where is it?'

'Hawaii.'

He began smiling to himself. 'Thinking about a vacation?'

'Not really,' Kronziac said, her mouth broadening in a cheeky little smile. 'Thinking about Magnum . . . *Magnum PI.*'

'The TV show?' Sedley asked.

'I used to be in high school when it was on,' she said.

'And you loved Tom Selleck?'

'He was okay – didn't love the moustache.'

'The car, a Ferrari, wasn't it?'

'That was okay too,' she said. 'It was the place that I loved.'

'Hawaii?'

'The pool,' she said, quietly and with the hushed reverence people hold for their most sacred memories or favourite fantasies.

'A swimming pool?' Sedley probed.

'A sea pool,' she told him. 'A beautiful sea pool, protected by the breakers.'

Stranski leaned a little closer, so he could keep his voice low, his questions more encouraging than demanding. 'What do you see?'

She answered readily and happily. 'The water, shimmering like thousands of liquid mirrors, the palms leaning over the beach.'

'Can you see anyone?'

'No.' Simply and without regret.

'You're alone?'

'On my own, but not *alone*. The pool is calm, the ocean's outside, noisy, constant, a distant roar – but not frightening. I'm on my back, floating in the pool in the ocean and if I want I can turn over and the world becomes quiet as I dive and I can see the sunshine, a wavering pavement of light on the bottom . . .'

Straightening up, Stranski leaned back from her.

'Okay, Nancy, you can open your eyes again.'

Her eyes opened gently, the lids fluttering softly.

'You said you didn't have an imagination,' he scolded her kindly. 'But you created a beautiful picture of a sea pool.'

She just smiled and seemed a little embarrassed. But she appreciated the relaxation she was feeling.

'Now we'll try and see if you can imagine a simple object,' Stranski began. 'When you close your eyes this time, imagine you are looking up at a full moon. Go on, close your eyes again,' he urged her.

Her eyes fell shut immediately.

'Imagine you're on the beach again or in the car or out on the veranda and you are looking up at that moon, bright but easy on the eyes. To see it properly, roll your eyeballs up, keep the eyelids closed. Roll them right up so you can see the lambent moon.'

He crouched over her and ran his finger lightly along her hairline. He could see her eyeballs revolving beneath the lids. Rapidly, he began giving directions in his ever-calm voice.

'Roll them right back up so you can see the moon. As you do this your eyelids will lock closed and the more you try to open them the tighter they will become . . . Now try, try to open them.'

He watched as her eyelids quivered but remained shut, tightening in wrinkles around the corners.

Stranski smiled to himself – *eye catalepsy.*

After nearly two hours of various relaxation and induction techniques Kronziac was under.

'Now, stop trying to open your eyes and just relax and sleep. Let the warmth flow over you like a wave – let every part of your body go limp. Breathe deeply and slowly – match the rhythm of the waves . . .'

He paused and relaxed himself, watching her chest rise and fall slowly with the sighing oscillations of her breath, her own brainwaves beginning to settle on an ebbing tide of alpha rhythms.

'How do you feel?'

'Sleepy,' she replied.

'Why are you sleepy, Nancy?'

Her words moved heavily in her mouth. '. . . Tired.'

'What made you so tired today?'

'No sleep,' she moaned.

'Couldn't you sleep last night?'

She moved her head. 'The Woodsmen . . . their brother's coming after me . . . Lucas.'

'He's coming after you?'

'I killed his younger brother.'

'You had to,' Stranski comforted her.

'He was going to shoot me in the forehead.'

Stranski took out a small notebook as quietly as he could from his jacket pocket and clicked his pen. 'Nancy, can you remember what happened? Did anyone tell him to shoot you? Did he say he was going to shoot you?'

'He was seventeen,' she whispered, her face taut.

'Did his brother give him any instructions before he left with Phillips?'

Kronziac's head moved again as if she was avoiding the sight of something. 'Told him to watch me. I could see his eyes were young . . . or maybe it was the way he looked at me.'

Her answers were short and simple. The classic child-like responses of what hypnotherapists call *trance logic* – the primary

377

processes of the brain beginning to exert themselves on the discretionary vetoes of higher brain functions that were now being sidestepped under hypnosis.

'Did he tell him to—' Stranski knew he had to be careful here. In her state Kronziac was highly suggestible. One of the most common criticisms of hypnosis – and the main reason why many judiciaries ruled information elicited under hypnosis inadmissible – was that the subject's responses could be hugely influenced by the operator.

'Did he tell him to do anything else?' he asked.

Breathing heavily she clucked her tongue at the back of her throat. '. . . Keep a close eye on the bitch,' she groaned, a guttural murmur.

'What happened then?'

'He took Phillips out . . . downstairs . . . called him a cowboy.' She was almost smiling. 'Told his brother to keep his cell phone on. The door banged downstairs. He told me to lay back . . . going to be a long wait. I held my gun beneath the sheets and I was shaking . . . he was watching me all over.'

'Did he do anything else while he was there?'

Her throat moved, swallowing hard. 'He sat down,' she recalled. 'Tried to be funny, the kid. Really believed Phillips and I were husband and wife. Asked if we had children . . . joked as he watched me.'

'Did he threaten you?'

'Asked me the time,' she remembered. 'He went into the closet and kidded around with a dress. He was laughing . . . came out with a pair of jeans for me. Told me to put them on . . . waited, watching me, waiting for me to take off the bedclothes. Told him I needed the belt and he went back into the closet.'

'You needed a belt?'

Kronziac's hand was twitching slightly and her eyes were watering from the corners of their closed lids. 'I wanted to stall,' she said, '. . . afraid he'd see my gun if I got out of the bed.'

'Did he get it? The belt?'

'No . . . he went into the closet . . . I was thinking of putting the gun under the pillow . . . he was calling from inside . . .

asking if I was bullshitting him, asking where he'd find it . . . then he shut up.'

'Why?' Stranski asked, intrigued. 'Why did he shut up?'

'*It shut him up*,' she replied, her voice strained.

'*What* shut him up?' he asked, poising his pen over the notepad.

It was apparent that Kronziac was struggling to remember or trying to understand the memory.

'The sound . . . a small sound . . . beeps . . .'

'Do you know what made the sound?'

She sighed heavily. 'I don't know . . . but he came out, running, putting something back in his coat, raising the gun to my head. I had to . . . I had to shoot.'

He could see she was having difficulty with the rush of memories that pierced the murky waters of her traumatized subconscious like sharp edges of wreckage.

'It's okay, Nancy, it's okay. You had no choice.'

But she continued to speak, a halting jabber, her breath getting away from her. 'He fell on top of me . . . I could smell smoke . . . burning wood . . . feel my hand breaking . . . hearing it snap like a stick . . . I pushed him away . . . his black mask falling away—'

'It's okay, Nancy, he's gone. It's over . . . rest now,' he told her, smoothing his tone as much as he could. 'Let the room and image of him fall away – imagine you are back in the sea pool . . .'

Slowly, her breathing began to steady again, the agitation subsiding.

'Outside the breakers the sea is calm and the water beneath you is warm and bright. You are floating on your back and drifting into a peaceful, restful sleep – resting, relaxing, lying in the warm arms of the water.'

Kronziac's eyelids ceased their flickering and her chest began to rise and fall in the steady motion of a deep sleep. Quietly, Stranski stood up from the coffee table and walked to the closed French doors to look over his notes in the bright light. He focused on her report of the beeping sound and the mention of a cell phone.

Arcana Celestia

FBI OFFICES, FEDERAL BUILDING, WILSHIRE BLVD

Stranski gently hooked Maggie by the arm as she headed towards Sedley's office.

'Sorry, Agent Ramirez,' he said quietly, almost whispering as he watched Ellstrom, Kronziac and Phillips go in.

She was surprised by his furtive approach. 'What is it, Dr Stranski?'

'I talked with Kronziac about her experience on the night of the Woodsmen bank raid.'

Maggie smiled cheekily. 'Oh yeah. She told me you tried to hypnotize her. Said you helped her have a good sleep, though.'

Stranski just nodded graciously. 'She mentioned something about Matthew Crebbs possibly having a cell phone and that his brother told him to keep it on while in the house. Later she recalled a beeping sound when he was in the walk-in, just before he rushed out to – well, to execute her.'

Her smile disappearing, Maggie tried to remember. 'I think Phillips said something about a phone that Daniel Crebbs had in the car and at the bank.'

'I know,' he said. 'I talked to him about it and he said Crebbs was going to send a text message to Matthew if anything went wrong at the heist. But when the HRT guys stormed the place it was chaos.'

'Why do you think it's so important?'

'If Matthew Crebbs got a direct order from his brother to shoot Kronziac, then that would show intent on his part and she was acting correctly under rules of engagement to shoot him in self-defence.'

'Yes, I guess,' Maggie said hesitantly.

'You were one of the first on the scene in the bedroom, right?' he went on.

She nodded. 'Me, Sedley and a couple of resident agents.'

'Could you see if Matthew Crebbs had a cell phone at all?'

She shook her head slowly in uncertainty. 'I really don't know.

Kronziac was in great pain with her wrist. I thought she'd been shot.'

Their conversation was interrupted when Sedley shouted from the doorway of his office. 'You guys want in or not?' he asked, holding the door open.

'Sorry, sir,' Maggie called back and began walking to the office.

Stranski stuck close to her side, his voice urgent. 'If there was a phone, where would it be now?'

'Should be held under sealed evidence,' she replied hurriedly. 'DOJ?'

'No. Internal, I'd say. Would be Westwood Park,'

Stranski was trying to squeeze his questions out as quickly and quietly as possible before they entered the room. 'Can you check it out?'

'I'll try,' she whispered anxiously. 'Taggart in Forensics might help out.'

Sedley's office was darkened, the blinds closed. As though preparing for a lecture Ellstrom stood in front of a bright rectangle of light on one of the blank walls, illuminated by the bulb of an overhead projector. On the glass platen of the projector he was writing in marker the plaintext of the Leo Pretaran cryptogram.

The rest of the team turned their seats around from the desk towards Ellstrom and the projector. Phillips, assigned to laptop duty again, had keyed up an Internet search engine enquiry field.

'I won't bore you with the details,' Ellstrom began. 'I'm a bit tired from being up all night with the NSA guys and I didn't get much chance to sleep on the plane back to LA.'

Kronziac was secretly glad that her house guest wouldn't have a chance to dazzle them senseless with a description of the NSA's new supercomputing facility at Fort Meade, its powerful Cray computers and attendant army of math boffins.

'Suffice to say,' he continued, 'that the ciphertext was indeed transposed ASCII code, which was further enciphered through a keyword, quite like the Vignere method in the "Ellen" cipher.'

Ellstrom had begun to call each cryptogram by the first name of the victim to whom it applied.

'After several million passes by the computer algorithms the keyword turned out in this case to be—' he paused for a second to say the word '—Yhuh.'

'What did you say?' Sedley asked, looking around to see if he'd heard it right.

'Yhuh,' Ellstrom replied and spelled it out. 'Y – H – U – H.'

'Doesn't sound like a real word,' Phillips observed.

'The Tetragrammaton,' Stranski said quietly, realizing immediately what it was.

'What, Dr Stranski?' Sedley asked, growing frustrated.

'That's right, Fred,' Ellstrom beamed. 'We looked it up. It's from the Kaballah. A derivative of Yaweh – the unspeakable name of God.'

Sedley just shook his head, reluctantly becoming accustomed to the esoteric nature of the whole case. He waved his hand, almost a gesture of surrender. 'Go on.'

'Using this as the transposing keyword,' the mathematician duly continued, 'we constructed the ASCII plaincode and translated it into English text.'

He moved out of the way so that his audience could see the plaintext riddle on the bright square patch of wall. The only sound in the room was the projector's fan purring.

if terrible + number = thirteen and
seven + sevens = square
then find him in 6751976 at the house of 21273 in the
only room number between a square and a cube his stolen
soul behind your own

I hope you know what he's saying,' Kronziac remarked. 'Because I haven't a clue.'

She looked around to see if the rest of them shared her perplexity. Their pained expressions gave her the answer as they read over the riddle again in their own minds.

Bill Murphy

'I must admit I was rather lost myself but the trick, as always, is to break the riddle down into manageable pieces you can *attack*. The first line seems to refer not only to a word equation but also to a numeral equation.'

The shadow of Ellstrom's finger pointed across the projected words: *terrible + number = thirteen*.

'Something to do with the unlucky number?' Maggie asked earnestly.

'Well, to do with numbers, all right,' he agreed. 'The structure of this expression is *alphametic* or cryptarithmic. The letters have distinct number values. Where ASCII is binary, this system has a higher base value, namely 10. Each letter is assigned a number from 1 to 10, 10 to 1, 0 to 9 or 9 to 0.'

Ellstrom realized he was beginning to shoot over their heads again. 'Anyway.' He moved on quickly. 'I worked out the letter values on the plane for this expression as the following.'

He put another plastic sheet on the projector platen to illustrate the calculation.

T = 4	N = 3	T = 4
E = 5	U = 0	H = 6
R = 8	M = 2	I = 1
R = 8	B = 7	R = 8
I = 1	E = 5	T = 4
B = 7	R = 8	E = 5
L = 9		E = 5
E = 5		N = 3

```
    T E R R I B L E
  + 4 5 8 8 1 7 9 5
        N U M B E R
  +     3 0 2 7 5 8
    T H I R T E E N
  = 4 6 1 8 4 5 5 3
```

'The same goes for the second line: *seven + seven = square*,' Ellstrom said and placed another sheet on the projector.

S = 3	S = 3	S = 3
E = 1	E = 1	Q = 4
V = 5	V = 5	U = 6
E = 1	E = 1	A = 7
N = 8	N = 8	R = 0
	S = 3	E = 1

```
      S E V E N
  +   3 1 5 1 8
      S E V E N S
  +   3 1 5 1 8 3
      S Q U A R E
  =   3 4 6 7 0 1
```

'This now gives us two possible alphabets for the number-letter values,' he continued, moving down the sheet.

```
0 = U, R
1 = I, E
2 = M
3 = N, S
4 = T, Q
5 = E, V
6 = H, U
7 = B, A
8 = R, N
9 = L
```

'On the third line of the riddle we have reference to two numbers: *then find him in 6751976 at the house of 21273.* I believe we now have the letter values for these numbers. There is some crossover as some numbers have two letters but the only two legible words that I could find are *havilah* and *mimas*.'

'"Havilah" and "mimas"?' Kronziac repeated the words, trying to figure their significance.

'Is "havilah" a word?' Stranski asked.

'Looks like it,' Phillips answered, tapping at the laptop. 'A town in California, just west of Bakersfield.'

'How about "mimas"?' Maggie asked.

He entered the word in the search engine and waited for the results.

Kronziac was still looking at the riddle, which Ellstrom had put back on the screen.

'*the only room number between a square and a cube*?' she recited.

Ellstrom looked back at the screen himself, his silhouette in sharp relief against the wall. 'It says room *number . . . the only room number . . .* the only number that I can think of between a square and a cube is 26 . . . 5 square is 25 and 3 cubed is 27.'

'Room number 26,' Kronziac said.

Ellstrom nodded, a little smile of appreciation at the simplicity of it.

'Any luck?' Sedley asked, turning to Phillips.

The search engine rolled up a list of matches and their summaries.

Phillips scanned through them.

'Mimas software . . . Manchester Information . . . Ah! Mimas, a giant in Greek mythology!' he exclaimed. 'Slain by Hercules.'

'Ties in with a lot of the Greek mythological references in other cryptos,' Maggie remarked.

'Try "mimas" and "havilah",' Kronziac suggested.

As Phillips typed in the new search, Stranski was reading the rest of the cryptogram projected on the wall.

'*His stolen soul behind your own* – seems like a religious metaphor . . . or spiritual.'

'Isn't directly mathematical anyway.' Ellstrom shrugged, unable to interpret its meaning.

'Got something here,' Phillips said. 'A hit on *havilah* and *mimas*. Though *mimas* is with an apostrophe – Mima's Motel, off the 483, Havilah, California.'

He looked around, grinning to see if there were any congratulations forthcoming from his colleagues.

'How many rooms?' Ellstrom barked.

Phillips returned to the screen. 'Er – thirty four single rooms, ensuite . . . cable.'

Sedley's mood seemed to have lightened with the discovery. 'If we do find Pretaran's body,' he said, 'then we might be able to add four definite murder-ones to Madsen's charge sheet before the psych evaluation on Wednesday.'

Kronziac swung around to Sedley. 'Wednesday?' she asked, shocked. '*This* Wednesday?'

'Yes,' he confirmed. 'Sorry you'll have to miss it.'

Before Kronziac could say anything else Sedley faced Stranski. 'I hope Wednesday is okay for you, Doctor. I've talked to Director Foley and the DA. Everyone agreed it should be as soon as possible so we know how to prepare the prosecution. Defence counsel has agreed.'

Stranski sighed. 'Okay,' he said. 'I will be looking over the video material and Madsen's clinical records from Grovehurst. Where will we conduct the test?'

'Hadco Neuroscience Building, USC,' Sedley replied. 'They've full PET facilities, like you wanted. Madsen will be transported at dawn under security from LA County for preparation.'

PLUTO'S BAR & RESTAURANT, MALIBU, CA

Resembling the hull of a galleon, the low ceiling in the bar was supported by thick varnished oak beams and decorated with hanging oyster baskets, brass navigation lanterns and tuna nets. The large window at their table framed a view of Malibu pier and the bay stretching south, separated from the city buildings by the thin belt of sand of the coastal beaches.

Secretly, Stranski was beginning to hate LA. The change from the grey east coast was nice for a couple of days but now he was growing weary of the city – or the mood it imposed on him.

Beside him Kronziac was on her cell phone and Maggie, sitting across from them, was prodding knubs of oyster, oiled with garlic butter, from her Sashimi platter. Ellstrom was at the pool table with a basket of fries, waiting for Kronziac to take her shot.

Stranski turned to the window once more and imagined what the city looked like from above, high above. A giant wound, he decided, on the side of the continent, a crazed pattern of roads strung together by a snaking frame of highways and interstates, all under an acrid gauze of smog that sucked the colour from the land. At least in Washington, with its drab white core of federal bureaucracy and teeming traffic on the beltway, time was marked by the changing temperatures and colours of the seasons. Here the passage of the months was notified to its citizens by the appearance of plastic symbols, such as Christmas trees, baking in the dry reflection of the sidewalks. Winter was just the idling tick of summer's hot engine. He glanced over at Ellstrom and wondered why the Englishman seemed to be thriving here. Perhaps the excitement of being involved with an FBI manhunt for a serial murderer? The buzz of the cryptogram chase? Kronziac? He began to think of his own partner in Georgetown.

'Don't you like your salad, Dr Stranski?' Maggie asked, speaking her words round a mouthful of sushi roll.

'Not hungry,' he answered feebly and pushed his Caesar salad away.

Fred Stranski had spent the morning watching the video files from Madsen's webcam. He had watched as Madsen played with his victims, killed them, laughed at them, clipped their fingers, dismantled their humanity like a mechanic.

Kronziac came off the phone and looked at the few scribbled notes she had taken during the conversation.

'What was that about?' asked Maggie.

'Taggart,' said Kronziac. 'Came back to me with information on the cream traces.' She squinted at her own writing. 'A linoleic acid dimer – called P-Block.'

'What is it?' Maggie wondered. 'A sun block? A moisturizer?'

'No. It's a prescription barrier cream. Specially formulated for sufferers of moth-dander contact dermatitis.'

'Say again?' Maggie asked, holding a rice-heaped fork at her mouth.

'For someone with a skin allergy to moth-wing dust,' Stranski explained.

'Did the forensic guys searching Madsen's place find any special creams?' Kronziac asked Maggie.

The young agent shook her head. 'Turned the place from top to bottom. No mention of it.'

Ellstrom was calling Kronziac to take her shot or she would forfeit her two-dollar bet on the game. She got up to join him, still trying to digest the information from Taggart, wondering if it held any significance in the case.

Stranski folded his arms on the table as Maggie finished her lunch and daubed her mouth delicately with a napkin.

'Did you talk to this guy Taggart about the cell phones from the Bitteroot raid?'

'Yesterday,' she confirmed. 'He said both phones used by the Crebbs brothers were under evidentiary seal at the lab.'

'Could he check them out?'

Maggie had anticipated the question. 'He's already at it,' she informed him happily. 'Both phones were damaged, but he's gonna check with the mobile service provider. They should have a record of any text messages sent between the units.'

Kronziac, despite her preoccupations, managed to hide the black ball behind one of her own, snookering Ellstrom. As he hunkered down to cue up his shot, she glanced at the clock in the shape of a brass helm wheel above the bar. 'Phillips should be in Havilah by now,' she figured. 'It's only a couple of hours' drive.'

'We should have gone with him,' said Ellstrom, one eye closed, calculating his stroke.

Kronziac smiled warily. 'Sedley wasn't having it,' she said. 'You miss and it's two dollars *you* owe me,' she said, trying to put him off his shot. 'I thought you said pool was all about geometry. Forgotten your math, Professor?'

Ellstrom glanced up at her. 'Double or nothing?' he challenged. 'If I hit the black.'

'You sure you can afford to lose four dollars?'

'Beats hanging around your place while you climb the walls worrying about your hearing tomorrow,' he said with a perceptive accuracy that immediately prompted her to agree. Despite Sedley's assurances that it was really just a formality for the sake of Bureau housekeeping she smelt something was up and hoped it wasn't her own hide slowly burning.

'Pass me down the mirror,' Ellstrom said.

'What?'

He nodded at a Coors mirror on the wall by the bar counter. 'The mirror.'

'Gonna do your make-up?' she joked. 'Want to look good when you lose?' She plucked the mirror from its hook, smiling at the waitresses. Kronziac was a regular so they let her do it.

'Now rest it on the side of the table, above the cushion,' he directed her. 'Perpendicular to the playing surface.'

Kronziac felt a bit stupid but placed the mirror on the table ledge as he told her, directly over the side cushion and at right angles to the baize.

'Now move it down to your right.'

She slid the mirror carefully along the table until the reflection of the black ball appeared in the silvered glass.

'Okay, hold it,' he said.

By now Stranski and Maggie, as well as the few other people

in the bar, were watching with interest.

'You like looking at yourself while you take a shot,' Kronziac laughed. But Ellstrom, with one eye closed, lined up the shot once more.

'All I have to do is aim at the reflection of the black in the mirror and—'

He stoked the white ball smoothly with his cue and sent it bouncing off the cushion just below the mirror and back around Kronziac's blocking ball until it rolled up to the black and nudged it in a soft kiss, a little click of contact.

Stranski, Maggie and the other spectators burst out cheering.

'That's cheating,' Kronziac protested, still holding the mirror in place.

'That's geometry,' Ellstrom replied smugly. 'Angle of incidence equals angle of reflection and all that . . .'

Stranski shouted across the bar to Kronziac. 'I should have warned you. He was always beating me at snooker.'

Kronziac was still protesting when Ellstrom stopped smiling and looked at himself in the mirror. He stood up quickly from the table.

'In mythology mirrors are supposed to steal your soul, right?' he asked.

ROOM 26, MIMA'S ROADHOUSE MOTEL, HAVILAH, CA

While other motels in the Kern Valley had, over the years, reno-
vated and beautified themselves to attract the most discerning
of visitors to the region, Mima's Motel seemed proud of its
cheap 20-dollar-a-nite rooms with basic conveniences. As the
other hostelries decorated themselves with Spanish Colonial or
Alpine rusticana, Mima's was content to offer its seventies-style
wood-panelled accommodation, hot showers and a colour TV
in every room. The building itself looked like a POW dorm from
the outside. Phillips stood in the middle of number 26 with
Mima herself, a portly lady in her sixties with long grey hair,
big eyes and a woolly cardigan. Agents Morris and Di Canio
carefully checked the room – behind the red crushed-velvet
headboard, under the yellowing acrylic curtains, the musty
cupboards and around the cigarette-scorched carpet.

Phillips kept his breathing shallow – the place smelt thickly
of stale bedclothes, edged with the astringency of turned
meat.

'Do you remember who rented the room last?' Phillips asked.

'I think so,' Mima replied, pressing her index finger against
her mouth and frowning at the ground. 'Big guy,' she said. 'A
bit younger than you – you know, late twenties, maybe.'

'Can you remember what he was driving?'

'Truck or a van, I think. Boxy kinda thing, anyway. He was
a delivery guy or something, I guess.'

'A brown one?'

'Coulda been.'

'When did he check in?'

She frowned in thought again. 'Have to check the register.
But it was sometime late last week. Thursday – yeah, Thursday
afternoon.'

'You sure?' It was Phillips who was frowning now. Thursday,
he knew, was the day when Kronziac and the Northridge detective had searched Madsen's van in Pomona. Before Mima could
answer his cell phone rang, bleating like an intrusive bug.

Fractions of Zero

It was Kronziac, talking excitedly about the 'Leo' cryptogram's last line.

Phillips nodded and turned to Agent Morris. 'Check behind the mirror on the wardrobe,' he said. With the phone still to his ear he asked the motel owner if there were any more mirrors in the room.

'The bathroom, of course,' she answered. 'Vanity mirror on the dresser and . . .' She began to smile coyly, her gaze turning up to the ceiling.

Phillips looked up quickly. He hadn't noticed the long mirror fixed to the ceiling.

Mima began giggling like a schoolgirl. 'We get a lot of couples,' she explained.

'There a trapdoor to the loft?' Phillips asked curtly.

'In the bathroom,' she answered, disappointed that he didn't find it funny.

395

2434 ABRAMAR, PACIFIC PALISADES, CA

It was late by the time they had left the office.

Stranski had gone back to his hotel to rest for the psych evaluation he would conduct with Madsen in the morning. But Kronziac and Maggie waited for Phillips to get back from Havilah and listened as Sedley debriefed him about the discovery of Leo Pretaran's body in the loft of room 26 in Mima's Motel. As far as Phillips could tell, Preteran had been strangled. Mima's description of the man who had rented the room was very vague and they discovered, running a check, that the name he had given in the register was false.

But the factor that worried everyone was the timing. Though the man had driven a brown van they knew he could not have been Madsen as Madsen had been placed under arrest by Cunningham at the time in Los Angeles. Maggie was still going through DynoTech employee records to see if she could find anyone else who might have been involved.

Even before Kronziac opened the front door they could hear the sound of Beethoven's Fifth Symphony blaring on the stereo. They found Ellstrom standing in front of the map and blackboard by the fireplace, a near-empty whisky glass in his hand. Hector scrambled behind a leaf as Kronziac turned the music down.

'You okay, James?' she asked, concerned as he stayed staring at the map. He had stuck a pin in the location of Leo Pretaran's dead body in Havilah and had drawn a large loop in red marker, joining up all of the other pins.

'Like Copernicus, in order to see the full symmetry of the heavens I had to look from the point of view of the Sun and not the Earth.' He spoke in the distracted tone of the insane – or the maudlin drunkard.

'I'll go make some coffee,' Maggie decided abruptly and headed for the kitchen, dropping her paperwork on the couch.

Kronziac gently took the glass from Ellstrom and put it down on the desk. She glanced at the computer screen, which was bright with a simple graphic of coloured dots orbiting a central point.

Ellstrom turned to her. He was smiling and she really couldn't be sure if he was drunk or not.

'Kronziac, you have nice symmetry in your face and a good hip-to-knee ratio, you know.'

She smiled. 'Are you trying to tell me I have a nice figure?'

'Beautiful,' he said. But he was now looking back at the map and the semantic table on the blackboard. 'It's just too beautiful not to be true.'

Turning to face her again, his eyes less filmy, more focused, he asked, 'It's not over yet – is it?'

She was taken aback by his piercing question. 'I don't think so. We have another killer out there. How did you know? An astute deduction?'

'More like induction,' he replied. 'We can calculate an infinity of related problems by solving just one – sometimes.'

Maggie's girlish voice intervened. 'Looks kinda like a spider's web,' she said, as she saw the convoluted red circle encompassing the pins on the map. She handed Ellstrom his coffee, steaming and black.

'I'm not drunk,' he said with a calmness and gentleness that suggested he was telling the truth. But he took the cup nonetheless. 'And that's quite a good observation,' he complimented Maggie. 'It *is* like a spider's web.'

The three of them looked at the map quietly for a few beats, Ellstrom sipping at his coffee.

'You never answered my question,' Kronziac reminded him. She had the feeling they were minding a fragile patient and wondered if the weeks of living in a strange city and the horrific nature of the case had finally crept up on the math teacher and assailed him from behind.

'At first I was thinking in lines,' he said. 'We knew there was some significance in the location of the bodies. I drew every imaginable line, constructed grids and linear shapes to connect them. But only as I looked at all the variables, the numbers hidden in the riddles, did I begin to see their *music*.'

He angled his head at Kronziac, knowing she would under-

397

stand the metaphor – or at least accept it without having to understand.

Quickly, he put down the cup and grabbed a piece of chalk, his speed of movement temporarily alarming the two women. As he began scribbling a string of numbers across the board, Kronziac and Maggie traded resigned looks of bewilderment at his behaviour. Maggie wondered if now would be a good time to excuse herself, take her paperwork and go home to bed. But it was too late – Ellstrom stood back from the board and urged them to look at the numbers.

0, 1, 2, 3, 5, 8, 13, 21, 34, 55, 89, 144 . . .

'Notice anything about them?' he asked provocatively. But he couldn't wait as they vacantly scanned the numerals, not really knowing what they were looking for.

'Each number is the sum of itself and the previous one,' he informed them excitedly as if he had just discovered it himself. 'They're called Fibonacci numbers and they occur everywhere around you; the number of petals on a flower, leaf arrangements – loads of things.'

'You said they were in the riddles,' Kronziac said him.

'Sure, they're all over,' Ellstrom replied. 'Ellen Holby's tether in the lake was eighty metres in length and she was floating fifty metres downstream, which gives us 80/50 or, simplified, 8/5. Peter Kelley was found at point number eight in the cave trail. The number on the Dürer painting was thirty-four, which gave us the answer to where Shayla Wilson's body was buried.'

'I don't know,' Kronziac said doubtfully. 'Though nothing would surprise me at this stage.'

'I understand the scepticism,' Ellstrom assured her and turned to the map. 'But it's the spiral that I believe proves my theory that whoever is behind this is placing the bodies according to a Fibonacci sequence.'

'Spiral?' Maggie asked.

'The Golden Spiral,' he replied with a reverential smile. 'In the Fibonacci sequence, imagine that each number is the unit value for a square. Starting with a square with sides of one unit in length, then two units, three units, five units, eight units, thirteen – and so on.'

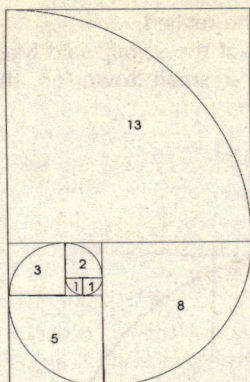

He drew the squares to illustrate it.

'And then you draw an arc between the corners of each square, each of the arcs join to form a spiral, more accurately a logarithmic spiral or the *golden spiral*. You find them everywhere,' he added. 'The edeira spider's web, the Nautilus shell, galaxies, hurricanes – all over.'

Maggie turned to Kronziac. 'Remember the engineer at Hyperion called the scraper at the bottom of the sewage tank a logarithmic curve?'

But Kronziac just mumbled unenthusiastically and stared at the map.

'The relationship between the Fibonacci numbers tends towards the *golden mean*,' Ellstrom explained. 'Three over two, five over three, eight over five – their fractions near a value of 1.618, which, as you probably know, is the most pleasing aspect to the human eye, the ratio 1 to 1.618, present in the proportions of everything from the Parthenon in Athens to your widescreen TV. You'll also find that many composers, Mozart, for example, used this number a lot. The famous sequence from Beethoven's Fifth, denoted in the Peter Kelley crypto, occurs in the symphony at exactly the golden mean point.'

'Okay, suppose all this is true,' Kronziac interrupted. 'What does it give us?'

'A centre point,' he replied.

'The centre point of the spiral,' said Maggie, catching on.

Ellstrom tapped a small town on the map. 'Kernville, California.'

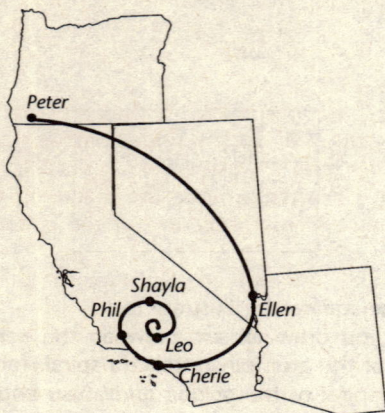

'Not far from where Pretaran was found,' Kronziac observed, noting the pin just south of Kernville.

Ellstrom went on. 'He's moving towards the centre of the spiral, or the bottom of it, you could say. That's why I don't think he's finished yet.'

'How can you be so sure?' Kronziac asked, frustration creeping into her voice.

'One simple answer might prove it,' he said daringly. 'Was there a marking found on the latest victim?'

Maggie nodded. 'Yes—'

Before she could say what it was Ellstrom shot his hand up to stop her. 'Was it an "equals" sign?' he asked them.

Maggie was shaking her head slowly with amazement as Kronziac gave him the answer.

'Phillips said there were two small parallel lines cut into his forehead. How did you know?'

Picking up the chalk again, he marked in the equals sign in the table next to Leo Pretaran's name.

Fractions of Zero

NAME	MARK
'Cherie'	b^n
'Ellen'	+
'Peter'	a
'Shayla'	/
'Phil'	n
'Leo'	=

'We thought that the mark on Cherie's forehead was "6" with a small squiggle,' he continued. 'It was actually a "b" with a small "n" and it wasn't a cross on Ellen's head but a "plus" sign. If you then arrange the marks on the victims in order of distance from the centre of the spiral you get the equation: $a + b^n/n = \ldots$'

'Equals what?' Maggie asked, faintly annoyed that the answer was missing.

Picking up from the desk an old math book he had got at the library, Ellstrom opened a marked page which bore a lithograph of a man with the bearing and attire of an eighteenth-century scientist.

'Leonhard Euler, a Swiss mathematician. One of the greatest.' Ellstrom described him with genuine affection. 'In an argument about religion with a French mathematician he propounded the equation $a+b^n/n=x$.'

'What was he trying to prove?' Kronziac wondered.

'The existence of God,' Ellstrom replied, with purposeful understatement.

She just looked at him, not knowing whether to laugh or get him more coffee.

'Of course, there's no such thing as a mathematical proof of God's existence,' Ellstrom said. 'The equation is merely a fanciful expression of the possibilities of maths. I told you, sometimes there's a thin line between mathematics and philosophy,' he added, grinning.

'In this case I think your Mr Euler fell right over it,' Kronziac said.

'So the answer is "x",' Maggie concluded. 'The next victim will bear the mark "x".'

Ellstrom nodded.

Kronziac suddenly thought of something else. Something she believed had ended with Madsen's arrest. 'Did anyone check last Saturday's lottery numbers?' Even to her own ears the question sounded absurdly comical.

'I got them from the lottery website about an hour ago,' Ellstrom assured her. 'But there didn't seem to be any valid SSN matches.'

'Unless he's changed the system of selection again,' Maggie suggested. 'We did think time seemed to be running out for him.'

Kronziac was more disturbed by the fact that now they had no idea who had kidnapped Leo Pretaran and strangled him and who was now possibly selecting his next victim. It couldn't be Madsen but someone he knew, a game partner.

'In fact, I think time *is* almost up,' Ellstrom said. 'Let's look at all the different places where the bodies were found. Cherie at the Hyperion plant, Ellen above the sunken boat called the *Iapetus*, Peter in a cave below an outcrop called Phoebe's Perch, Shayla under The Snowball, also known as Tethys Rock.'

He picked up the photo Phillips had taken of Phil Chavez's burial site at Soda Lake. In the background was a sign over a mine-shaft entrance.

'Phil was found near the DION-E mine—' he read the letters on the sign '—and Leo was found in Mima's Motel – Mimas.'

'All Greek mythological figures,' Kronziac said.

'Yep,' Ellstrom said and leaned over the computer desk. On the screen the bright dots were still orbiting, prescribing concentric circles around the central point. 'They are also the names of satellites,' he told them. 'The moons of Saturn.'

Kronziac's attention jumped between the computer screen and the map, marked with the locations of the dead. 'Is he trying to match their orbits?'

'I think so,' replied Ellstrom and began prodding the keyboard. Having at last mastered one of Kronziac's never-used graphics packages he called up a map of the western states on screen. On it he had placed large black Xs, marking the locations of the body sites, replicating the *National Geographic* map over the fireplace. With a few more deft taps on the keys he superimposed the Saturnian lunar system over the map so that the moons of the ringed planet now wheeled in the skies above California and Saturn itself was positioned directly over the town of Kernville.

'Watch this,' he said as he slowed the spinning dots, inching them closer until they coincided with the X marks on the map.

'Almost an exact match,' Maggie said, staring in awe at the screen.

'Yes,' said Ellstrom proudly. 'The Saturnian moons of Phoebe, Iapetus, Hyperion, Dione, Tethys and Mimas coincide with the burial sites. This not only gives us a locational correlation,' he informed them. 'But the conjunction is also *temporally* specific. The designer of this—' he searched for the right words '—this macabre celestial choreography has set his system in the fourth dimension too.'

Kronziac raised her eyebrow at the mathematician. The fact that he had got everything right so far regarding the cryptograms and the riddles forced her to listen seriously to his theories, however bizarre. But he still had the knack of bugging the hell out of her with his long-winded explanations.

'You mean time?' she said, wearied.

'I guess that's why he changed the selection system with the lottery numbers.' Ellstrom nodded and tapped the corner of the monitor that showed the date and time of the orbits. 'He was working to a deadline. The conjunction occurs at twelve midday, February thirteenth this year.'

'The thirteenth's tomorrow,' Maggie pointed out and moved away from the desk.

'Why tomorrow?' Kronziac wondered.

Ellstrom just shrugged, his bag of answers empty. 'Thirteen is a Fibonacci number,' he suggested weakly. 'And February is the second month of the year. Two is another Fibonacci.'

As Ellstrom and Kronziac stood at the computer, looking at the screen, their minds racing to try and anticipate the killer's next move among the figures and movements of the heavens, Maggie was staring at the blackboard.

'Could the X be interpreted as a cross?' she wondered aloud

as she concentrated on the semantic table, listing the names of the victims and the unfinished Euler equation.

NAME	LOCATION	CRYPTO	RIDDLE	MARK
'Cherie'	Hyperion WWT	Caesar Shift	Keats – poem	b^n
'Ellen'	Iapetus – L. Meade	Vignere	Mythology	+
'Peter'	Phoebe's Perch	Enigma	Beethoven – 5	a
'Shayla'	Tethys Rock	Beale	Bible	/
'Phil'	DION-E mine	Linear B	Dürer	n
'Leo'	Mima's Motel	ASCII code	Alphametic	=

'Yes. I suppose it could,' said Ellstrom, joining her at the blackboard.

Margaret Ramirez came from a good Catholic family and knew her movable feasts. 'Tomorrow's Ash Wednesday,' she said quietly. 'First day of Lent, when the penitents must bear the sign of the cross on their foreheads.'

HELIPAD, ROOF OF FEDERAL BUILDING, WILSHIRE BLVD

Kronziac got some venomous looks from Sedley as the helicopter slowly ascended into the bright blue morning, the checkerboard of buildings and streets spinning below them.

'You've got a section chief from Inspection Division waiting for you in my office right now,' he snarled, 'just twiddlin' his thumbs.'

'I know, sir,' she replied contritely, raising her voice to be heard above the chattering blades and the whistle of the engines. 'I apologize. But I think this is far more important.'

Everyone else in the confined cabin remained silent. The Deputy Assistant Director's mood pervaded the air like a thick smoke, discouraging anyone from opening their mouth.

'Wait till Foley finds out,' he remarked and glanced disconsolately out at the lines of the city drifting below. Then he turned swiftly back. 'I mean, what in God's name makes you so sure about this?'

Kronziac realized that Sedley was addressing her directly, and only her, to place her now as the prime mover behind the whole cryptogram murders case – not so she could benefit from the capture of Madsen but to crucify her in the eyes of Foley and the rest of the office if Kernville turned out to be a turkey.

She slid a glance in Ellstrom's direction.

'Because it's too beautiful not to be true,' she said with a smile.

The reply furrowed Sedley's forehead and his stare grew murderous.

Even Ellstrom wished she hadn't said it. 'The original marks to be placed on the foreheads of the penitents,' he said, intervening quickly, 'according to the early translations of Ezekiel, were to be *tavs*, not crosses.'

Sedley's glare shifted away from Kronziac and focused upon the mathematician, softening only slightly. 'So?' he asked.

'A *tav* is from the Hebrew alphabet,' Ellstrom explained loudly, reciting the information he had gleaned from the Internet in the small hours. 'In the ancient scripts the *tav* resembled the Greek letter *chi*, which is the first letter in the Greek word for Christ – *christos* – and it looks, not like a cross, but an X.'

Sedley exhaled through his nose, almost a snorting scoff at the idea. 'And this is your Ash Wednesday theory?' he said imperiously.

Ellstrom nodded weakly, his own faith in the idea beginning to deflate rapidly.

'It can't be Madsen,' Sedley muttered sadly. 'So do we have any idea who this second killer might be?'

Taking her cue, Maggie fumbled through her DynoTech employee files and pulled out some paper-clipped sheets. 'Eric Klim,' she said.

Sedley frowned in her direction. 'Who's he?'

'Works with DynoTech,' she said. 'Out of the Petaluma office in San Francisco.'

He had his next question already lined up. 'And how do we know it's him?'

As the chopper banked over the San Fernando Valley, Maggie struggled to keep all the papers on her lap.

'He drives one of the company's brown Chevy Expresses, like Madsen,' she explained, shuffling through the files for more specific information.

'Which would explain the asbestos traces and the sightings of the van in Palo Alto and the tyre marks in Oregon,' Phillips chipped in, helping her out.

'And outside Leo Pretaran's apartment, according to police witness reports,' Sedley admitted, reluctantly adding some credence to their belief that there had been a second killer working all along.

'But how did you come up with this guy?' Sedley had to shout to be heard above the whine of the engines as they climbed through a low cloud bank.

'The cream traces found in Shayla Wilson's bedroom and on Peter Kelley's clothes,' Kronziac replied, 'were identified as a barrier cream for a very rare moth-dander-associated skin allergy. Klim's employee health-care plan showed regular stubs for reclaiming on a prescription cream – the same as was found in the crime-scene traces.'

Sedley began nodding in tacit acceptance.

'They were a double act,' Kronziac continued. 'Both worked for the same company. One in San Francisco, one in LA. So they both covered the length and breadth of the state – and beyond. Both took out three victims each.'

Maggie seemed at last to find what she was looking for among the files. 'Their partnership goes back a long way,' she told Sedley.

'How far?'

'Back to when they were kids,' she answered. 'Klim had a similar background to Madsen. Given up by an unmarried mother. Spent time in the same foster-care house in San Francisco with Madsen. Both did stretches in juvenile for gambling, substance abuse, violent attacks and . . . both ended up in the Grovehurst Institute for psychiatric care.'

'Jesus.' Sedley shook his head. 'Two of 'em could have been planning this for years.'

'Like evil twins,' Ellstrom remarked. Phillips, next to him, nodded in full agreement, for once.

'What the fuck is it all for?' Sedley wondered.

'That's Stranski's area,' Kronziac replied.

'Do we have a description of Klim?' he asked.

Maggie handed him a poor copy of Klim's company ID photo.

'Even looks like Madsen,' he remarked.

'The Petaluma office said he went on a job in Fresno about four or five days ago and they haven't heard from him since,' she said.

'We reckon he's in Kernville,' stated Kronziac, not with the confidence of certain knowledge but the bold assertion of instinct. 'St Dominic's. The only Roman Catholic church in the region.'

The Deputy Assistant Director's eyes drifted up from the photograph of their suspect, blotched with black spots of ink, as he considered the thin threads of evidence indicating Klim as the second operator.

'Better call ahead and clue in the local police,' he decided.

'Kern County Sheriff's Department are already looking out for him and the van,' Kronziac said, having pre-empted Sedley's decision. 'I took the liberty,' she added softly.

All Sedley could do was shake his head and smile at Kronziac as he sat back.

The black helicopter followed the snaking line of the I-5 over Tejon Pass, its thumping blades urging them towards the white-capped ranges of the southern Sierras, the small town of Kernville – and the centre of a corpse-strewn spiral.

POSITRON EMISSION TOMOGRAPHY (PET) LAB, HADCO NEUROSCIENCES BUILDING, CAMPUS PARK, U.S.C.

Those in the audience chamber arranged themselves on the three rows of tiered benches according to their allegiance, as they would do in a courtroom. Usually the setting for teaching or clinical demonstrations, the lab this morning hosted the State's pre-trial psychiatric evaluation, as agreed with the court and the defence, of alleged serial murderer Emery Madsen.

District Attorney Mary Scholte, dressed conservatively in a black trouser suit, her hair less voluminous than usual, sat on the front bench with her number two, Aaron Cole. Barely out of law school, with some apprenticeship in community practice, Cole displayed a dull-eyed smile that belied an incisive legal intellect which Scholte hoped was not about to be snatched up by one of the downtown private firms.

At the other end of the bench huddled the defence, a baggy-suited man with unruly steely hair who called himself Sol Koepicknicki and his aide, a long-limbed Ivy Leaguer, with an exquisitely tailored blue suit, who had been introduced as Shawn Blackney.

Along the back seats sat ADIC Foley along with some cronies from the DOJ, there mostly out of curiosity, not having had a serial-murder case for years. Fidgety without his morning coffee, Foley surveyed the white spaces of the lab itself, which was separated from them by a wide pane of glass – reinforced, he hoped. In the centre of the lab sat a large white cube with a hole cut in the middle, big enough to allow a human body to be inserted. There was a noticeable lack of wires or control consoles and the place had the sterile vacancy of a morgue.

'Looks like the inside of an empty fridge,' remarked one of the DOJ guys. Foley nodded non-committally as the door opened and Bob Vesoles entered, taking a seat at the end of the back bench near the door. Scholte turned around and nodded an appreciative hello to the pathologist. He would be one of her main expert witnesses and she had persuaded him to make the small journey from the coroner's office to see Madsen in the flesh. Vesoles had reluctantly agreed, none too enthusiastic about having to see the man whose handiwork had been laid before him in the form of three mutilated bodies.

The attention of those in the gallery was focused on the entrance to the laboratory as Madsen entered, cuffed, and flanked by prison officers, a couple of FBI agents and some state policemen. Madsen had changed out of his LA County Jail overalls, and was dressed casually in jeans and a plain white shirt, tight on his muscular frame.

Stranski followed them to the middle of the floor and motioned for the prisoner to be seated on an armless chair, directly facing the partitioned-off gallery. Stranski conversed with Madsen while the prison guards uncuffed him and he took his seat. Those in the gallery watched closely since they couldn't hear what was being said in the soundproofed room. Madsen nodded respectfully, politely listening to the psychologist, but occasionally glanced at his assembled accusers, seeking each of them out as if to estimate the mettle of their intentions.

Stranski smiled finally and left Madsen, who stayed seated, guarded by the two armed prison officers at the door. The prisoner, like a restless adolescent, looked around and up and down, his eyes sweeping the bland confines of the room.

From the side door Stranski entered the viewing gallery with his usual loping gait, his lanky figure moving across in front of the audience.

He gave a small wave in Foley's direction. 'Morning, Len,' he said quietly. The ADIC nodded back as the psychologist went on to exchange pleasantries with the legal representatives.

Stranski finally sat down at the long white desk at the front, facing the lab. The desk, unlike the lab itself, was lined with computer screens and the squat monitors of the psychological reads, all their green lines running dead, no vitals to report.

Pushing some of his papers around, Stranski began nervously and cleared his throat so harshly that he had to swallow hard before he could speak.

'I'm sure we've all been introduced but – er – just for the record my name is Dr Frederick Stranski and I am here to conduct a psychiatric evaluation of the subject on behalf of the State and Federal prosecution. I'm sure,' he continued with a crooked grin, 'that you are all acquainted with the subject's history so I don't believe it is necessary to give a clinical preamble on the case.'

Scholte and her junior nodded encouragingly as Stranski spoke, while the defence inspected him coldly. It had been a long time since he had had to give expert testimony under the hot glare of legal scrutiny, and it was showing.

'Anyway, I intend to conduct the structured interview on the subject to establish a foundation for a clinical diagnosis of Dissociative Identity Disorder. We will further explore the case-specific phenomenology under narco-synthetic regression, with attendant psychometric evaluation with EEG and PET study.'

'Are you qualified to reference PET studies psychoanalytically, Dr Stranski?' Koepicknicki asked, showing his courtroom teeth.

'We conduct PET evaluations as well as other neuro-imaging techniques at the Civil Aeromedical Institute to show cerebral blood-flow in pilot-reaction assessment when subjects are undergoing multi-tasking and cockpit environment interaction,' Stranski replied. 'As part of the FAA's Human Factors Study Group it is my job to assess the results and correlate them analytically.'

'We're not deciding whether our client can fly a plane, Dr Stranski,' Blackney pointed out.

'Stop sniping at our man,' Cole intervened, shooting a wary look at the defence. 'This is our show. You're well aware of Dr Stranski's background in this research and criminal profiling. You'll have ample opportunity to cross-examine his credentials at the trial.'

In a deep area of Stranski's own mind he was sticking pins in Kronziac's effigy for getting him into this situation, his jabs softened only by the knowledge that she should, at about this time, be undergoing her own inquisition over in the Federal building.

'Just protecting our client's physical and mental welfare,' Blackney asserted, palms raised.

'Then let's get on with it,' Scholte chipped in and gestured at Madsen, sitting impassively in the bare white lab, unable to hear the wrangling in the gallery. 'Let's not keep your client waiting any further. Go on, Dr Stranski,' she urged him. 'Please continue.'

Picking up some stapled sheets of paper, Stranski began to explain the first step of the process.

'The clinical interview conforms to the criteria as outlined in the latest version of the *Diagnostic and Statistical Manual of Mental Disorders* or DSM. The subject, I believe,' he glanced in the direction of the DA, 'has signed the consent form.'

Scholte nodded and Stranski searched the desk for the switch to activate the two-way microphone that would allow him to instruct Madsen in the lab. Before flicking the switch he turned to the legal teams again.

'In this situation it is better that I refer to him by his first name as this will relax the subject and promote more natural responses.'

Even the psychologist's proposed informality had a clinical reason behind it.

'The questions are structured on multiple-choice responses, so the likelihood of leading the subject is therefore further reduced,' he explained.

He pressed the microphone button. 'Emery, can you hear me?'

Madsen looked up at the ceiling. The psychologist's voice came from a small speaker embedded in the tiles like an air vent.

'Yes, sir! Loud and clear,' he shouted back, his voice loud and raspy over the speakers in the gallery booth.

'Okay, Emery.' Stranski smiled. 'You can speak at normal volume.'

'Sorry, Doc,' Madsen replied, still a little too loudly.

'As I mentioned to you earlier, I'm going to ask you some questions,' Stranski explained. 'Some questions only require a simple positive or negative answer, others are multiple choice. They are very straightforward, with no need for you to explain your responses. Okay?'

Madsen nodded. 'No problem.'

'Would you like a glass of water before we begin?'

'No, thank you. I'm fine.' Madsen grinned, the pale flesh of his face rough with a day's growth of ruddy beard.

Stranski poised his pen over the questionnaire sheet to mark the reply boxes.

'Question One. Do you ever experience headaches – yes or no?'

KERNVILLE, CA

'Whiskey Flat Week,' Sergeant Bildshaw told them as he drove them in the Kern County police car from the landing strip through the centre of town. 'Our midwinter festival celebrating the old Gold Rush days.'

A high-desert lake-resort community, Kernville sat on the northern shores of Lake Isabella, the largest freshwater lake in Southern California. A gateway to the Sequoia National Forest, the town enjoyed a diversity of landscapes, from desert plain to alpine woodland, with fishing and rafting facilities on the river Kern, which flowed through the centre of town, and skiing in Shirley Meadows to the west.

'This is probably our busiest time of year,' Bildshaw remarked. He was a heavy-set man with a thick moustache and a wheezy voice. He drove the patrol car slowly through the thronged streets; Maggie, Phillips and two other agents followed in another car behind. 'Get quite a lot of folks up from LA,' he said, thinking it might somehow please them. 'And down from Frisco – from all over, really.'

As Kronziac glanced out the window she found it hard to see what the town was actually like since the main street's buildings were hidden by a tented boardwalk, with stalls and souvenir shops dispensing Old West bric-a-brac and arts and crafts. Men dressed as Old Forty-niners in chaps and trappers in squirrel-tail hats posed with raised musketry for the visitors. A parade of women and little girls in pinafores and bonnets tramped along behind covered wagons, cartoon floats and doleful mules. There were carnival rides and mock gunfights in the side streets, the occasional gunshot piercing the cacophony of background sound. Marquees with signs like 'Golden Gulch' hosted country-and-western hoedowns jumping with energetic reels or line dancers moving in precise patterns over the wooden floors.

Kronziac found it faintly disturbing, all this activity so early in the day, not even eleven o'clock yet. The fact that they were

414

looking for just one man amid the crowd she found even more unsettling. But her attention was directed forward as the sergeant announced the appearance of St Dominic's, about half a mile on the main road running north.

The church's wedgelike Gothic form loomed over the town and stood out against the gently undulating ranges of the mountains beyond. Its flinty dark towers pierced the hazy blue sky, rearing up from its Roman basilica and cruciform transept. The sharp pyramidal roofs and pointed pinnacles, adorned with tendril-like stone decorations, were supported by a black trellis of flying buttresses, topped with spires. The whole edifice suggested a fearful rectitude to those approaching, its gargoyles soundlessly reminding them of the painful possibilities of the afterlife and God's retribution. Any visitor who came to the town was struck by the huge church's appearance and Bildshaw catered for this with a practised recitation of its history.

Built in the late nineteenth century, he explained, by prospectors and ranchers who had profited hugely in the Gold Rush, the church was based loosely on the Gothic cathedral of Amiens in France. Through their patronage, the gold and cattle barons hoped to consolidate their earthly prosperity in the afterlife. They stoked the ambitions of the Irish Catholic missionary priests who had hoped Kernville would extend their congregation of worshippers among the influx of new families attracted by the secular riches the region could provide.

But the church was stranded when the ebbing tide of the Gold Rush left the town as nothing more than a rural settlement whose future would depend more on the patronage of tourists than on glistening nuggets in pans of river silt. And so, alien even amidst its immediate surroundings, and egregious in a state whose native religious architecture, though Catholic, was simple, earthy Spanish-missionary, St Dominic's could now hardly populate ten per cent of the pews in its vaulted nave with the ever-dwindling Catholic congregations of Kernville and the neighbouring communities of Lake Isabella and Wofford Heights.

The avenue leading up to the entrance was lined with coaches and cars, young peach-faced schoolboys emerging from the vehicles in robes of sackcloth, smearing themselves with burnt cork as if dress-rehearsing for a pageant.

'Catholic Congress of Jesuits,' Bildshaw said, inching the patrol car between the buses. 'Various YMCAs and the Union of Catholic Communities are all putting on a penitential procession for Ash Wednesday. Probably our busiest day in ten years,' he added, shaking his head, but with the benign indifference of the truly unconcerned. These groups hardly constituted a threat to the civil peace.

Both police cars had to park a considerable distance from the entrance to the church and their occupants got out, joining the sackclothed crowds on the avenue.

As Sedley talked business with Sergeant Bildshaw, Kronziac and Ellstrom looked at the front edifice looming over them as they neared. On its dressed sandstone stood canopied statues, the Gallery of Kings, looking imperiously down, carved invocations in Latin chiselled along the granite trims above them.

From the side of the building a County Sheriff's policeman ran to Bildshaw.

'Sorry, Sarge,' he panted, looking at the FBI agents. 'We found the van matching the bulletin in the back parking lot.'

'A brown Chevrolet Express?' Phillips asked.

The policeman nodded.

'Any sign of a driver?' Sedley asked anxiously, alarmed by the prospect that Klim was moving stealthily among the crowds.

'No sign,' the policeman told them. 'And the van's locked.'

'Can you place your men at all the exits?' Sedley asked the sergeant.

'I'll try,' he replied doubtfully. 'We're pretty stretched today. Who the heck are we looking for, anyway?'

Sedley tried to disguise his annoyance at not being able to give them a good description by delegating the task to his subordinates.

'Phillips, you, Morris and Di Canio talk to Sergeant Bildshaw's men and try and give them an idea who we're after. We'll go and check out inside. We need to talk to someone who knows the church layout.'

As they climbed the steps of the church, Kronziac and Ellstrom lagged behind as they entered under the giant rose window, adorned with a concentric whirl of rounded triangular arches and stained glass.

Around them the schoolboys, dressed in their hooded robes made out of sacks, were being hushed by their leaders as they entered the church.

'Spooky,' Ellstrom remarked in a reverent whisper as he looked at the dark corners of the edifice and the moulded gargoyles on the granite quoins, a vomit of green slime on the walls beneath their grotesque mouths.

Kronziac kept her head down, suddenly aware of her own position as a lapsed Jewess as the arched portals darkened over them.

POSITRON EMISSION TOMOGRAPHY (PET) LAB, HADCO
NEUROSCIENCES BUILDING, CAMPUS PARK, U.S.C.

Stranski thanked Madsen over the microphone.

'Can you let in the neurology team now, please?' he asked the prison guards. They opened the door of the lab, admitting a doctor and a staff nurse who were wheeling an instrument cart.

The psychologist turned the microphone off and began scoring the interview results.

'Any idea?' Koepicknicki asked, unable to wait for Stranski to complete his marking.

'I'm not sure how reliable the results are, anyway,' remarked Scholte, aiming her remark at the defence. 'He probably didn't want to incriminate himself.'

The defence lawyers were about to rebut this when Stranski swivelled around in his chair.

'Actually, I think he was quite truthful,' he said. 'Perhaps the opposing impulses of avoiding self-incrimination and a presumed willingness to go along with his defence plea of insanity might have cancelled each other out. In my judgement, he *appeared* truthful and the questions were not designed to catch him out.'

The implied admonishment seemed to quell the petty exchanges between the two sets of lawyers and they sat silently, waiting for Stranski's verdict on the first part of Madsen's psych evaluation.

'The subject scored positively on somatization – headaches, stomach complaints, etc., which marks towards DID and schizophrenia. He also scores positive for substance abuse, Schneiderian First Rank symptoms, trances and sleepwalking. Positive scoring also for childhood abuse, Borderline Personality and dissociative amnesia. He scored fully positive on the Dissociative Identity Disorder questions.'

'So what are you saying?' Cole asked impatiently.

'Well, there is a degree of overlapping with features that characterize schizophrenia but there are positive indicators of DID.'

'He has the disorder?' Blackney insisted, a pleased smile on his face.

Stranski found it hard not to smile himself. 'All I can say is that this subject displays an elective responsiveness that suggests further clinical investigation for DID.'

The prosecutors looked decidedly glum. Foley and the DOJ boys shifted restlessly in the back benches, their butts growing numb on the wood.

'Is it possible that one of my client's dissociated identities was in control during the crimes?' Koepicknicki asked, fishing for more encouraging news. 'In your opinion,' he added sweetly.

'That's not for me to say.' Stranski fended off the question with a gesture of his hand, but he knew it was the central question of the whole case. Was Madsen aware of what he was doing when he stalked his victims, toyed with them and executed them? Did the responsibility for their deaths rest squarely with him, his conscious, sentient self? Though juries were becoming less and less tolerant of insanity pleas, desperate defence teams still saw them as viable, and sometimes the only, options for their clients. But it was still possible, given a sympathetic jury, that a successful dimunition-of-mental-faculty argument could be rewarded with a sentence of psychiatric care, instead of a cell on Death Row in which to await lethal injection and a higher court of judgement.

'As you can see,' Stranski gestured out the window, 'he's being prepped for the next phase.'

Madsen was having tiny pick-ups attached to his chest and skull and clamp sensors put on his fingers by the nurse. The doctor held his elbow, piercing an arm vein with a needle to attach a tap for the administration of tracers.

'We'll be monitoring not only his physiological status but his brainwave pattern and regional cerebral blood flow,' Stranski explained.

The door of the viewing gallery opened and a young man in a lab coat stepped cautiously in, hunching down almost as though he did not want to be noticed.

'Excuse me, Dr Stranski,' he said. 'You need me now?'

The psychologist seemed to be delighted and welcomed the young man in.

'This is John.' Stranski introduced him to the room. 'He's a resident technician here at the lab and I hope—' he smiled '—that he is able to work all these . . . gizmos.' He glanced over the monitors and keyboards on the desk.

The technician took the seat next to Stranski and powered up the computers.

'I know you all have notes on the matter,' Stranski continued. 'But I will briefly explain the theory behind the PET machine.'

'Please do,' Scholte urged him, articulating a difficulty all the lawyers were having in digesting the technical information provided by the lab on Positron Emission Tomography, the tracer kinetic assay and its mathematical computer modelling.

'PET,' began Stranski, 'is a non-invasive imaging technology for measuring *in vivo* the metabolic activity of cells – in this case, brain metabolism. Unlike x-ray, CT scanning or MRI, which show anatomical structure, PET produces images of the cells' actual biochemical action. It is a very potent tool for diagnosing disorders such as Alzheimer's and schizophrenia as well as the pathology of tissue abnormalities such as tumours. We will inject a radio-labelled biologically active compound called a tracer.' He paused to read his own notes. 'In this case, 18F-labelled fluorethylspiperone, or FESP, a D2 dopaminergic receptor ligand. The formulary is in your notes,' he assured them. 'The tracer tags itself to the normal chemicals of the body. Over time, the radioactive tracer decays, emitting positrons that are detected in the gamma rays of the scanner. The pulses are interpreted through the computer modeller to produce an image of the bloodflow, along with the metabolic consumption of oxygen and glucose, membrane transport and ligand receptor activity in the brain.'

'I thought you were going to help us understand.' Cole shook his head lightly, raising smiles among all the lawyers.

'I hope you're not going to turn our client into the Incredible Hulk,' Blackney remarked stiffly, an awkward attempt at levity.

'There is absolutely no risk of adverse radioactive exposure inherent in the process. Simply put, we will be able to monitor the activity of the subject's brain chemistry.'

Madsen, whose shirt had been replaced with a hospital gown, was helped onto the scanner bed by the nurse.

'Once Mr Madsen is settled I will be testing his working memory, not only to calibrate the detector field of the scanner and software but to get a baseline on his brain's functioning.'

The technician was busy at the keyboard and the main computer monitor blinked to life with a blank screen and a numbered colour bar along the left margin.

'A spectral analysis will be used to show the level of activity.' Stranski pointed at the screen. 'White and red indicate most activity, blue and black the least.'

In the laboratory itself, the doctor and nurse left Madsen, retreating with the armed guards to a control booth at the back of the lab. Madsen's body moved on the gantry until his head and shoulders were inside the aperture of the PET scanner.

Stranski pressed the microphone button. 'Everything all right with you, Mr Madsen?''

'I'm fine,' he replied loudly, his voice booming over the small microphone in the scanner.

'Can we turn on the visual?' Stranski asked the technician.

'Sure,' he replied and with a flick of a switch a small monitor above the computer screens came on. Madsen's face appeared, filling the frame, his features slightly distorted with the wide-angle close-up. His closely shaved head was festooned with electroencephalograph pick-up patches and their wires.

The technician looked over all the computer screens and monitors. 'EEG, cardiograph and body temperature all reading normal,' he stated.

The main screen in front of Stranski flickered as the PET scanner began to hum with activity in the laboratory. 'This will be our main point of interest,' he said, pointing at the screen.

They could all see Madsen on the video monitor, his eyes rolling, blinking with slight apprehension as the cyclotron about him purred into life, accelerating charged particles in a spiral path between two sets of magnets, all hidden in its smooth white housing. The outline of Madsen's cerebral structure began to slowly fade up on the screen, an area of fuzzy blue about the hemispheres, some patches of red and yellow beginning to show on the reticulated lobes of the brain.

The technician began tweaking the software and detector sensitivity, balancing the 'noise' on the image, sharpening the pixel resolution.

'The subject's head is aligned along the petrous ridges,' Stranski explained, pointing at a black area between the cerebellum and inferior temporal lobe. 'Once in this position the camera on the scanner is aligned with the entire brain construct.'

The image began to flare in various places, with colour casts from red to blue showing scattered patches of activity across the brain, from the thalamus to the basal ganglia and the auditory and visual cortices.

'The tracer is now beginning to be metabolized in the plasma component of the brain tissue, and starting to report back, carried with the blood into the most active areas of the brain.'

'Can abnormal brain activity point to DID in the subject?' Scholte asked.

'Not positively, of course.' Stranski was quick to point this out. 'The neural workings are too complex. A psychiatric disorder is not a brain tumour, lighting up like a bulb on the scan. Instead, the PET study should contribute to an overall evaluation of the subject's psychopathology, from which a diagnosis of DID could be inferred.'

Foley, at the back of the gallery, was beginning to wonder what the purpose of the psych evaluation really was. Just put the son of a bitch on the stand and take him apart with the evidence.

'To calibrate the image acquisition and to assess the memory processing of the subject I will perform a verbal-pictorial working-memory test,' Stranski informed them. The legal teams scribbled notes, trying to keep up. Pressing the 'on' button of his microphone, the psychologist addressed Madsen, now more relaxed in the scanner tunnel.

'You still comfortable, Mr Madsen?'

'Yes,' Madsen replied, smiling into the video camera.

'Okay,' Stranski began. 'I want you to think of the numbers

one to eight but place them in a random order and assign each a picture. That would be, for example, two dogs for the number 2, three cats for the number 3 and so on.

'Any order?' the subject asked, his auditory and motor cortices pulsing with activity.

'Yes,' the psychologist confirmed. 'Any order and any picture you can think of.'

As Madsen went about his task many areas of his brain flared in rainbow hues as the cerebral arteries channelled blood to fuel the thoughts. With the microphone off, Stranski asked the technician to pull back the sensitivity of the scanner and to record the image, placing it on an electronic clipboard for comparison.

'Thank you,' said Stranski after a couple of minutes, as he saw the activity subside, signalling the subject had completed the task.

'You want me to call out the numbers, Doc?'

'No, that's fine,' Stranski said, disappointing Madsen a little. 'Now, I'm going to give you a sequence of numbers from one to eight and will then ask you a simple question on them. All right?'

Madsen nodded at camera.

Stranski began calling out the numbers into the microphone. '7, 5, 2, 1, 8, 6 and 4. Which number have I left out?'

Mental activity spread again across the globe of Madsen's brain image on the computer screen.

'Er – 3, I think,' he replied, his small eyes narrowed in concentration.

'That's correct,' Stranski told him. They could see Madsen grinning on camera.

Turning around, the psychologist explained the simple experiment as the technician posted the second scan to the other computer monitor.

'In the first exercise the subject was instructed to generate the numbers visually,' Stranski explained and pointed at the first scan, patches of colour dotted in the middle and front part of the brain image. 'As you can see, we have bilateral activity in the mid-dorsolateral frontal cortex, always present in memory processing, but here in the general region of the PZ and Broadman's area 7 – in the middle of the brain,' he translated, 'an area known as the precuneus, we also have activity.'

A bristled yellow blob hovered over the medial part of the image. 'Documented PET studies associate the precuneus activity with visual imaging in episodic recall.'

Stranski moved his finger to the second scan. 'In the second scan we see just activation in the frontal cortex. The absence of work in the precuneus supports the non-visual mechanism of the second memory task, which, in simple terms, was verbal only.'

Koepicknicki was shaking his head. 'Sorry, Doctor, but—' He searched his own notes with a look of suspicion. 'I'm not sure what the distinction is or what inference is being drawn with the exercise.'

Stranski gathered his thoughts for a moment to explain. 'Basically, the evidence of activity in the precuneus shows that the memory is visually based, with the same mechanism as an experience – what is being remembered was actually *experienced* through the sense of sight. The lack of precuneus activity would suggest a verbally based memory, an externally instructed memory. The subtle distinction will form the basis for our next step.'

Everyone shifted wearily, their own brains wrestling with the difficult concepts Stranski was trying to demonstrate. He always found it harder to convey psychological findings to anyone other than his peers in the shrink industry. It took a considerable amount of interpretation to put complex psychological ideas in terms that they could understand.

'And what is your next step?' Blackney asked sceptically.

Stranski leaned closer to his assistant and mumbled in his ear. The young man nodded and set about retrieving a video file from a mini-DVD that the psychologist had passed to him before the session.

'I feel I should warn you,' Stranski mentioned gravely, 'that the footage we are about to see, taken from the suspect's computer by FBI specialists, contains graphic pictures of the murder of Cherie Blaynes.'

He directed his warning specifically to those on the back bench, who had no legal necessity to be there to see the pictures. But no one moved, no one took the option of leaving, steeling themselves instead out of morbid anticipation.

ST DOMINIC'S CHURCH, KERNVILLE, CA

As with all Gothic churches, the eye of the entrant was drawn instinctively along the narrow axis of the nave to focus on the sanctuary and the altar. As if through a natural geometric perspective that human vision cannot resist, the attention of the worshipper was immediately focused on the distant repository of the Holy Cross and the canopied niche of the tabernacle.

Having been led up the spiral stone stairwell from the narthex, Kronziac, Sedley and Ellstrom followed the police sergeant on to the organ loft and the gallery of the church where he left them again to find a priest. Ellstrom began to detach his gaze from the carved pinnacles of the altar screen to roam the heights of the vaulted ceiling, towering seventy or eighty feet above them, where the saints stood, frozen in marble statuary, like sentries. Ribbed in double hammerbeam timber, the ceiling reminded him of the Oregon Caves. He shuddered for a moment, under the dizzying altitude of sainthood and the vision of Peter Kelley's burnt body.

Kronziac turned away from the altar to look at the rose window, now behind them, illuminated from without by the morning sun, its coloured stained-glass lens projecting a coloured mosaic on her face. Underneath, fringing it like a fan, was the three-manual, eighty-five rank organ, the pipes gilded with gold leaf of Paduan design.

Sedley's attention was focused on the floor of the nave, where rows of schoolboys and novices were being herded single file into the pews, their hooded uniforms of brown sackcloth assembling in two dark rectangles beneath the pointed arches. In the minor arcades sat the congregation, families and older parishioners or pilgrims, a mumbling chatter of prayer and reverent conversation rising from the aisles, the occasional yelp or sigh from a bored child, restless in the arms of its mother. On the outer aisles beneath the triple archways some of the *penitenti* knelt among the laity, waiting for their turn in the confession boxes. The transepts were lined with chairs for the senior clerics and in the chancel the sacristants were preparing for the mass and administration of the ashes. In the centre aisle at periodic intervals stood tables heaped with palm fronds, their spiced scents wafting through the resident odours of brass polish and candle smoke.

'Where is he?' Sedley whispered to himself as he surveyed the crowded seats below, their occupants still restless in the hushed patter and shuffle like an audience before an opera.

Morris and Phillips joined them in the organ loft and, after their moment of taking in the immense dimensions of the church, they confirmed that the police officers were now placed outside all the exits of the church and near the cloister, the old school and the residential clerical buildings that were attached to it.

'We'd better start a search pattern,' Sedley commented, looking out on the church, daunted by its vast recesses.

'What time is it?' Kronziac wondered.

'Nearly twelve,' Phillips said. 'The mass will be starting soon,' he added, noticing the choir assembling below the triforium in the eastern transept.

Bildshaw came up the stairs, followed by a priest in his black cassock.

'This is Father Fabien.' The sergeant introduced him. The agents were unsure if it was protocol to shake hands with the young priest. Kronziac figured him to be not much more than twenty-four. But his expansive smile put them immediately at ease as he displayed a wide expanse of white teeth with a large gap in the middle of the upper row. His features were so dark that it was hard to make out the other details of his face in the dim light. He spoke good English but in the pursed-lipped accent of a Central African. Nowadays the most fertile grounds for vocational recruitment were the old missionary countries of Africa and South America. Kronziac wondered how the hierarchy of Rome really felt about the fact that the continuation of the faith in the first world now depended on priests from the countries that had been the last to be converted.

'Welcome to St Dominic's.' Fr Fabien smiled graciously.

'Thank you, Father,' Maggie replied quickly and with a respectful deference not quite as evident in the responses of the others.

'These people are agents from the FBI's Los Angeles office,' Bildshaw explained, causing the priest's smile to fade somewhat.

'Is there something wrong?' he asked, looking at them closely, hoping to single out the spokesman.

'We're not quite sure,' Sedley said awkwardly. 'We're looking for a man in connection with some . . . serious crimes.' Whether it was the solemnity of the location or whether he didn't wish to introduce a note of hysteria Sedley refrained from mentioning that the man they sought was responsible for killing three people.

The expression in the priest's eyes narrowed further. 'You think he seeks sanctuary in the church?'

The agents looked at each other in surprise.

'That only happens in the movies, right?' Kronziac asked lightheartedly but hoped nonetheless that there wasn't an official policy that Catholic churches could provide a haven for criminals.

'It does only happen in the movies.' Fr Fabien agreed readily. 'I have never heard of it in real life. I suppose it would depend on the nature of the crimes. What has this man done?'

'Murdered three people,' Phillips said curtly, hoping to shock the priest into immediate cooperation.

The priest regarded him uncertainly as Sedley tried to explain more calmly. 'He is a violent man,' he said, 'with a psychiatric history and, yes, we believe he was involved in the deaths of three people.'

'You're sure he is here?' Fr Fabien asked, startled.

'No, we're not sure,' Sedley replied truthfully. 'But we have good reason to believe he might be.'

The young priest jerked his thumb in the direction of the altar. 'The monsignor is preparing for mass now. Should I go and tell him to cancel it and clear the building?'

Sedley smiled a little to signal his appreciation. 'That may not be the best course of action. This man is probably armed and any change in proceedings might – well, we don't know what he's going to do.'

'We've posted officers outside the doors,' Bildshaw said hoping to reassure the priest.

'I'll go and talk to the monsignor, of course,' said Sedley. 'But, for now, everything should go ahead as normal. Our agents will be keeping a close eye on the congregation.'

'Do you know what he looks like?' the priest asked.

'We have an idea,' replied Sedley. 'A young guy, not much older than them,' he said, indicating the few hundred school-boys sitting in the pews, their heads covered by their sackcloth hoods.

'We are having a special penitential procession today,' Fr Fabien explained, almost apologetic for the event's timing.

'We need to know what the order of proceedings are,' Kronziac said to him. They moved nearer the balcony of the gallery to look down on the nave and altar.

'Well, as you know—' the priest looked at them '—today is the Day of Ashes, the beginning of Lent and forty days to Good Friday. We are preparing ourselves for the Wedding Feast of the Lamb. The procession of the *penitenti* is held to re-enact the sacramental absolution of the Ninevites and also to commemorate the blessing of the sackcloth of the *penitenti* by the first bishops of Rome at St Sabine's on the Aventine Hills.'

'Will they have their foreheads crossed with ashes?' Ellstrom asked.

'Yes,' the priest replied. 'They will be marked by the ash in the form of the cross to symbolize their devotion to God and their acceptance of their own mortality in being turned out of the holy places. The ash is a biblical symbol of sorrow and penance.'

'Are they just – I dunno—' Kronziac smiled awkwardly '—ordinary ashes from a fire?'

'We burn the old palm fronds from the previous year's Palm Sunday when they symbolized Christ's entrance into Jerusalem and the unwitting fanfare for his crucifixion. The burnt palms remind us of his sacrifice.'

'Are the ashes kept on the altar?' she asked, surprising the others with her particular interest in the ashes.

'They are in the clerestory now for the oil to be added, to make a good smudge, but will be brought down shortly before the mass begins,' he told her. 'Which should be very soon now,' he added.

POSITRON EMISSION TOMOGRAPHY (PET) LAB, HADCO NEUROSCIENCES BUILDING, CAMPUS PARK, U.S.C.

'Is it ready?' Stranski asked his assistant.

'Yes, Doctor. On the second computer monitor,' John replied, gesturing at the smaller computer screen next to Madsen's face, waiting patiently under the scanner. The muscles on his jaw seemed to be quivering as he hummed a tune to himself and his motor cortex was rippling lightly with glucose and oxygen consumption.

'As I observed the subject's responses to questioning by the investigating detective about the events of the night Cherie Blaynes was abducted I was struck by both the content of the subject's own memories of that evening and the manner of his recall.'

The others in the room just nodded in silence and let him get on with it.

Stranski turned the microphone on again. 'Emery, I'd like to talk to you about the night of September second last—'

Before he could go on Madsen began to complain. 'I already told the detectives everything I knew or could remember,' he protested, staring directly at them through the small screen, his body exhibiting slight signs of stress.

'I know.' The psychologist tried to placate him. 'It won't take very long.'

'Okay, Doctor.' Madsen's heart rate and EEG plots calmed again.

'Did you go any place that night?' Stranski asked. 'Out for a drive or to visit friends?' He knew the answer would be negative but had to get the subject to begin relaxing and talking.

'No,' sighed Madsen. A slight decrease in resistivity on the galvanic skin monitors indicated an increase in sweat-gland secretion. 'I was at home,' he said. 'Watching TV or something, I guess.'

'It was a Sunday evening.' Stranski tried to press him. 'Sunday, the second of September.'

431

'I know,' Madsen replied, his heart rate jumping, his respiration growing more shallow.

'It is important that you try to remember.' The psychologist persisted, gently but firmly. 'What were you doing on Sunday, the evening of second September last?'

They all watched as Madsen's face tightened, his eyes fixing on a point in the centre of the camera. Electrical and metabolic activity sparked throughout the frontal lobes on the PET scan, burning in the medial and inferior frontal gyri.

'I was at home,' he said stiffly, his vitals receding to a quiet base-line functioning, cerebral activity also quietening. 'I had to do some work at home.'

'What did you have to do?' Stranski probed, quickly checking all the monitors, appraising the subject's eerily calm state.

'Fix one of our filtration pumps, for cleaning asbestos fibres from the air. Was up most of the night with it.'

Stranski motioned for his assistant to run the video file from Madsen's webcam – recorded the night he killed his first victim.

Those on the benches leaned closer, straining to see the dark image that appeared on the monitor between those showing Madsen's face and the electronic brain-map of his mind. They could just about see the figure of a young girl, bound to a chair, her head moving this way and that, the band of tape across her mouth, her face glistening with tears. Madsen, oblivious to what they were watching in the gallery room, waited impassively for the next question, all his body signs calm.

'What was wrong with it? The pump?' Stranski enquired.

'Motor was acting up,' Madsen replied coolly. 'I didn't know if it was an electrical fault or what. I tried but it just wouldn't work. I was checking through the spec cards but . . .'

On the video footage they could see Madsen's shoulders, darkly silhouetted under the cone of light over the small table, the metal surfaces of the shelves and tool chest framing the scene. If those in the benches had been hooked up to the monitors the screens would have flickered and jumped, registering racing heartbeats and active sweat glands.

Vesoles, out of professional curiosity, leaned forward to get a better look as Madsen dealt Cherie the playing cards on the pathetic little table in the dark confines of his van.

'What did you do to try and fix it?' Stranski asked.

'I took out the wire cutters to release the electrical wires from the clamp.'

On the video Madsen stood up from the table and, leaning over the tool chest, pulled out a drawer and played his fingers over the contents like a surgeon selecting the proper instrument. They watched closely as he moved to the chair and clipped the electrical flex that bound Cherie's right hand to the arm of the big wooden chair. As she spread her fingers, grateful for the freedom of movement, however small, Madsen returned to the game of blackjack, talking to his victim who could only respond with tearful shudders and muted screams of anguish.

'*Come on, Alison . . . Hit, Stand or Double-down—*' They heard him shout, his voice choked and reedy on the small speakers of the computer.

Scholte began scribbling in her notes.

'I tried several times to get it to work,' the live Madsen continued, his brainwaves and neural patterns still calm.

Stranski directed his audience's attention to the PET scan. The frontal cortex flared in red patches, with haloes of hazed yellow and green indicating some memory activation and stirrings in the motor regions along the central fissure. But the precuneus remained silent, barely shimmering with the cold blue of passivity.

'I tried many times.' Madsen repeated himself with only slight variations. 'To get it to work. It was really pissing me off.'

Stranski searched for but couldn't find any real signs of activation among the structures of the limbic or emotional centres of Madsen's mind.

In the video Madsen stood up from the table once again and reached out, grabbing Cherie's right hand, her arm struggling with all her strength, trying desperately to wrest it from his grasp.

'I decided to cut one of the wires,' he continued, his mouth calmly reciting the events, a steady tide of brainwaves running on the EEG read. 'Thought there might be an electrical short,' he said.

Foley and the Department of Justice men watched, grimacing tightly as they saw Madsen, the girl's squirming hand in his strong grip, take the wire cutters with his free hand and bring them close to her index finger.

'So I clipped the auxiliary cut-out switch wire,' he said, expressionless and without emotion.

On the video Cherie's body bucked in a spasm of pain as her captor snipped her finger off beneath the dim cone of light. Her hand fell limply to the table, dribbling blood, and her head seemed to slump forward as he resumed the game.

'What happened then?' Stranski asked, as the people in the gallery were still trying to comprehend what they were seeing.

'Still wouldn't cooperate,' Madson replied as his earlier self on the video dealt the cards, their edges dipping in the liquid on the blood-soaked tablecloth. 'Still wouldn't work,' he said again, unconcerned in the small tunnel of the PET scanner.

Cherie was wobbling back into consciousness, her blonde hair streaking over her face as she looked up, her eyes hooded, to meet the gaze of her tormentor who waited for her with the cards. They seemed to stare at each other for a moment. She began shaking, tears dripping down her features, mingling with the blood. He looked down for a moment. Then his black shoulders seemed to dance with rage.

'I lost the rag a bit with it,' Madsen said, without any hint of frustration or embarrassment. 'Gave it a punch,' he added.

They all watched in horror as the video showed Madsen shoot up from his chair, the black length of his arm swinging across Cherie's face, her head jerking sideways in a fan of blood, then slumping forward once more.

'Forgot I had the cutters still in my hand,' Madsen went on in a flat, even tone. 'Split the goddamned oil bottle.'

The words registered no excitation in the limbic region and galvanic measurement detected only the slightest sweat secretions, more likely because of the heat under the cyclotron.

'The stopper fell out,' he said.

'What is that?' Stranski asked, keeping the subject talking.

'A rubber float-ball in the oil reservoir,' Madsen explained in an uninterested manner. 'If the oil pressure in the pump goes down it covers the cock, keeps it from flooding the motor.'

On the computer screen Madsen was standing over Cherie's form, obscuring her from view. But they could see him lean down over her and flick her blonde hair to the side, much like a lover would do as they fondly watched their partner asleep. He angled his head to the side for a moment and they could glimpse the gaping wound on her face, a wet mat of blood soaking on her hair and the white glistening ball dangling between her cheek and nose.

'Jeezus!' Blackney recoiled. 'Is that her eye?' he gasped.

Madsen moved swiftly away from Cherie's motionless body and with diligent industry selected a long-necked scissors from the tool chest. He stood over her again, balancing himself like a dentist about to perform a delicate extraction.

'I cut it from its tether,' Madsen said suddenly, activity flashing through the frontal lobes and in the central areas.

'Some limbic responses,' Stranski muttered to himself. 'Why did you cut it?' he asked swiftly over the microphone, as the Madsen in the video placed his feet apart, providing space for something on the floor beneath him.

'Slight agitation in EEG and heart rate,' the technician observed quietly as the subject's vitals displayed a small measure of excitation.

Stranski also observed more complex enterprise in the frontal cortex and flashbulb flickers of yellow in the precuneus.

'Why did you cut the string?' he asked Madsen again.

The subject seemed to consider his response for a moment.

'I wanted to see what sound it would make,' he replied.

Scholte and her number two exchanged inquisitive glances.

'You just wanted to see what sound it would make?' Stranski repeated, keeping Madsen on the point, observing more global activity in his cortices. His facial features had also loosened, with a bit more animation in his head and eye movement.

'To see if it would bounce,' he continued. 'You know, with a flat *thub* like a squash ball or a meaty splat!'

Stranski saw a good deal of working now in the sensual areas

435

of Madsen's brain. On the video they could only see his black shape in the dim light as he worked on Cherie. Then his head dropped, his gaze following something as it fell to the floor of the van. Then his foot moved to stamp on it.

'It crunched like . . . a pickled onion,' Madsen said and his face blanked again, resuming an expressionless gaze in the monitor.

All cerebral metabolism subsided again to the calm flickers of neutral thought patterns.

The psychologist realized that Madsen had slipped into the autonomic demeanour he had displayed prior to the 'ball' interlude. He attempted to bring him out again.

'What did you do with . . . *her*?' he asked, prompting an objection from the defence that he ignored. The mention of the word 'her', he hoped, would ignite the hidden memories of the attack on Cherie. But there were no signs of emotional response across Madsen's brain patterns.

On the video, Madsen moved away once again from Cherie, allowing them a view of her face, slicked with blood, the trailing sinew of her optic nerve sticking to her cheek.

'It was no good any more.' Madsen stirred. 'I got my drill to mark the nameplate. We always do that in the company. Mark it to show it's no good to us any more.'

Stranski realized Madsen was now possibly referring to the experience of drilling the mark in Cherie's forehead. But the video footage blanked out as Madsen turned the webcam off.

'What mark did you put on it?' the psychologist asked. But Madsen's face was just as blank as the computer screen next to it.

'I can't remember,' he intoned flatly.

'Where did you dispose of the machine?' Stranski persisted, trying to prise out any further recollection from the subject.

'I can't remember,' Madsen repeated vacantly.

Knowing they wouldn't get any further, Stranski decided not to push the matter. 'Thank you,' he said evenly into the microphone. 'Would you like a glass of water?'

Madsen accepted and Stranski instructed the nurse to get the water for him.

The psychologist turned around to the others in the gallery. Their faces looked drained and they were sighing and murmuring half-sentences of disbelief to each other.

Foley felt that he could definitely do with a coffee and wondered if he should get back to the office anyway to check on how Kronziac was doing with the inspector. But an irrational curiosity kept him in place, like it did all the others in the room.

'What was that all about?' Koepicknicki wondered, his mind still spinning from what he'd seen on the video file. He realized that if a jury saw it his client would have little chance of beating a murder-one change.

'It's quite complicated,' Stranski replied as he stared out at Madsen, still lying under the scanner, the nurse placing a glass to his lips, flanked by the two armed prison officers.

'Well, we know that,' Cole remarked. 'But what is your *opinion*?'

Both legal teams were at least united in their abhorrence of and confusion about what they had just witnessed and both were looking to the psychologist to give them guidance on how they might prepare their respective cases.

Stranski paused to think for a moment, running his eyes over the comparative brain scans that the technician had arranged on the main screen.

'There were great correlations between Madsen's reported memory of fixing the machine and the actual experience of killing his victim,' he said. 'The cutting of the wire seemed to be an inaccurate but related memory of cutting off her finger and so on.'

'You think he can't or just doesn't remember it the way things actually were?' Cole asked.

'The scans showed that his reported memory did not display the character of an experienced memory. Little or no activity was seen in the precuneus or the complex and nuanced frontal cortex activation that makes up a real memory of an event. Instead, his memory of things was like the test I performed initially, having the less active profile of an externally instructed, non-visual, verbal-based memory.'

'A learned memory?' Scholte wondered. 'Such as an alibi?'

'Possibly,' Stranski replied, but without much conviction. 'It was more like a screen memory. A memory constructed to mask the recollection of the real events. The conscious Madsen whom we have here with us today is amnesiacally dissociated from the Madsen who carried out the atrocities on his victim – or victims,' he added, remembering that there were two more video files of Madsen executing Ellen Holby and Phil Chavez.

'So you might be saying he didn't know that he was actually committing the crime?' Koepicknicki asked, gleaning some hope from Stranski's speculations.

The psychologist became aware that he had to be very careful about what he said. '*Part* of him seems to be unaware of or dissociated from any accurate memory of the crime. This does not mean he did not know what he was doing at the time. It just means the memory of it has been sublimated and replaced by a false one, the narrative of which runs parallel to the real event – the float-ball and the eye, the specification cards and the playing cards, the oil tank and – the blood.'

'You're suggesting he has programmed himself not to remember?' Cole asked, an expression of hostility on his face.

'Well, we might, and I stress *might*, be able to find out,' Stranski replied.

'How?'

'Regressive intervention. We had a sign of leakage that we might be able to exploit as a portal through the amnesia and screen memories.'

'What leakage?' Blackney asked.

'When he described cutting the float-ball, he exhibited signs of emotive episodic memory, as if he beheld the image of a simple stopcock float-ball but was experiencing the thrill at and curiosity about how a human eyeball sounds when it is dropped on the floor and squashed underfoot.'

Stranski noticed that some of those in the room were beginning to look at him in the same way they had watched Madsen, with a distant gaze of doubt and disdain.

But Scholte was scrutinizing her notes, underlining something she had scrawled with her pen during the session.

'He mentioned a name,' she commented. 'He called her

Fractions of Zero

"Alison" at one point. Any idea who he was referring to?'

Stranski shuffled some of his case files on the desk. 'I think I have an idea,' he replied cryptically. 'Perhaps it's more important to ascertain *why* he mentioned that name.'

ST DOMINIC'S CHURCH, KERNVILLE, CA

The old priest muttered the act of contrition, his head bowed as if wearily taking on the burden of penance himself. In the wan shroud of light his bald head shone, placental almost, a smudged cross on the forehead, framed in the black hatch of the confession box where men and women whispered their sins and the darkness whispered back. The last few strands of his silver hair, metallic and mauve in the light, conspired to hide the dented scar of an old, old injury over the left temple.

He gave the boy three Our Fathers and five Hail Marys for the unimaginative confession of taking the Lord's name in vain. The priest knew that teenage schoolboys were guilty of just about every sin in the book – bar the capital offence of murder, perhaps. Though he had known of those too in his time. He dismissed the boy, who covered his head with the hood of his costume, and checked the time. Mass was about to start and the priest was going to turn off the light that signalled the end of confession and join the other clerics in the transept when he heard another penitent enter the cubicle on the other side. This would have to be a quick one.

He snapped open the hatch, only a thin veil of net curtain separating him now from the confessor – another schoolboy dressed in a robe and faceless beneath the hood. Though his sense of taste and smell had been dulled by time the old priest's nostrils flared at the noisome odour of a skin emollient.

'Go on, my son.' He urged his visitor to get on with it.

The voice of the robed figure was low and purposeful, rising from the close dark. 'Bless me, father, for I have sinned.'

Along with the words came a black, right-angled shape. It moved across the veil, its shiny tip pointing.

The dead air of the church quivered as the voices of the choir rose with the opening strains of 'Kind Maker of the World', from *Jesu Dulcis Memoria* and silenced the idle hum of the congregation.

440

Fractions of Zero

A young mother seated under the pointed arches near the rear of the western arcade was thankful for the start of mass: her two children, whom she had brought to see the pageant, had become restless and wanted to crawl over the wooden pews. But her attention was suddenly directed towards the varnished triangle of the confession box across the aisle. The insistent whine of a drill resonated from within its motor struggling in a grinding scream as it bore through something hard until that something gave way.

The recessed lights were dimmed in the laboratory and the aperture of the scanner glowed with a soft blue halo around the subject's head.

After taking a fifteen-minute break the spectators reassembled in the gallery for the final act of Stranski's show. He had stayed at the desk while the doctor and nurse topped Madsen up with the radio-labelled tracer and administered a mild hypnotic.

The legal teams settled in their respective positions. Koepicknicki had sounded out the possibility of an Alford Plea, essentially a murder-two, with Scholte. But she'd shot it down with a dismissive flick of her hair at the coffee-vending machine in the lobby outside. The state wanted murder-one and believed they would get it on the counts for Cherie Blaynes, Ellen Holby and Phil Chavez. The defence still had only one option: diminished mental responsibility. Madsen was insane. As Sedley had said in his office at the Federal Building, everyone knew Madsen was crazy. But was he crazy in the *legal* sense?

Even Stranski couldn't be quite sure.

Foley and the DOJ men also came back after the brief break, even though they all had plenty of work to do back in their own offices and departments. But no one seemed to want to miss out on how Stranski was going to probe the mind of Emery Madsen.

As they settled down, the psychologist turned around. 'Okay,' he began, his voice hoarse. 'We have administered a small dose of Alprazolam, an anxiolytic hypnotic – the pharmacology of which,' he pointed out, 'was agreed by all sides.'

Koepicknicki and the DAs nodded to confirm.

'According to all of the subject's clinical records, he has scored very highly on both the Stanford Hypnotic Clinical Scale and the Harvard Group Scale. Studies point to a high level of correlation between DID sufferers and hypnotizability. Therefore, I believe a hypnotic intervention is our best option to try and create a channel through his memory screen.'

'Is one symptomatic of the other?' Scholte asked.

Stranski compressed his lips in concentration. 'They both stem from the patient's ability to sublimate memories and feelings. It might be better to say that someone with DID is more open to suggestion or manipulation under hypnosis.'

The last part of the psychologist's answer caused some concern among the prosecution team. They didn't like the faint suggestion of outside influence acting on the suspect.

'It is generally thought that about seventy per cent of us are hypnotizable to some degree,' Stranski informed them.

'Seven out of the ten people in this room could be hypnotized?' Blackney asked, a note of disbelief in his voice. His gaze took in the others in the gallery in a gesture obviously meant to include them as sceptics along with himself.

'Yes, Mr Blackney,' Stranski replied, meeting the lawyer's scepticism head on. 'I think you see hypnosis as a means of making people act like chickens like the stage or TV hypnotists do. But there are more subtle forms of – mind concentration,' he said, happy at that moment with his choice of words. 'In everyday life we experience dissociation and amnesia in many forms, losing the car keys or . . . have you ever found yourself driving along the highway and suddenly realizing that you can't really remember the past minute or so?'

Stranski hoped he wasn't the only one who had experienced this. But some of the people in the room gave barely perceptible indications of agreement.

'That has the same phenomenology as a trance,' the psychologist continued. 'Part of your mind was able to coordinate the – ah – *motor* skills needed to carry out the complex operation of driving a car while your upper, thinking brain was preoccupied with something else – dreaming about a fishing trip, say. Here the fisherman and the driver were dissociated from each other, yet both were occupying the same mind.'

Koepicknicki leaned forward, interlocking his fingers in a solemn judicial manner. 'And hypnosis can create this sort of separation?' he asked.

'Not *create*.' Stranski corrected him. 'But . . . exploit it,' he said, with the anguished look of someone unable to adequately explain themselves. 'You can't make people do things they don't want to. You can't just hypnotize them and tell them to go out and kill someone for you.'

His statement raised eyebrows all over the room, like warning flags on a minefield.

'For instance, when I was at college,' he said, lightening his tone, 'guys were always asking me if I could hypnotize girls and get them to take their clothes off.' He affected a theatrical thoughtful expression. 'They were mostly law freshmen, if I remember,' he recalled, with a wry smile that only Scholte returned. 'But I, being the responsible psych undergraduate, told them that it was both unethical and impossible to just put someone under and then order them to strip. What I didn't tell these horny college kids was that it *might* be possible, under hypnosis, to suggest to a girl that the room was very warm and that she might be more comfortable if she removed her clothing. This approach would bypass her modesty and regulatory belief systems and give her a moral licence to disrobe.'

Blackney began smiling slyly, his body language again making it look as though he was talking for everyone. 'Dr Stranski, I'm sure your college days were a hoot and gave you a veritable treasure trove of charming reminiscences. But I fail to see how what you just told us has any relevance to our client's case.'

In twenty years of research, study and practice of the subject, Stranski had yet to find a simple sentence or idea to explain satisfactorily the theories of hypnosis or hypnotherapy.

'Yes, I think we'd better press on,' Scholte suggested, looking at Madsen's face, strangely tinted blue on the video monitor. 'Before he falls asleep on us.'

'Very well,' said Stranski. He turned back to the laboratory and his subject who was lying quietly under the blue crescent of the PET scanner tunnel.

ST DOMINIC'S CHURCH, KERNVILLE, CA

Ellstrom stood with Fr Fabien in the organ loft as they watched the celebrants call the worshippers to the Prayer of Invocation. Sedley and the other agents had gone below to prowl the aisles while Kronziac had rushed to the clerestory, Sedley insisting that the police sergeant go with her since she was unarmed.

As the celebrants invoked contrition for the penitents the young priest turned to Ellstrom.

'You are not one of them?' he asked in a flat tone that indicated more a statement than a question.

Ellstrom, taking his gaze away from the altar, smiled in reply. 'No, I am a mathematics professor.'

This amused the young priest whose face radiated with a wide smile, his teeth as brilliant as the alabaster ornaments on the altar screen. 'What are you, a mathematician, doing here?' he asked with serene curiosity.

Ellstrom could only smile himself as he recalled the weeks and months he'd spent in Los Angeles, with Kronziac, the cryptograms, Hector the lizard, the heat and the spectacular ocean views.

'I don't really know,' he said feebly and rolled his gaze around the floodlit columns of the high nave and its stony rows of saints until it returned to rest on the open face of the priest. 'I know it sounds crazy in a place like this but we have been drawn to the centre of a spiral – by a deadly conspiracy of numbers.'

To Ellstrom's own surprise his words produced little visible alarm or amusement on the features of the priest who was now looking out over the crowds of people below and the hair-shirted *penitenti* arranged in rows and columns.

'Professor,' Fr Fabien said, keeping his voice low because the priest at the lectern was reading from the Book of Joel. 'This is a church based on the concepts of medieval builders who sought to glorify the house of God through the geometric pattern of the cross, the rectangle of the nave, the square of the transept, the hemicycle of the apse and the curved triangles of the arches. Its design was inspired by an early tradition of mathematical study, when men such as Nicholas of Cusa believed the way to God's mind was through numbers. The windows, paintings, frescoes and sculpture all reflect the Renaissance imagery of Euclidean perspective and the geometric expression of God's creation.'

Fr Fabien turned to the rose window, the sunlight liquid in its coloured patterns, threaded with lead. 'Look,' he urged Ellstrom. 'The Seven Sacraments depicted in a circle of light.'

Then he turned to the nave again and gestured at the areas beneath the columns. 'The windows on the side arcades. On the east the Five Joyful Mysteries and on the west the Five Glorious Mysteries. Above them the oil and tempera paintings of the fourteen stations of the cross – the Ten Commandments, the Seven Deadly Sins, the Holy Trinity . . . you see?' He turned finally to Ellstrom. 'It is a temple to the divination of God through numbers and the geometric beauty that governs the Earth and the heavens. Mathematics is the purest of sciences, its study the discovery of the beauty of all God's creations. For, like God, numbers are immortal.'

The young priest dropped his head and began laughing lightly to himself in embarrassment. 'I apologize, Professor. You see, the order here has a tradition of math teaching and scholarship. You must forgive my enthusiasm.'

Ellstrom had worn a fond smile throughout Fr Fabien's description of the church. But now his expression hardened in focused concentration on an old problem. 'Doubtless, Father, you have heard of the Fibonacci sequence?'

Sedley patrolled the columns of the narthex at the entrance of the church with Agent Di Canio. He could see Maggie in the distance, near the top in the eastern transept to the side of the chancel. She kept herself low behind the arches of the chapel, its ceiling capturing the light under the watery colours of a reproduction fresco cycle of de Voragine's *Golden Legend*, the story of the wood of Christ's Cross.

In the western transept Phillips loitered with Agent Morris by the octagonal font in the baptistry. Just up from them, Kronziac and Bildshaw stood at the exit to the vestry, scanning the lines of *penitenti* as they trooped like Trappist monks in their scratchy russet robes to the sanctuary where the celebrants waited for them with the ashes, behind the brass fretwork that fenced the chancel from the sanctuary and the stone garden of the altar. The main celebrant mouthed into the microphone the blessing of the ashes.

'Almighty God, from the dust of the Earth you have created us. May these ashes be for us a sign of our mortality and peni-tence . . .'

And so the penitential procession approached the chancel, each hooded boy bearing a palm frond as an offering, each lifting his forehead to be marked in a cross of ash.

Kronziac watched each boy closely but it was hard to see the faces beneath their hoods. She began to make her way down the side aisles of the transept behind the seated clergy as the *penitenti* returned one by one from the altar.

Phillips stopped her as she passed. 'We're not going to find him among all of these,' he whispered anxiously. 'They all look the same, for Christ's—' He stopped himself from saying anything more.

But Kronziac didn't stop to talk. 'There might be just one thing to single him out,' she muttered and carried on down the side of the church, the sergeant from the Sheriff's Department dutifully following.

Phillips frowned at her, wondering what she was up to, and then turned back to watch the seemingly endless procession, now joined by the rest of the congregation as they went up to receive the anointment. He could see Maggie, across on the other side of the chancel, and nodded at her in a gesture of frustration. But he wasn't sure if she'd seen him over the vast width of the transept.

In the real western corner of the church, Ellstrom followed Fr Fabien along the side wall of the outer arcade. It was quiet, almost empty but for a few of the onlookers in the pews at the back and well away from the pageantry of the nave and main aisles. A young woman glanced at them as they stopped in the aisle opposite her seat, next to the confession box. Her children, bored again, were climbing over the wood but the appearance of the priest made her fuss over the kids to get them to settle and behave.

'The thirteenth station of the cross,' Fr Fabien announced to Ellstrom as they stood beneath the huge oil painting above the confessional. The painting depicted the bloodied limp figure of Christ being lowered from the cross into the arms of Mary Magdalen. In the Renaissance technique of tempera underpainting with a glaze of oil colour, the wounds wept in a vivid claret from the pale blue, lucent flesh.

'There are eight rungs in the ladder to the cross,' the priest said, so quietly as to be almost whispering. 'Eight symbolizes resurrection. Notice the wounds,' he said, turning to Ellstrom whose neck was craned to study the painting. 'There are five,' Fr Fabien informed him, 'the number associated with sacrifice. Three is represented by the cross, the Holy Trinity. Two symbolizes the duality, Christ's body and spirit now ascending into the Kingdom of His father, the true One, to live with Him for eternity, the endless cycle of zero.'

The young priest turned to Ellstrom, his dark face waxy in the gentle gleam of nearby candles on the altar of Our Lady, flickering beneath the Virgin's benevolence like petals of light.

'Fibonacci numbers – all of them,' he said as if they shared a secret denied to the droves of worshippers and *penitenti* who filled the church to receive the ash. 'We use numbers to teach the schoolchildren the wonders of the Bible and the story of Christ,' he said. Then he tilted his gaze up at the slumped torso, the pierced breast and the thorned, blood-drizzling head. 'Or perhaps we use Him to teach the magic of the Numbers,' he reflected, feeling an unease in the hull of his soul.

Ellstrom had shifted his attention to the stained-glass window beneath that depicted an old man with a long grey beard and sorrowful eyes, carrying a sickle in a field of green. 'What does the window mean?' he asked, drawn to the wide eyes of the humbled old man.

'The weakness of our mortal lives,' answered the priest. 'He represents chastity, morality, death and melancholy. A Christian version of Saturn, the ancient Roman god of agriculture, or his Greek equivalent . . . Chronus.'

Fr Fabien's words tailed off as he noticed the red taper of light still on over the confession box.

'Fr Ignatius must have left the light on. He's as old as our friend up there.' He smiled at Ellstrom who stared at the stained-glass figure of Saturn, realizing now that he was standing at the centre of the golden spiral.

Kronziac was halfway down the side of the church, struggling to get by as the people from the side aisles made their way up to the altar. She stopped at one of the arches that cordoned the central nave from the western arcade. In a pew further down, one of the *penitenti*, sitting on the last place on the long bench, was bowed like all the rest of them but was rubbing his forehead vigorously as though the ash was burning his skin.

Kronziac turned to Bildshaw, motioning for him to catch up with her. It was difficult to move or to see with the line of worshippers shuffling upstream against them, so they moved around the column, which stood like a giant granite tree trunk, to get a better look.

'Shit!' Kronziac cursed, attracting a volley of reproachful looks from some of the people nearby. The end seat of the pew was empty. She glanced up and down the church but could only see the congregation slowly making their way to the altar or resuming their seats, their faces lowered and reverent. She could also see Sedley near the main entrance of the church, Di Canio watching the doors.

With Bildshaw, a little bewildered by her haste, following, Kronziac rushed to the vacant seat and looked around again. But there was no sign of one of the hooded young men scurrying anywhere: they all remained kneeling in the pews.

'Where does that lead to?' she asked, seeing a small door leading out of the arcade.

'Downstairs to the crypt – I think,' replied Bildshaw, trying to remember.

POSITRON EMISSION TOMOGRAPHY (PET) LAB, HADCO
NEUROSCIENCES BUILDING, CAMPUS PARK, U.S.C.

Stranski turned the microphone on. 'Mr Madsen, I trust that you are comfortable.'

On the video monitor, they could see that the subject's facial features were calm, the pick-up wires trailing from his crown and temples like garlands of ivy, his eyes already heavy with the mild and pleasant effects of the hypnotic drug. The monitors all showed that his vital signs and brain patterns were reflecting a similar calmness in his mind and body.

'I feel fine,' he drawled, grinning slightly, his eyelids hooded, a glistening meniscus on the pupils.

'Good,' said Stranski, matching the subject's soft tone. 'I want you to feel relaxed as possible.'

'I can do that.' Madsen smiled dimly.

'Good. I want you to fix your sight on the topmost blue light on the scanner, above the camera lens. Can you do that?'

'Sure.' Madsen moaned with the effort and they could all see him on the screen, moving the focus of his gaze above the camera. The gentle glare of the light and the effort of keeping his eyes looking upward seemed to be further inclining him towards sleepiness. His eyelids began to flutter.

Stranski was marking a clipboard on the desk in front of him, ticking off the subject's responses and reactions. 'Now, keeping your head steady, just let your eyelids close,' he said in a tone that suggested to the subject that his eyes *wanted* to close.

Without any further encouragement, Madsen, keeping his eyes in the upward position, let his lids come down.

The psychologist marked his clipboard. 'Good, now you can open your eyes again,' he instructed him. Madsen's eyes blinked open.

Stranski turned off the microphone and turned to the lawyers. 'The subject displays high facility for the eye-roll test with the attendant activity in the thalamus, posterior commissure and other zones.'

He gestured at the PET scan that was confirming the activity. 'Activation of these zones correlates the ready ability to eye-roll and enter a trancelike state. Ninety-nine per cent of all hypnotizable subjects show a positive eye-roll.'

The lawyers scribbled in their notepads and listened attentively.

The psychologist switched on the mike again. 'All right, Mr Madsen. I would like you to let your eyes fall closed once more but you can continue to listen to my voice.'

Madsen's eyes immediately shut.

'Begin to be aware of your breathing. Try to slow it down. Begin inhaling, in slow, deep breaths that will start to give you a nice relaxed feeling all over as you take in the air.'

On the respiratory monitors they could see the patterns of deep, rhythmic inhalation.

Over the speaker in the scanner they could hear Madsen's breath as it ebbed and flowed with the effort.

'As you breathe you will feel more and more relaxed.' Stranski continued speaking in a rhythmic tone to match the subject's breathing. 'You will feel even more comfortable if you flatten your palms against the bed and let your arms go limp, to let them relax themselves.'

Already the psychologist was subtly introducing a dissociation between the rest of Madsen's body and his arms. Witnessing the falling heart rate and activation in the motor cortex, Stranski knew his subject was willingly complying with all suggestions.

'Good,' he said. 'Notice that your arms are so relaxed now that they are becoming light and that your hands can barely feel the bed under them. Keep breathing in and out, slowly and deeply. You are noticing with each breath that your hands are getting lighter and are hardly touching the bed.'

There were some flickers of action in Madsen's motor cortex but without much regulation from the upper voluntary regions of the frontal lobes.

The psychologist kept his voice low and even, allowing no hint of alarm or surprise to be communicated to the subject.

'It is quite interesting now that your hands feel so light. It is as though helium balloons are attached to them and want to rise up in the air, your arms going with them. Do both of your hands want to rise or is it just one?'

Madsen hardly seemed to want to answer, lost in the drug-induced relaxation that was being further enhanced by the psychologist's voice.

'Good,' Stranski went on, looking away from Madsen's image on the monitor to his figure lying under the cyclotron in the lab. Madsen's left hand was raised in the air.

Stranski turned and smiled with some satisfaction at the others in the gallery before addressing Madsen via the microphone again.

'You can now let your arm lower gently to your side again, slowly, and as you do this you feel yourself even more rested. You have reached a state of total, unimpeded relaxation.'

Madsen's arm slowly moved down to his side again. He remained silent on the scanner bed, his eyes still closed.

'To my mind,' Stranski told his audience, 'this subject, even allowing for the drug administration, is a hypnotic virtuoso. His ability to "go under" is very high indeed, as indicated by the ideo-motor exercise and his records.'

'Is he asleep?' Cole asked, watching, on the screen, the subject lying motionless.

Stranski gestured at all the monitors. 'There is no skeletal or muscle paralysis. EEG exhibits increased alpha wave patterns such as Sleep Stage One but without any eye movement. We have a slight increase in regional cerebral blood flow in the caudal area of the right anterior cingulate, sulcus and bilaterally in the frontal gyri. Also, the subject is still responsive to auditory stimulus. So, in a word – no. He is not asleep, but many of his mental functions are at a state of rest with basic regions working to provide homeostasis. There is no one definite physiological indication that one is in a trancelike state but the combination of all these signals—' he gestured with a long hand towards the computer screens '—suggests that he is in a different state from normal conscious activity. Psychologically he is now much more open to suggestion and as we have shut down the upper, regulatory areas of the mind he is much more willing to accept inconsistencies and perceptual anomalies. He is now more liable to be controlled by the emotional areas in the limbic system.'

'More accessible to outside influence?' Scholte asked, to make it quite clear to herself.

'Yes,' replied Stranski. 'I hope we might be able to tap into his emotional life story, as it were, and possibly circumvent the screen memories to get at the truth of the factors that motivated the killing of Cherie Blaynes and his other victims – *I hope*,' he reiterated, lest any of the lawyers might get the impression that all the questions about Madsen would now be perfectly answered.

Stranski returned to the man lying under the cyclotron once more. 'You're feeling relaxed, Emery?'

On the monitor, Madsen nodded, his lips moving but not producing any words.

'Cicumoral pallor,' the technician whispered to Stranski, observing a paleness around the subject's lips. Another sign of Madsen's altered state.

'Emery,' the psychologist began. 'I want you to imagine yourself in your favourite place. The only place in the world where you feel safe, the place you feel happiest. It could be somewhere from your childhood or it can be from now.' They examined the scans as green and yellow patches stirred around the brain, in the frontal cortex, the visual areas and the precuneus. Madsen was gathering his memories in the soft greens and golds of pleasant reminiscence. It was the bad memories that burnt more fiercely in human minds, flaring redly each time the trauma was recalled.

'Can you describe it for me?' asked Stranski, trying to assess the visual acuity of Madsen's memory.

The subject started slowly, like someone turning in their sleep. 'The cherry trees,' he began, his words loading his mouth thickly. 'In the gardens.'

'What else can you see?'

Madsen was slow to answer, almost as if he was savouring the experience of the visualization before recounting it. 'The grass lawn leading up to the ferns and the conservatory. All the others prefer to stay in the heat of the conservatory. But we like the air and the privacy of the gardens. The grass and trees protect us from them – they can't hear us . . . or watch us.'

Madsen was talking in the basic childlike delivery Stranski had hoped for, another positive indication of hypnotic regression.

'What are you doing there, Emery?' Stranski asked, gently coaxing the answers from the subject.

'Oh, the usual,' Madsen replied happily, his brain radiating gentle flickerings of happiness in all the sensual centres.

'What's that?' the psychologist asked cheerfully, taking his cue always from the subject's demeanour in his responses.

'Chess . . . backgammon . . . or my favourite.' He moved his head in a slightly embarrassed, almost coquettish manner.

'What's your favourite?' Stranski asked, smiling purposely to relax his voice.

'Blackjack,' Madsen confessed, like a child owning up.

Blackney leaned close to his partner, whispering. 'Was that what he was playing with Cherie in the video footage?'

Koepicknicki shrugged.

Stranski turned around swiftly and nodded. 'Yes, it was.' He hushed them and turned back quickly to the microphone.

Madsen was still rambling on. 'Of course, I like roulette . . . and Keno . . . poker – all the bad games. We never played for money, though.' He was shaking his head in amused denial.

'Who are you playing with?' Stranski asked gently, his soft tone downplaying the possible seriousness of the answer.

They waited as Madsen's eyes flickered under his lids. His systolic blood pressure raised slightly and red cores of activity scintillated through his hypothalamus, indicating increased memory retrieval. The technician also noticed a slight increase in skin conductance with sweat secretion.

'Eric, of course,' Madsen finally said and opened his mouth as if about to say more.

Stranski quickly pulled out the files on the desk containing the state records on the foster-care house Madsen had stayed in when he was a child. He ran his fingers down a list of names until he found it.

Eric Klim.

He'd been one of the foster kids, Stranski explained to the lawyers before turning on the mike again.

'Who else is there?' he asked. 'Can you see anyone else there?'

The technician was watching the monitors as the subject displayed increasing signs of agitation in the limbic brain centres, his emotions beginning to churn. His brainwave patterns were jumping with a higher frequency and there was increased venal blood flow in the limbs.

As no answer seemed to be forthcoming Stranski decided to confront the subconscious directly.

'Is Alison there?' he asked breezily, as if the question was of little importance, more an expression of casual curiosity.

'Alison?' Madsen asked back, a note of surprise in his voice.

Stranski glanced quickly at the file and the list of names of the other children at the foster home. 'Alison Winders,' he reminded Madsen, who was now shaking his head.

'No – no, she's with the other crowd, from the other place.'

Stranski, perplexed, asked, 'What other place?'

'Foster home – in Oakland,' Madsen replied frostily, the mention of the home stirring black memories in his frontal cortex and red streams of emotion in the hypothalamus.

'Did you ever play cards with Alison?' Stranski asked, pinning him on the subject.

Madsen seemed reluctant to answer. 'The Jack made us play,' he said finally, his mind tossing with memories.

Stranski turned to the lawyers. 'I think he's referring to Albert Jackson, the caretaker of the foster home in Oakland. He was charged with multiple counts of sexual assault on the foster kids.'

Madsen continued with his painful recall of the foster home. 'She beat me once,' he said, the words heavy, loaded with hate. 'The rules of the game were that she could leave the shed and I stayed with The Jack and he played with me – and he always won.'

Storms of traumatic emotion flurried throughout Madsen's mind and the skin sensors picked up a large increase in sweat secretion.

'He's trying to subvert the memory of the trauma,' Stranski explained. 'This is the genesis of his dissociation, his escape from the horrors of being raped by the caretaker.'

Scholte was about to ask a question when they heard Madsen speak on the video monitor, his face relaxing a little, the hint of a grin stretching his pale lips. 'I beat her, though,' he said, with low, deadly calculation.

'When?' Stranski asked.

'Few months ago,' he bragged.

Someone in the room whispered Cherie Blaynes's name.

'What happened?' Stranski urged.

The shy and mischievous demeanour seemed to take hold of Madsen again. 'It was kinda fucked,' he gasped. 'Lost my temper – forgot I had the clippers in my hand. Friggin' blew her head out.'

Madsen was like a boy describing a fight sequence from a violent action movie that he thought his inquisitor would find amusing and cool.

'You cut her eye out,' Stranski reminded him flatly.

'Yeah. I just wondered what it would sound like when it bounced. She deserved it, the bitch.'

'Why?'

'Telling everyone on us.'

'Telling who?'

'Everyone – that I was The Jack's butt-boy . . . that I enjoyed it – we had to get them all.'

'You had to get who? Who did you get?'

'Mrs Jack . . . Bobby – Eric got the others.'

Consternation grew among the lawyers. Foley and Vesoles were straining their ears to try and hear Madsen's responses over the speakers.

'Who are these people?' Cole whispered to Stranski.

The psychologist turned to the lawyer, his file open, and pointed out the names. 'Mrs Jack was the caretaker's wife – Mrs Freda Jackson – and Bobby Myers was another boy at the foster home,' he explained.

'But these aren't the actual people he went after and killed,' Scholte protested.

'No,' said Stranski, acknowledging her confusion. 'But he *thought* they were.'

'Unless this is all bullshit,' Cole threw in.

Koepicknicki leaned closer to Stranski. 'He thought Cherie was this girl Alison, that Mrs Jackson was Ellen Holby and Bobby was Phil Chavez?' he asked, beginning to pick up the insanity scent again.

Stranski, on receipt of a warning look from the DA, was reluctant to agree with this opinion totally.

'Maybe.' He shrugged. 'Or someone led him to believe they were these people.'

No one said anything in response to this theory, sitting back in their seats to consider Madsen as he lay motionless beneath the scanner, his thought signals having calmed again to run in neutral.

'What did you do with her?' Stranski said into the mike. 'After the game. What did you do with her?'

Madsen moved his head to the side, as if in deep concentration. 'Drilled the mark into her head,' he said simply. 'Took her out to the sewage works and dumped her in the tanks like I was supposed to.'

'Like you were supposed to?' the psychologist repeated. 'Did someone tell you to do it?'

The subject on the video monitor appeared restless. 'EEG raising in alpha, beta and delta waves,' the technician called out as Stranski observed increased bloodflow in many areas of the occipital lobe. The frontal cortex was also bursting with activity as the subject seemed to be struggling with a blockage in his memory stores.

'Post-hypnotic amnesia,' Stranski said to himself.

'What?' asked Blackney, just picking up the psychologist's murmur.

'There seems to be a screen.' Stranski tried to explain as fast as he could. 'Like a block placed on his memory. It could be post-hypnotic amnesia.'

'Someone's made him forget?' Scholte wondered aloud, grimacing with shocked incredulity.

Stranski slowly pressed the button of the microphone. 'Who

gave you the instructions? Who told you Alison was telling stories about you?' he asked, doubtful that he would get a straight answer.

Madsen's mind registered a flurry of activity throughout, the complex neural networks flashing with confusing signals.

'Where did you get the instructions?' Stranski persisted, shifting the emphasis a little.

In the usual place,' Madsen replied. 'Under the cherry tree.'

'In the gardens?' Stranski asked hopefully, buoyed by the sign of progress.

'Yeah . . .' Madsen nodded slightly. 'Every week we have our game . . .'

'Where?'

'The hospital,' Madsen replied dismissively, as if it were unimportant.

'Is Eric there?'

'Yeah – usually.'

'Is he the one who gives you the instructions?' Stranski asked, provoking a storm of activity in Madsen's mind. But no answer was forthcoming.

'Is he the one who told you about Alison and what she was saying?'

Madsen struggled to answer. His respiratory rate and heartbeat increased, the sea of brainwaves beginning to churn.

Koepicknicki was considering calling a halt to the session in the interest of his client's health but was reined back by the possibility of them discovering who was controlling Madsen, making him kill – if there was anyone at all.

'We play for hours,' Madsen started to say. 'Sometimes for the whole afternoon – in the garden. We don't play for money . . . just for the sweets. They taste like shit but we . . . we don't want to offend him.'

'Who, Emery? Who?'

Madsen continued talking, his speech beginning to stammer, his vitals quivering erratically. 'You see, he took care of us since we arrived – he told us about them . . . about what they were saying . . . he even found out where they lived – gave us the instructions – how to find them – gave us the drugs to knock 'em out . . . we'd spend weeks watching them before we took them . . . and now they won't be talking about me any more.'

Stranski continued to try and intervene to engage the subject directly, to calm him down. He knew that through the hypnotic regression he had unleashed Madsen's dissociated identity, the subverted violent persona.

Madsen continued, oblivious. 'He gave us the letters for the police – would tell them where the bodies were – they would fear us but never find us . . .'

'Who gave you the letters?' Stranski said in desperation.

Scholte started to caution the psychologist but the defence shouted her down. They had to get a name. Perhaps their client was a victim of someone else's influence – a new angle to the insanity plea.

The technician too was beginning to voice urgent concern. Madsen's vitals were now jumping with high levels of sporadic mental agitation.

'He always takes care of us – gave us the magic of the game – told us about the magic of the numbers . . .'

'Who?' Stranski asked.

Madsen's PET scans showed flashes of all colours from blue to red, winking like lightning across the globe of his mind.

'Heartbeat skyrocketing!' the technician warned. 'High level of conductivity, he's sweating like hell!' he said.

The two legal teams were beginning to shout at each other, Scholte arguing that what was going on was inhumane, the defence replying that their client might have been coerced into the crimes. They had to find out who it was.

Foley, Vesoles and the men from the Department of Justice sat with concerned expressions, themselves torn between wanting Stranski to call a halt to it and their curiosity as to what Madsen was going to say next.

Stranski looked at the face on the video screen, festooned with wires, shiny with sweat and contorting as Madsen's fragmented identities fought for control. On the PET scans a red storm raged in the heart of his brain, the emotional centres in the limbic propagating blue arcs of thought around the spheres of his frontal lobes.

Stranski turned to the mike to talk to Madsen and bring him down but strained his ears as he heard the subject say something.

'Uncle Frank takes care of us . . .' Madsen whispered.

Stranski, close to the microphone, waved his hands frantically to try and silence the legal teams, who were noisily slinging arguments at each other.

'Jesus!' the technician cried, as the heart monitor's alarm began bleating.

On the video screen Madsen's eyes snapped open in a frozen gaze of raw terror.

'He's embolizing!' the technician shouted and hit the emergency button on the desk console, setting off another alarm in the laboratory. The doctor and nurse ran out of the control booth, pushing a crash cart.

The bickering between the lawyers subsided as they all stood to see what was going on. Foley and the other spectators shouted aimless questions about what was happening.

Stranski pulled back from the microphone, staring at the PET scan of Madsen's brain. A red tide of blood was spreading across the hemispheres from a white core in the centre, flooding the last sparks of thought in the frontal lobe.

For years afterwards the psychologist would keep to himself his conviction that he had witnessed a physiological impossibility. And that he believed Emery Madsen had triggered the bursting of an artery in his brain, and had in this way caused the self-destruction of his own mind.

ST DOMINIC'S CHURCH, KERNVILLE, CA

Kronziac quickly descended a narrow set of stone steps from the western arcade where she found a small drill with a battery compartment snugly fitted into the handle for mobile use.

'They could be doing some maintenance work around here, I guess,' the sergeant remarked, looking at the drill. Kronziac pointed at the gnarled bit, streaked with blood and with squabs of pink tissue in the whorls.

Glancing up, she could see the door into the crypt slightly ajar.

'Better call for back-up,' she said to Bildshaw as she moved towards it.

After tapping on the door of the confession box the young priest smiled at Ellstrom, whispering.

'Fr Ignatius is one of our senior priests.' He winked at Ellstrom. 'Been here since the fifties. Sometimes he falls asleep in there.'

As he opened the door its bottom edge swept over an emulsifying pool of wine-dark blood. They found the old priest with his head leaning back against the wall of the box, his shirt an obscene red, stiffening bib. A dark hole gaped in the centre of his ash-crossed head, a stringy pendant of brain flesh hanging from it.

Bildshaw found the light switch by the open door and they entered, Bildshaw's .38 Special held out in front of him in the classic two-handed grip. The crypt of St Dominic's had started out as a repository for the Earthly remains of the early rich prospectors and cattlemen who had funded the church, as well as for the priests and one bishop who had enjoyed its magnificence. Their memorial stones and epitaphs lined the walls, the humble visage of the bishop carved in sandstone and scowling like one of the gargoyles on the roof. Nowadays the crypt acted as a subterranean storeroom, holding a collection of paintings, relics, church artefacts, vestments and sculptures, all of them caged in the centre of the vast vault like toys in a baby's cot.

'Is there another way out?' Kronziac whispered. The police sergeant kept his gun pointed straight ahead as they inched forward.

'At the other end,' he said. 'But I'm sure it would be locked.'

As they moved forward slowly they could hear faintly the sounds of the church, muffled by layers of stone, from the nave directly above.

Kronziac went down one side of the cage while Bildshaw crept down the other. Between them in the store cage were the leaning rectangles of oil paintings depicting everything from Adam and Eve and the Expulsion from Paradise to a towering copy of the Polyptych of the Misericordia with a solid gold background and featuring John the Baptist and St Sebastian, his body used for target practice by his men for his imperial contempt. Arranged on tables were chalices jewelled with opaque stones and alterpieces of fine brass and enamelled mosaic. In a bin stood a rank of swordlike crosses with flattened edges of hammered steel and copper hilts.

Kronziac had just glanced over to reassure herself that the policeman was still there when the lights went out and the door they had come through banged closed. The room became pitch black and they both stopped in their tracks.

'Shit!' Bildshaw wheezed. 'Has he locked us in?'

'I don't know,' Kronziac shouted back, her eyes trying to sensitize to the dark, her pupils widening to admit any available light. 'We'd better make our way back to the door. We've both got guns,' she added loudly. 'So if anyone wants to make a move at least one of us will have a clear shot at him.'

She heard the wire cage rattling – and footsteps.

'Is that you?' Bildshaw whispered fiercely, his voice shaking.

'No,' Kronziac replied, feeling her way along the cold smooth ground.

'Is that you?' the policeman shouted again, as if desperate for a truthful answer.

Kronziac was about to answer when she heard the thwack and reverberant ring of iron on bone. Bildshaw shrieked as another blow struck him. Then his voice faded in a gurgle that tailed off into a slow dying gasp.

Shaking in her shoes, her heart pumping in her ears, Kronziac stayed perfectly still as she heard movement at the other side of the cage – some shuffling, the rustle of rough fabric and the gentle swish of rushing liquid flooding across the floor.

Taking her shoes off, she crept slowly towards the door but stopped as she heard movement in front of her. Bildshaw's walkie-talkie chirped and a small crackling voice asked him where he was. Kronziac made her move and ran to the sound. A shaft of light from a small hole in the crypt wall illuminated the floor for her and revealed the body of the Kern County Sheriff's Department sergeant lying on a spreading sheet of blood. His arm had been cut off at the wrist and elbow, his chest skewered by an iron cross that loomed over him like a headstone. Open-palmed, his amputated hand lay on a nest of gristled bone and flesh, robbed of its weapon, the forearm lying next to it, its cleft bones bursting jaggedly through the packaging of skin.

Kronziac moved away from the spot of light to cower in the dark of the crypt among the dead priests and gold barons, their bones walled up in the foundations of the church they had built. Above, in the nave, she could faintly hear the choir begin 'In the Cross of Christ, I Glory', their plaintive voices muffled by the stone as if smothered by the clouds of heaven.

Kronziac could smell him coming, the odour of his skin cream raising a sharp note over the dead iron reek of the policeman's blood still gouting from the elbow stump and gored chest. Through the narrow funnel of grey light she could see his hood emerging, like a wraith materializing in a swarm of airborne particles. His robed arm was raised towards her, the glinting steel of the .38 seeking her out in the dark.

Kronziac clutched the policeman's severed arm tight in her small hand and pounced the moment she heard the banging and the voices of her colleagues outside. In that microsecond, as he hesitated in surprise at the pounding on the door, she launched herself up – and thrust the radius bone of Bildshaw's slashed-off forearm through the right eye of Eric Klim, daggering it all the way through, lancing his brain, so that only its own thick sheathing of flesh prevented it from travelling further through the socket.

He staggered back, screaming, and let off a shot that dug a hole in the crypt wall. Then he sank to the floor, writhing, wrestling with the sword of bone in his eye, splashing around in a jetting cataract of blood until his twitching body finally became still.

Reductio ad infinitum

2434 ABRAMAR, PACIFIC PALISADES, CALIFORNIA

Kronziac closed the door of her house behind her and as she threw the car keys into the rosebud bowl she found the small clear plastic bag in her pocket. In it were some scraps of moth wing that she had tipped into the ashes as they were being prepared in the clerestory of St Dominic's two days before. The plan had worked as she hoped it would when the wing-dust had aggravated Klim's skin allergy when he received the sign of the cross on his forehead and had sent him running from his seat in the church. She tipped what was left in the bag into Hector's cage and he flicked his tongue out to grab the scraps of dried moth, retiring to his perch behind the hibiscus to munch on his surprise treat.

Kronziac turned on her computer and looked around the empty room, part of her happy that things seemed to be back to normal, another part already beginning to miss the upheaval in the house that her guest had created in the few months he had stayed there. She checked her e-mail and found a message from Ellstrom who had arrived back safely in Boston. The message told her to check the blackboard.

Glancing across the room she found the blackboard in its old place by the Hawaiian bar. Wiped clean of the cryptogram table, it now displayed just a single row of digits. A most important number, his e-mail told her, one she should not forget, for it was the telephone number for his new office at Harvard, where he was now a permanent member of the faculty, the Professor of Number Theory.

Smiling, Kronziac went to the bar and made herself a margarita to toast Ellstrom's promotion and her own change of luck. She had just left the office where Sedley and a very friendly Assistant Director Foley had told her that Inspection Division were dropping all disciplinary inquiries into the Woodsmen raid and the death of young Matthew Crebbs. Taggart at Forensics had extracted the memory chip from Crebbs's mobile phone and, together with the phone company, had deciphered a text message sent from his brother's cell phone just before they were both shot. The message had seven letters, two simple words – KILL HER. This showed intent on the part of Matthew Crebbs and she had had no choice but to defend herself.

Foley had rewarded her by inviting her back to work as head of the Domestic Terrorism Unit again as soon as she wanted. Jones's surveillance operation up in Montana had picked up signs of movement among the Woodsmen in the Bitteroot Valley. Sedley warned her that Lucas Crebbs might be on his way to Los Angeles.

The sky was a bright airy blue and a slight offshore breeze caressed her face as she took her drink out on to the veranda. She thought of the day when she'd found Jerry Blaynes's card folded among the aliases of poor Jimmy Soton, the day the whole cryptogram case started. She was glad it was over. On the way home she had stopped by to see the Blayneses, Jerry and Cynthia both worn and faded after the months of grief. They had looked at her with sad disbelief when she'd told them that the only reason their daughter had died was because the digits of her Social Security number had come up in the lottery. She'd explained it again and again and had tried to comfort them by saying a great many victims of this type of crime were really the victims of unfortunate circumstance – wrong place, wrong time, wrong number. She'd further tried to console them – or at least help them put it behind them – by confirming that Cherie's killer Emery Madsen now slept with a life-support system at the California Medical Facility in Vacaville, brain-dead and relying on the machines to keep him 'alive' until the Department of Justice decided what to do with him. His accomplice, Eric Klim, was even more dead.

So Kronziac left the Blaynes with their grief and their gratitude. She met Cunningham on the way out. He still professed an interest in joining the Bureau but she told him to stay put with the LAPD – the vacation time was better. As she drove away she passed Donnie and Jared, working together on Jared's mom's car, laughing and joking around like kids are supposed to do.

Fractions of Zero

She sat back on the lounger and sipped on her margarita, figuring she had enough time to herself to take a quick nap before Phillips and Maggie arrived with fresh bagels. They were picking up Stranski from his hotel so he could drop in on his way to the airport for an hour or so before the flight that would return him happily to the city of Washington and his job at the FAA taking care of airline pilots.

Before Kronziac closed her eyes she heard Mrs Peters opening her bedroom window and calling hello to her, eager for a chat, maybe even to share a cigarette. But she stayed put on the lounger, sipping her cocktail, thinking about potting the flowers for the spring as Mrs Peters chattered on about her daughters and asked Kronziac about the man staying with her. Had he gone? Was he coming back? But Kronziac felt her eyes close, as if the warm sun had brushed her lids with a soft hand, and she was drifting to her favourite place, lying in the warm waters of a sea-pool on the edge of the tumbling, boundless ocean.

Inside the house, as Hector crunched a last shred of mothwing his eyes swivelled wetly towards the computer screen that flickered as the screensaver scrolled over Ellstrom's e-mail, the letters spelling out the daily quote:

> '*Nature is an infinite sphere of which the centre is everywhere and the circumference is nowhere . . .*'
> Blaise Pascal, *1623–1662 (Mathematician)*

Spring brought the patients out. In their robes and gowns they padded about the grass and the paths, treading the heavy half-world of their minds as if swimming in honey. A nurse led one of the newest admissions to the picnic table beneath the cherry tree whose black branches were budding in little bows of green.

'Can he join you guys?' she asked in the most perfunctory manner. She set the kid down on the seat before running off to cover up one of the patients who had stripped off and was urinating on the ferns in the conservatory in front of the visitors.

At the table a white-haired man, in his sixties at least but with the sure, steady animation of a man much younger, sat dealing cards to a teenage boy who stared at his hand with the glazed stupor of someone heavily sedated.

'Sit down,' the man said, looking at the disturbed new boy as if appraising his suitability for something as yet unspoken.

The boy sat down reluctantly, the edge of his paranoid belligerence only blunted by a heavy regime of lithium.

'What are you in for?' the man asked.

'Bipolar, borderline and some other names,' the boy snorted. 'They think I'm a schizo,' he added, looking curiously at the other boy who sat staring at his cards as if the king, queen and jack were dancing a jig in front of him.

'Here, have one of these,' the man muttered quietly as he took a small capsule from a bag. Inside the capsule was a dull maroon liquid, its colour much like that of a morello cherry.

'What is it?' the new boy asked, excited at the prospect of some recreational narcotics.

'Cortisol cap,' the man smiled.

'What the fuck is that? A popper?' the boy asked, hoping for something a little stronger.

'Makes you forget,' the man said temptingly. He passed it across the table, watching out for staff.

'Hear about the woman with multiple personality disorder

470

who complained to her shrink about the bill?' the man asked.

'Yeah,' the boy answered, flicking the capsule into his mouth. 'He charged her group rate.'

The man nodded his head in smug satisfaction. 'Good, you're smart. Know how to play games – card games, number games?'

'Not really,' the boy replied, chewing on the capsule.

'Well.' The man leered. 'Uncle Frank will have to teach you . . .'